Thoughts on Vacation

a novel
by

Michael Lyons

Vol. 6 of the Sextet
My Years of Apprenticeship at Love

Hitmotel Press
www.hitmotel.com

First Edition

Library of Congress Cataloging in publication Data

Lyons, Michael
Thoughts on Vacation
Vol. 6 of the Sextet *My Years of Apprenticeship at Love*
I. Title

ISBN: 0-9655842-6-7

Published by HiT MoteL Press

Designed by Michael Lyons

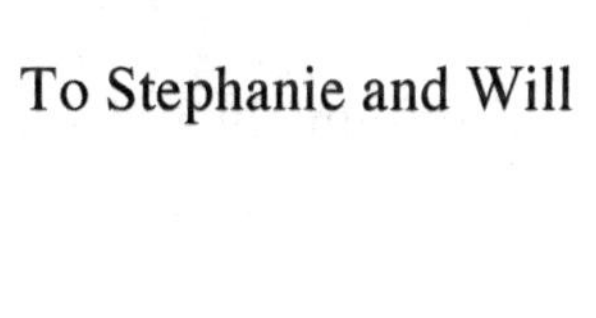

To Stephanie and Will

When I’m flying in an airplane,
I get the feeling
of being
well-educated.

---Roux Underwood

Table of Contents

Blood and fire and thunder and something awful in the middle of it

"Walker, take care of the baby." My wife would say this on her way out the door to let me know I was on my own with the wee lad. I liked it when it was just me and the kid hanging out.

Sometimes we got a kind of game going where we sat in separate chairs facing off with each other: baby Bill sitting in his battery operated swing and me in the rocking chair. There are pictures of this. Me—Walker the new dad—in moccasins and sweats, with a big grin on my face and the two of us looking at each other with admiration. In the game we rock back and forth sometimes zooming in toward each other then flying back away from each other. Or sometimes going in the same direction, forward and backward in rhythm. Wild Bill, as I was fond of calling him, thought this was hilarious. His eyes would get big, and he got the joke and really laughed and delighted in it. Me too. This was before he was even walking. We'd be rocking back and forth at each other and I'd be singing to him: "I'm a lone cow-hand, on the Rio Grande. And I learned to ride before I learned to stand."

He loved to scramble up and down the carpeted stairs from the living room to the bedrooms upstairs. Then one day, my wife and I had her cousin and his girlfriend in to baby-sit, and this cousin was from a really big family some nine younger brothers and sisters. And while we were out he taught baby Bill how to slide downstairs, on his butt. Just by making himself rigid like a bobsled, he'd shoot down those stairs. We were shocked and amazed, and since the cousin came with such impeccable credentials we thought it was all right. Little Bill was so proud of that.

Everything was of interest to the child, and his enthusiasms were contagious. I had read a little Piaget, and it was fascinating not only to observe the growth of a human mind, but also to be invited into their world of play. Hanging out with him was like a mini-vacation. Dealing with their small concerns made me feel like a giant who could control the world. It also made me feel I was in the service of something great. The future.

Sometimes we would just wander around the house and look at stuff. Or I would pack the micro-hellion into his car seat, and we'd go to the mall and look at ourselves in the big mirrors and store front windows. We'd play with the trains at the toy store. When we were at home, there was a while there when we'd play loud music and dance around the place. One song was "Rhythm of the Saints" on a later Paul Simon CD. Bill like it when I did large martial arts moves, to the phrase "thrust of a knife."

Now Bill was two years old, and he had had a very good day-care provider. The lad was showing his father one of his paintings. It had some fish and a bunk bed. For Wild Bill it was a kind of machine.

"OK," he said, "this is how it turns off."

Intrigued at how the child's mind makes sense of the world, I interviewed him a bit. The little Billy Boy was great, pushing beyond his limits, establishing himself as a kid in his father's eyes and arguing me out of seeing him as a baby. It happened around the word 'cradle'.

Dad: Cradle?

Bill: It's not a cradle. It's where the baby sleeps.

Dad: *O-o-OK*. And this is me with my big hair?

Bill (indicating a toy box): You get the toys out from here.

Dad: I see Mom has got a beautiful face. She's smiling.

Bill: I miss mom too. And I'm sad and Kevin's sad because we're sick.

Dad: What made you guys sick?

Bill: Kevin caught the worstest virus ever and I caught the worst ever virus, ever. And mom had to pay a hundred dollars to get some juice.

Dad: Special good juice? With soy milk in it?

Bill: It's called Bestest Juice Ever. The bigger better juice ever. Whoever. . . Kevin intended to have milk at school. It is called Logo.

Dad: Logo. What's in Logo then?

Bill: It has Vitamin C, butter and vitamin A. And I got the specialist juice ever.

Dad: Well listen, tell me. Does the balloon help hold the bed up? . . .. Or is it just . . .

Bill: The balloon helps hold the bed up.

Dad: And also what? . . . It sings you lullabies?

At this Bill disengaged and looked around his dad's office.

Bill: Dad you have a cool room.

I was afraid I might have been a little aggressive in my questioning and offended him; but I persevered. I like to push him a little because it can be like listening to Chagall or Kandinsky when he explains his art.

Dad: Can you tell me, do you remember the lullabies the balloon sings? How does it go?

Bill: It goes . . . I changed the song.

Dad: That's OK. .*(softer)* . Tell me.

Bill *(sings)*: Cradle cradle cradle rock rock rock: I know you intended to be well if . . .in the twilight I am. *(low tone)* it will give you a big hug and kiss / I'm delighted to help you miss.

I as often, was melting at the sweetness of it.

Bill *(singing)*: She's gone away / she'll be back tomorrow. . . When your mommy gets sick . . .

Dad: Ha ha. Ha.

Little Bill explained the picture by saying, "See this part up here on the right with the red fence, that's the devil in hell. *(I see that here the lad has blurred the paint with his finger into some amazingly interesting randomized fiery kind of thing.)*

"And this part down here, the H, I put two hearts on it, that's for mom and dad." *(By now my heart was melting. I was feeling so much love from this little boy, that it was easy to feel it imbuing all my life.)* He said: "And that line there is God! He's trying to keep the devil from coming down."

The picture was of the Red hell domain floating

above, writhing. It would come across except for a kind of "fence" or boundary which he called the yellow wall. There was a Man with big hair—the Dad and a Woman with smiling face—the Mom.

Then my little boy said: "The movement of god falling down on the earth and this blocking in the yellow fence here will never die. Will never go away."

And I thought for a moment it WAS like being in the presence of Kandinsky; it was like listening to a great artist talk about one of his paintings. I enjoyed it immensely.

Children put their entire world into their paintings. I think they follow the steps of creation or the steps of the emergence of the archetypes of perception and order into their world. Every painting for them is like the dawn of creation, a young god creating the world. First we notice the light. Then the next thing we notice is the great space. And we are starting to draw lines from our eyes to the things we want to see. And then we notice the objects in the space, the seas and the sky, and the wind-riffled grasses and the flowers and the swaying trees. *(The space is all in motion, like a spirit moving through it).* Satoris of space.

The way the archetypes of order come into our world is just like how they lay out the way God created the world in the Bible. First there was light, then space, then the plants and mountains and waters, and then further on in the distance the stars, and then he filled the world with creatures. And on the 6th day he made man; on the 7th day he rested.

And then, after putting the little angel to bed, it was back into my own world. August the 8th —thinking about my sister. This, her birthday.

And thinking about the primitive life forms they found and had all kinds of press conferences about, even President Clinton mentioned it. And it *is* amazing: the rock came from Mars and landed on Earth.

And I was thinking about my sister fighting for her life against cancer. She had started having it looked into about the time I brought my bride-to-be to meet my family in Texas. I know she is in good hands. They have some of the best hospitals in the world in San Antonio. That's why my mother lives there.

There's been a lot of death in the air lately with the explosion of flight 800. A lot of people think it was the ragheads again. It was an act of terrorism. And a week after they found evidence of life off-earth—microfossils in an ancient, ancient rock blasted off the surface of Mars, circulated around the solar system for a billion years, then crashed into Earth—in the Antarctica. And there it lay until someone found it. Why the Antarctica?

The Yellow Park at the Heart of St. Francis Wood

Me and Bill, on our way to the park. We bounced down Ocean Avenue, which was worse than any washed out country road at the end of a long winter, with the K-Ingleside streetcar rails, now even more torn up from work on the sewers. I usually take him someplace everyday after I pick him up at daycare, either to a park, or to the ocean, or to the mall, unless the weather is really bad, and then I take him home, and he watches TV. We turned up into St. Francis Wood heading for what Bill calls the Yellow Park. We've been going there almost every day lately since it turned spring when a little light is left at the end of the day.

The park is in the lee, at the bottom of one of the great hills of San Francisco. Up the hill wealthy houses are situated so that they appear to scramble, climbing on top of each other, thrusting their great windowed facades up to the sky all around the little park couched down below. I turn up the street that runs along the park, drive past the park, and my boy gets excited about going around a loop at the end of the street and turning back around so we can pull over to the curb across the street from the park.

It's a tight squeeze parking and getting him out of his car seat, because the people whose houses are across the street from the park are growing hedges all the way out to the curb to discourage access. This is a park in the wealthy section of San Francisco, not that many people use it. I hear that nannies come during the day, but I only come over here in the gloaming with my wild child. I like to sit on the swings because you can get a really good view of the sky from inside this hollow, and look off at the clouds foaming over the sea. Sometimes there is tinny electronic bell chimes wafting across the way from the church below, diffusing through the cypress trees into the park, of St. Francis Wood.

"Here, take my hand," I said.

And the little fellow put his hand in mine. I held it tightly as we walked across the street. And as soon as we were safely across, he pulled it away—for he is a fiercely independent three-year old. He started unaided down the steps toward the gate leading into the children's sand-lot.

Inside, he turned and said, "Be sure the gate is locked."

He is worried about dogs occasionally barking the back yards of the extremely elegant houses of St. Francis Wood.

For some reason, these houses give me the feeling that they were looking down at us from their wide-eyed windows like perpetually shocked Victorian dowagers with opera glasses endlessly looking over tiers of balconies at the spectacle below.

Inside the children's park, we walk past the swings and always step up and walk like tight-rope walkers balancing along with arms extended on the upright 2x4 forming the edge that boarders the sand lot. It leads to the play structure with its twisting yellow slide. The yellow slide with the yellow railing was butted up against the big wooden structure.

When we first started coming here, Bill couldn't climb up onto the big wooden structure which served as the platform for the big slide. The rungs were too far apart. But I showed him how to use the rungs at the corner. Now he can climb up onto the highest part of the play gym where he couldn't before and come zooming down the big slide. And he had been doing it over and over with great glee. And encouragement from me.

I first noticed the couple out of the corner of my eye as the youth was teasing the maid at the gate, not letting her open it. She was beautiful, young sixteen or seventeen maybe, could be a sophisticated and very well developed fifteen. As Bill played and I watched over him—the young and the old, something magical happened. We were joined by these young lovers and the physical attraction between them imbued the park.

She was on a walk with her young beau. She had him beguiled, although he sometimes feigned indifference which lasted about two seconds. It was part of their game.

They couldn't keep from touching each other, or rubbing up against each other, or bumping into each other, or putting their hands on each other every few seconds, as they swirled around each other in the park. It was like they were two porpoises moving gracefully in sync through an ocean of sexuality side by side, touching each other was surfacing for air. Then they would stop the casual touching and clutch each other in a long passionate embrace, their lips locked in a hungry kiss.

And all of this love and young horniness of spring was swirling around in St. Francis Wood.

Seeing that my little son was safe doing something, I couldn't help but look beyond him through the monkey bars over toward her. And, lo, the beau had gotten her down on the ground and was astride her, and they were wrestling, and he had her arms pinned down and was kissing her, and she was tossing her head back and forth enjoying it.

Then they stood up and rode the spring horses, and I could see her dark and wild hair was long, falling down past her shoulders. She was like a ballerina in vermillion lycra top above tight, worn blue jeans with bell bottoms and raggedy knees almost torn through.

As their teasing and folderol circulated closer to us, I could see that her slender little wiry teenage body supported these breasts that, under a tight lycra danceskin top, were a little too ample and yet that well defined. She might have been wearing padding or support for they looked like two balloons tied to her slender teenage body. Do young girls know about such things? And yet they were so heavenly, as though they might just lift her off the ground.

She had a checkered flannel shirt she had taken off and wound around her waist. Though it's hard to tell about families and wealth, especially as the grundge aesthetic democratizes all, her clothes were of a finer cut than his. Regardless of where they came from, love had made them into a prince and a princess, and I was struck dumb by a glance from her large smiling sensitive brown eyes. There, right before our eyes, a lovely young female was undergoing a metamorphosis from a girl into a woman, and there was all this tenderness and vulnerability about her.

Bill's eyes were wide with awe for this beautiful woman. I wonder what he thought. And I think she became awed by my child. He attracted them to us.

I was helping Bill climb, and he was so proud doing it over and over, and the couple came over to play and jump around on the bars. The young man crawled onto the climbing structure and seized her, at every opportunity and she leaned over and let him. And like Jack and Jill they tumbled down the big slide together. Bill looked on in wonder as all of this love and young horniness of spring was swirling around in the park.

She was not that skilled in makeup, and the eye shadow and the eye liner on this child's fun face seemed a little out of place on a girl so young. But young girls really seemed to go for that these days. Her lipstick rose above the lip line, giving her the appearance of large lips like the singer Sade, or maybe she really did have large lips, might have been from kissing a lot.

The young man was very attractive too, smooth of face and very handsome like a matinee idol, couldn't have been much over sixteen, but maybe as young as thirteen, a big sophisticated thirteen. They were so cute.

And I wondered what these young people in love were saying to each other these days, learning to talk the ancient language of love, invisibly transmitted down the generations through the genes. There sure were lots of squeals of delight intermixed with the swoons, faints and teases going on. The young man climbed up to the very highest part of the monkey bars and balanced there. You could tell that the beguiled heart of this youth, long kept in a cage since the first love of the divine mother, had escaped and was now feeling the awesome power of this new found unity under the influence of this lovely young girl. She had him walking along the outside edge of the very tip-top of the structure; it was a horizontal ladder from which kids hung by their hands and move hand - over-hand, rung to rung. He was up there like a tight-rope walker. And she was smiling back at him, impressed. Her smile had driven him to the heights of the ecstasy of youth blessed with good looks and the confidence of success at early love.

I was excited about the success the young man was having with the girl, and I hoped this kind of success comes to Bill early in life. Things would have been so different for me if I had not to been cursed with such a great shyness. My son has certainly the cutest little face of any child I have ever seen. Maybe it will develop into teen appeal. O, I suppose I have, in my youth, experienced some form of this passionate adolescent love. Maybe everyone has. This love brings you through the timeless age of just-peaking adolescence into adulthood.

And who wouldn't be turned on by this Romeo and Juliette. She was lovely, young, long dark hair, maybe Mexican. At one point they were sitting on the bench, he reclining with his head in her lap and she was bending over to kiss him, and run her hand over this fine young animal she had in her possession, and she arched herself up, and leaned over him some more, so that I could appreciate her back side under thin denim, and I was thinking *what a lucky young man.* And all of this love and young horniness of spring was swirling around in the park.

Later, I was trying to get Bill to go to the other side of the park and get onto the swings to give this darling young couple, who just kind of sparked my heart making me want to encourage them, some space. And too, they were engaging in some behavior I was not yet ready to have Bill see. It was really shocking when they were on top of the slide up above Bill and I; they were flickering their tongues back and forth across each other's tongue in an open mouth kiss like two horizontal candle flames in a fit—until she burst into a giggle, and smiled shamelessly at me and Bill. But Bill had to be coming around where they were all the time.

Perhaps little Bill was quite shocked, because he started whining about wanting to be up there where they were, using the slide—and I wanted to get him away from there, because by now I just about thought of them as the Divine Couple. It was getting past his supper-time and his whining turned into a keening wail as I had to carry him back to the car and take him home.

And all of this love and young horniness of spring was swirling around in the park of St. Francis Wood.

Ambivalent Man to the Rescue!

I wanted to tell my kid stories he would like. Kids are totally and naturally into the hero archetype. The stories they like hook into their aspirations of greatness, for their morality is black and white. My kid was crazy about the Mighty Morphin' Power Rangers TV show. This had everything a boy would like: great physical fighting choreography, hideous operatic monsters, explosions, and the amazing technology of transformers. Whenever we could, we explored construction sites, investigating the hydraulic ability of front-end loaders, admiring the huge claws of trenchers, and fantasizing about the squat stance of bulldozers. He was an infallible expert on the names of every type of dinosaur. (I'll never forget the first time we took him to the zoo. The plucky three year looked eager and at the ready: "I want to see the triceratops," he said, waiting, with his hands on his hips, ready to go, fully expecting to see one, too.)

My kid looks up to me to be his hero. I wanted to tell him the kind of heroic stories I knew he would enjoy. But I usually just felt manipulated by most heroic literature. I liked lyrical Beatnik writing but wasn't about to start him on that downward path of anti-hero wisdom. That's something you do on your own. So I started telling him the stories of old black and white Flash Gordon movies and Rocket Man serials. He liked that. (I used to tell the lad that I came from a time before there was color. You can tell by the old black and white movies.)

I did get going for a while on one story that had aspects of the Laura Croft /Tomb Raider video game set in old post WWI Vienna. Except cavorting in the ancient city of waterways was a character based on the elegant Ezra Pound crossed with the evil Doctor Sax escapading and shape-shifting from within his flowing cape among the shadows and sunlight falling on ancient columns. Little Bill seemed to like it.

But if I were to try and depict myself as some kind of comic book hero, I would have to be Ambivalent Man. Though outwardly you might think Ambivalent Man should be a character with two heads, one a shrunken, sulking, insipid, rude, sub-human, monstrous, snarling, cry-baby head budding out of Ambivalent Man's neck and wobbling, squalling, flopping around next to the real head, it is more subtle than that. Ambivalent Man has warring sub-personalities vying for dominance. His body is possessed by the spirit of two animals: one a frightened silly goose and the other a tiger. These spirits are constantly pulling Ambivalent Man in two directions at once. And worse, leading him places:

and there abandoning him by switching so that he is the goose when he needs to be the tiger.

Ambivalent Man lives on an island in the Sea of Fantasy.

Summer—I'm in an old house. Its paint is flaking. It has a wonderful verandah open to the sea. The house is situated on the strand somewhere. There are cushy old chairs—I'm watching the breezes off the sea move the bamboo blinds ever so slightly. Beyond, the endless blue sky sees the ocean eternally convolving with the land. The island fantasy comes on me to counter the malaise when I don't feel much "drive" (sexual or otherwise). It's kind of like I'm going through the routine, just trying to put one foot in front of the other. Maybe we all do this, but perhaps I'm more aware that something is missing. Things are very even, but kind of "flat." My emotions are very subdued (I wouldn't say repressed). I laugh. . . Sometimes. Somehow I am able to live out there. I think: you could be happy here. It only requires thirty five hundred dollars a year.

Lately I've been reflecting on how to regard my current state, perhaps it is not even a state—an island, a small island, I am the dictator—the United States of Hysteria. How to know whether one is up, or down, or somewhere in the middle (or maybe "in the muddle"?) of a great big puddle. But no man is an island. I feel somewhat removed from people and the human society around me, and I'm too shy to engage. Most adults are un-understanding, trying to do too much. We all have to work so hard creating excess wealth for the owners of production that you are left staggering around in a cloud of quasignosis. Which is a state somewhere between hypnosis, which is being in an advertisement-induced trance, and ignorance which is not-knowing - anything. Whew, how can I be so dull, ignoring the world?

Children are never like that. At times I feel like an anthropologist from another planet, unable to comprehend the ways of humans, their enthusiasms, the things they collect, how they fill their time. I'm reasonably content by myself. And I have come to see how in marriage you can trust being able to show the vulnerable, defeated side of yourself. I seem to have drifted from my friends, but I notice it feels good when I really do connect with someone "simpatico." Then I remember that I am human after all.

But to be on a tropical island . . . Yes, a major change would be good. St. Thomas in the Caribbean? Maybe flip over to the southern hemisphere. Somewhere in New Zealand? Nah, too many Australians. An island off the coast of Thailand. . . My level of interest in various things seems lower than it was a while ago. I have so little patience! I love my kid, and my wife is a good person, but I don't seem to have the requisite . . . sense of paterfamilias required for family life. I don't feel like I'm enthusiastically engaged in life. Why must I always Be Ambivalent about being parents; about buying a house. About committing to a direction of action. After all, you might fail.

I have a strong sense that being in a warmer place will be good for me, will help me to feel more comfortable in my body. Yes, an island off the coast of Thailand. One of the Spice Islands. Bali, where there is a lot of spirituality, and the music. I could end up my days a raghead in a sarong, playing the gong, jammin' along, in the Balinese Gamelon men's group. I haven't yet made any major changes in my life circumstances, in part because I am so drawn to familiar habits. And because I don't want to miss one minute of my kid growing up.

Why must I always Be Ambivalent? Because you are not really committed to any path of action but your own. Yet for the sake of getting along, you feel you need to hide your real feelings about something and present another set of feelings. Ambivalent Man lives his life *somehow*; it is like a kind of defense. He has found living in ambivalence a compromise solution to make his life and the life of those around him easier.

Ambivalence comes from protecting the inner child as it tries to grow in efficacy. We all have this inner child we are trying to accommodate. We all go through that time when we think: I must be adopted. I must have been captured by these people. These people are weak and pathetic, I can not be from them. In fact, they say if you want to know what your Muse looks like, you should look for pictures of yourself when you were about ten or eleven years old. Right at the cusp when you still had the beliefs of a child yet the savvy of an adult. Look for a picture that shows you to be both accomplished and defiant, and try to remember that time.

All superheroes are a variation of Ambivalent Man. He is the Uber-hero, the archetype for the rest. Take Superman. How ambivalent can you get?—"And WHO, disguised as Clark Kent, mild-mannered reporter for the Daily Planet" was really Superman in disguise. Yes, underneath the meek, whipped-into-submission exterior is a being with almost omnipotent powers, able to leap tall buildings in a single bound, see through walls, and fly around faster than a speeding bullet. I preferred to be affiliation free.

I get my inner child together with my real child. He

is three years old and is alternately charming and manipulative, only he is not yet so good at it, and it is obvious, and yet he is learning. It is amazing to see the personality unfold.

Ambivalent Man has many roles; they are the subpersonalities inside of him. One is Poor Me. Poor Me says I don't have any choice. Or: It's not really a choice I would want to make.

How can you turn things around and feel like you have a solid identity and have the freedom of choice and the means to pursue these dreams?

Or . . . I seem to be in a double bind.

Ambivalence—it is so energy draining. Couldn't I ever just really get wholly behind something, unequivocally be with it?

Becoming Ambivalent Man was a survival strategy in a world when all the choices are not to your liking. When I was younger, I used to rationalize it philosophically: ambivalence was some kind of hip new multivalued logic, not the black and white world of our parents who came through the depression. But a world of all gradations of shadow in between.

Maybe where I'm at now is dealing with a "normal" level of existential ennui/malaise? How much of it is the result of so many years of depression? How much of it is connected to the functioning of my neurotransmitters? I must admit, I sometimes experience the anguish of depression and the accompanying sense of hopelessness. I also must admit I don't experience very much pleasure. I wonder whether I should try Prozac. Or should I try another medication—L-Triptophane? Vitamins? To see if they do more? Or does a certain level of ennui just go with who I am at this time of my life?

The Buddha taught most of us live our lives in a state of sleep and have not yet awakened to the source that spawned us and is taking care of us in every breath. But instead we prefer to give up in the face of this awesome terror, and let some other agent take over and control us in a numbness to being that leads to suffering. And we accept this. The old man in the Tao, too, says give up your idiotic sense of self-importance, pay attention to the enormous gifts flowing out to you from the source. Let the flow of the Way carry you along. And that's just what the island fantasy is. To be less attached to our world. To be out on a rock in the middle of the sea, winds rising, hurricane coming. To be out there in it, to stand up with this strong sense of being someone apart from the rest.

Dreamcatcher

My sister Anne has some really sharp boys, Mark and John. And on our annual trip back to Texas, taking our own little Wild Bill to visit his grandparents either on Thanksgiving or Christmas, I enjoy seeing these nephews, because they help me keep in touch with what's happening with the young people these days. They play a lot of computer games and are very good at them, and I get input on designing new games from them. Mark is the younger, preadolescent, and we had lots of good talk about computer games and Greek mythology. He was really into Greek mythology. He especially liked the exploits of Hercules and was recommending books for me to read. John is the older, and we were able to get into one of those high-speed, animated, data-transfer, quick insight talks that occasionally a teenager will let you be part of. This in spite of a disturbing and perplexing set of complications from a punch in the face he took during a run-in with a gang at a swimming hole. Complications from the blow were making his speech slur and for him to tire a lot. He is a very intelligent boy, turning into a fine strapping young man, writes poetry. He's so attuned to me, and I can see I hold an undeserved place of greatness in his heart, for I am, after all, the maternal uncle. I love where this boy's mind is going. He's studying Latin and mathematics and thinking about getting into medicine.

My other sister Karen had successfully fought off cancer; it had gone into remission. We were celebrating. She got us this fabulouso condo to stay in, down on the San Antonio river walk. Right across the river from the old Ursline Academy, a few blocks from the Alamo. So my wife and kid and I were downtown away from the families in the suburbs. My brother was bringing in his kids and his ex-wife from Houston. Downtown San Antonio was not doing too good those days. It is a always bit surreal anyway: the buildings are a cross between European art deco with a heavy Spanish twist brought in from Mexico City, mixed with Southern and Yankee building and Aztec rocco. There are some fine examples of the Mexican and German stone work on the buildings down on the river. It has always been a fantasy of mine to get a big warehouse with high ceilings and lofts and plenty of room.

We all got along pretty good. Only my sister Anne and I had a minor set-to over her minors. I was talking about possibly bringing those boys out to San Francisco some summer when they are older and getting them jobs testing computer games. I could just see these guys spending a summer in a room full of teenage game testers, drinking cokes, eating chips and candy bars, and playing games fourteen hours a day, while getting paid handsomely. And she was being all worried about them getting bad influences in their lives. And I said a wrong thing.

When she asked, "You wouldn't let them smoke any marijuana, would you?"

I said, "I think it might be nice to get high with them some day."

"Oh you wouldn't."

And I still didn't take the hint and went ever further with, "Yea. Everybody should at least try it once in their life."

"Oh no, I don't like that at all," she said, and was kind of hurt and shocked and mistrustful of me after that. "I'm not going to let them come out and visit you."

I got to make one side trip back up to Austin while my wife and sisters went shopping. I hooked up with a dear old friend from my careless youth, Wild Bill. We took his dogs for one of those great long marathon walks along the Colorado River like we used to. As often happened in our conversation, the topic turned to How the West was Lost. And we got to thinking about a kind of fictional alternative history of America based upon people getting kinder to one another.

We talked about what would have happened if the old guys in the cavalry knew about marijuana. Wild Bill said the cavalry did actually, "They called it Goof Butt, a hip term back then." We wondered what if, when they got off duty, they went out behind the corral and smoked some Goof Butt.

He said, "What if the mostly white cavalry had

gotten off their high horses and smoked some weed with the Indians."

He added: "And maybe, some of the Mexicans who smoked it, too, had come over, and they all got high. And maybe even some of the men and women got naked and jumped into an irrigation ditch together to cool off in the sweltering heat. That would really have fixed it wouldn't it?

"Yeah, they might have accepted each other. And what if some newly freed Negro slaves who owned property in the area, that "forty acres and a mule," came over too, and brought out some of that good gage and whipped out some bodacious barbecue, and they all had a picnic. That would have REALLY fixed things."

They would have created a whole new alternative history for America. It would be a kind of science fiction in which the white men were able to see from the perspective of the Indians, could travel into the underworld of their spirits and have visions and come back again, able to integrate into their rational science the unfolding harmony of nature. Basically, the Indian could have taught the white man how to live within his bio-niche, and about community; and the white man—with his northern-European angst-driven technology—could have brought the Indian out of the third world. Or better yet, the two could have developed a really useful, spiritual technology. That would really be something, wouldn't it?

My wife and I even got a couple of hours off by ourselves. Left little Wild Bill at home with my brother and his kids, and we wandered around in some of the shops near the Alamo. We found one store that sold

Indian curios, in particular they had a Dreamcatcher. I was shocked and amazed. I had never seen anything like that.

A Dreamcatcher is made by bending a resilient green branch into a circle to join itself, like a snake devouring its tail, and tied end to end. Then, using animal gut, one strings a spider's web inside the hoop. It is a kind of mandala. The web is the same kind of weaving technique the Indians used to make the mesh of their snowshoes—a brilliant kind of technology that allowed them to spread their weight over a wider area, thus they could walk over the surface of snow without sinking in. Did they get the idea from water striders? The weave uses one long strand going back and forth from the center to the edge, interlocking at nodes, forming a kind of star mesh. It is quite a delicate feat of knot-tying technique. Then the hoop is wrapped in leather or fur, and from it is hung bird feathers. What a marvelous spiritual technology. It was first discovered among the Iroquois. At the center of the web is a crystal, or a seashell, or some other magic mass. The Dreamcatcher works by binding the spirits of nature present in the materials that go into making it; the trees, the animals, the birds, the great mother of the gods—sea, the capricious and generous earth, are invoked to only allow the good dreams to pass through and to trap the bad dreams by focusing them into the crystal. The Dreamcatcher is hung over the sleeper's bed at night. What an incredible technology of the sacred. Look at that circular mandala as it is attempting to capture the warp and woof of dreams.

Anyway, I was telling my nephew John all this in our high-speed, data-transfer talk. I wanted to go back and get the original anthropological literature and go through the process of building one for myself, because then I would invest it with a lot of my own spirit and it would become mine, and I thought it would get into my dreams more easily. He caught onto my enthusiasm.

Also, the Dreamcatcher reminded me of the Smith plot. This is a graphing system based on polar coordinates in electrical engineering. It is used to defend against noisy losses in broadcasting and receiving antennas by tuning. The coordinate system is a skewed, warped polar plot of the real and imaginary parts of the associated solution or system model of a circuit with capacitance and inductance. The zeroes are resonances of reflecting how the system was made from these physical parts producing capacitance or inductance. It was about how a signal passing through a media was attenuated, or otherwise trapped or influenced by noise. The warped grid looked exactly like the mesh of a Dreamcatcher.

Now for Christmas in our family, we draw lots and send one gift to one person (well, usually everybody gets something for the kids). My sister Anne got my name that Christmas. And sure enough, long after we were home from our trip I got a Dreamcatcher in the mail as my present! To be given one is almost as good as making one.

I was delighted. I took it upstairs and hung it centered over our bed. Then I went up to a tanka painting hanging on another wall in the room, a real tanka from Tibet with a curtain or shroud you can lower over the picture because their pictures are spiritual objects. And I covered the picture.

My wife noticed this and said something about it, and I explained: "To me it's respecting the energy of the artworks. And now I am pulling my energy out of the Tibetan Buddhism of the tanka and focusing it into the natural religion of the American Indian." And it seemed acceptable.

That night I had this dream. It is a recurring dream I keep having about looking for home. I am traveling out of San Antonio up the Austin Highway, going past the old Bun and Barrel that we used to hang out at back in the days of hot rods when I was a teenager in the sixties. And in the dream, I am somehow cruising in a car up along the San Marcos River into Comal county and some of the beautiful old aquifers full of cold water that stream out of the earth up. They formed beautiful jade pools where we used to go swimming. Some parts of the Texas hill country are as pretty as any country on earth. What I mean is not just that it is pretty as different from the hot, burnt-out wasteland that people assume Texas looks like in the movies, what I mean is the idea of the sylvan glade. That is, you might come upon a small lake in Quebec, or a hillside in Vermont that is an arrangement of nature so pleasing there is just a presence of place to it that always makes you feel good just to be there. There are places like that in Texas, too. In the hill country, there are grottos where the aquifer comes up from inside the earth, or little slopes where you meander under the ancient live-oak trees whose leaves almost shine in the cool moonlight, and the real beauty of the place becomes present.

In the dream, I am standing on the sweeping verandah of a big monastery. It is high up on a bluff overlooking a river. It is a big building made of stone, and the verandah on the second floor is up on pillars. I keep on coming back to this place. There is a commune there. Mostly women. And this time I went to dinner up on the second floor. When I went there to eat, I had to walk past plates of leftover buns from the breakfast the children had been served. There was some kind of a daycare on this verandah. I went into the main dining room and all the women were done up in purple. Some even had their faces with thick purple and lavender masques with sequin sparkles on their faces. It was wild. I looked out onto the town from a rampart of the monastery. When I say monastery I mean the image of the monastery in the dream. The image is ambiguous—a condensation of, a constellation of stone buildings from my past: my uncle's house in Ontario, the pavilion at Garner State Park, a Texas road house like the ones at Medina Lake, Deep Eddy pool in Austin and others. Each building brings with it its own meaning.

There is a river flowing through the town. And a big drive-in with fast cars. There are orchards of pecan trees. At dinner, all the women were being served by the men. The men were in natty cummerbunds and bow ties. The women were wearing gossamer flowing purple robes, faces rouged in a light purple, their cheeks dusted lightly here and there with a sprinkle of sparkle stars. They were in some kind of ritual sisterhood dinner. But I had been invited, too. I don't know why. I know somehow this place is something I keep coming back to, it's like home, or it's like a utopia of some sort.

Trying to understand this dream, I began to ask what would a technology of the sacred be? I tried thinking about a kind of skull cap, you know one of those long, old-time, sleeping caps (mama in her kerchief and I in my cap) that they used to wear—like a sock. A kind of cone hat that stretches up and attaches to the Dreamcatcher. But really the cap is a wire mesh, a web of fine wires intricately laid out on a Smith plot mesh so that they resonate with the energy flowing through. In the band of the cap are encephalopods that pick up brain waves, and the Dreamcatcher is like an antenna. An antenna for tuning in and displaying dreams. Some of the details get kind of fuzzy here, but the Dreamcatcher is like an antenna, or like a transducer, or a satellite dish that picks up the dreams from the Collective Unconscious and transmits them down to the brain, or going the other way, picks them up from the brain, and sends them out the transducer Dreamcatcher which, like an antenna, braoadcasts them out to where they are picked up by a computer. The Dreamcatcher does a Fast Fourier Transform, extracting the energy in the brain wave patterns and transmits that out to a big computer in the next room which does an analysis on this energy and looks for thresholds so it can distinguish between bad dreams and good ones.

I didn't get an insight into the dream until a couple of months later.

My teenage days, cruising the Austin Highway in fast cars, were so different from my world now. There was no such thing as a personal computer, nor pot. We drove to the hidden swimming holes coming up from the underground aquifer and laying at the bottom of canyons in the hill country. I recalled once spending the night in Garner State Park. Us boys got as buffed and shiny as we could, for campers and went to the country dance on the big pavilion overlooking the forest. (I was to shy to ask the lovely Texas daughters to dance.) That might have been the building in my dream—the big old Texas roadhouse made of stone. This dream was bringing me back around to see myself as a teenager, now removed, looking at the teenage rights of passage from the role of the big brother, the role of the uncle, to the role of the father.

But what is the meaning of the lavender women being served by men in bow ties and cummerbunds? Well, it's about the strategy of domestic peace. That ongoing commitment to family going down the generations. We are part of the dreams of our parents, and we inspire our children with our own dreams.

The Man Who Glowed in the Dark

Note: I am really embarrassed by this story. It expresses fears and feelings that are too painful to touch directly; they made me feel like a lowly character. So I invented Pharley Pizmo a character, (a garbage pail) into which to dump the feelings. The story is valid I think because it represents a man's efforts to de-sacralize the Goddess archetype for making him feel so abashed, sloppy, gawky, stupid, ugly and *unworthy* in her presence.

Vacation. His wife was happy. His kid had been looking forward to it with such anticipation. Pharley Pizmo didn't know. What does he know, he works all the time, was straight from six solid weeks of night and day jamming with the programming as a mouse potato. His wife comes from a family where it is understood that you must take a vacation every year. Certainly before the end of August. So here they were at camp. Pharley

Pizmo was apprehensive. It is not easy for him to spend a bunch of time with his family, and even more difficult to be in a large group setting of strangers. But he knew he must make the trip if only to help his wife take care of their little micro-hellion.

They drove their little station wagon east from San Francisco, across the Bay Bridge, past Oakland, worked their way up from the lowlands of the Delta, up over Altamont Pass, marveling at the great windmills, up into the high country of the Sierras, across great bridges over rivers, working their way up past China Camp, up Priests Grade to the mountain meadows, then onto narrow roads winding through countryside and over cattle guards amid tall pines and the great massive rocky upheaval of cliff faces until they came to the camp and checked in at the window of the main office.

The little family had to immediately unpack and get the car back up into the parking area off the highway because they locked up the roads down to the cabins at night. They carried their stuff into the cabin amid foreboding realizations: 1. They were right next to the dining hall—called the Lodge, and there were a lot of people making noise, enjoying long sophisticated California dinners with wine there; and 2. There was a peculiar odor emanating from the dining hall. They kept looking at their feet to see if they had stepped in something. Pharley Pizmo figured it was probably only the grease suckers cleaning out the traps and that it would go away. Besides, to raise a stink and change cabins was way too much trouble and there was no policy for it anyway. They decided to settle for what they got.

Pharley Pizmo's wife was driving him nuts with her maniacal organization energy, and he just wanted to get down and look at the creek and let her passion for organization run its course. So he took the wee lad, and the boy and his father slowly walked the little creek just down the hill from their cabin. The creek wended its way amid rocks and boulders under the tall alpine canopy. The sound of flowing water was restful. Pharley Pizmo tried to interest the boy in the watercourse way but the lad's only desire was to drop rocks in and make a splash.

The boy and his dad sauntered among little old dogpatch cabins situated here and there, every 20 to 30 feet or so through the woods. These little one room "shacks" (upgraded now to a single room dwelling) had once housed workers on the big public works projects—dams, railroads, tunnels—during the Depression.

Pharley Pizmo just wanted to get himself down to the lake or the pool as soon as possible to cool off his stunned and jammed-up body, so he got himself back to the cabin to change. There he collected his wife and the wee bairn collected his mother and the three headed out to walk across the entire length of the site headed down to the lake. The camp is several clusters of one and two room cabins with the large communal bathrooms in each cluster. Walking among the little cabins and seeing people on their porches is like walking though an Appalachian Peace Corps scene, everybody is dressed loose. The whole place didn't cover more area than the site of a large shopping mall.

At the lake, children were catching tadpoles and chasing dragonflies with little nets. The way they swathed the nets back and forth made them look like little cherubs flapping their wings. Some of the little blond-haired angels were floating on rafts. Two enterprising young girls were hard at work blowing and blowing to inflate their raft.

As Pharley Pizmo was walking to the lake with his wife and child in tow several paces behind him, the slim, gracile figure of a tall young woman emerged from a group of young women and walked straight at him. She made eye contact with them. It caused all around her to suddenly become arrested in their tracks. Some kind of recognition occurred as she came closer, along the road through the forest. As he watched her walking toward him, Pharley Pizmo suddenly felt sort of stunned, like a rabbit or other small rodent momentarily paralyzed in the headlights of a car. Her face had an aura of radiance about it. She was the picture of glowing health; here was the face of summer itself, smiling, tanned, carefree, on this lovely lithe young lady. Pharley Pizmo kept glancing at her.

She looked up directly at him. Here was a personage truly touched by the gift of beauty. The flashing of her indigo eyes, set in whites against tan, belied the presence of some entity other than a human being - a goddess or some other perfection of animal deception - driving the vehicle of her body. It shocked him. She seemed to *glow* from inside. His pulse quickened, and a sudden emptiness was left behind as his stomach went for a free fall down an elevator shaft. He needed to get out of the way or be run over. His knees might get weak and he might fall down in adoration before her. He tried NOT to think of how beautiful she was as she confidently stepped right up, stood before them. She was looking past Pharley Pizmo toward his wife. He was surprised when she struck up a conversation. She shook her long flowing hair free in all her girlish wonder, and said, “Hi. I’m Shawn’s daughter.”

He kept glancing at this animated young beauty as they spoke. He became painfully aware that he must have gawked for a second or two too long. She giggled.

"Hi," said Pharley Pizmo, trying to a overcome severe speech-impediment suddenly brought on by his awe. It has never been easy for him to talk to beautiful girls, but he had to talk to her, not just because she was gorgeous, but because his wife would start to become suspicious at his awkward bashfulness and suspect something was amiss. Pharley Pizmo tried NOT to think of how beautiful she was.

A brief animated introductory woman's conversation ensued. Pharley Pizmo tried not to appear tongue tied, awkward and ancient. She was only seventeen years old; her name was Lenore, she was the daughter of his wife's friend Shawn Greendraw. Her face had been graced, had been touched by the form of immortal beauty; it was beaming from her forehead. And her fraternal twin sister, Monica, waved shyly from a distance. She was equally beautiful in a more shy sort of way even though her hair was smoothed back in a more severe business look; her silky, peaches and cream complexion needed no make up. Pharley Pizmo tried not to be obvious watching them. The forward one turned on a dime and headed back to her tribe—the teenagers. He looked after her straining to see the shape of her chest, as she turned.

Pharley Pizmo thought about losing twenty pounds, getting a flat muscular stomach and being able to talk to these young beauties. Then a deeper problem occurred to him: how could he slough-off twenty years.

That night Pharley Pizmo's little family sat at Shawn Greendraw's table. Meals were served cafeteria style either inside or on the big deck at the central lodge, and were fantastic. It was packed at dinner. God, thought Pharley Pizmo, all these people from the same city fiercely recreating. They all hold secrets interesting and dull. The teenagers ran with their own crowd, and each of the twin daughters came over to the father's table to hug and tease brownie points out of their dad. Pharley Pizmo's heart skipped a beat when he was introduced to the twin's older sister, Diane. She was a couple of years older, very good looking with short red hair. And feeling, Clara Bow eyes.

Shawn, their great big old dad, said, "The girls are staying in tents across the creek." He was a kindly paterfamilias with a fastidious moustache and a good shave, like the old gent in tails from the Monopoly board game. "They have three seventeen-year-olds in one tent, and my oldest daughter, there, the one with the short red hair—she's a sophomore in college, don't you know,—is staying in her own tent right beside them. 'Because,' she says, 'these teenagers make too much noise.'"

Pharley Pizmo felt uncomfortable around these young girls. He had always felt intimidated by beautiful young women. He found himself wondering what would it take to overcome that. But then too, he was a married man and therefore rendered, or grandfathered in as a family man.

The next morning, Diane, the twins' older sister, came by to chat with Pharley Pizmo's wife. His wife introduced them. He tried to look nonchalant, yet he couldn't help trying to get a closer look at the young woman's eyes—were they really azure turquoise eyes, or were they contacts.

Try to talk to them, Pharley Pizmo urged himself. You are a married man and a father, you shouldn't be any threat. Use your status of being married and therefore rendered inert, to talk to this young lovely. "Your father tells me that you're going to UC Santa Cruz."

"Yeah."

"Do they still have that History of Consciousness Program there?" he asked.

"Yes," she said. She seemed excited that anybody knew about it. "I've even take a class in that department."

"Oh, what was that?"

"Well, it is called: *The Presentation of the Self through the Body in Space*."

"Wow."

"Yeah. It's about the localization of body image. We read a lot of Heidegger and stuff."

"Incredible," he said. He sighed and thought: these young people are so smart.

As she turned to leave, Pharley Pizmo watched the rising and falling of her behind as she walked back to her father's encampment. He found himself being amazed at how tightly her jeans fit her. Pharley Pizmo watched after her with a mixture of protective fondness and lust. Young. Attractive. Bright. On the way up to a splendid womanhood. His mind drifted into a fantasy about him having concourse with the goddess in the forest. She's a powerful, unforgettable, a devastatingly beautiful teenager who lures him—not against his will—into a grand indiscretion at a sacred place in the forest. Then she vanishes back to high school, never to tell anyone about it.

Later as Pharley Pizmo was walking across the compound, he composed a letter in his mind to the advice columnist:

Dear Abby, What am I getting myself into? I'm a 43

year old married guy. My wife's friend has two 17-year old daughters, and I'm unable to control my feeling of attraction to them. I find them extremely engaging and their older sister too. Although I'm many years older, I only look 37. I'd really like to bend one of these young lovelies over a picnic table and take her from behind. But what about my wife? My wife's friend?—their father! Many things worry me. What must I do to escape the torment of these longings. Doubtfully yours, Pharley Pizmo

Pharley Pizmo saw the proud student of psychology Diane again the next day. She was with her father's girlfriend, also an attractive redhead. Diane was sitting on the grass directly in front of him, sitting in her bikini. She was relaxed and she had let her legs fall open. It was very sexy. She had wrapped herself in a long beach towel and he was looking up a long sarong between the legs of a beautiful exotic woman in a southern clime. She was spreading her legs, for him, letting them loll back and forth innocently. He couldn't see her chest from here, couldn't tell if she had a large pair. While I'm at it, he thought, I'd like to inspect if she's a real redhead too. Christ if I could only think of some way to get closer.

Reckless desire was sending Pharley Pizmo into insane paroxysms of lust, and he felt he had to do something to negatively offset the spell of the glow surrounding this young beauty. He countered with self-loathing. I would drag her down, he told himself. If only she had a flaw, some imperfection, something to catch hold of, something to commiserate about.

His reverie was interrupted by a loud commotion

coming from one of the moms out on the raft. It was a huge woman in a floral bathing suit, one of those truly large mammas, a vast panoramic mountain of flesh, an amazing Amazon of a woman—the size of a walrus. She was ark-arking at her children. She had a rubber swimmer's cap from under which long sprongs of unwilling curls spilled out and ran like snakes down her neck and face. Pharley Pizmo shuddered and watched in shocked amazement as she jumped up and down on the raft rocking it. She bellowed, admonishing one of her many children in the lake swimming out toward the raft, "Swim, honey! Swim! You can do it!"

Then another great large Amazon mother ambled past. Pharley Pizmo looked on in horror and dismay, unable to take his eyes off her ass, hanging out of the back of her bathing suit. Either the woman doesn't know or doesn't care, he thought. The way her asses moved from behind looked like a fat jowly man, with a moustache, chewing a bathing suit like it was a big piece of spinach.

Somewhere in between the pillar and post of being on vacation, Pharley Pizmo got a little time to himself swimming in the lake. Oh well, what the hell. Jump in and join them. He loved the white noise avalanche sound that the leaves of the tall sycamore trees created undulating in the breeze around the lake - a sweet skiffling staccato, each leaf doing little rhythmic drum pats in a great aeolian orchestra when the wind rifled through their spangling leaves.

The next evening as Pharley Pizmo was coming back with his family from the pool and the lake, all four young women came sauntering, tall and tanned and young and lovely, by. He realized their attire went way beyond casual camp clothes, that in fact these beauties dressed down in the style of grunge - to de-emphasize their feminine beauty? Not possible. One of them was carrying a boom box on her shoulder and they were all dancing to some Grateful Dead tune. Jerry Garcia had just died the week before.

That night after dinner Pharley Pizmo decided to take a walk over to their tent site and see what he could see. Now, Pharley Pizmo was kind of worried about bears. Do bears prowl around at night. No, they only came out in the morning, he told himself. Hell no, another part of him argued, that's all they do is look for food. They can kill you with one swipe. Males eat their young. He crossed the creek on a wooden bridge and walked along the edge of the tent encampment. A man can take an evening stroll, can't he? What was wrong with that? He hoped to perhaps see a silhouette of one of these tall young beauties undressing in front of the light from a lantern at their tent. Who knows (his fantasy went), maybe one of them might spy him, and order the others, "Have that soldier washed and oiled and brought to my tent. So that he may be presented to me."

Pharley Pizmo lurked around the campsite, but began to feel creepy. Strange doing this, like a voyeur. He felt less than human, like some kind of animal looking through the bushes at people. He began to forget who he was. He was an animal of two minds running in the night, he had the night vision of the wolf or the cat predator. Looking at the scene lit by the moon, it was almost as bright as day, or like seeing it from inside a lightning flash, motion and movement leaped out and grabbed you as you ran by. He was on the trail of their scent; it was so strong he could almost see them by a synesthesia of scent for sight, see them standing, taking off their bras in the silhouette of tent light, their little sexual triangle hidden. He falls forward, he is running on all fours now, low to the ground feeling the grass like it was the hair on an animal's back, like there was no distinction between him and the being that was the earth, moving through the woods like a ballet dancer on point, soft as trout slipping through the stream. He came to the tent sight on all fours, tongue hanging out, hot on the trail of cunt. A great storm was fomenting to the north, swirling shadows and moving tree branches, but it was nothing like the push, the rush of energy in his body: it was the Infinite—needing to propagate itself through his animal seed. He crouched in the shadows, an animal on the earth in the great obscurity of night. The infinite must have their sex in order to penetrate space; we must procure sex so that matter can evolve into pleasure. And just as the body advances us through space underneath a sky that is like a skin around the world, we try to enter under the skin of the other. He oozed, he poured forth, he flowed, he elongated himself on the earth - became a snake slithering through the underbrush.

What fun it would be, he thought, to just plunge into the middle of all that feminine pulchritude like a barbarian. Then he remembered the joke, about the old bull talking to the young bull while looking at a heard of cows. The young bull wanted to run down there and get one of the heifers, but the old bull said, Let's walk down there really casual and slow and get all of them. Yeah. That would be cool. Pharley Pizmo tried to formulate a plan. How could he sneak into one of the tents where the wild girls were; especially the one with the young college girl in it. This camp is a small tribal community. I'd have to use magic or some kind of ruse or both, he thought. But he was an old married man and she was a sweet young college girl, the daughter of a friend of his wife's! It was obvious that the only way he could do the deed was if he put on some kind of disguise. But then that probably would mean some kind of rape if not at least deception.

Maybe If I shocked her. . . Presented her with some archetypal animality. Like a bear. That would get her attention. I'd need to get something that would at once paralyze her resistance and, moreover, turn her on. What if I made them think I was a bear? How could he go about it. First he'd have to cover his body with pine pitch grease and stick millions of cinnamon colored pine needles to his body. Then burst into her tent and GROWL! Maybe that would stop her in her drawers, and appeal to the twenty-one year old libido. . . Suppose I had a bear suit and lumbered into her tent. She might just lie still, trying to feign being an object—objectivity. And before she was aware I was not a bear, I would have her curvaceous bod stripped bare and could put it to her.

Pharley Pizmo went back to his cabin. A little later Shawn, the girls' father! came over for drinks and a visit. Pharley Pizmo was happy the father couldn't read minds; the father of the girls would have had him publicly horse-whipped for degeneracy. Shawn taught Pharley Pizmo how to tie a mantle on a Coleman lantern.

That night Pharley Pizmo lay awake looking up at the ceiling of the little cabin he shared with his wife and kid. Thinking: Rather than be a bear, what if I were a Radiant Being. I'd need to shed twenty pounds and twenty years and get something to make my body glow. Glow like moonlight on water. Like the way he used to in those old black and white movies with Gina Lolabridgetta and Giselle MacKenzie. How could he make himself into a Luminous Being. Yes! With the phosphorous that they have inside TVs! TV screens glow because of phosphors that decay just slowly enough that successive pictures blend into each other. Yes, phosphorous. But there aren't any TVs around here. What about fluorescent lights? He could steal a bunch of them, break them open carefully, collect the little bit of phosphorus they contain and then paint his body with it! Maybe if he greased his body up in pine pitch, he thought. He'd wander through the night - the Glowing Man. Phosphorus. Light Bear(er). Yes, maybe if he greased his body up in pine pitch, and then rolled in pine needles until he had a big furry coat, a shaggy white coat like it was just out of the wash, washed with Wisk or one of those old detergents that his momma used to use that made shirts glow in the dark. The Light Bear. Yeah, right. I get all cut up from rolling in the pine needles, then the cuts would mix with the pine pitch and the ooze would glow. Yuck. This is crazy! he thought. And you'd need a black light to make it glow, wouldn't you? Well fire light might work, it has ultra-violet in it, doesn't it? Or the weird glow from a Coleman lantern. He could see it. An eerie glow wakes up Giselle Mackenzie from her deep woods slumber and she opens her eyes to find the man with glowing skin standing in her tent. It might end up in the news. He could see the video clip in his mind:

Newscaster behind the desk looking up with abhorrence on his face. Sierra Occidental—Camp authorities and rangers heard reports of a mysterious "glowing man" who single-handedly seduced and /or raped a group of three young women camping in the Sierras.

No one else except the victims saw the brightly glowing man slip into their tent and start talking to them one at a time, apparently putting each of them into a hypnotic trance with his voice. The man then calmly carried each of them, one at a time into the forest. "We were paralyzed and unable to move," they said. The Glowing Man carried off first the two youngest daughters, then the older daughter, of Shawn Greendraw. The three victims, emerging from the forest after the ordeal, non-plussed but safe, said they felt they had been put into some kind of trance. They said, "It was the most amazing thing we have ever seen." The Glowing Man is reported to be about 6' 3" tall, in his late 30s, white and of average build with dark hair. He was not wearing any clothes but his entire body was reported to be everywhere covered with pine needles; that glowed! The Bear/ Man took them to his lair, a grotto hidden in the woods. It was a kind of altar, they said. The women said the glowing man carried them in the dark, up the draw, slipping down narrow deer trails until he came to what the girls all said they saw at first was a dim glow in the bushes. The oldest daughter said, "It turned out to be a small shrine built of rocks. It was totally abandoned. No candles. No pictures of saints with their haloes glowing, no swirling energy clouds of all known hue and brightness trumpeting the emergence of some tantric deity. Nothing but very, very old, lichen-covered, rounded stones, in a small arch, with an alcove-like space in the middle." The Glowing Man placed each woman on this stone alter one at time, as though making some kind of offering. On the altar he penetrated each of them. They could see him glowing there in the dark. "The damned thing glowed all by itself," the oldest daughter said.

Maybe. . . thought Pharley Pizmo. Wait a minute! His kid had some glow-in the-dark marks-a-lots. He could just color himself up with that! Maybe. . . In his mind he sought refuge from these elaborate insane fantasies by continuing the letter to Dear Abby: *What about her father? Would he find out? He doesn't seem to be keeping that close a tabs on her. But of course if it was rape, even if by my alter ego, my double, my ulterior motive, what would their father do to me if she told him. But all the same, a man is allowed to have a life, supposed to get a little every now and then. It's not like I am some uncaring, carefree eighteen-year-old looking for a fine sweet piece of teen-age ass.*

Actually it is, Pharley Pizmo told himself, shaking his head sadly. I have no grounds for defense.

He took up the design of a luminous being again. Maybe something like the way the mantle works on a Coleman lantern, he thought. Maybe I could make a sheath, tie it around my penis, and strap on a butane tank, onto my back. And just the skein of the sheath supporting the gas would burn, the way it does on a Coleman lantern. How hot does it get inside the mantle. Maybe it is just the fuel that burns, for the mantle is never consumed. You never know unless you put your finger in and light it. My penis could glow luminous bright in the dark, yet not be burned. Yes. The Man Who Glowed in the Dark. He imagined being in another news clip.

Sierra Occidental —Firefighters were stunned to hear a story from four young women campers about an illegal pyrotechnical display from a mysterious "glowing man" who might have accidentally started a forest fire burning in camp vicinity.

The four astonished witnesses, young women living at the camp, saw a glowing man with a very bright light blazing at the end of his erect penis calmly walk into the college student's tent. Seconds later streams of light were seen inside the tent, and jets of flame spurting out the door. The witness said, "The light emitted by the Glowing Man's light-tipped battering ram began to increase in both size and potency. The light got brighter and brighter until he let off an incredible blast and a stream of roman candles shot out like tracer bullets across our tent." The man then returned to the forest leaving a bright trail of light behind him.

The Glowing Man smiled. Well. It was better then spending all that time sticking millions of pine needles into your skin, so that they hung like coarse fir. And waiting for the puncture wounds to scab over. Crazy. I must be losing my mind.

The next day Pharley Pizmo was feeling extremely alienated. Looking at the people at camp disgusted him. They all come from San Francisco. Almost everybody has a kid or two. People our age have teenagers. Our kid is just three. They walk around. Everything is taken care of: Meals, lodging. There is swimming. The lake. Horseback riding. All these kids have their bikes. It is a cool place for kids. You could let even the little ones run free. Everybody dresses in funky colors. Can't tell how much money people have. Because the place is not expensive. Very democratic. Everything seems to please these people, the food, the games, the pool, the lake. Rocks for the kids to climb, even the squirrels. Pharley Pizmo was going out of his mind with boredom.

He was certainly out of his element. Vacation. Either he was losing his mind or trying to make the transition from being a wage slave to being a mage knave—a sorcerer's apprentice. Ah, to be invisible. That would be good, or to at least be immune from prosecution. How could he protect himself from other people knowing.

What other people know about you and what personal information about yourself you seek to present to the world are two different things. The right to a private and a pubic self are only as good as your ability to protect your privacy. The kind of jobs you get and the ability to earn, to learn and to yearn are based upon the "perception" of your worth. Someone once said: Money is the sixth sense. Without it the other five are not operative.

Pharley Pizmo thought about the job hustle he was constantly up against. Human resources, what a name. Give me a break. Why don't they just call you a machine or a stack of lumber. He pictured a human resource person going around introducing the new worker, "and here in this cubicle, sits a number crunching lawn mower." Pharley Pizmo recalled a recent program on NPR about this guy who worked as a temp at a desk near the laser printer. The guy was shocked to find out that the people he interacted with - some of the individual co-workers as often as forty to sixty times a day - didn't know his name. They were not curious to know even that little bit about him. From his vacation Pharley Pizmo wrote a postcard to Dear Abby in his mind:

Life here is so hard that I don't think I can make it through. Sometimes I want to cry. I want to escape... I want to go out. I thought again about killing myself. It's stifling here. I want to see my friends outside ... God please help me.

A party of his wife's friends, Mr. Greendraw and his lovely daughters, and others loaded up in several cars and caravaned to O'Shaunessy Dam. From on top of the great dam forming the Hetch-Hetchy reservoir they could see below a small brick pump-house, about the size of a small brick duplex, attached to the wall of the dam. And a huge spurting gush of thousands of gallons of water per second was blasting out of a two-foot wide duct in the face of the pump house. It was like a great wide mouth going O, spewing forth a torrent of water shooting 150 feet straight out with a great force of exhortation before it fell 500 feet onto the chasm below.

It was weird. Pharley Pizmo had forgotten that he was one of those people that suffer from height-induced psychosis. It manifested in suicide fantasies. His mind got taken over by some elaborate suicide plot, in which he leaped off the top of the dam and fell the eight stories down onto the roof of the pump house. He saw himself trying to crawl, dragging his broken legs behind him over to the edge of the pump house, crawling painfully, while tourists pointed and screamed, saw himself lifting his broken self up over the edge of the pump house and throwing himself into the blasting gush of water, actually trying to straddle it like a horseman or like the guy in Dr. Strangelove riding the A-bomb down at ground zero. Whew. Pharley Pizmo shuddered at the thought. Where on earth did that come from?

No particular reason really, came the answer. Just giving in—to the air. The air wanted to feel his body shoot through it. The air wanted to see if he would make a huge explosion of blood at the bottom of the long fall of the waterfall plume. Or maybe the air just wanted to see if the huge plumes of foam kicked up by the shoot would buoy him up. Ah, hah, not bloody likely. The facade of the pump house looked like a face with water gushing out of the mouth. Pharley Pizmo looked at the face on the dam. And looking down from that height at the gigantic plume shooting out of the center of the face of the dam, he was dismayed and shaken to find such a mad thought about what it would be like to commit suicide had inserted itself into his mind. Detached, he speculated: if, in the chute, in the fall (he could see himself leaping off the dam and his trajectory taking him into the gushing torrent spewing out from the overflow) would I struggle, would I scream for the brief moment of the fall: my mind accelerating at 32 thoughts per second per second as my feet walk across — through — an invisible door into a metaphysical world. There is water, I am falling into water. I might be able to . . . there might be . . . just enough up-splash from the falls, that the upward force would support me. I'd have to enter it just right, rotate and get to the perfect angle, the same angle light has to achieve in order to glance off of water and become a rainbow in the chute.

Pharley Pizmo was able to turn this from dire to dry by seeing himself come up in an MTV bungie jump commercial and some young announcer gives me high five and says, "Way to go dude."

When Pharley Pizmo got back to camp, he started noticing how much his little boy was enjoying the camp. Pharley Pizmo started getting more into the swing of things. He enjoyed the cold lake with its green-plank, oil-barrel raft. He enjoyed the huge, marvelous, red dragonflies that patrolled the shores, hovering like helicopters or darting off like harrier attack jets to hoover up the mosquitoes. His boy was having a wonderful time, chasing tadpoles, playing in the pool with water wings, learning how to climb the many large boulders around the place. One was called Pride Rock and it was the place for children to climb in order to go from being babies to kids.

Pharley Pizmo took a crafts class that afternoon and made a Dream Catcher for his son. It is a net of weaving, attached to a sapling frame bent into a circular mandala. There is usually a spiral nautilus shell, or a crystal in the web. It was first invented by the Iriquois, for capturing and banishing nightmares. Pharley Pizmo found a shell while walking in the woods. He understood this mountain too had transport with the ocean at some point in the deep aeons of pre-history.

Pharley Pizmo realized the nicest thing about the camp was how architecture informs community. The cars are left parked up on the highway and people use paved footpaths (wide enough for the garbage truck) or walk under the Alpine canopy forest on the bark covered grounds. After a while everybody starts letting their kids run around free, playing basketball, tennis, riding bikes, playing ping-pong, climbing rocks. The parents one by one were letting go a little, feeling a terrific sense of relief to be able to trust the community of parents.

Pharley Pizmo's wife had them worrying about entrance exams to kindergarten for Christ's sake. The boy has wonderful language skills, thanks to his mom, and they were going to push him into a bilingual preschool this year. Pharley Pizmo got him a little Mac plus, and was teaching him to mouse around on the PC clone. He can mouse around with the best of them, he'll be all right. Just buy him a bunch of CDs.

Pharley Pizmo thought he might use the momentum of the upswing in his mood, to carry forward his campaign to bed one of those teenagers, especially the co-ed, the older sister.

What about talking her into appearing in an art

photograph in the nude, he thought. I could tell her I could get it in a magazine. Women do have a lot more vanity for that.

He practiced his spiel:

—Hello. I hope you don't think I'm too forward but I think you're really beautiful and I'm a pretty good photographer and wondered if I could interest you ... in sitting for an art photo.

(Pause, give her time to consider.)

—Well there are some lovely old smooth trees that have half fallen down the hills over here, and they are all worn smooth and they look like legs and arms and I thought I might pose you near them. See, people would associate the shapes of the trees with the human body shapes better if they had a human body in the picture.

—I was thinking of something like that famous Wyeth, of the girl crawling in the fields. The trees are like the girl in the painting. Only ours would have this obviously healthy girl —you—and she is nude. It's a statement.

Yeah right. Instead, Pharley Pizmo gave himself another field trip, a walk along a stream that split itself over little islands or boulders. He was able to leap or carefully ford from island to island. He had his recording equipment and tried to do some recording. With his ears Pharley Pizmo could hear the burbling of the stream like tabla drumming of the water echoing and slapping over the rocks. But his recording just came out white noise. God damn, what I wouldn't give for a good portable DAT with digital I/O, he thought. He coveted that new Tascam just out for $1650. The folks at Lucas bought the first one from Bananas at Large in San Rafael. But I'm just a dilettante, a dabbler, and that's too rich for me.

When they got home from vacation, Pharley Pizmo helped his little son write a letter home to his sister, the boy's aunt. It went:

We had a nice vacation. I liked climbing the rock best.

I made a rainbow candle, in the wax and the water.

I put on the water wings and I floated in the shallow water of the swimming pool. Can't go in the deep water. No sharks in the deep water of the lake. Frogs and tadpoles and bull frogs like that water, plain water has crocodiles in it.

No sharks, no crocodiles

Daddy is batty, he put a feather in the dream catcher and he put a big fat piece of moss on my dream catcher, to collect the nightmares so they don't bother me.

I'm going to start at Little Star school. Because I'm going to study Cantonese language.

We made sun angels when we got out of the cold pool. We lay on the hot concrete. It felt hot. Good.

I slept in the sleeping bag.

Wolverine Man had veins of blood on his body. His hands were like shredders. Wolverine Man fought with Batman. Batman lost and White Ranger threw his vehicle at Wolverine, and he tumbled to the ground. He knocked the bullfrog, he knocked the tadpole.

Some Thoughts on Vacation

Summer in America. At a camp for San Francisco residents in the Sierras. I sit in a folding chair on a rising slope in the lawn overlooking the diving board at the little lake. If I can quiet my ego and be present, I can hear the little skittle-tittle shash of the waving sycamore leaves in the trees. Sounds of the pond at a sweet spot. But instead I shout: "Echo!" The sound skips across the flat lake surface and resounds off the dense redwood and pine tree-line in the distance and comes reverberating back. Echo. The little lake has an echo. A big black bird rises, then plummets into the shoreline where it disappears in the shadows.

I didn't expect to see a man die on vacation.

Now, I was saying good-bye to the place, and trying to have some *other* thoughts, some other recollection of the vacation besides the incident—like the insights walking around in nature, or what I experienced being close with my kid. Or even just the power of the place—as you pass through huge, massive granite cliffs, staring down on you from some 4000 feet straight up. Or getting sun burnt, mosquito bit, lip-chapped, swimming a lot. Or the conversations I had, the reading I did in a book about the emergence of rhythm in nature's clocks and the insights it gave me. Anything to make it feel like a normal vacation—the fractal pictures I took of reeds growing out of the lily pond and the branches coming out of the fallen sunken log in the water juxtaposing the generosity of nature against the art of the little man-made Monet bridge. The incredibly clear night sky in the high Sierra: at night you can see the whole cross section of the Milky Way. And oh, the scary walks through the forest in the dark.

Oooh I just inhaled a mosquito!

And that reminds me of the book I poured over on this vacation: *When Time Breaks Down*, by Arthur Winfree. About how he reset the mosquito's internal clocks and that gets me to thinking about the heart—my heart, your heart—and when it, or something else as important, might give out.

And with this, the drowning incident would replay again.

We were, many of us, sitting around the lake. I had been bumped out of my sweet spot by a loud tourist with an annoying Brooklyn accent. I had been trying to concentrate on Winfree's book about, ironically enough, the circadian rhythms of nature and the topology of defibrillating arrhythmias. And to escape this voice, I had swum out to the green raft about 30 yards from the deck. I was sitting on the glossy green-painted planking of the oil-barrel raft with my legs outstretched, trying to warm up in the hot air, lake water dripping off me into little puddles beading up, when I heard the shout a good distance off.

Help!

We turned to look across the lake and saw the danger. A man was floundering way out in the lake. Come to think of it some sort of agitated activity on the periphery had been kind of noticed. A man had managed to raise an arm in the air and shout Help!

Someone yelled across the lake at the people of a tailgate party on the other side (they were so much closer) that there was someone who needed help. They didn't seem to respond - perhaps they could not hear us?

Next thing: I, along with several others were moving towards it. Hikers on the other side of the lake were moving toward the edge too.

There was another shout HELP and the lifeguard, an attractive young woman named Sandra, holding court in front of a team of tanned volley ball players (all male) turned to give her far-off stare at the lake.

Some others stood on the raft platform with me. There were others on the lake: some people in a little yellow inflatable canoe, wearing life jackets, three teenage girls hanging onto a big air mattress, an older woman swimming her long laps, a couple of young boys. I used to be a lifeguard in my youth, but sadly, due to a life of stress, insanity and inactivity, eternally geeking out in front of the computer, I've become overweight and short of breath. So now, it did cross my mind not to go after him. Let the staff and other younger people go. I'm not in much shape to rescue this nearly three hundred pound floundering man who I had recognized—just before I hit the cold water and the shock brought me to my senses—as I started swimming toward him. I had seen him drinking beer with his buddies, grinning a charming, shy grin, a fat, nay rotund, man. Hanging out with the good old boys in the rocks next to their trucks and fishing gear. I had not heard of the good Samaritan law; I don't recall making any conscious decision. I just dove in after him. I was closer than the lifeguard, and the man was shouting HELP!

It was sheer idiocy on my part. What could I do? I could barely swim well myself and had forgotten most of what I knew about lifesaving. I wouldn't even have attempted it, if it had been a couple of days earlier.

Yes, a couple of days before the tragedy yesterday, I had decided it was time to swim all the way across the lake to the rock sticking out on the other side. I had to roll over on my back and float a couple of times, but I made it! So now I felt like I owned the lake, its cool fresh dark-green waters were so much better than the nasty chemical itch at the swimming pool. And when duty called, I jumped in.

We were white figures moving through the blue-green water, rushing toward a central point like beads of dew sliding down the radial strands of a spider's web to the center. The encounter that would unhinge us was minutes away, its enormity disguised from us not only by the barrier of time but by the buoyant media threatening to take us down under it.

What I describe is shaped by what my wife and little boy—they happened to have wandered down to the lake to look for me—saw too. By what we told each other and what other people told us in the time of obsessive re-examining that followed. What happened is this, as determined by what the police said—and many of the residents at the camp were either police or firemen themselves or were somehow related to disaster and city workers—so they knew the investigators.

The drowned man's name was Hans Otto, a mason from Danville who owned property in San Francisco. He along with his wife Milvia, a licensed practical nurse from Danville, and their son Mendle (nicknamed "Mack"), age thirty-one, and some other families who were friends of the Ottos had gotten a couple of the big cabins far away from the lodge for a happy summer getaway.

It was past lunch and a bright sunny day and lots of people were out on the little lake. Only moments before, some people had sort of noticed something amiss across the lake, but it wasn't until he called for help that people started moving to his aid.

On the land somebody was saying something to the son, "Yo Mack, what's up with your old man out there in the lake? He looks like he's having a cramp or something."

Mack didn't know.

Mack's father, Hans Otto, was a huge, cigarette-smoking, six-pack-drinking mason. With a huge potbelly. He had had too many drinks at lunch, and he had lumbered down among the big boulders on the far side of the lake and putting a little yellow inflatable canoe into the water, he flopped down on it. The inflatable split at the seams under his weight and promptly started sinking in water over his head.

Some of those in his party noticed it and were moving toward him even before he cried out. He was going under fast, his plastic inflatable lifeboat loosing gas, it had sprung a leak and air was seeping out as he was slipping in. They thought he would be able to work it out himself. Those closest to him could see the man struggling to hold on to what was left of the inflatable, which was soon mostly underwater. This was when he yelled for help. Soon there were several of his friends and party on the far shore shouting and screaming.

I'm lingering in the prior moment because it was a time when other outcomes were still possible. And the convergence of five figures in a flat green space has a comforting geometry from the raven's eye: the knowable, limited plane of the green felt pool table, where all outcomes are decided by pure Newtonian mechanics of collisions. We were coming in from all angles of the compass, converging on a drowning man who was thrashing in the middle of a little lake. We were moving toward a catastrophe which, if we could see it in higher dimension, is an event in a phase space of many folds, where perhaps one could drill through this manifold to some other outcomes.

This was the moment, the vortex at the center of the curl, where time and destiny were being pulled into a black hole. The black bird flying over could see us from two hundred feet up: five distinct groups of people—the girls, the man in the canoe, the hikers from the other side and last Sandra from the lifeguard tower, and me—moving across a green one hundred acre lake toward the white splashing, not far from the spillway at the deep end. Some dipping oars, some paddling on floating devices with their hands, some swimming in the cool dark green water. I approach from the raft, Sandra is behind me.

I am swimming from the raft; the man in the yellow canoe with a hat is turning and starting to dig in; one of the girls raises up on her forearms and destabilizes the mattress. They are all three sisters, Shawn's daughters—young women, just starting in college—beautiful and courageous: two of them break free of the mattress and start swimming toward the man, who was now screaming Help. Help me! Sandra, the lifeguard has jumped into the little aluminum row boat all set up at the dock for just this life saving situation. She had deftly pushed off, and is rowing like mad across the lake. She knew an adult can easily drown in a minute. A child can drown in 20 seconds. Others are running toward the shore from the woods on the other side.

Right now, in retrospect, I am holding back trying to see maybe the shape of destiny perhaps. I knew the three young women swimming heroically toward the drowning man from earlier vacations here at the camp. They were Shawn's twin daughters Monica and Lenore, twenty-one, spending a few days in camp with their dad, to celebrate his birthday. Along with their slightly older sister Dianne, twenty-four, the three beauties were spending some rare time together for what was supposed to be a carefree outing, floating and hanging out on this lovely little lake in the California alpine. The girls all went to different schools, one at UC Berkeley, one at Yale, and the wild one at Santa Cruz. They had capsized themselves, and while Dianne scrambled to clutch their raft, Monica and Lenore—both expert swimmers—broke free of the mattress and started swimming toward the man in trouble, at the moment he screamed Help. Help me!

The closest person to the drowning man, and the first to reach him, was John Nolan, a father, who had his young son with him in the same kind of little yellow inflatable canoe that Mr. Otto had. Mr. Nolan's six-year-old boy is trying hard not to de-stabilize their canoe; his eyes bugged with fear, as his father paddled hard in the direction of the drowning man.

Coming from land was a bus driver and a couple of the man's friends, Dave Pinochot, a young guy in his thirties, big into Sierra hikes but not that much on swimming. He has dropped his back pack and canteen and is running in his hiking shorts and heavy hiking boots toward the rocks at the water's edge. They are the drowning man's friends.

At present I am on a stretch of line trying to make it across the lake from the raft to the drowning man. It doesn't matter how deep it is, it is all over your head. All I could do was my painfully slow crawl. Sandra, the lifeguard plowing through the water like a pro, quickly overtook me.

The drowning man's float was hemorrhaging at the seams. Obviously way past being worthy, it had started to fold, and only a last billow of it was sticking up, and the man grasped it and rolled over on his back and went under kicking madly.

John Nolan was moving smoothly toward the point of intersection, paddling the canoe fiercely and was the first to reach him. Later as he described it when he was coming toward him, he and Mr. Otto were looking eye to eye: John Nolan said, "For a moment it felt as if there were only the two of us in the whole wide world, that there was nobody else on the lake or in the camp, that everyone else had simply disappeared. And I was excited because I was going to get there in time—I was going to get him." He said, "Mr. Otto seemed to be floating vertically—smiling, but there was a look of fear on his face. He had a shocked expression behind the smile. I saw the panic on his face, and I shall never forget it. I was just a few strokes away! But I looked at my boy FOR A SECOND, to make sure he was OK and to figure out what we would do when we got to him, and on looking back I saw only the top of Mr. Otto's head! He had gone under as though he were looking for something." We were later told it was probably at this moment when Mr. Otto had the heart attack.

There just wasn't any more of the float to hang on to, and all the struggling got Mr. Otto caught in the fern. He had somehow gotten a foot entangled in the mass of water plants growing beneath the water at the edge of the lake. The fern, yes, I too, had encountered the fern. It is a thick knotted mass of long, hardy, green, snake-like tentacles floating just beneath the surface, twisting and turning in some parts of the lake. They are nasty, large, rangy, prickly, pipe-cleaner like plants, and it hurts to rub up against them. They are almost predatory. They aren't everywhere. It is like a hedge in front of the rock. A hedge you have to get over. The Fern. I might have to go to a psychiatrist and tell him about the fern, its griping tentacles, its mindless nemesis. The drowning man was in that part of the lake close to the shore where the green vines and weeds and underground plants were quite thick and rough, and he had become entangled in them. Because, in his panic, the drowning man had thrashed his legs, and this had gotten himself even more ensnared in the thick tangled mat of water-plants growing like ropes close to the other side.

It was only a couple of days earlier when I, myself, had made this swim across and encountered the fern growing at the far side of the lake. I had actually had something of the same experience, I was caught by a strand of the fern. You can't see where you're caught, but you can feel it. The best thing to do is not panic, and stop movements. That will often allow the fern to let go. But Mr. Otto was already panicking. His anxiety must have quickly grown into fear and then panic, and when panic comes in the door, reason and your ability to solve problems go out the window. Panic knows only two responses, fight and flight. Neither is much use under water when you are trapped in the fern. This sudden over-amping stimulus must have been what pushed him into a heart attack.

John Nolan and his boy in the little yellow inflatable canoe were on him at that point. John reached into the water to lift Mr. Otto. The drowning man made a desperate grab onto the salvation of the canoe, and this caused the flimsy floatation device to immediately capsize. John Nolan said, "He must have felt the float touch his shoulder or something, because his eyes were shut tight in pain; just his hands came out of the water and grabbed onto the float, and he pulled it down. And that knocked Tommy out into the lake! I had to go after my boy."

"I saw the man, clutching onto our float. He nearly grabbed me! I felt his fingernails claw my back. I turned to look at him and saw a face all puffy and red, his eyes bugged in terror. He was frantically heaving and wheezing, and choking, gasping for air. It was terrible."

John Nolan tried to right their own situation by grabbing onto the inflatable, which had slipped out of the drowning man's grasping reach. Later we understood that the drowning man was caught up in the reeds, and even if he had wanted to reach down and untangle himself he had been trying to grasp and hold onto the air-filled boat in a panic. For now he had to deal with the chaotic arrhythmia in his heart coursing through his chest, and circulating out, disrupting muscles and severing control to the parts of the body, freezing them up. While at the same time his breathing was moving into eventual quiescence. He could not have kicked and struggled himself free from the tentacles of the fern that held his legs.

I, myself, had to stop and tread water for a moment to get my bearings. Then I had to roll over on my back and float for a while and try to relax. I was getting short of breath. I could see that some others were trying to save the man, and I didn't want to become a burden. Sandra the lifeguard, pulling hard, knifed past me in the rowboat.

The twins Monica and Lenore got there next, at about the same time as a couple of young guys did. Monica said, "I tried to reach around behind Mr. Otto while reaching to grab onto Mr. Nolan's float, and the drowning man grabbed me around the neck! This big man grabbed me and was trying to use me to keep himself afloat! And he was hanging on to me, and I was way out of air, and I panicked and went under. I just did manage to grab a breath and went under. Luckily that is the thing to do because a drowning man will not hold onto a sinking object. He was thrashing and struggling and kneed me in the side trying to climb out on me. I could feel the plants scratching on my body."

Monica came up gasping, she had pushed him off. Her sister Lenore was trying to maneuver Nolan's inflatable canoe over to them. One of the boys, noticed Mr. Otto was caught and dives down to try and untangle him. Mr. Nolan was rescuing his panicking boy, towing him out to the edge.

Monica said, "And Mr. Otto was still thrashing about. He had become entangled in the water plants and was making it worse. He sunk, and I tried to swim around behind him, and we ended up butting heads."

The other young men swimmers at the scene were Rick Yen and Bob Zemack. These young men were diving down and trying to unravel the vines from around his legs.

Now Sandra the lifeguard reached the core of the catastrophe in her boat and saw that the drowning man was nowhere to be seen. People on the shore were shouting: "He's under the canoe, he's right under your boat." There was no sign of the drowning man. One of the guys from Mr. Otto's party, who had jumped in with his clothes and shoes on, was there. Sandra immediately shouted at him to hold the boat, and jumped into the lake where the drowning man had last been seen. The lifeguard was shouting instructions at everyone there, and, though I was not at the scene but close, was doing all I could to keep myself afloat and could not hear her. I was gasping for air and held onto the rowboat like it was a buoy, and one of the other guys had a hold of it and was trying to swing it around.

And the big guy was sunk under.

I saw him. I put my face in the green brown lake water to see what I could do to help. I was doing the dead man's float, trying to calm myself down, and I saw the drowned man under a couple of feet of water, and he looked weird and white under the green water in that strange light. He wasn't kicking and trying to claw his way back up for air. He wasn't struggling. He hung perfectly still and floated—drifting in the half light of the murky water.

Coincidences of time and place, and a predisposition to intervene had brought us together to hover over the sinking man. The lifeguard was in charge, but she was underwater. I was exhausted, I'm sorry to say. I should not have been there and realized I could end up being a burden and causality too. I might easily get caught up in the deadly fern. I felt my own heart about to leap out of my chest and wondered had a made a mess of things? I don't know whether the others were exhausted or slipping or what, but I knew in my mind that I had to do something to save myself; I was not going to make it.

Monica and some of the young guys from shore were diving under and had managed to free Mr. Otto's leg from the weeds. I saw Sandra dive under and get him. And I wondered if there was some freak break in the laws of physics that might let a man breathe under water. Finally, one of the young men managed to get his legs free. Sandra got the right hold, her left arm over a shoulder and her other under the other shoulder. Somehow she had managed to drag the heavy man up. She must have a powerful kick for a swimmer.

There was a lot of shouting and confusion. We were all talking. I wasn't talking. I was starting to gargle water. Someone said, "She's got him."

We didn't know what to do. Sandra brought him up—a tiny woman holding up this huge bear's head, and barked an order to hold her boat steady and to use it as a platform to hold us up and to pull him onto the boat. Sandra was red-faced, bawling out orders at us; she was the authority here, and we tried to obey.

"Help me hold him up , I can't lift him out!" she shouted.

The drowning man had passed out, had had a heart attack. We didn't know it at the time, we thought he had just fainted. The man lay slumped under Sandra's arm as she was attempting to stretch around his wide girth in a hug. Someone else was holding his other hand, trying to use the row boat as a lever to pull him up. I tried to get a hand under his arm, but still had not gained purchase on the rowboat, which was swinging around wildly as Lenore and others tried to maneuver it into position. Sandra shouted, "Somebody needs to get into the boat and we need to pull him up onto the boat by the back end."

And now Dave Pinochet makes a great pulling leap and manages to heave himself over the back end of the rowboat and flop down onto its seats. He had shoes on, and he scrambled and turned around and reached down to grab his drowned friend's hands and pull him into the boat. Others were below in the water trying to help push the big man on board. And thank god I was able to get one hand on the rowboat and use the other hand to help with the lift. Dave was trying to not let it capsize from all the hands that were helping and holding and we were glad to get this boat to give us some leverage because of course, we couldn't stand on the bottom to lift him up. A drowning man is never tall enough.

Someone shouted, "PULL him up onto the boat, and we'll get him to shore."

Sandra was getting exhausted, as it was taking all her strength to hold the man up, and the other fellow reached across the canoe, and had hold of the drowning man's other hand, and was holding him up. We were panicked - freaked out. It had all happened so fast and the drowned man was beyond participating in his own rescue. And finally with a great heave, we managed to beach this whale into the back of the boat.

Sandra shouted up to the young man pulling him onto the boat: "Try to turn him over so that he is face up, so we can start CPR. The guy yelled back "Hold the boat steady," and we just did manage to turn him as we wrestled Mr. Otto up over the stern and onto the floor of the boat so he was sprawled out on his back over a couple of seats, face up.

With a great heave Sandra pulled herself up on the stern of the boat and over the drowned man's unconscious body. She started basic life support—mouth to mouth CPR. She said later, "I could tell that the prognosis was not good." Sandra shouted at one of the camp workers on the shore to go back around the lake to "get the CPR kit in the lock-box behind the lifeguard tower. It is unlocked!" Hans Otto was brought to shore, pushed to shore; pulled to shore. The boat had to be pulled in through some trees because we had to go around the side of the rocks to a better place to land. Many people had gathered around to help lift Mr. Otto off the boat and carry him onto the grass and lay him out on the ground. Sandra got down there and started doing CPR while another camp worker pressed on the chest, and they called out time numbers. I staggered out of the water with some help from a kindly camper extending a hand.

The man's wife Milvia Otto was standing beside the rescue workers looking on, a frightened expression on her face. Her best friend held her hand.

By the time the runner got back with the Emergency CPR equipment—pumps with bags and clamps and tubes, Hans Otto was without breath; nor did he have a pulse. His eyes were open with fixed, dilated pupils. CPR was continued. The camp doctor had arrived from the clinic and rolling Mr. Otto over first on the right side and then on the left, had inserted an endotracheal tube down his throat. Using a suction catheter, he tried to open up a passage, but it didn't work. They kept working for another fifteen minutes, until the camp doctor, Dr. Smith, pronounced Mr. Otto dead. He took Mrs. Otto's other hand and looked her in the eyes and said, "The breath is not going down. We tried to pump it out, but it is hopeless. As soon as the lungs fill with water, that's it."

The dead man's wife was by his side. The Highway Patrol came. An EMS unit came and took him away. The wife rode in the back, and their son followed in a car driven by a sober friend. The other couple camping with the Ottos were close and of some consolation. It was about 2:30 in the hot afternoon when the officers took her and Mr. Otto to the hospital in Sonoma by EMS vehicle. And we headed back to our cabin – a forlorn group, freaked out and in a state of our own shock. Shawn was there helping out. He is a disaster coordinator for the city and knew one of the highway patrol cops. He told us that as they were getting ready to leave with the body in the EMS vehicle, Milvia's friend gave Mrs. Otto a gift. She hugged her bereft weeping friend and held her close. She said: "It's nobody's fault. God's gonna pick who he's gonna pick. It was Otto's time. God don't make no mistakes."

We felt a kind of horrified shame at not being able to save this man. I still can't get this image out of my mind of the man half-floating, half-sinking in the eerie light of the murky green water. He was just a couple of feet away, and it was not that much closer to the shore where we would all be able to go ashore, but we were surrounded by the deadly weeds. I was extremely bummed out that I had let myself get into such awful shape and seemed to be unable to turn this part of my life around, even now after the death of this man due to my inattention to the physical.

He might have been able to save himself when the float collapsed and started to lose air and buoyancy, but then the shock and the gravity of the struggle apparently precipitated a heart attack. It might have worked saving someone who maybe had temporarily had a cramp and could at least hold his head above water; this guy was totally incapable of that. He had had a heart attack. It must have been awful. Getting tangled in the water weeds, the panic, the heart attack. We know that alcohol and maybe drugs were a big factor. He was overweight and diabetic, and he had a heart condition. Still, if his friends had kept a better eye out for him. How different things might have been if he had stayed with his friends and not gone in the water. Or at least if somebody had gone in with him. How different things might have been if his weight had not exceeded the capacity of the inflatable canoe or if it had been more seaworthy and able to stay afloat.

What had started out as a simple, pleasant summer camping trip for a week in the California Sierras had ended with a terrible, heart-rending drowning. Some one should have seen it coming. People knew nothing about the tangle of water weeds at the edge of the far side of the lake, or the precipitous drop off in depth there. There was no warning sign; nor was it brought up in orientation around the campfire that first night.

The Dance at the Deck, that evening, which is usually the most joyous affair, crowning the week with a blowout on the last night of camp, with all these moms in tie-dyes dancing with their kids, was canceled—out of respect. It was a subdued somber evening with people hanging around their cabins in small groups, and some just packing to leave. They would later instigate a mandatory swimming test for anyone going into the lake.

As we were saying good-bye to the place the next day before the long trip home, I was again going back over the events previous to the incident to see if I could find some clue as to how to prevent it. Or just to have some better memories of the place.

I remembered when we arrived after a long drive from San Francisco. We were thrilled and pulled up to the little Cabin, 25. It seems to be at the crossroads of basketball central. Carrying bedding, ice chests, first aid kit, lights, polywogging gear, suitcases and back packs with clothes we get situated, I have a huge array of tape recorders, video camera, CD player, CDs and books.

I am always filled with my natural fear and loathing around strangers, and it takes a lot for me to confront that at camp. Nor is it easy for me to be cooped-up with my family for a week in a small one room cabin. I try to be Buddhist about it (dealing with adversity is the price you pay for a lesson in love): going through the camping adventure with loved ones brings you close. And my boy, Wild Bill, just loves coming to camp so much.

It *is* crowded. People living in little one-room cabins and tents, might have lived like this in refugee times. That is part of the charm of the place. The little old dogpatch cabins are situated here and there in clumps among giant spruce and redwood trees, every twenty to thirty feet or so through the woods. They had once housed workers building the Hetch Hetchy dam, one of the big public works projects that pulled us out of the Great Depression.

There is a calendar of days and activity times posted

under glass in front of the big timber lodge. Days of crafts, face painting, making friendship bracelets, making pine cone bird feeders, tie-dying, candle making, button making, swim lessons every day. Tomigochis are left being watched by moms while the kids go pollywogging every day. There is lanyard weaving. Endless games of table tennis played on the many outside tables scattered here and there among the trees in prep for tournaments among opponents sorted by age. And the almost continuous basketball games are prep for tournaments. The climax sporting event of the week is the big baseball game between the young staff and the old guests; it satisfies the American hunger for a showdown of greatness from both camps.

Evenings are taken up with the several talent shows—there's one put on by the staff, one put on by the kids at the camp, and one put on by adult guests—and movies. We made the mistake of letting our five-year-old see the one about lizards and reptiles. He was up most of the night. The other one was *Grease*, the musical, which he loved and knew the music. There are campfires with delicious s'mores and the Fuzzy Bunny mouth cram skit, and hayrides. The whole week leads up to the grand finale—the Dance. Here are the most joyous scenes of moms dancing with their kids in a swirl of The Makarena, the Hokey Pokey, the YMCA, and kids wearing earrings and necklaces made of glow sticks, to be part of the new tribal unity.

The food is quite good, old-time, hardy, rural, American cuisine; the menu has remained unchanged for nearly 75 years, though this year Thai wraps occurred and they claim they have gotten more serious about the coffee. Food: strawberries, Lucky Charms, bagel and cream cheese, cannelloni. Pizza Friday. Baked potatoes, ice cream, chocolate brownies, chocolate milk, marshmallows roasted, apple pie, p. b. & j sandwiches, dining alfresco while showing off your California wine on the large deck.

Our first evening there, Bill hadn't met any one yet. He spent much of the time carrying over a big fantasy from home—the Sailor Moon story. Our cabin fronted on the main path by the lodge #25. It was the closest cabin to the basketball courts. Don't rent it unless you love the endless thump. . .thump. . .thump of round ball. Beside the little cabin, Bill had figured out how to use one of these little pull-string disk launchers as a scepter from the Sail MOON story. There he was, Lonely Boy with the launcher doing "Moon Crystal Magic!" in front of the little cabin 25. Right beside the basketball court and right next to the main path to the lodge. We were at the crossroads central, but maintaining a civil indifference.

"Sailor Moon!" he shouts. He wasn't strong enough to pull the launcher hard enough to really make the spinning disk float out, but he had figured out how to sweep his arm across the horizon and that made it float out. And it fit in with his story. That's the way Sailor Moon launches her tiara.

It was a creative use of this toy—little fellow there with his parents. Not yet ready to hook up with anybody.

"Sail-or Moooon!"

"Moooon Tiara Magic."

"Moooon Scepter Healing power!"

"Bazook Pshueeeieiei."

When Bill plays by himself, as he often does because he's an only child, he usually plays all the parts.

He includes the guns and sound effects.

"Mars Fire & Might."

He goes into playing the part of another sailor scout—Sailor Jupiter: "Sailor Moon we need your help!"

"What do you want my help for?"

Sailor Venus: "She needs some power!"

"We're both doing fine."

Then back to Sailor Moon: "In the name of the Now I will right wrongs and triumph over evil and that means you mega-trash!"

I wonder what goes through his head. . .

Once he asked me out of the blue, "Is that chaos? Daddy."

I've been kind of obsessed with a study of fractals and chaos lately. I recalled the time I took him to stand by a fountain, and we had been mesmerized by the frothy turbulence at the foot of the waterfall, or at least I was, and I told him then, "That is chaos."

Another time we were looking at some machine and he asked me, "Is it fractals?"

"No," I said. "It's just a machine. Man only makes machines. They are linear. Nature makes the best chaos. Only nature makes truly beautiful fractals."

Come to think of it, Sailor Moon is about the struggle between Chaos (the forces of the Negaverse) and Love. Sailor Moon even fights a character Chaos/ Galaxia if I recall. And she does it with a power upgrade: non- confrontation, stepping aside.

As soon as I can, I leave the camp area and get off-road, walking into the hills, heading for my favorite place. I know the way by heart. You start off walking up the edge of the meadow, staying in the shade of the edge until you have to cross it . . . feel—the sun is warm on your back . . . the bugs are zooming . . . walking up the fire road . . . cutting across on the dusty horse trail . . . notice the cob webs on the un-traveled deer trail . . . the air is calm and there's hardly any movement and the blue sky goes on forever. Eventually I come to the steep part at the edge of the patch of land I love . . . a very long tree perhaps forty feet has fallen and I climb on it and walk along it, up, onto the back entrance of the land . . . I find myself in a beautiful piece of land, a sylvan glade under arching trees . . . there is a driveway curving out to the main road for access to the old wooden water storage towers up there, and above them crowning this land sit some giant boulders. I make for that, for that is where I fantasize I will one day have my house. I climb higher until I am in this inviting place. . . in a grotto of huge slabs of granite. . . and there my fantasy starts, there are gardens below and flowers growing where they have seeded themselves, vines climbing over a fallen tree and up the side of stone. . . there is a green lawn out to the road and shade trees. There is a breeze up here, I listen to the sound of the breeze blowing gently in the tall pine trees . . . the sun is filtered through the leaves. The air feels mild and a bit cooler. I breathe deeply of the dry clear air several times, and with each breath, I feel more refreshed. I find a comfortable place to sit, a perfect niche in the crook of a twisted oak tree, all covered over with a velveteen carpet of moss . . . like a throne fit for a king. I am. Relaxed here I feel it all flow through me . . . coherency, no noise just a clear channel . . . It feels good to allow myself to just enjoy the warmth and solitude of this peaceful place.

Kids are really nice; they help you get into all kinds of conversations. They are great icebreakers; they are something to have in common with other parents; they are like balloon extensions of our own egos out there bumping into other people's balloon extensions.

The wife has been packing and getting ready for months. They so look forward to it. I go out with her, and she talks endlessly because she runs into people from her church, from various bureaucracies of the City—she is one of the many city employees here. And since my wife comes from an old San Francisco family, many old school chums are encountered. I don't know what to say when they get into their conversations about who they used to hang with or about city politics.

I usually try to ignore these people. I fortify myself with books. This time I had brought a real doozie *When Time Breaks Down* about pattern formation in matter governed by topological physical constraints. (As they must be). That was quite a thing to contemplate. Basically, I live in books.

There I was walking down to the swimming pool with this great ponderous tome on topological biology under my arm. I'm thinking what would America be like if mathematics were made a lot more accessible with modern media.

I had noticed that some teenagers had brought SKATEBOARDS to the forest. Well, what are you gonna say, these people are TV babies. They have the attention span of a sound byte or a rock lyric—that means it's got to be short and 87% monosyllabic and repeated in refrain. And they're getting into my face. I'm walking around kvetching about the city dwellers, bringing boom boxes, bikes and skateboards to the forest.

Walking among the sun bathers, in their dark brown bodies and minimal bikinis with their romance novels, and their oleaginous sunblock and their striped Costco beach towels, I felt proud and fiercely protective and chagrined at this attempt to read this book.

A great fat brown cow of a woman in a skimpy brown bikini lying in the middle of traffic was dominating the conversation with a voice that could be heard all the way from Brooklyn about the novel she was reading: "It's about a guy who goes around stuffing his live kidnap victims into sturdy, clear-plastic body bags that are air-tight. It's really gross and dramatic as he watches the victim slowly struggle with the diminishing air supply, and just before they suffocate to death he un-zips it a bit to let a little air in, and then it starts all over."

Great literature! I thought, folding up my chair and heading for anywhere away from that voice. When did murder become the most popular form of American entertainment? This is more or less the type of people here, I conclude. I am reading a heart stopping book, too *When Time Breaks Down*, The three dimensional dynamics of electrochemical waves and cardiac arrhythmias. Winfree's book starts with studying circadian rhythm in fruit flies and moves into the whole theory of how natural clocks are organized around a singularity (a phase singularity). All living beings have working within them a tell-tale internal clock that marks them as having evolved on this our planet, Earth.

I can't believe I brought this tough nut to camp. It is all this topology applied to rhythmic systems. Don't know how I managed to get hold of this book. It leaped into my hands while I was cruising the remainder table in the Stanford book store. I suppose it was the color plates; it had these colored isoclines that looked like tie dye bleeds of primary colors. Winfree is trying to make it easy to grasp the phase space of rhythms. You can see the color hue being shifted in the blend, and the color is the frequency of the rhythm. Well, a guy's got to do something to keep his mind a little sharp, and this treatise was definitely gonna give the old logical sectors some pushups. I felt the slick shiny cover and read the blurb on the back cover in yellow text against a black background: "Without recourse to explicit mathematics, he illustrates his fundamental ideas by coloring diagrams so that the phase of a rhythm is indicated by a corresponding color. Geometric intuition then serves in place of equations." *Yea*, maybe I *could* muddle my way through it. I need to get speeded up, need to get pumped up to read a book like this. It's not so strange really. I had just come off writing this weird novel that gets into some wild *poesie concrete* where the syntax might be spread across two pages, as well as reading down one page, and often goes into notation to work with the idea of language as object.

It was about the idea of language becoming object, in the sense of object-relations that the mind relates to, and the objects of programming. It was about a guy wandering around in the fields on peyote looking for what he called the manifold. It had a section with the ponderous title *Hyperspectral / the Dirac Satori*. This was a strange poem about Onto/slashology, the combining of opposites, and many other things.

I often thought of what America would be like if mathematics were made a lot more accessible with modern media. If it were made something people could talk to each about like they talk about rock music stars. If people gave it a small fraction of the obsessive attention they give to TV. We'd have this perfect rational utopia where everybody spoke perfected logicality to each other in a kind of Leibnitzian binary ratiocinator language. They'd talk about Norbert Wiener and David Hilbert; about applied mathematics & the pure; about Rudy Rucker and the archetypes of perception. Then I realized I'm walking around kvetching about the city dwellers, bringing boom boxes, bikes and SKATE-BOARDS! to the forest. There seems to be some program for bringing inner city kids up. I should have gotten to know some of them.

My wife had asked me, "What's the book about?"

I told her that the book is about the search for a universal biology that is not so much concerned with quantitative measurement, the linear, but more with the topology of movement and connectivity. I could see her mind quickly going blank on me and I added, "It was written by that guy back in the 70s, who gave a bunch of mosquitoes jet lag. He wanted to see if he could reset their internal clocks. He would wake them up at odd hours with flashes of blue light."

SAM jeered: "Great! That's ALL we need—a bunch of mosquitoes with jet lag!"

I like my wife's snotty-bitch humor—except when it was directed at me. "Yea that would be terrible," I said, "nothing's meaner than mosquito meat—except jet-lagged mosquito meat."

"Ha ha." We shared a laugh.

As I was reading the Winfree book it struck me that the camp was in the shape of a four-chambered heart. It was like I got this view of the blackbird from higher up. I began to try and see the topological forces governing my world. After the 3rd day I figured that the only way I was going to survive this vacation was to go off-phase. I had this vague sense: my happiness or sense of ease is changing over time. What is the rate of change due to? It changes at a rate proportional to the local density of tourists around my person, and there is a constant sense of pressure due to the spatial location of the cabin, right across the footpath from the most populous place—the basketball court and the lodge. When I was at that cabin, I felt that I was constantly under scrutiny. To go off-phase meant that I had reached a point in the book that allowed me to visualize and understand the forces that animated my movements through the camp and that also contributed greatly to the happiness factor. It was a question of timing. To be going DOWN to the lake when people were leaving and coming UP for supper. That was the best time, when you had the lake almost to yourself.

I started trying to nap during the heat of the day and generally tried to be out of phase with the movements of the crowds. I had to do something to escape the endless thump thump of basketball. I found confirmation of this thinking in the book I was reading, what I thought were just the movements of the automaton on vacation were actually governed by the geometry of the situation.

⌘ The whole camp is shaped like a kind of heart!
The atria on top and ventricles at the bottom.

The little office was right at the center, at the heart where all roads crossed. The upper left part went to the lodge and their campsite, campsite B. The lower right part, where the lake and the swimming pool were in the ventricles. Thus the atria, were where the food and lodging were, and the bathrooms were—each campsite was centered around a common bathroom and laundromat facility. And people basically moved back and forth, like a fluid being pumped along roads from one area to the other. And these feelings more or less governed my movement between the atria and ventricles of the water and food. What a silly metaphor! The whole camp a heart, pulsating in circadian rhythm, phase locked to the sun.

When I was telling my boy Bill about it he said: "Kinda like fractals, isn't it dad?" My little philosopher. He was trying to share my enthusiasm and use the word fractals in any context to get a better understanding.

"Well actually it's like cellular automata," the dad said. My poor kid. I must have waxed enthusiastic over fractals and chaos many times with him. He gets exposed to all these ideas, because when I am with him, I feel like sharing my child-like enthusiasms for the mysteries of existence. I remember telling him: "Plants are fractals, clouds are fractals, only nature is smart and clever enough to build fractals. We mostly work on linear machines." And another time, we are walking though the forest, and the dad picks up a handful of dark rich humus at the foot of a tree. "Look at this good stuff," he said pointing into it. "Look there's an ant coming out, and there's, another bug." He paused for a moment. "There are molds in here, and beneath that bacteria, trying to recycle everything. There's more life in this handful of dirt, than there is on all the planets in all the rest of the solar system."

But this time talking to him at camp, I was really getting excited. I was having a realization of the immensity: all living things have internal clocks that mark them as having evolved on this planet. "Circadian rhythms, phase-locked to the sun! We are on a piece of rotating machinery. It is an Egg!" I was flipping out on the idea of the big earth-egg, that we walk around on, hatching ideas and isms. "And here you are, right here, parts of this rotating machinery. Mountains and oceans and such do not have intrinsic daily rhythm, although they are part of the rotating, they are not the same as the living parts of this rotating machinery that do—these beings endlessly engaging in daily time organization by evolution phase-locking them circadian. I'm a Circadian! You are one too!"

He's an amazingly smart little fellow. Once he floored me when we were looking at the names of the planets in the charts on his wall and the mobile over his bed. He said to me, "Dad, did you ever think about the U in the planets: MercUry, VenUs, JUpiter, SatUrn, Uranus, NeptUne, PlUto. All but two of the planets have the letter U in them." The Parent beams and the child beams back. Who would have noticed that but a five-year-old?

The more I got into the book, the more I began to see my small life as a trajectory in a much larger phase space. I was a circadian - most basically. I was a concatenation of many oscillators, all trying to keep themselves going, and keep the species going. I was just a projection of these topological entities living in a higher dimensional phase space. A phase space started in the rotating earth, rotating around the sun. Day and night. Winfree is trying to get to the place where arrhythmia comes from, the place where time stops, and he pictures it like the North Pole, around which the world revolves but which itself does not, the un-wobbling pivot where all the longitudinal lines come to a point and it is ambiguous what phase of the rotating world you are in.

So I'm out of phase and trying to at least present the appearance of being caught up in the camp life activities. I'm in a hurry. I must get back to my kid's talent show when I walk past this beautiful young woman in blue shorts lying on the shore of the lake. Nice tanned legs. Blonde hair. It is not all so restful and innocent around here. Walking by I felt this ring on my finger like a thread binding me to . . . What. What? A community that has mucho pressures to help you maintain. Much pressure, a prison actually. I am walking along carrying the big blue tuber a five-foot long floatation device, Styrofoam cylinder about as round as a tennis can, curved like a long banana. It is sticking out in front of me, and I wonder how I might look from the side, while I see a fine looking woman in blue shorts, walking. How did we get from these simple circadian beings to these entities constantly moving between the poles. My fantasy is not all that well conformed with the restriction of marriage. I like meeting women. Motherhood is an ancient spell from which I am trying to awaken and maybe one of these other mothers might help me. But we are just passing in the evening. I hope she doesn't get mosquito bit. (Yes, campers, mosquitoes really do perk up around dusk. Every twenty-three hours, mosquitoes buzz around intensely.)

Winfree started the topology book with the notion of life at the poles, where all the colors merge. It is a singularity—the place where time stops—and we are distributed around poles: reason and passion, mind and body, culture and nature. Poles. Singularities. Sources. Sinks. Sex is like a battery: one side the opposite of another, and sex is the continuous short-circuit of the battery. Is that the same thing as holes, the genus of a torus, the genus of a phase space? Attractors in phase space? What did Freud say? With this ring I thee wed.

I was feeling that I had this ring through my nose, that I was some kind of dancing bear being lead around.

Marriage is a kind of singularity in which evolution stops, I mean you've got to work together. What did Freud say? The price of civilization is renunciation of the instinctual. We are all out here trying to be in a community, and for a little while there at the dance, when the old and the young together were dancing the Macarena, when the young were instigating the old to dance the Macarena, the thing came together, a utopian community together in the country, trying to get body, land and psyche together.

What is this, the other, which we seek out, seek to be caught up in for a while. A fruit is a plant's way of spreading seed. They are rooted and can't move around, so they have to get animals to move stuff around for them. What is an animal for, besides being an agent to move seed around. These hideous biology forces use us, make us want - moreover need, each other. We want to, oh so dearly, find beautiful chicks with long legs and generous breasts who parade and prance on our arms and bare our beautiful off-spring. It's comical. We are a lonely species and at the same time we simply don't really get along with each other.

Marriage has been promoted far too much. It is really a hard thing to maintain with the most mature of people. They either have to be so very honest and flexible or in complete denial and rigid. Much of the time marriage is a kind of carefully allotted mutual poisoning. It's called security. Security is a tar pit.

What would it mean for this entity, Nature—to have it renounce that kind of knowledge of herself, the instincts—for a much more symbolic and codified knowledge. What is the seed that *we* are carrying forth? Well, our ability to be social, to continue to work in groups, because surely that is what has led to an advantage. Men had always cast women as the primitive, as the erotic other, whose bodily sensuality threatens to annihilate the autonomous ego, forcing it back to helpless infantile dependency on the mother. We are here trying to find an intimacy with Nature, a sense of community. The community of parents is the community here, constantly thinking of your children. But it is hard to have a sense of community with Nature.

Later that day, I was way out in the middle of the lake, relaxing back with my arms draped over the tuber. Out on the lake, I own the lake, I'm floating out in the deep green water as if hovering magically in the air—waiting stoically for the rest of these assholes to go up to dinner; so I can breath an expanse of relief and have the whole lake to myself. I don't know. I guess I'm just not a nice person any more. I'm becoming heartless.

It seemed like the whole camp turned out for the tie dye. I was doing tie dyeing, thinking of the target and the spiral and the wave, as I was reading *When Time Breaks Down* and under the influence of its colorful intuitions into phase space and electrochemical waves. For my design, I wanted to make one of those spirals zooming into the center of the shirt. The crafts instructor told us how. You stick a fork in the middle of the shirt and by twisting the fork in one direction you cause the shirt to wind around itself into a spiral. Then you band this circle together tightly with rubber bands, so that they are like the crisscross sections of a pie. You color the sections across from each other to make the continuous swirls of color spiraling into the center of the shirt.

It was a teeming confusion with just about the whole camp out there on the volleyball court waiting for the squirt bottles of color to color the sections. I got some mixtures going. And I got the idea to work from the center blue out to yellow and in between to mix them for the green. And from the yellow out to a purple, by mixing a band in between for an orange. There were folds that were not touched by the color and these moved all the way through the T-shirt, and would make it look like lightning strikes were spiraling out from the central sector. It would be cool.

I wondered if there was an application of topology. Maybe I could write a paper, The Topology of Tie-dyeing. Yes. . . how folding protects, how expanding spirals. . . how the center of the shirl (did I just say shirl?) is a kind of organization center for the unfolding spiral. Shirl? Maybe I could start a new business, in honor of Art Winfree. Selling swirl shirts—Shirls?

Everything revolving around a singularity, a black hole, a sink, a drain, the place where time runs out. It is at the poles, singularities where all the tangent lines shoot off to infinity or otherwise become unstable. It scared me to think of the end.

I had just come off writing a short poetical novel. It was supposed to take place in the time it takes to be on a psychedelic trip, a peyote trip. It went through the stages of perception dissolving and archetypes of energy emerging. Call them Mescalito, Carlos did. Some parts of the book had this really blown-out syntax, spread across the two page spread. One wants to attack the traditional concatenation powers of language to reflect what the book was about: some guy on peyote wandering in the woods under the tutelage of mescaline. It was about the idea of language becoming object, in the sense of the object-relations that are the currency and the landscape of thought, which the mind relates to. And also in computer languages, the self-contained subroutines—the "objects" of programming to which and from which parameters, variables and iterative counters are passed and checked. He was wandering around in the fields (of time and number and symbol) but also the real fields of the farm looking for what he called the manifold. I wanted to... I was still on the search for some kind of strange and natural language of chaos and fractals that I thought was some much more primary language of BEING that might talk to me if I were somehow prepared to listen. I wanted a poetry that prepared one to transcend syntax. And metaphor. That took you down to the Worfian bedrock. And took you into a spatial thing—but I did not want mathematics (because of its bad rep for being too difficult and its bad rap for being unfeeling). I don't know. It seem like Winfree in his book was trying to do something like that with his colored isoclines of equal time in phase space. He found the twist—not a linear move—but how there is the helix, in all circadian rhythms.

And now I was thinking about going into the tie-dye business, applying some of the biochemical clock experiments in the book. Scroll waves oscillating in a petri dish back and forth bouncing off the boundary like a tiny inland sea. The book makes a huge contribution to the study of biology, by laying the foundation for the oscillator, the clock, driving all the computations in the flesh. The book develops Winfree's research into arrhythmia; we follow his twenty-five years of exploring the role of biological clocks in ecology and behavior. From the way daylight regulates timing of Drosophila's clock, to the phase resetting of pacemaker neurons, and to the mechanisms in space and time of biochemical clocks. The biochemical clocks led to two-dimensional pattern formation experiments in chemical liquids and in fungi containing biological clocks. Rotating waves of chemical oxidation. The famous Belousov-Zhabotinsky reaction is studied again. I remembered it from the cover of Prigogene's books. I felt like a stumbling but practical Leopold Bloom. I wondered if there might be a practical application of those sweet scroll clouds like marbleizing paper or even a kind of tie dye, upon which you could make these beautiful rotator swirls. Winfree gives the recipe in his book. I felt extremely lucky to be studying this material, like I was present at a new kind of abstract art. My mind gets all excited by this stuff. I wanted to quit everything, abandon wife and kid, and go off and live in a warehouse and work out this color field time and phase singularity painting method. Truly this is hyperspectral.

It was a couple of days later when I finally made a bit of contact with one of the population. She was a lovely Jewish princess, dark Adriatic looks, a small intelligent face framed with tightly waved jet black hair. I'd seen her in the camp and was delighted when we turned up in the laundromat together washing out our tie-dyes.

I started the conversation with, "So are you a full time mom? Or do you have a job on the side."

She looked a little hesitant. "I teach," she said.

"Oh... What?"

"Linguistics."

"Linguistics. Wow! What Language?" She probably thought I thought she was a little old school teacher.

"English," she replied.

I was about to say, 'English as a second language,' and said, "In a university?"

"Yes."

"Oh, cool. Linguistics is fascinating."

I was half thinking about putting the make on her, but I really do like linguistics. I told her I do technical writing, and she mentioned linguists were doing a lot of work in that area using structured generalized mark-up language.

Somehow I steered the conversation around to semiotics. "Yea. I really enjoyed semiotics when I was in school," I said. "I liked it for art and literature. It wasn't until much later, when I got into using it for interface design—you know, reading icons and signs, I've even been thinking about using petroglyphs—that I really got a lot more experience with it."

I humbly and sheepishly admitted to her that I never got to use metaphor in my technical writing. "I never did get to use one metaphor in technical writing. I once tried to say a certain screen was a "gateway" to the rest of the application, and they just fell out of their chair."

"Well, have you read Markoff?" she asked.

"O yes, it was about metaphor. What was the title?" I asked, fishing. "Fire...?

She gave me a confident glowing smile, "*Fire, Women, and Dangerous Things*," she said.

I gave her a sympathetic smile of admiration. For beautiful women really are dangerous things. I thought: she must know I'm flirting with her.

It came out she had worked with Labov, because I recalled: "Another guy I read when I was in school was Labov." I said the name, pronouncing the 'v'. She looked puzzled.

"It was *Rules for Ritual Insult*," I recalled. "That was the beginning of Discourse Analysis!" I preened, proud of my memory.

She seemed pleased at that. "Labov, you mean Lay-bow," she corrected.

"O yea." I said. "I've never had anybody to talk with about this stuff before." *I wondered if she would suspect that I had read that book, to try and understand some way of being cooler around blacks.*

"Labov was my advisor!"

"Wow!"

Then I went into a real faux pas. I said: "Labov isn't black is he?" Oh, oh. She's giving me a look that says, what a stupid question. *I could almost kick myself. Duh, of course not with a name like Labov.*

Giving me a smile of chagrin for my stupidity, she said, "He's Jewish."

Uh oh I thought. Hope I haven't blown it. She probably thinks I'm a racist, anti-Semitic, male chauvinist pig. A long pause ensued. Then it came out that she had also studied with Irving Goffman. "Wow, he was really a wild guy." I said. "He was a hero of mine. His books are extremely funny."

She smiled, politely.

"Like, *Stigma, the management of spoiled identity*," I recalled. *I had a painful memory of how I had at one point in my life felt like I was suffering from a spoiled identity and had read that book to try and find some help. Not the best avenue of thinking when trying to chat up a good-looking woman.*

There was another awkward pause.

"Do you have a web page?" I asked, thinking of trying to get some way to look her up. *I thought, here might be some kind of project we could get into so that we could get to know each other better.*

A long awkward pause ensued.

"Do you get into Charles Sanders Peirce?" I asked, "in any of your classes?" *I'm always looking for some help with Charles Sanders Peirce. Trying to find any-*

thing from anybody about him.

"Oh yeah, a little."

Since I didn't get to go into graduate school, I'm always trying to use words in a context to learn. And I've noticed how my kid does that too. This got me to worrying that I was putting myself into such a supplicating position. "Wow. I though I knew something about semiotics, until I ran into that guy."

I got closer to her by leaning against the washing machine next to her. *I felt like I might be a graduate student, talking to a professor. They must lead such cool intellectual lives in the university.* I leaned over and with a teasing smile on my face, said, "I bet I've got one of your books!" I said this while pointing my index finger as though interjecting a challenging point. "It's the one where these women are talking. They are together for some weekend, and one of them is a linguist, and is analyzing what they are saying. Yeah."

She thought for a moment: "That's a book by a colleague of mine, Deborah Tannen."

"Oh, yeah right," I said, though I couldn't remember. "Anyway, I bought it because I wanted to spruce up the dialog in my writing."

There was a shorter pause in which I considered synesthesia as semantic rock and roll. *I don't know, but I think I've always felt meaning moving around in my head, like I think the way some people experience music. I might have autism. And writing, and now beginning programming, provides a kind of way I can shake in my chair, groove back and forth, in a kind of nominal music trance.*

We talked about the synesthesia, and I told her about a class I was taking in the visualization of music. She talked about how her eldest son could listen to a tape recording of the musical soundtrack for any Star Wars movie and narrate the entire story, in time with the soundtrack music. I mentioned the funny story of how my Bill, when you read him a story he has heard a few times before, can tell if you leave out even one word. "Is that normal?" I asked.

Scene: Walker and his wife are looking over the railing of a porch attached to a simple one room cabin. A mother and a father are watching out while their child Bill is playing with another child Leigh. Leigh, a girl, is a year younger, four. The father is sitting in a white plastic lawn chair on the porch with his legs stretched up onto the railing. The mother is sitting beside him. Below the porch railing, the children are playing with little plastic action-hero figures distributed across the top of a little green-plastic fold-up picnic table.

Bill: The blue ranger is trapped! He is in a cage! He needs the help of the other rangers.

Scene: The Father sits bolt upright. There is a shocked quizzical look on his face.

Father's thoughts *(in Voice Over)*: I am picking up a kind of lilting rhythm in the way Bill is laying out the story. I was obvious there was something going on with this rhythm of concatenation and the linguistical production of play. I couldn't believe my ears! A typical one was something like this.

Scene: The child Bill is directing thoughtfully.

Bill: Suppose the evil emperor changed them into icicle bad guys and the blue ranger had to come along and melt them with his lava ray.

Scene: The Father thinking.

Father's thoughts *(VO)*: Bill's sentences were something like Suppose the da da was da and then the da da was da. It was upturned at the end as if inviting the girl to participate, but it wasn't upturned at the end like Valley-girl speak. It was said with authority.

Scene: The child Bill is directing thoughtfully.

Bill: The one-armed ravaged man, has been through war and living with him has made the pink ranger sad.

Scene: Looking over the Father's shoulder at the children.

Father's thoughts (in voice over): Bill was going on with an elaborate concatenation of story about the situations his hero (The Blue Power Ranger) was in. Leigh was playing with the Pink Power Ranger. What was amazing was the way Bill was laying out his story. It was in a series of lilting sure sentences, that were almost all of the same length and I thought they are almost the same prosody. I didn't dare jump up and get my recorder for fear of disrupting the flow, but I had never heard such a marvelous verbal display from his boy.

Scene: The man's wife, the boy's mother says:

Mother: They're saying El Nino is going to be really bad this year. Going to be the rainiest year ever.

Scene: She bends the paper and shows the man the front page. It has a color graphic of the world, with parts of the ocean looking yellow to orange to hot red. The Father reads the headline caption out loud.

Father: SCIENTISTS FEAR ECOSYSTEM DISASTER

pause

Father:*(says with relish.)* Mummmm Chaos. I love Chaos.

Scene: Looking at the picture on the front page. It shows how on the earth storms are driven around the poles. The woman snaps the pages. And keeps looking at them. Pause

Mother: We've got to get that dry rot work done on the front of the house, because it is going to be a really wet year.

Scene: A storm of consternation and cognitive dissonance rolls across the Father's brow.

CUT TO:

Scene: We see a quick animation of branching neuron trees trying to fire off in different directions.

Father: Oh. Wow, Yeah.

Father's thoughts *(VO)*: Now I'm thinking about the horror of more financial hemorrhage, and how much work it would take to come up with the money to do it! I really shouldn't be on this vacation.

Scene: The father shifts and squirms around in his chair as he tries to get back into his amazement of the way the children are playing. We follow his gaze to them.

Father's thoughts *(VO)*: Now part of this was the boy and *girl* playing. I think playing with girls lets Bill have a lot more fantasy going. Usually the boy games degenerate pretty soon into physical contests between the heroes and the bad guys. Bill would concatenate a scenario with perhaps a dozen such sentences, very elaborate detail. Leigh would get impatient, and say try to get control of the game.

CUT TO:

Scene: The child Leigh is looking petulant.

Leigh: But can we get back to the game now?

CUT TO:

Scene: A pained, shocked expression on Bill.

CUT TO:

Scene: A look of commiseration on the father's face indicates he feels for how the male is being constantly interrupted.

Father's thoughts *(VO)*: And Bill would look kind of miffed, (as if to say this IS the game) but hiding it well in his good nature, and zoom over into her game. She wanted the Pink Ranger to marry the Blue Ranger and they had a quick wedding and a hug before the Blue Ranger had to fly off to another planet (A big boulder that was ten feet away from the table). And there he had to have some more adventures. Bill was extremely at ease, and affable, almost big brotherly, with weaving her game into his.

Scene: The mother is shaking her head and looking—staring ahead. She snaps her fingers angrily into the paper.

Mother: They still haven't caught that rapist in the east bay.

Scene: Father's shoulders go up in sheepish guilt.

Father's thoughts *(VO)*: I felt guilty for all men. Men are nothing but a penis with eyes.

Scene: The father looking thoughtful observes:

Father's thoughts *(VO)*: My boy child usually plays out the parts, but now he has spent a bunch more time laying out the precepts of the story of the game; it is almost like he was laying out an argument and expected it to be challenged. I think knowing that the *girl* would also be kind of interested because a year makes a great deal of difference in verbal ability at this age. Wow the game seems to have morphed from Power Rangers into Sailor Moon. Sailor Moon is always about power with them. All about trying to get power back.

Bill: "Power of Saturn!" Whew, shew whew,whew, *(laser blasts)*

Scene: Extended sword fighting, with great hacking swaths being carved in the air; Bill is playing some kind of samurai sword fighter. Then abruptly

Bill: " I didn't know!
Sailor Venus are you OK."
So we must...

Father's thoughts *(VO)*: And again he was called back into Leigh's game which now involved a large stuffed skunk.

Leigh: (... "but it didn't smell bad.")

Father's thoughts *(VO)*: Anyway, it was wonderful, and I hope the opportunity presents itself again to record this play, but I rather doubt it will. I'd like to have better linguistical tools to analyze this text and interaction. There is much to learn there.

Scene: Mother looking thoughtful

Mother: When we get back, I've got to take him to get his shots.

Pause

And did you hear about how they are having to have homework for kindergarten?

That evening after supper I went down to the lake to hear the Frog Symphony in the setting summer sun. I sat in lotus at the edge of the pond listening, as the Frog Symphony tuned up to greet an early rising full moon. With eyes open, I let myself become entranced. And dissolved into the soundscape. My perception opened up: looking at the flashes of sunlight on ripples of concentric interfering circular waves—made by the multitude of water striders and other beings, disturbing the glassy lake surface which was reflecting the sky and the dark forest across the other side. (It's not technically a lake; it's a large pond.) With my eyes open, I began to meditate on the surface of the lake, taking it in with my whole being. The idea is that the perception is wide, beyond the eyes open,—whole being—instead of having the eyes closed to look for internal lights. Just letting in the scene, letting it fall down through my eyes like a long waterfall, and cascade on the center of my breathing.

It's quiet . . . with no people. I began falling into a kind of love for the landscape, or feeling the love in the complexity. But then the mind started going into states of awe and bliss over this, and then the ego got into *its* struggle with the body for supremacy; ego wins and poses an interesting math problem. Contemplate: Quadra-pole moment sound of the frogs in stock tank with START UP FROG being any one, though tended to be the more dominant. OR the one who had found the sweet spot—one frog seems to have found the place where his song is exactly the right frequency to resonate the whole lake, turning the lake into his guitar cavity. Trying to draw females to their Elvis, Jerry Lee Lewis, Donnavan, Jimi Hendricks, Jim Morrison, drawing attention through sound. Let us consider the problem of the Frog. Boy frog has to make his sound AND attract girl frog AND avoid the wolf dog fox who is also attracted to the sound. AND Girl frog has got to find him AND throw her tadpoles off. The family is a lifeguard tower, a preoccupation covering over the contemplative scene, covering everything. The human family is the most highly evolved biological structure on the planet.

But then luckily a sensation arose. I started to feel my shoulder under the linen shirt with no under shirt buttoned up. *Commo los tehanos* But I digress. I say mantra to pull me back: Being as feedback, being as body as feedback, body as being, body as path; mantra to let me get myself into deeper esthetical states—*shimmers into the water of vibrations:* body as feedback, body as being, body as path.

Ahhh, so . . . Glassy surface with ripples, seemed like a 2D map of Venn Diagrams of intersecting influences—mutual probabilities.

(A ↔ B) ↔ X / A ↔ (B ↔ X) / (A ↔ X) ↔ B

So many intersecting circles on the surface that they made the surface almost choppy with little shimmer waves.

This abstract, but simple, diagram of overlapping influences is an objective correlative (Image) of the state of mind I'm talking about. I think: Maybe the ego isn't exactly winning after all. Maybe abstraction is really the only language supple enough to speak to an art of being, as opposed to visual or audio or logical language. It's a picture of perceiving by your being. Not just looking at the surface of things or what is going on in your own mind but at the *way* it is absorbed into your being. Making you realize you are a part of all that is going on at the Moment. Later, with Jung, I understood that I was in the presence of a *mysterium coniunctionis*, that the intersecting Venn diagram of Baysian inference is the *mysterium coniunctionis*. It's not the Frog Symphony, it's the Frog Quartet. Actually it's the zero-sum Frog Game.

But at night the incredibly clear air seemed to reject my silly entrapment in the heart of the camp as I wandered away from the people and had to find my own way and be off from them. And wander around Mud Lake. It is terrifying to walk through the big woods at night. Man's mind is hair-trigger wired to jump at moving shadows in the dark forest (and I was worried about bears), to react before you are attacked from the side or behind. I was ready to jump first, and ask questions later, and that is exactly how I felt walking out to Mud Lake by myself. In the dark I could see Cassiopeia in the firmament. Cassiopeia what a lovely garment you have!

Saw bats zooming in going jeet jeet and off in the distance big frogs and crickets all around the pond and the stellar constellations . . . Cassiopeia the Northern Cross, the big triangle of summer. They are also present around the pond and only we know they are part of it.

It blew my mind to read this heart-stopping book: *When Time Breaks Down*. The three dimensional dynamics of electrochemical waves and cardiac arrhythmias. I can't believe I brought this tough nut to camp. It is all this topology applied to rhythmic systems. It starts with studying circadian rhythm in fruit flies and gets into the whole theory of how natural clocks are organized around a singularity (a phase singularity). We are in phase space now. And he uses colors to give a sense of this space for the coloring of maps is a good way to illustrate phase behavior in this abstract space. Why is that? You might ask. Well, suppose you think of a 2x4 structural beam being pushed from above until it buckles. It can fracture into the left and right. Those are like sinks or drains around which its struggle to maintain integrity will oscillate until it finally buckles. It is the set of all possible ways to buckle, and it is like a continuous color going down a density gradient. Fractals! These are the force fields of an abstract space!

And how the singularity is vulnerable to arrhythmias and fibrillation. Winfree goes on to develop a theory of organizing centers for natural clocks, "the internal clock that marks us a having evolved on this planet earth."

It is like we are a visible source of rotating spiral waves distributed out into tissues made of clocks. A filament, a tornado-like filament arching through 3D space to close in a ring. If that isn't the dynamic manifold at the heart of nature, then what is?

Winfree talks about ". . .topological exactitude , indifferent to quantitative details of shape, force, time."

Wow. What an incredibly profound insight into who we are on this planet. It seems to point to this world of Platonic beings, like a bestiary of equations governing all things in a kind of phase space of all possible outcomes.

In what Platonic dialog does the old philosopher speak about the archetype of giants? These bodies that float in some kind of fluid. Yes, that would be getting back to the first, most ancient, take on all this stuff.

I thought about a book I wanted to write, *The Church of the Coincidental Metaphor*. It could use some of the ideas from these topological dynamics. Phase singularities and asymptotic isochrons. The criterion for an event happens to coincide with an isochron.

I wanted to write my kid something like Sailor Moon, something he could really love and be wild about. Sailor Moon, Sailor moon, it began to sound like phaser swoon to my ears. That was the only kind of symbolic semantic complex of idea programs that thrilled me down to my roots. It was about the phaser $e^{i(wt-\phi)}$ the winding basis, the rotator vector—the phaser—the basis of all rhythmic spaces. The story I wanted would be something like the Harry Potter books that used magical incantations (but these would be talking through equations) to go from one dimension of reality to another.

It would be an attempt to reconstruct for others the Pythagorean feelings I get from sensing the god as mathematician working in nature. And the way in, is the Fibonacci spirals and the golden ratio. It is everywhere. It is the source of our understanding of harmony and beauty. It is the source of our experiencing harmony and beauty. The way life superheterodynes on top of matter which has as its own agenda—the production of life.

Like for example, when I contemplate a flower I go into the spiral head, and think of them as fruiting body to propagate seeds / genes. Or I look at the topology of its branching and flowering. There is a notation, a kind of algebra that some botanist figured out. The Botanist's Branching Algebra. An Algorithm for the Beauty of Plants. What was it? The L-system, for the orientation of branching in 3D space. Now how'd that go? It had an arrow —> and some function. It looked one way if the plant is leggy and keeps elongating and not branching.

And it was the flip of that if it is bushy and keeps branching off at every node. Wonderful stuff. It was like a function but the argument was a replacement rule. It had this really complex ideas expressed in a simple string.

I could animate the development of the plants of the forest in my mind. The branches growing on trees were all being driven from some centralized kind of fractal function iterating in many different ways in plants. It was like a whole new way of looking at things, this biologically-oriented consciousness. I was seeing what FORM did. There is an inherent form to the real plant that the algorithm captured. I'm excited about really seeing the plants this way, formally, mathematically even, though most people would say this is dry and dull and too stiff. But I just see magnificent ripples on the lake of matter - ripples that grow and make flowers which stream off particles of scent and attract bees which get the powdery mildew to percolate across space and time one way or another.

Mr. I

(Crossing the Brain / Blood Barrier)

During the years 1991 and 1992, my sister Karen was diagnosed with cancer. She began a round of chemotherapy and it went into remission. She was pronounced cured, and we thought she was one of the increasing numbers of lucky ones who had beat cancer, thanks to advanced treatments. I am sorry to say I was not as attentive as I might have been. I was going through a severe economic depression my own self. It was right after I had given up 43 years of bachelorhood for marriage, and my wife got pregnant in the second month of our new marriage. My sister's cancer had started about the time I made the trip out to San Antonio to introduce my bride-to-be to my parents. My sister was complaining of a pain in her back. I was scrambling to adjust to the responsibilities of parenthood and marriage, and meanwhile was unable to get any work at all. I was actually on the verge of selling my computer equipment! There just wasn't anybody around who believed enough in what I was doing with interface design and web design (let alone with my writing), to stop me from such a drastic fate. I also developed tinnitus, a constant ringing in the ears. It just happened one day after driving back from a job interview in Silicon Valley: this shrill high frequency scream developed in my neurology. At first I thought it was from having the window down, and that it would go away. But it didn't go away. It kept me up nights, made me smoke more pot to get some relief from it, and basically drove me crazy. I was running around from doctor to library trying to get some help for it. I had always been able to hear the high frequency motion detectors in department stores when I was a kid, I thought every one could. But when I got into a ginko biloba study at UT Med school, they matched the frequency and sure enough it was shrill. This I already knew. Finally some big ENT doctor—the head of Kaiser ENT—followed me down the hall, raised his fist and yelled at me in the hall in front of god and everybody: "I've had it for 30 years! You've just go to learn to live with it!" So I had my own problems, and though they were small compared to those of my sister, they occupied my mind.

Perhaps to assuage my guilt over being the big brother and not being able to help my little sister, I began writing a story about an invented character Jack, an engineer who got onto a project about heightening the body's own immune system to fight against diseases. The story was called Crossing the Brain-Blood Barrier. In the story Jack invents a system that uses visualization in a biofeedback situation with MRI images to enhance the body's own miraculous healing processes. It would ask the reader to use his mind to move his attention into places a few scientists have gone before. In my story, the machine that Jack built was potentially capable of curing cancer. It was a way of holding out some kind of hope for her. We believed that high tech would save us.

It wasn't long before I realized that my story presented the reader with monstrous complexity. It is way too technical for the novel to support. As I went along the story became like a piece of artificial intelligence, like Topsy, it just growed and growed. I felt like I was in some kind of 60s aesthetic of a self-aware work and that at times it was mocking me.

Writing is supposed to be a flawless seamless presentation, in which the author doesn't present any problems to the reader that he doesn't work out or find neat solutions for. Nor should a work go on overly long, because the modern reader has deadlines and very little time to read, except perhaps the vacationer, but what they want is a page turner. They want characters with traits, and above all they want drama. What I want is intimacy and truth served by fiction. And fiction in the service of enlightenment. If I were to classify it into a genre, the story has some affinity with hard-science sci-fi. To me it was a mind-blowing stretch of speculative fiction, a stream-lined information space with the most interactive design element ever invented—the character. It weaves together many, many ideas. It makes up an advanced theory of evolution called solution theory. It poses the idea of a teleomatic (organizing) principle exploiting the property of water to create life. It is an actual description of imprinting on water. But presents way too much technical stuff to the literati and gets too literary with the scientific reader running the risk of confusing and alienating both camps. My only hope was in poetry, modern avant garde poetry. I took some encouragement from old Ezra Pound. How poetry was the vehicle for thought. I used to try to read Ezra Pound as a young guy. I certainly did not have all the languages, nor the steeping in world lit to appreciate what he was doing. I just liked how his lines cleaved space and were so much like speech. How he didn't have saccharine sentimentality. Then I would get critical commentaries, the concordances—there weren't any Cliff Notes or Classics Illustrated, but I needed some serious concept tenderizer—and see what the learned commentators said. And as I studied these I began to appreciate more and more what ole Ez was doing. For one thing he tracks the same myth across many cultures and many languages through many times. And he would do this in a few lines. What an amazing thing, you get the sense of language as this great sea circulating about the world into all cultures and times. Talk about fugal, this sense of language is exactly the place poetic literacy should be going into. He called it rock-drill, and saw the work as drilling into the bedrock of language, flinging up phonemes and semantemes and words and phrases and gems of extraordinary beauty along with the debris. It becomes the thing you are talking about. It becomes self aware. This is a great 60s art form, like the put-on. Old Ez practically invented hypertext. For me the things that I didn't get in Pound's work became like semantic objects worth trying to understand. (Because it paid off with thrilling experience of beauty, and a much greater appreciation of the thought created on this earth.)

I

When Jack arrived early at work that morning, he drove past the entrance gate through the new cyclone fence that the company had recently wrapped around the place. The fence had three strands of barbed wire pulled taunt across the top of it, and just came up to the giant boulder at the entrance gate. As usual the feeling of ennui mixed with dread and danger he got when coming to work started to imbue his being. He parked "his" company car at the back of the Field Service building of *LightWrite*, the giant semiconductor fabrication company. The building was one of many identically similar buildings in the campus, made of tilt-up concrete walls, designed to span the maximum space for the minimum cost. They were every where in the semiconductor sprawl of Silicon Valley.

As he got out of the car he noticed that the Director of Human Resources, flanked on each side by two big cops, had advanced towards him and were standing right in front of him. It was around 9:00 AM. Formally, the director addressed him: "Jack Corvic. Your employment here has been terminated. Further, you are to be escorted,"—he indicated the cop on each side of him—"from the premises. And criminal charges MAY be pressed against you. An investigation has been conducted."

Jack was shocked. His eyes opened wide in fear.

The HR honcho continued: "You are to go with these officers, to gather up your personal property. Then your are to be escorted OFF the premises."

Jack thought: *What the hell is going on?*

When he got inside, there was an uptight mood about the place. Ashen-faced people shot furtive glances, dashed about as though everybody suddenly had to pee. As he was escorted to his desk, Jack noticed some of the cubicles had the openings leading into them taped shut with yellow hazard tape forming a big X. Inside these cubicles the desks were also taped shut with the same yellow caution tape blocking their drawers. So was his! Again he thought: *What the hell is going on?*

Jack was told by one of the rent-a-cops that there had been an undercover worker somewhere, who had made elaborate notes about people in the shipping department dealing speed. Some of the engineers had been involved. No fewer than 60 heads would roll in this mass firing. Even some executives were summarily dismissed because they had known about the drug abuse and not turned anybody in. It was even thought that some people had traded RAM for speed. There might be a criminal investigation.

People who walked by the opening of Jack's cubicle saw him—resigned, red faced, clearing out. He did not have his usual sweet little catfish grin curling pontifically up from under his moustache. Jack had dark Italian good looks. He was short, powerful, swarthy, with curling dark hair that fell just to his collar. His left ear was pierced with a small diamond. Usually Jack walked around the place in a calm capable manner like a little sultan, secure in his environment. He had a way of putting people down sometimes; he could look upon you with suspicion; he could appear smug, but it was only a cover up for a basic shyness and sincerity that had not served him too well in the business world. Jack was versatile, he was an engineer.

Jack gathered up the last of his possessions: a few personal reference books, a potted plant. He noticed people looking at him. It was shocking to see the fear and loathing in the eyes of coworkers who just yesterday he had thought of as friends. Jack felt stupid and suspicious. He didn't like people to suspect him. It made him feel like he'd done something wrong, like something he did in the past and thought he got away with. (And in fact he had been doing speed at work, because there was so much work. But he had also been able to own up to his addiction and gotten himself into a company-sponsored drug rehab counseling program). Jack tried not to feel the suspicion, because people become suspicious of you when you look suspicious. But he couldn't help it with these two big cops marching him, red-faced, out the door.

Jack Corvic found himself kicked out of the kingdom of high-paying, high-tech work —out onto the street where he had to look for a job. And forget about unemployment benefits; they don't give you even the measly little dole they do have, when you get fired.

The first few weeks of being unemployed weren't so bad. The initial shock of his wife that day had been terrible though. But Jack was an excellent engineer with some background in radio, some in digital, some in computers. He had done work in magnetic resonance at school, and worked in hospitals around radiology and biomechanics. He had worked all around Silicon Valley, even in banks, as part of both hardware and software development.

When the Light*Write* company refused to readmit him—even though he had been in a company-sponsored drug-rehab program (paranoid Jack wondered if this wasn't where they got the information to do the bust in the first place)—his loathing for the corporate hegemony in modern life was further inflamed.

As if he didn't have enough trouble, it was right about that time that they learned the news that Jack's sister had cancer and was to start chemotherapy treatment. He knew how sick this made patients, and he feared for his little sister. He had to be confident she was in good hands; there was nothing he could do for her.

He began looking in the Monday business section of the Mercury News for jobs, calling buddies in the business, networking, telling everyone he was available. Having to tell people he was looking for work began to get old real fast. All this rejection. He began to feel like a pariah. Then he started going to the agencies and they were even worse. He had never in his life encountered such stupid people. What a bunch of ninnyhammers. Kids just out of school, without even a clue about anything, trying to represent him, trying to match his technical talents with what the employers wanted. It was just a word game for them and they didn't understand the meaning of the words. But the jobs just weren't coming.

His new Mantra became: "Your Job must be first on your list of priorities for the good life. Without a Job, you have nothing. No home, no wife, no family, no church, nor recreation, no car, no boat, no second home—nothing!" Over and over again. Sometimes the mantra came with admonitions, old saws: "The idle mind is the devil's workshop." And "The harder I work, the luckier I get." And so the weeks passed. Jack going around to agencies, sending out resumes. Some good drunks helped. He smoked pot more than usual. He used the time to let his mind wander the realms into what he called the mystic systems religion or Vedanta-vatic.

Jack was actually a very spiritual person underneath the overly-mental (but thick-skinned) engineer nerd persona he projected. Jack's interest in healing and metaphysics stemmed from an out-of-body experience that happened to him quite by accident. The incident occurred when his parents were getting divorced. During that awful period of his childhood, he'd occasionally wake up at night not knowing where he was, or with a feeling of being in two rooms at the same time. But worse, with a sense of some dreadful tentacled monstrous presence close by. One that immobilized him in its ubiquitous grip. The experience initially frightened him terribly, and there wasn't anybody to talk to about this stuff. He got into looking for answers in books and psychology and eventually accepted that the splitting of his parents had caused his own unconscious to open up, and let some ungodly primordial energies to seep out into his world. They threatened to devour him. This bifurcation of interest not only sparked his psychic abilities, but also as a defense against them, made him a very rational engineer. He never got into the hippie hallucinatory explorations scene: the idea of losing control like that was too terrifyingly real. But he had looked into transcendental meditation as well as other religions. Other out-of-body experiences, happened to him spontaneously once or twice over the years.

Jack had been fooling around and now he was paying the price for it. But idleness is the devil's workshop and he started getting ideas. Tormented by the thought of his little sister dying of cancer, he thought to somehow turn his programming efforts into creating some distracting computer activity, perhaps a virtual reality type program or game to help people with cancer take their mind off their troubles. He even thought about how some doctors were having good results curing cancer using visualization. Maybe there was some way he could couple visualization with virtual reality. He knew that alternative health was about the body healing itself through, among other things, meditation and visualization. It was like words or thoughts—or perhaps it was the lack of them, as in Zen—could effect a cure through crossing the brain-blood barrier somehow. He wondered if that were truly possible, or was it just a dream. He had to find out for his sister's sake.

Jack's idea was to build a machine. Or a system of machines, to use Magnetic Resonance Imaging, (MRI), along with real time feedback. The feedback would be used to present the MRI images that were being taken—in real time—to the subject so that he could use them to enhance the body's own ability to heal. Eventually the feedback would be used to control the MRI machine as well: applied to both the magnet and the radio waves pulsing the tissue being imaged, to cause changes to that tissue. The basic theory is that only the mind body heals itself. This machine would use the mind's ability to visualize and move attention to parts of the body that were being imaged in MRI. This feedback would be presented as images through a pair of virtual reality goggles to the user. The system would be able to pick up signals from the glove and brain, and present these images so that the patient could, by a kind of visualization program, affect his own cure. His process answered the question: What would happen if you showed the MRI to the *subject* in real time. And you taught the subject to enhance his own body's healing capacity using this feedback. Would a better image produce better results? Would a very interactive and therefore more engaging experience enhance the body_mind's ability to heal itself? Of course it would. It was a good idea; the implementation, of course, would be filled with many obstacles. He thought to maybe, at some point, interest a venture capitalist in his designs. Virtual reality had entered its creative heyday. It was turning up everywhere. Jack was on all the mailing lists and it seemed like every other week there was a seminar or convention or poster session or brown bag luncheon in various fields of interest that he would like to attend, somewhere in the country. These were extremely interesting times. But he also knew that venture capitalist did not usually invest in unemployed bums with big ideas. He knew it would take a lot of money, so he set about starting to get the money.

The idea of how to get the money suddenly came to him one day as he was wandering around in the aisles of the Silicon Valley Surplus, way up in Oakland. He had gone there to get some respite from the endless self-torment of being Mr. Unemployed. It made him feel better looking at the machines; he easily understood them . And there they were! As advertised—boxes of credit card readers for only $9.99. The ad, cut out of the newspaper and pasted in a placard on a chrome stand, read: "We got these from Crocker Bank as excess inventory, when Wells Fargo bought them out. Brand new units still in the factory box. / Only $9.99 (originally over $400) to own the same type of credit card reader used by the banking industry for credit verification."

And there it came to him—Jack, trying to think of a way to turn his luck around, began thinking of turning the card reader around—make it a card *writer*! It's the law: any transducer that can read, can be made able to write. Hmmm, might be as simple as changing the polarity of the current. Ahaa! That's what he'd do. He'd write himself up a bunch of ATM cards and go around checking money out of the ATM machines at banks. If the fucking Machine wasn't going to pay him to work, then he was still going to make the fucking Machine take care of him anyway. He didn't create the world the way it was. He didn't ask to be born into the economy so interdependent and complex that you could fall through the cracks.

Jack knew from having worked at Visa about the pathways of authentication and clearing and key encryption, and what an old pal at Wells-Fargo had told him about Jackpotting an ATM machine. Jackpotting was where you got an ATM machine to spit up all the 20s it had, or at least as many as you asked it for. You had to get (or synthesize) the special card that the technician supervisors who worked on the ATM machines used to get access to deeper architectures of the ATM machine.

He went over the design requirements for Jackpotting in his mind. What I have to do is interrupt and take over the line between the ATM and the Host. The ATMs are connected through dedicated lines to a Host computer. Luckily they are not doing key encryption, and I don't have to spend hours running a cryptoanalysis program to get the key. I will have to use a war dialer to try all the number combinations to get a PIN, but there are only 4 numbers and a modern laptop could eat that right up. What I do is insert my laptop computer *between* the ATM and the Host. My computer would be attached to the special super-user ATM card that I write. A data cable leads from that card to my laptop. Like that kid had in the movie *Terminator*. But now laptops were much more powerful. I would need that because I would have to run the Host environment on the laptop, in effect masquerading as the Host connected to the ATM machine.

Jack stepped through the procedure. Basically I begin by inserting my fraudulent ATM card into the ATM.

I have the Host computer now effectively connected through the card to the ATM machine.

What the ATM does is: send an authorization

request signal to the host, saying "Hey! Can you authorize me to give this guy money? Or is he broke? Or is his card invalid?"

What my laptop does is: intercept the signal from the host, discard it, and send a Not Engaged signal to the Host, which host interprets as, "There's no one using the ATM" signal.

What the Host does is: get the "no one using" signal, send back "okay, then for God's sake don't spit out any money!" signal to ATM.

Then what my laptop does is intercept the signal (again), throw it away (again), send "Wow! That guy is an ATM technical supervisor! Give him as much money as he asks for. In fact, give him ALL the cash we have! He is really an ATM technical supervisor" signal.

What the ATM does is—what else? Obediently dispense cash 'till the note-cassette is empty.

Running the Host environment on my laptop I modify the status & number of the card directly in the Host's memory. In effect I have turned the humble user's card into an all powerful trusted officer of the bank security card, used for testing purposes. At that point, the ATM does whatever its operator, its super highly-trusted security administrator operator, told it to do.

The next few weeks of idleness were a terror and a blessing. To fill the time Jack engaged in an orgy of technical creativity, hacking hardware and software. With no Unemployment money coming in, his household was going to hell in a handcart. So he hid from his pressing economic and social problems by burying himself in the absorbing technical problem of jackpotting the ATM machines. The first thing he did was reverse engineer the card reader to write an account number of his choice on the magnetic strip. He wrote his own number on it; he duplicated his own card because he knew the PIN number associated with it. He tried it at his own teller machine, a typical pay-point in Berkeley. It worked. He realized, though, that he was vulnerable to the bank's cameras. Not to worry. He came home and with his soldering iron built a set of infrared LED encrusted sunglasses (High output LEDs, Opto Diode Corporation OD-100s, effectively saturate or 'OD' or 'blind' surveillance cameras which typically don't filter infrared). So he would appear as a glare of light on video tape; while to anyone on the street he would appear to be wearing those strange flashy sunglasses that gay divas sometimes wear.

He was excited about his success on this first foray into the netherworld of information crime.

"OOOhhhh how sweet it is!" Jack exclaimed at his cleverness that evening while at home on dad duty. The idea is to have this intelligence working for you but without leaving any kind of trace. Intelligence without representation.

"OOO, yea! Sensor suite!"

"What's 'cent's are sweet' daddy?"

Jack laughed as his son Dan struggled with the words. The lad was so smart.

Regular work had allowed Jack to marry and he liked the stability, companionship and focus it brought to his life. Eventually they had a little boy. Now four years old, he was the delight of Jack's life. And he felt the little person as a sparkle in his blood.

"Well anyway, it's sensor. S-E-N-S-O-R. You've got some really nice sensors." Jack said.

"I do? Where."

"Well, your eyes are sensors, and you're ears are

sensors."

He reached out and took the child's little hand. "You're fingers and toes are sensors." He touched the lad's nose, "And your nose is the cutest little sensor I ever saw. Anything that lets you feel the world is a sensor."

"Well if I feel the world, then I'm a sensor too."

"That's right. You're whole body is a sensor."

Jack's plan was to visit ATM machines, and get them to dispense as much cash as possible without causing alarms to go off. He knew that the ATM machine command language was based on a 3 digit code, and that they all—even those from different banking institutions—would have the same code. Basically, you had to get the ATM machine to accept these three codes: First, Message 604, Supervisory Mode. This was where the ATM has been set to the Supervisory mode. It is for when the ATM maintenance personnel are monitoring the ATM. There is a time out on being in Supervisory mode. The terminal owner will be called. Second, you have to monitor and take control of the bill dispensing with Message 630, Bill Count Warning. This warning alerts the ATM that it has dispensed an undetermined number of bills, causing the ATM to go out of service. The bill condition may be inadequate. Jackpotting relied on the fact that the cash dispensers and their states were monitored. If one cash cassette became empty during a cash dispense, the ATM switches to the next cash cassette and continues dispensing. And last, you had to be sure to log off with Message 627, Supervisory off. This tells the ATM that the Supervisory mode has been exited. The ATM maintenance personnel have completed the needed repairs.

Jack needed to be able to adjust the amount of money taken from a given machine, and not just take it all. It was a question of time spent in front of the machine. During the day he wanted to just spend at most 2 minutes in front of a machine, for if an ATM was dispensing 20s at the rate of 2 per second it would take a little over 2 minutes to dispense $5,000 if the money cassette inside the ATM had that much. Two minutes was an AWFUL long time to be standing in front of an ATM machine—shivering in the fear of committing federal felonies, as it relentlessly went about dispensing money at you! Throwing money out so fast that you had to repeatedly empty the tray, lest the dreaded Bill Count Warning message 630 called powers that be to come and nab your ass and throw it in jail. You had to stand there with one hand up near the card port, and a data cable running down your sleeve to the inside of your coat, and your other hand trying to grab the pile of 20s that were piling up at the little tray door—before the pile got so thick that it became wedged in the little door because the rapid 'phut, phut phut' spew of 20s fed out so fast and furious that it exceeded the limit of what could be pushed through onto the tray anyway. When the ATM started dispensing it did not stop spitting out the pile of bills and wait till they were taken away, but spit out money continuously until it was done. It turns out that the thickness of the pile is the limit of $300 or 15 twenties. So he had to wait for 16 or 17 piles! of lucre before he could flush his presence out of there. All kinds of warnings were detectable, but his program had control of the machine and intercepted them.

If he could visit 10 machines a day, and get $5000 from each, that was $50,000 a day! He might be able to visit 20 machines. If that was all he did. In any given metropolitan area, Chicago, Boston, Los Angeles, he could find 100 cash machines in a week, that was half a million dollars! Then move on to the next metropolis. In fact he could get detailed digital city maps on his laptop and a GPS signal indicating with a little beacon and driving instructions to get from bank to bank. That would make him much more efficient. It would take trips to only 4 or 5 major metropolitan areas, to get a couple of million. That ought to be enough. A million should be enough money to get started in the big game of life. Maybe I'll retire to Sonoma and grow grapes. Be healthier anyway.

He got the Host Operating system software from a friend at Wells Fargo—told the guy he just wanted to mess with it. The guy was a trusted old friend from the school, and had been Jack's mentor in programming and didn't believe Jack for a minute. So Jack had to tell him about that he was just interested in doing it for the technical hack, and that if he did actually see any money from the project he would share some of the loot with him. Jack actually said, "I will shoot you some jack."

From a Hacker bulletin board he got the war dialer program to try all the combinations of 4 numbers so he could get the PIN number of the supervisory ATM card. He used that to find the PIN for the supervisory ATM card by going at night to a busy pay-point location. He had the glasses on. He had the especially prepared card. He had taken the laptop apart and re-connected the components with data cables so that he could hide the components of the laptop strapped to various parts of his body under his coat. The motherboard with its CPU, was under his shirt; the hard drive in his back pocket. He fed the video out to a pair of 3D classes. It was just like having the laptop screen in front of his eyes and your hands were free. He could also look through these glasses, all the while with the LEDs saturating the security camera. The keyboard he replaced with a small keypad. With lots of macros mapped to the keys. He ran the war dialer on the distributed laptop connected to the special card and easily got the PIN number for the supervisory ATM card. He used the authentication on the Host to accept the password.

Finally he began his run. His wife had been giving him more and more of a hard time since he had done nothing about searching for work. Instead spending his time in front of his PC, or working in his shop making cables, soldering, programming, blowing ASICs, punching magnetic cards onto plastic. Finally he was ready for the first trial. He reached the ATM on Shattuck in Berkeley. Now he was afraid. This was for the money not just for the technical hack. He began walking back and forth, in front of the Neutron Cafe, or circling around the BART Station at Center. $2,000,000! His fear always held him back so that twenty times he was on the point of approaching the squat ATM deity, which began to appear to him as scowling like some kind of awful iron toad going to suck up all his freedom. What if he got caught, sent to the federal pen? What good would he be to his son then? But he was even more scared of his wife leaving him and taking the kid with her. Abruptly he made up his mind, crossed the street running, so as to allow no time for reflection, snapped the zap shades over his eyes and flung himself in front of the ATM machine.

He plugged the magnetic coded card in. He keyed in the PIN number. He waited a long few seconds not knowing if some alarm would go off. Then the automatic teller made the phut, phut, phut, phut, phut sound

10 times. Each one a twenty dollar bill. Ha! ha! It worked. He addressed the machine, his worthy opponent: All right, now you gonna pay.

Following a pre-plotted, digitally-displayed, satellite-guided itinerary, Jack traveled all over the Bay area. He got more and more excited about pulling all this money together. He crossed the bay, went to all the little towns off highway 101: San Carlos, Redwood City, Shallow Alto, Melo Park, Lost Altos, Mountain View, Sunnyvale, San Jose. He re-crossed the Bay, coming up the other side, Fremont, Hayward, San Leandro, Oakland, crossed again, regained San Francisco, worked in and out of all those neighborhoods, and crossed the gate on up into Marin, working all the tellers in a non linear progression without any clear cut pattern. He didn't feel any remorse because he knew the celebrated man-in-the-street would not have to bare the brunt of his indiscretions. He did think the bank security would figure out what was going on. They would probably recoup the loss in a day's round-up of hundreds-place decimal points. He knew he had to move fast and relentless, continuously.

Jack had to deal with long (2 minute) cash dispensing times. It was truly hideous and grotesque, the time he had to spend in front of each madly-dispensing teller machine. It was like something out of I Love Lucy, that one where she is working on a chocolate assembly line and the chocolates start coming too fast and she has to stuff them in her mouth and down her bodice and still they keep coming, falling on the floor and she had to look up all panicked to make sure she is not being watched and she doesn't know what to do. There couldn't be any one else in the bank line.

After hitting 100 tellers averaging, 5 per hour: that's

one every 12 minutes, taking him 20 hours —he was on the move constantly all the time for a whole day, he had $20,000 bucks. He pulled into a truck dealer on Hayward's Auto Row. He bought himself a new truck —one he had always wanted. Completely decked out, a 4x4, high off the ground. Blue, with a fine stereo system, quiet, powerful and economical. After he drove it off the lot he pulled over in a quiet neighborhood under and giant tree and just let himself bask in the new car smell. It smelled like freedom. From there he set out across country. He could just camp out in the truck. It was so elegant and new, the cops wouldn't hassle him, if he just didn't fuck up.

He averaged nearly $100,000 a day, even including travel times, polling for numbers, writing new cards. Jack got his routine down pat. He got good city maps. He ripped pages out of phone books for the addresses of the ATM machines, and marking their positions, then plotted minimal paths between them. Away from his home turf, he no longer feared linear short paths. He went into Hack Mode—moving into machine phases, out of cycle with the waking world, missed meals to the point of malnutrition, always driven by an obsessive passion to *finish the run.* Nights on the move in a hallucination of numbers. Grim, unshaven, his mind became a scramble of highways and exits, ATM paypoints and a cabalistic mishmash of transactions processing. He looked the part of a bum as he sat on a bench in another town organizing the shortest paths from one ATM machine to the next.

Every night he'd call home and talk to his little boy.

"Why do you have to stay away so long?" Dan asked.

"Because I've got to work little man. But I'll be

home soon, and we are going to move to a nice place up in the country. We are going to have a big garden, do you like that?"

"Why kind of plants are you going to grow?"

"Whatever kinds you want. How about grapes?"

"Grapes! That would be great."

"And you can have a dog."

"O really daddy. I want to get a beagle!"

"Yep, we'll have to get a dog, and maybe some horses too. And me and you and mama can go for long rides and we can camp out and sleep in a tent if we want to like we did last summer."

Jack traveled all around by truck, paying cash, staying in cheap motel rooms near various strip mall where the ATMs were. He reached New York walking around with figures, sums of money running around constantly in his head. Like a machine, calling out the address of the next Bank Of America teller with which to engage in transaction processing.

Los Angeles gave him 350 thousand dollars

Santa Fe—200 thousand Phoenix, San Antonio, Dallas, Fort Worth, Houston, New Orleans—one million. New York—a half million. It took him 40 days and nights of non-stop unholy hack frenzy to pull together nearly $2,000,000.

It was never reported in the media—banks just didn't like to appear lacking in security measures. They just quietly made good all the sums. Probably recouped it in a minute of the foreign debt round off.

When he got back to San Francisco, he looked up at the Pyramid building and found himself wanting to scale it like King Kong. He felt like getting into a gladiator wrestling match with the one-eyed giant Sutro Tower.

He had lunch at Chez Panise with his wife and son and bought wine at 40 dollars a bottle.

He invited some of his old colleagues of the Field Service Department at *LightWrite* out to lunch —had himself driven down there in a limo, and took them out to dinner at the finest restaurant in Mountain View, *Ling Chou's*. He told them that he had inherited some money and said he had plans to retire somewhere in Sonoma and raise grapes.

II

But now that he had some money, it was time to fund (what else?) some science. Jack set about fulfilling his dreams of building the non-invasive healing system. He used a two-pronged attack. The idea was to 1) develop the necessary tech: hardware and software and 2) to begin establishing himself in some way in the medical community. To become an expert at (1), he started going to VR conferences to learn what equipment to buy. Then to make inroads into (2) he engaged his old friend and roommate, Paul McWhirter, who was a don at UCSF medical school research labs. Jack knew he would need to develop some kind of liaison with medicine and health, if only for the cache of being able to write proposals and grants on letterhead.

Jack had been a pretty good interface designer, and wanted to get into 3D. He bought expensive software packages for 3D and CAD. He bought books and took classes. He set about drawing characters in 3D. At first it was little blobby aliens, developed from applying a mesh- smoothing modifier to a box, to make the being a lot more rounded, like a sausage. He learned the basics. To give the sausage a neck, he learned to edit just the polygons of the neck mesh, and this he scaled down to shape into a torso with neck and head. He would work on one side then duplicate it by mirror symmetry on the other. Arms and legs followed. He could view his creating in top, side, front and back views. He became adept at the polygon modeler, NURBS. He advanced from cartoon characters, to the more realistic. He tried various methods. Some character generating methods start from the eye or mouth, assembling the pieces into a full head. Others build the entire body as a rough shape first, then hack it into shape by slicing and adding detail. Since he couldn't model facial details yet, he simply applied a texture map to the shape of a head. His first character models were all done using this mapping method. As he progressed in modeling skill, he began to create the eyes, mouth, etc, using actual geometry. He built the facial features point-by-point and polygon-by-polygon. With infinite patience he alternated between the front and side views to create the profile, adding depth to the flat face outline he started with. Stretching poly mesh grins. Chamfering sockets into which to set spherical eyeballs. He downloaded models off the web and built composite creatures. It was like Frankensteins's workshop there for a while. He learned subdivision of the mesh to get the geometrical facets of the polygon parts to become continuous and smooth surfaces. And do you know they began to look more and more like a real faces. Some were actually quite beautiful. He thought to incorporate his own face into his computer generated character. He added eyebrows and hair, and clothes and dressed them up, and rendered them into scenes. Then he sought to add bones and to animate them. To move the lips and make the characters talk and have facial expressions was really difficult and he spent a lot of time with it. He put his own head on a game character who wore a long duster and stole cars and was a magician. He called him the Animage. It felt great to animate his own avatar in cyberspace.

To educate himself on what VR equipment to buy, he started attending conferences on Virtual Reality. At the Cyberthon in San Francisco he met Jaron Lanier creator of the data glove. He saw William Gibson whose novel *Neuromancer* inspired many VR developers and designers. They were called Spacemakers and he would be one of them.

He started buying VR equipment: high powered computers, a Silicon Graphics machine, the dark video goggles and the black glove. These are packed with sensors and trailed wires to a high powered computer or workstation. Through the goggles you can see a computer graphic representation of a room; turn your head and the graphics update to make it seem as though your head turns in the alternate reality too. This feedback feels like what happens to you in reality when you turn your head in a room. It is very convincing. To move in this world all you had to do was point the finger of the glove in a direction and the world seen through the video goggles moved past you, giving you the feeling that you were moving through it. "Outside" you could fly through the air as little puffy clouds went slipping by. Point the glove in a room and zoom through. You could pick up objects in the room and throw them and watch them bounce. The objects could be rendered through a Physics Engine that imparted to them the actions and behaviors that looked more like the way you would expect, for example in the inelastic collisions off surfaces. It made things behave the way they should, as if governed by the laws of reality. He was now an explorer of virtual reality. A space maker, which was a new kind of entertainment creator. See so that we may see. Point the glove like some thoughtful philosopher making a point. Jack set out to create the supreme computer game. It was an obvious direction to take computing —merge computer modeling with virtual reality. He wanted to make his game into a space of real time so that you could get in a feedback loop with what was actually the current state of affairs in the game and have instantaneous feedback effect on it.

To get further into the medical world, objective (2), Jack started hanging out with an old roommate friend at UC medical center, Paul McWhirter. Paul was a respected scientist at the UCSF medical research center, a post-doc fellow doing research in molecular genetics. When Jack would ask him about what he does in his research, Paul would get condescending and short, a common situation with the scientists of esoterica. Paul explained it was what switches in the genes turns hereditary diseases on and off. As roommates, Paul and Jack had been thrown together out of necessity and had learned to appreciate or at least tolerate each other's difference. Paul was sort of a friend but had the supercilious know-it-all-attitude of BIG SCIENCE. After all, he had become a biomed engineer before that was even understood. He had a PhD. in Molecular Biology, with minors in Immunology and Biochemistry. He had been growing and maintaining an immortal line of mammalian cells for years. His main job was screening for and constructing a library of how genes expressed themselves. He was experienced in both transient and stable transfections. Slide techniques for cellular immunofluorescence were second nature to him. He had in situ hybridization work going on in his lab. He authored papers using microscopy assays and digital imaging. He processed tissues for cryopreservation. He did all kinds of serum analysis and blotting, and plasmid construction.

When Jack hinted at his idea of using biofeedback to go from the mind to the body, Paul patiently, somewhat condescendingly, explained the Blood-Brain Barrier to Jack. He said: "Long ago they injected a bunch of blue dye into the bloodstream of an animal. They found that all the tissues of the body EXCEPT the brain and spinal cord would turn blue. So they realized that there is a barrier to keep blood born contaminates out of the nervous system. It protects the brain from hormones and neurotransmitters but of course people have found ways across it. Marijuana is a fat soluble molecule that gets across; as do barbiturates. And stress."

Jack asked, "What about going the other way? From the brain into the blood."

Paul looked perplexed and shook his head as if to say No*ooo*.

Jack continued: "Well what about these mediators that can control their oxygen absorption rate in the blood by slowing their breathing way down."

Paul caught his meaning and was quick to nix it. Dubiously, like a scientist forced to present both sides of the issue, he said: "Yes, well it's not exactly clear how that works."

Yet Jack was convinced that he could do this. Go across this barrier from the brain to the blood, from the mind to the body. The word will be made flesh. Jack swallowed his personality and began to become quiet around the doctors. They were such an arrogant bunch. Jack did take some hope from Andrew Weil's work especially the *Spontaneous Healing*, and the holistic practices he was trying to bring into traditional American medical practice. Jack felt his whole generation moving toward a more holistic view of life on this planet. There had been this kind of feeling in the air during the human potential movement and Jack still subscribed to it. You had to. They were searching for the new indigenous myths everywhere—in American Indian studies, in shamanistic practices, in UFOs, in eastern mysticism for a deeper understanding of the meaning of life than what was offered in the west by the culture of science and consumerism.

Jack talked his old friend Paul into letting him get involved as an unpaid intern in his lab. Frank hoped the situation would lead to him becoming a co-worker. To seal the deal, Jack offered to buy and build a virtual reality system to help them visually manipulate molecules in 3D. Paul was hip to that! And there wasn't anyone around with the technical savvy to be doing it for his lab. They just weren't that sophisticated about computers. Jack soon found, as the new tech support guy, that some of the doctors —though brilliant in their area of medicine—were so thick when it came to computers that they were not even able to write letters longer than a screenful when on AOL because they didn't know about the screen scrolling down. It seemed to be way beyond some of them to type a URL into the browser; they wanted to just click on links or find them in their favorites. One of the doctors eventually proved to be unteachable.

So Jack and Paul were once again thrown together to walk the same path out of need. For Paul saw the value of being able to use the computer in his molecular researches. Jack kept his cards close to his breast though, for he knew his post-doc scientist friend would be shocked by the bold moxy of Jack's intentions to explore microcosmic healing at the edge of possibility. The administration gave Jack a couple of cubicles worth of space out of their warren off to the side and at least not in the stinky chemical room with the rabbit cages and the titration equipment. Jack bought and put together a state-of-the-art 3D imaging and virtual reality multimedia system for them to share.

Jack felt good to be part of the working world, part of a team again, even though he was only an intern, and a paying one. But from his little cubicle with a window in the UCSF lab he could see the Golden Gate Bridge and even past it, all the way over to the Marin headlands. Some afternoons the light shining from the sun setting across the Pacific imbued the canyons of the city with a honeyed magic, like the cool sound from brass horns. Jack started pulling together a fine library of training animations and videos that were available in the medical universities around the country.

One night the name of the machine he would build came to him: PHASER. This acronym emerged after a little time fooling around with words to describe what he wanted to be able to do. He rejected (ASVSCMRFEIELA) for Autoimmune Stimulation by Visualization and Simulation Controlled Magnetic and Radio Field Enhancement for Inverse Etiological Local Application project. Luckily this got worked into a better acronym: PHASER for Phenomenal Healing Amplification by Stimulated Emission of Radiation. He knew this was nothing less than a revolution in consciousness. Of course the inspiration for this had come from Laser. And he had always admired the mathematical object phaser, which was a supremely elegant way to de-convolute waves into their harmonics and phases. And there was the futuristic phaser from Star Trek. But really, for Jack the meaning of the phaser was the idea that phase locking of spins, and rotations and vibrations that held together and became something did so because of the golden ratio ϕ (phi), the number that coordinated the mean and the extreme of things back into itself in a way that its center could hold and it would not fall apart. The yoking together of the mean and the extreme was that which defined harmony and coherence.

Jack started building an online library and learning center for the Molecular Genetics Group Laboratory, whose team he was now part of. He used the UCSF Med School letterhead to further the team's experimental work in molecular biology (as well as his own). With the caché and letterhead of a prestigious medical school behind him, he started pulling together all the microscopy and animated images people were sharing in that community as part of an advanced visualization and training center. While this was going on he began to pick up what he could from the students, lab workers, scientists, and from classes at the medical school. He took a class in mammalian cell culture. His fellow co-workers who worked with this stuff at the lab were amused by his humble beginnings, but this made them more accepting. Jack did a lot of reading. At first the knowledge driving this community seemed strange. His own background had been in engineering; he knew circuits and some physics. He recalled struggling through maybe one course in biology and one in chemistry while at college, but had not done well because they seemed to require so much memorization and classifications. There was never any theory. By contrast he loved the grand rational presentation of theory in physics and quantum mechanics, where you defined the basic objects and calculated them from scratch—and where you only had to remember a few equations. It all came from F = ma. For Jack, calculus was surely the finest piece of thought ever put together on this earth. It was a kind of enlightenment to understand the general behavior of functions as they went about convolving dimension, and see how this understanding emerges out of the concrete description of all motion in the universe. No wonder they called that time from Newton and Leibnitz through Laplace and the Bernoulis, Lagrange, Poisson, and Euler: the Age of Enlightenment. This lineage carried forth by Gauss, Maxwell, Hamilton, Poincare, Mandlebrot.

Jack was not completely unfamiliar with the modern area of biology. In college, about 25 years ago, he had read some interesting stuff, trying to gain a background on Quantum Mechanics. He read books and papers co-authored by Jung and Wolfgang Pauli, about the archetypes of order in number, the mandalas in atomic models of radiant energy and in speculations on time and dimension and synchronicity. He had read Shrödinger's 1960s paper "What is Life". This was, after the 1954 discovery of the most famous molecule of all, the double helix spiral of DNA. Schrödinger compared the genetic material to an aperiodic crystal where information could be coded in a linear array. But to Jack, the life sciences all seemed so messy, compared to neat little switching circuits representing logic equations and programming. Although at one point, when he was going through a lot of psychological study and turmoil in his own life as a young person, Jack began to try and imagine an information theory of life. Also he had spent a great deal of time thinking about von Neuman's self-reproducing automata, and trying to see them as an archetype in the cannon of mathematics. Like a circle or a kind of simple machine, a wedge or an inclined plane on the nano level. But there was a huge gap in his understanding between the molecules of the code of life and say a hip bone.

The Molbio class was taught by a cool teacher, a ruddy, healthy-looking, man in his 40s who on the first day showed them how to use meat tenderizer (because it contained papaya enzymes that penetrated the nucleus), dish soap, and distilled water to extract DNA from wheat germ. Jack immediately liked him. The instructor lifted weights, went on vacations in sunny places, and was a gene hacker. From him Jack learned sterile lab procedures. He learned what a protocol was, and got some formal, supervised experience working with the centrifuge. Much of the time Jack felt like the class was over his head but the administration let him sit in on it anyway.

It wasn't until he got the good simple analogy of the cell as a factory that the life-sciences world-view started to settle in for him. The cell was a factory, and it had production lines inside of it, and had to have material delivered to it, and had to have products taken away. Little loading docks at the cell membrane, truckloads of raw material coming in and product going out. . . . while the machines inside the cell factory were these stations that made proteins. The machines were all governed and watched over by *information* directed to them from the DNA, which was distributed throughout the factory in chromosomes on genes. All these cell factories are always working at maximum capacity and top speed with just-in-time inventory. And all the factories in the nation, the united nation of cells, were ALL governed by some central authority. Jack wondered What is this thing called life? Suddenly life becomes redefined for him in an entirely remarkable context. How could something called life appear so well coordinated and designed? Who was the CEO who was responsible for it. Just physics? What intelligence or network of intelligent agents had designed this splendid machinery? It was an honor to try to understand that question.

They used powerful, expensive electron Microscopes to see cells. And there were all kinds of 3D modeling of cells to aid with visualization. With these training animations you can fly over a pimple like it was an island seen from an airplane. Or you can zoom down into a cut like one looks at a canyon fly-by. As you hover and fly over it, you look at it from all angles. Being able to look at the terrain, and models of the terrain, and recognize things, helped the student know in much more detail, the place he needed to go to in his mind to integrate the knowing.

Then one day on a walk by the reservoir, Jack was stopped in his tracks when he saw the analogy between the cell and the city. It was one of those visions that all students of molecular biology must get when they have been studying too much: It was like the cell was some huge domed-over city. The cars were the molecules moving around inside the cell. The houses were the Ribozomes that took the delivery of things from the trucks on ladders of RNA, kind of like the way material is delivered off the back of truck at supermarkets on those ladders with rollers for rungs inclined to roll packages into loading docks. What an image he was pulled into! Cellular structure writ large into the work-day world of the cityscape! He kept driving the buildup of the image with his questions, magnifying the splendid machinery of life at work in real time. Everywhere there were these invisible endoplasmic reticulum structures, predefined passageways that things had to squeeze past. It was quite a vision. Like roads and curbs and sidewalks and invisible private property laws. Here he was in a San Francisco, in which a single protein molecule would then be the size of a family car. To scale it up he recalled the liver. He had read there were, in a single liver cell, about 200 million average size protein molecules if all cellular space was used for packing such molecules. And in San Francisco? What were there, about 200,000 cars? And the invisible property boundaries of the city, the streets, the curb, the sidewalks, the driveway and the foyers form an invisible urban cytoskeleton across which you do not trespass. They were like the invisible structure of the inside of the cell. There was all this egress and ingress and congress among the people of the city, there were influences bowing out, and pressuring in. What if instead of doors, people emerged through the walls of their houses, like osmosis, diffusion, endocytosis, exocytosis—floating off like a very large food particle through a leak channel where you came up to a wall and just stood there until a vacuole opened up and a vesicle formed around you and you just floated off. He got this vision of a Magritte painting of myriad men in suits and bowler hats with umbrellas floating toward downtown.

It all really came clear to him one starry evening when he went up to the top of Twin Peaks Mountain, and stood looking out onto the city, dazzling like jewels against the black waters of the San Francisco Bay. He could see all the way down to San Jose; the Bay was encircled in a garnet of sparkling lights, the lights shimmering and refracting into the night. He knew all the lights were driven by the 60 cycle push-pull of the AC power company, coming through the wires like the push-pull of a reciprocating saw, delivering in lock-step the world-driving shape of the future. Matter wasn't flowing in those power lines, just force moving in and out like a piston supplying energy to the machines by dropping voltage across resistances. At that moment he saw the city as body, the body electric. The human body of a trillion cells. Hundreds of times more than all the people on earth! Cars and trucks in the street were cells moving in capillaries. Houses and buildings were organs that didn't move—they were factories to which raw material and from which products were taken. He assumed that all students of biology at some point in their study must have these visions. It binds them together. He thought: Jack, the more deeply you looked into it, the more in awe of it you become. I want to know where the boundary is crossed over between the molecular machines in the factory and LIFE. What is this thing called Life? Who designed these exquisitely tiny molecular machines and the great feedback cycles of metabolic pathways. Finite automata emerging, but there platonically, *a priori* just waiting for an opportunity to enact itself.

He learned about plasmids which are vectors, usually viruses with transgenic payloads grafted into them acting as vehicles to carry designer DNA into a host. There was the transgenic shotgun approach in which tiny gold beads coated with DNA that can be shot into a cell with a "gene gun." Though these don't *even* compare with sex which is nature's best way of exchanging genetic material between organisms.

Then Jack got going on another analogy of life. It was the Cell as Brain. It was right after he had gotten up from working at his computer and was taking another walk through the woods. He looked into the trees and his imagination zoomed down through the plant tissue to the working of the cells. There seemed to be an intelligence to the cells. Working, signaling. It wasn't just physics. It is was an intelligence. It was computation and information, and this intelligence was always watching him. Always.

It was at that moment he saw the interlocking panoply of life that is the ecology, surrounding him as brain. He suddenly realized he knew what was going on in the heart of every tree, every plant and flower, ever bush and blade of grass. The great mitosis raga. Dividing and Separating, passing on the library of instructions, on to the next generation across time. The Mind. It was writing itself into time with the cell. The cell was like a section of memory. A tract on a hard disk. An intersection, a node in a semiconductor RAM array. Everything in front of him, everything in existence now was in a giant memory, all interacting.

Nucleotides were like infinitesimal currents governed my myriad internal clocks sweeping around in the small space like tides in the involution ocean.

Each cell has its own copy of the organism's genome. Every cell was a computer with a code, a language built on an alphabet of only 4 letters. The program had a beautiful physical architecture, a spiral looping through the dimensions of a many faceted substrate, whose surface behaved like switches set on the surface of silicon—except this is pattern written in carbon, with its polyvalence —reaching, extending. So, we are RAM, holding a pattern for a while. A little calculation thinking about the four basic acids linked together in DNA, taking the four in binary parings over the space of some three million nucleotides, showed each cell carried the same amount of information as a CD ROM—650 megabytes.

Nature storing data and material in a binary system. It was like RAM; the panoply in front of you was like RAM, you could eat it, live in it, it was there for you. The Great Quantum Designer had built a world for you. It was organized into objects, just the way a program was "objects" are self contained modular program units communicating with other objects like routines calling functions, subroutines invoking global variables and checking against states current and past. (Or like the human mind with its objects relations.) Everything is communicating with everything else. Messages and instructions come and go across the cell wall, as does material. Or across the synapses of the human brain as does thought. And way down inside of every cell was the genome, the entire library replicated in every cell, a vast spiral that someone said was 6 feet long, inside every cell. How can such intricate, exquisitely nano design be going on. Someone else had said that if the DNA were stretched out across America it would be like vast stretches of highway with a few roadside attractions and cities along the way. There would be vast stretches of unused nucleotide strata. Jack had entered the nanoscape. In the nanoscape there is a highway, the DNA highway, and one can travel it for miles and miles, and not see a rest stop or any new or interesting feature. And yet look at all that comes of it. Yes the nanoscape, the new platonic world of self-reproducing automata as archetypes, equivalent to the circle and the line. The nanoscape was an ocean of form, a sea world of perfect platonic solids—the viruses. For the viruses make their shells out of discretely stacked molecules that are relaxed by physics into their platonic symmetry.

What *is* this nanospace? Viruses range in diameter from 20 to 400 nanometers (one nanometer equals a billionth of a meter. Ten to the minus ninth power, meters). Oddly, virus shapes are more often geometric than biomorphic. Jack had seen photos of an AIDS virus crashing into a cell, and it was like a meteor crashing into a planet. Spewing out recombinant life stuff all around the impact site. What is this nanospace? I am trying to understand how life emerges out of matter. They are saying nanospace is a space of state machines, little finite automata. There before, *a priori*. There already in the structure of the universe, waiting. Waiting for the nucleotides of the involution ocean to have some way to form the molecules of life, to write life into matter, to carry form across time. The question was, at what point do these molecules of life becoming self-sustaining. The way the foam flops up at the edge of the shore sometimes, a suspension of sand and salt water, a gel of air, its shape determined by randomness and initial conditions.

One could compare the geometric and biomorphic shape spaces but both are contained in the fractal—the expression of one dimension tunneling and branching into another. The old high-school geometry of Euclid is embedded in the modern fractal geometry of limit sets and permeable boundaries and recursive, feedback-iterative functions.

And yet there was a digital memory in the code to remember the shapes served up by randomness, a pattern that abides so that they could be reproduced the same, time and time again across time Molecular Biology approached this complexity straight away. Beginning with raising petri dishes of bacteria. Jack had even extracted his own DNA. It was an easy procedure, just needing an enzyme to cut into the nucleus of some cells he scraped off his own tongue. Later Jack learned how to create plasmids which are cells which had been injected or otherwise infected with snippets of genetic altered material of his choosing. He felt absolutely omnipotent when he was able to control the evolutionary pressure to obtain the results he wanted. He followed how they infused worms with a jelly fish enzyme that made them glow green in black light. They had even used this technique to make the pathways in the endoplasmic reticulum of cells stand out. It blew Jack's mind because the edges of the channels of the organelle looked just like the way the lacy veil of constellation densities are draped over the bulges and currents and vortices of turbulence in spacetime.

One day Jack bought a glowfish off the internet. Some enterprising outfit made Glowfish. He brought it home and put it in a little aquarium with a black light. When Dan saw it in the aquarium he said, "Wow, that's really cool, Dad." Then Jack explained some of the ideas of cloning to the lad. Later Jack asked the boy, "Would you like to clone Crystal?" (their beloved kitty). Little Dan had no reservations what-so-ever. He was all for it. For him it was grown-ups breeding animals and creating live toys. Jack wondered what kind of world this younger generation would create.

By the end of the year Jack had set up a system of molecular modeling using VR. A very sharp young scientist from the Stanford Research Institute on Ravenswood was loaned to them and Jack learned a lot. So he started pulling together the other elements of his agenda by setting up a research foundation. He hired a professional grant writer and got matching funds and equipment. He felt legitimate writing on UCSF medical center letterhead. Jack started getting lots of high powered equipment for the lab. And he started going around the country with his group of peers, the Molecular Genetics Group at UCSF, attending various seminars, and trade shows, having meetings with professors.

Then Jack's sister's cancer started up again. No one knew why. He went back to Texas to visit her. He spent time helping her cope with the rigors of chemotherapy, and saw some of their procedures. How (in the big heavy-metal particle-beam theatre) they used the MRI (Magnetic Resonance Imaging) and P.E.T. (Positron Electron Tomography) scans of his sister to align molecular x-ray beams with tumors so that you could get a much more accurate sighting of the disease agent in the cross hairs. They showed him pictures of the tumor. What once was the color of healthy youthful tissue was now black and shredded. Her breathing no longer imbibed of the spirit but was strained and forced

It shocked Jack; made him depressed. First he went into denial. Then he got mad. Then he went to work. He must do something to stop this. He must explore it with a vengeance for his sister's life was at stake. Somehow there must be another reality that would have effect on this one, a parallel reality. People had been looking at using virtual reality to let doctors zoom around inside virtual cadavers: the doctor-in-training guides a probe using real images of PET scans as though they were x-ray flashlights. The medical training community was big on using virtual realty and you could see why. Molecular biologists were starting to use the data glove to manipulate complex proteins, to reach out, touch and wrestle the molecular models into position for binding with other models. You could use the data glove to hone your surgical skills in a simulation, just like astronauts going through procedures in a training module for an extra-vehicular excursion on the moon. Maybe that would let him somehow reach out and grasp this evil tormenting his sister and stop it.

Jack knew that his project of building the natural healing system he wanted was way too big for one man. Yet he wanted to get started immediately. So he began looking to put a team together. Things really started to come together when, in the quest for the human software side of his experiment, he was fortunate to start at the source: studying visualization with Dr. Carl Simonton in Texas. Simonton, who was very well-known as the grand old man of using visualization to help with the natural healing ability of the body, was also a hard-science radiation oncologist and medical director of the Cancer Counseling and Research Center in Dallas. A seminar on visualization was given by Simonton and his wife, Stephanie. She was a psychotherapist and director of the Center's intensive psychotherapy program. Dr. Simonton impressed upon them a most important fact: "What goes on in a patient's mind is often the key to whether he will get well." Jack learned visualization is using your imagination to see yourself in a situation that hasn't yet happened, picturing yourself having or doing the things you want, and successfully achieving the results you desire. They used visualization to help patients invoke their own body's immune system to fight cancer. The Simonton's patients had a survival rate twice the national norm, and in many cases have experienced dramatic remissions or total cures.

While there in Dallas, Jack Corvic met Frank Drown. Frank was a student and collaborator of Simonton. Frank was a tall, heavy set, prematurely balding, darkly-bearded man. What hair he had was black and slicked-back. Though he wore a suit; his shirt was rumpled. Jack and Frank hit it off during a break from the seminars. The two men let their initial conversations go a little deeper than the talk of students. In that kind of way two proud fathers talk to each other about their kids, they became closer.

Jack said: "I got my kid a Gameboy a while back. All of the kids we know had one. Especially his closest friend."

"Yeah, I got mine one too. They all have to have them. It's part of the Pokemon phenomenon."

"Yep. My boy Dan is crazy about Pokemon. That's the killer app they have for these little handhelds. It is an amazing little program, with all kinds of attributes, like health and power associated with these cute little designer entities."

Frank said, "They hook it in, too. With watching the TV series." He sang: "Gotta catch em all."

Jack laughed. "Yes!" he said. "And now they've got the trading cards. Last week Dan blew fifteen hard-earned bucks buying game packs so he could find one with a Charizard! But I still like the Gameboy. It is an amazing little handheld, in spite of all the hype. I swear my 5-year-old learned how to read from it. He taught himself how to READ! Just so that he could read the dialogs in the Gameboy interface!

Frank said, "That is amazing, isn't it?"

Jack said, "Yes it is. Imagine if the school district had that kind of development money that Nintendo has to design learning programs like that."

"Wow, yeah. That would be incredible."

Jack said: "Yea it is amazing what their mind can absorb at that age. I'm studying Molecular Biology, and god, all these proteins and kinases. It would be so nice to have some kind of cool knowledge machine that made it super-interesting to understand and remember this stuff. Pokemon is a world teeming with hundreds of creatures. And the animals walk around and compete and they grow in their power and evolve; they metamorphosize into more advanced versions of themselves. Each with different powers. It is amazingly complex. The Pokemon creatures are a graphic designers tour-de-force. I wish I had some way of keep track of the world of Molbio the way they do in Pokemon. I must confess I like Bulbasaur. Usually the creatures represent an impossible cross sorting of phyla, like you have with a Bulbasaur. It is a cute little dinosaur with a large bulb on its back; this can open into a flower! It is an entity that is an amalgam of a dinosaur and an onion! And we are privy to the budding reproductive capabilities of these little creatures. I rather think its sets up burning questions and gets a child's mind to wrestling with some pretty big issues. For example the Bulbasaur can evolve into a something, what is it, something in its same genus anyway, that has more attribute points and greater powers. The game has a simulation of evolution.

"And the cuteness factor of Pickachu," said Frank.

"Oh I know, he has almost achieved the cuteness of Barney."

"Oh, god. Barney. We survived Barney. And Power Rangers. And now Pokemon."

"I like Hitmotchan myself."

"Yea, it has an aspect of Charley Chan and Jackie Chan. Jeez," Jack said. "I'm surprised I know that. I guess I am spending way too much time watching my kid's TV shows. You know I am always trying to come up with good bedtime stories to tell my kid. I found that he really likes stories based on TV shows. So I just try to follow what I see in the show."

The two men continued walking back to the lecture. Jack said: "Some of my kid's best cards—and I'm surprised I know this—well I guess I shouldn't be; he can't stop talking about them and I try to show interest—are: Kangaskhan, Beedrill, Mewtoo, and let me see, . . ." and here Jack wrinkled up his brow looking into his memory, "Oh yea, Snorlax, Poliwrath, Hitmonchan. I guess I must really be an OK dad."

Frank smiled in recognition and confirmation. "They are getting this whole idea about evolution."

Jack said, "It is kind of sad. The entertainment model of education."

Frank said, "I'd like to blow up the TV." He looked kind of cynical and said, "But I suppose it is necessary for the poor to learn how to watch the rich at play."

Jack was a little taken aback by this strong critique of the American way, but wrinkled his brow, changed the subject away from what looked like it might get political and continued. "You should see when two of these Pokemon addicted children get together and talk the talk with each other. And when they play. They lay out the cards in an elaborate game. I've seen Dan play it, he makes up these elaborate games and drags me into playing them with him. Poor kid, he's an only child. The other day, on a play date I overheard him say something like this—he was describing Venomoth's power: 'Once during your turn you may change the type of Venomoth to the type of any other Pokemon in play other than Colorless. This power can't be used if Venomoth is Asleep, Confused, or Paralyzed.'"

The men laughed. Frank made some comment about colorless quarks and quantum chromodynamics that

Jack was delighted to hear.

"I lived through the Power Rangers," Frank said. "And have seen this addictive behavior before."

"Me too! *That* was a craze. But this is something else again. It's an incredibly elaborate, detailed, information-rich environment, which is why it's so absorbing. Nine-year-olds are capable of sustaining a conversation of several hours on the subject. Every day!"

"These kids are intense. Dan had a card stolen at school. There have been conflicts about whose card is whose—fights! Because some kid made a trade, then took it back! St. Stephens, where he goes to school, sent home a notice the other day banning Pokemon cards. The note said: 'These cards are extremely disruptive.'"

Frank said: It is really insidious. The coolest and most valuable cards are extremely hard to find in store-bought packs."

"That is true."

"So kids buy pack after pack, trying to find the one or two cards they don't already have."

"I heard here was even some kind of a lawsuit! They claim that it is too difficult to get the really desirable cards and that you have to spend a fortune to get one."

Jack said, "He is always bugging me for cards, and I feel bad when I don't give in to him."

Frank said, "It's a craze. There was an article in the paper the other day about how some parents have blown thousands of dollars. Can you imagine having that kind of money?"

"Not for cards. Instead of "gotta catch 'em all" you just, "gotta say no."

Jack said: "But man, they become such avid collectors. It becomes a second-order obsession: just having all the cards in a book, and organized and thought about.

He has these big photography books filled with cards. They are amazing works of art, little paintings, bright and shining and full of energy and magic."

Frank said: "The sad fact is that children—like adults, by the way—are basically obsessive. The difference, if any, is that children have even less tolerance for delayed gratification: In fact under the right circumstances, a few minutes between now and my kid getting what he wants seems intolerable to everybody. So the pressure that a kid can bring on his parents makes one nervous: Is she / he gonna blow?"

Jack said: "Nevertheless, though it's a pain in the butt, you can just say No."

Frank said, "Well it is probably a good idea not to give in to their obsessions. This situation points out how children are really susceptible to being infected by memes."

"Memes?" Jack looked puzzled. "What are memes?"

"Well, maybe think about it as a craze. Or just a way of doing something. A meme spreads through a culture like a craze. Fire and the ability to make it and control it was the first meme. Or the wheel is a meme. Some guy attached a plank to a wheel and made the first wagon, and look at what all THAT has become. It is a way of doing something that everyone who sees it mimics it. It is the intentionally of culture. Or like an invention: the teller machine. Or, like the ritual of making sure there is coffee in the morning. Or how we have to have a cellular phone now. Or a tax loophole making businesses possible. A meme is a way of being and doing that is culturally transmitted. You can say a meme is a kind of Movement or Reformation, or just a Procedure or Method."

"Hmmmm."

"The word was invented by a guy, a biologist named Dawkins. In a book *The Selfish Gene*."

"Oh, yea, I read that. As part of the (and here Jack made air quotes) 'concept tenderizer' activity I need to undergo to get ready to study Molecular Biology."

They both laughed.

"I don't exactly remember it though."

"Well I think it kind of ties into what I am doing with Visualization," Frank said.

"Oh yeah? How's that.?"

"Well, what is the thrust of my practice? You may ask. What are memes and why should we care? Visualization is about the education of the imagination. It is also about finding, and uncovering the memes that have a hold on your life. My own area of interest has to do with the question about how do we constantly take ourselves out of our body through our self-talk. It seems to me that this kind of take-over possession has something to do with memes. That becomes so apparent when you meditate.

"Do you meditate?" Frank asked.

"No, I don't," Jack answered. "I have thought about it, but haven't gotten the time for it."

"Well if you meditate you begin to understand that the endless chatter of thought-forms that arise in meditation are the flowers of what they called seed-thoughts—these are memes. That's what I think. Well anyway, people have done a lot with the idea of memes since that book came out in the '70s."

As the two men were talking a young university student ambled slowly past them. Frank nodded to the young dude and continued: "Memes are everywhere, they are ubiquitous. Like take that guy walking by with his pants pulled so far down below his waist that they almost are around his ass, and his hat on sideways. You never saw that until a few years ago."

"Yeah that's true."

"Bill caps. You never saw them to the side until 10 years ago, and before that it was about 25 years when people started wearing their hats on backwards."

"It signifies youth," Jack said.

"Right. Then you hook it into genetics and procreation. Attraction. Appropriateness. Belonging to the right age group or social hierarchy. The genes are seeking outlet, and the memes facilitate that."

"Hmm, Well . . ."

Frank said, "The first hit I got on memes was in *The Origin of Consciousness in the Breakdown of the Bicameral Mind* by Julian Jaynes. He has the reader imagine an ancient hunter making arrowheads. This neolithic man," —the two men stopped and looked at each other. Jack had put on a bit of weight, and grown a beard since he was working in the lab. He looked a bit Neanderthal. Frank was more professional looking, tanned with bright teeth. Frank continued: "This neolithic man, who lived at a time when the Left and Right Brain were not so well sutured, heard his own thoughts as a voice outside of his head in a feedback loop with the audio cortex. He heard his own thoughts as a voice and thus was able to admonish himself, as he hit the flint rocks together: "Sharper. SHARPER! Make the blade sharper."

"Wow that *is* pretty basic isn't it."

Frank said: "Memes are the voices, or directions—the intentions we have that strive to accomplish actions. The discovery of fire would have been an early meme, and it would have spread through the population like a, well like a wildfire." He continued: "The word meme comes from mimetic, or mimeme. To copy, to do like. Dawkins wanted to get a system like genes, though being different from genes, that could explain genetic structures outside the body; like a termite's nest or a beehive or a beaver's dam.

"Oh yeah. I read that. Now I remember."

"He defined memes as the units of *cultural* inheritance and selection, rather than natural selection. The meme is the way that Darwinian evolution based upon random mutation of genes undergoing the selection by Nature, gets speeded up to Lamarckian evolution where things learned are passed on to succeeding generations. Memes are like genes: just as an animal is colonized by the genes, indeed is the way for genes to pass themselves through time, so a meme colonizes or dwells in human minds. Memes are patterns of information that can thrive only in brains, or the artificially manufactured products of brains—books, computers and so on. Media is their substrate. In a way the mouth in speech and the ears in hearing and the eyes in reading are the sexual organs of memes. A meme wants to propagate!"

They both laughed.

"But isn't that just an idea," Jack argued.

Have you ever had a song stuck in your head? One that you just can't get out. Like the other day I was playing that one of 'Your so vain. You probably think this song is about you' over and over. It was driving me nuts. A meme is a *contagious* information pattern. It has to leap from one human to another. If you are just thinking and examining your thoughts then those are *ideas*. The meme replicates by parasitically infecting human minds and altering their hosts' behavior, causing them to propagate the pattern through the patter of those who become its promoters; if it is not replicated, then the meme remains only an idea or a thought. Individual slogans, catch-phrases, melodies, icons, inventions, and fashions are typical memes.

Jack looked a little perplexed.

"It's true," Frank said. "It's true. A lot of philosophers and others have explored how memes replicate themselves, how they share certain fundamental characteristics with genes: longevity, fecundity and copy fidelity. Even talking about allomorphs and phenotypes as having analogies in the dialectic of how ideas form into memes, and large meme complexs. Like Marriage is a large meme complex whose main theme is "Thou shalt not commit adultery." Or the Boeing Aircraft company, or Visa are large meme complexes—so big that one person can not see the whole entity. A lot of college professors have mined the gold of analogies between genes and memes for cultural and psychological research. And semiotics too. We have the meme root in phoneme, the fundamental unit, the atom of speech sound; we have morpheme, the most minimal grammatical unit, like *the*; we have semanteme the fundamental unit of meaning in a sign, like the sign of the cross has to have the basic +." (And he made a cross in the air.) The meme and the seme.

"Like the other day. My wife took all the signage off the refrigerator to give it a cleaning, and it was a beautiful thing to see that massive white surface without all the documents stuck on it in layers: photos tugging at the heart, the little magnet thingies holding up notes and cards, the cork board with schedules and commitments. It was like a Zen experience. For a moment we got a little respite from the kitchen memes. I could really appreciate the connection between a clean Zen environment and a liberated mind."

The two men continued walking side by side, leaning in to talk to each other earnestly. They were in a quadrangle of the university hospital. Jack, with a nod of his head, motioned for Frank to notice a huge bird, a big black grackle crow. It was one of a whole gaggle; they kept leaping out of a big live-oak tree down to the ground below, then leaping back up into the tree again. "I wonder what it would be like to be a bird flying over a modern city. Imagine the sense of liberation from signage. The bird would be able to soar above the same world that I live in, the same panoply of buildings making statements, statues of heroes and politicians making statements, the same electric signs that I see, the same pictures, and words floating up into the air and other symbols that assault the human city dweller every waking moment. These are physical meme vehicles and they require representation in human intelligence—for the bird they would have no meaning other than being fortuitous poop targets."

The two men laughed.

Frank said, "Literacy is a meme complex based on the alphabet which is a meme. One meme complex that we really try to propagate very accurately is classical physics, with it's Newtonian dynamics which we try to propagate exactly from generation to generation. Inventions are a meme, as are tax loopholes. Just anything cultural passed on from person to person is a meme. Go to a baseball game, and there are people coming together to ratify and behave in the meme of TeamSpirit. Or like in the Israel and Palestinian confrontation, the primary meme that they live under and that generations of Palestinians transmit to their children is OpposeIsrael. There is a certain obsessive, or behavior-driving aspect associated with the meme. Look at the Fatwah. Now

THERE's an institution. Give me that old time religion. With a Fatwah, a cleric can unleash the sadism of a terrorist who, in the throws of divine conviction, can enact the death instinct beyond any moral bounds and feelings of guilt. It is the most exaggerated example of a religious meme complex. They get themselves all hopped up on Fatwah & Jihad incorporated. In fact, some would state it stronger and say a meme is a kind of Mind Parasite! That literacy itself is a mind parasite, a language parasite that has infected the left brain and taken up residence there. In fact there are some neuroanatomists and brain scan researchers looking for the cross cultural, cross-language characteristic shapes of brain activity and jaw micro-movement from internal speech to get a physical representation of memes. And there might be some truth to it. Poetry has always recognized the connection between sound energy and sense. That is where onomatopoeia comes from. The codification of energy in memes may be at the cross-cultural heart of music. I am so grateful for having studied poetry! Especially the representation of sound energy at its mimological heart. But we might be better off considering meme as metaphor or analogy. They try to talk about pre-literate hunting man as having more perception, living in a much more spiritual world, and that man has to give up more and more of that. I guess that is something we will never know.

"Memes are personality. They organize behavior and energy and interest."

"And if they are personality, they are . . . a child can't help but being infected by the personality of his parents. If we are to find liberation, we must liberate ourselves from our parents, though it is sad to see them go."

Frank was an open, ebullient and forthcoming sort. He told Jack that he was from Russia by way of England. It turned out Frank was the son of a famous parapsychologist, Judith Drown, who had emigrated from England to the Soviet Union to become a socialist. Now her son Frank was a Russian émigré who had fled Russia following harassment from the K.G.B, for his background in psychic phenomena studies. They had a huge program of PSI research in the 60s and 70s. Kirlean photography of the bio-energy auras around living things was one of their famous results.

While they were in Dallas, Jack learned that Frank Drown suffered from Multiple Sclerosis, an autoimmune disease of the central nervous system. As Frank explained: "In Multiple Sclerosis, inflammation of nervous tissue causes the loss of myelin, a sort of protective insulation for the nerve fibers in the brain and spinal cord. This de-myelination leaves multiple areas of scar tissue—that's what the word sclerosis means, scar tissue—along the covering of the nerve cells. This disrupts the ability of the nerves to conduct electrical impulses to and from the brain, producing the various symptoms of MS." Frank rattled off the litany of symptoms; he was used to explaining the disease. "Fatigue, problems with walking, bowel and/or bladder disturbances, visual problems, changes in cognitive function (including problems with memory, attention, and problem-solving), abnormal sensations such as numbness or 'pins and needles', changes in sexual function, pain, depression and/or mood swings."

The two men regarded each other in silent recognition of mortality.

Frank told Jack about how he used visualization to help him cope with the disease: " I use visualization to mitigate the disease. I've got a whole routine. I meditate twice a day. I use visualization to keep the MS symptoms at bay. Basically I picture the myelin around my nerves, regenerating. I work down my spinal cord, then around the brain visualizing all the scarred tissue disappearing. I go to my eyes and clear the blurred vision. Then finally I give myself the reward by imagining myself running down the beach to my waiting family and friends." Frank said that the visualization technique is simple and that the main condition of its effectiveness was that it taught one to be reliant on persistence. "You have to change your life-style. You have to be able to draw into yourself at least twice a day for 15 minutes. Religiously. No exceptions. The more vivid the picture in your mind the better. It does take time and commitment, but then what doesn't?"

Jack was very touched by this. He understood how Frank's routine, or practice, (or was it methodology?) was the product of fear and ingenuity. Frank had developed a practice in psychoneuroimmunology. He was living proof that you could turn back the inevitable degeneracy of the body with healing that began in the mind. Frank had learned and become an expert in what Jack was now just beginning to learn from studying with Simonton: how to apply the discoveries of biofeedback to visualization. Jack decided at this first meeting that Frank was the person to be point man for the Phaser project.

At the seminar, Jack learned about other similar relaxation techniques with cognitive enhancements. They all traced their roots to meditative practice of Eastern religions. And indeed for Frank it *was* like opening a third eye, the eye of the imagination, the eye that communicates with the psychic senses, a third eye to live in the present.

Frank wanted to help Jack with an induction. He said: "Well, first let me just say you have to get fully into the present. And I've found the key to being into the present!—the now moment of existence. And it is this, do it with me: 'Let time past and time future be exhaled with the "out" breath; and let time present be inspired on the "in" breath.' Do it with me."

Frank took a big inhale and moved his hands in a gathering motion, as though he were a container for all things around him present. Then he slowly exhaled while his hands made an ameliorating, spreading-out, pushing away motion as though something were flowing out on the out-breath and flattening out to make all things on an equal playing field; or maybe to be strewn and sewn as seeds for the next future. As he repeated the in and out breath, Frank invited and indicated to Jack with his eyes to do likewise. And they did. "Say it with me: Let time past and time future be exhaled with the out-breath; and let time present be inspired on the in-breath."

Frank summed up what Simonton had explained this way: "Through breathing you are meditating. After you become present through breathing, the meditation can go two ways. Contemporary meditation theory classifies the meditative experience into concentrative and receptive. Receptive refers to openness to all thoughts and sensations that occur. This is the Active Imagination of Jung. Concentrative involves directing and fixing attention on a stimulus—the mantra. Guided Imagery is Concentrative, while Visualization would be more receptive."

In the Center's extensive library, Frank and Jack delved into the extensive literature about how these techniques and psychological systems —autogenic training, progressive muscle relaxation etc, had been used in clinical applications to reverse many syndromes: anxiety, phobias, depression, phantom limb pain, hypertension, heart disease, Raynaud's disease, diabetes, hemophilia, headache, dysmenorrhea, childbirth preparation, cancer, drug abuse, athletic performance, seizures, sexual dysfunction, asthma. People from all walks of life used these techniques for general well-being.

Frank had a couple of CDs out. They were recordings of his voice, speaking various guided imagery visualizations and hypnosis inductions. The CDs, —one had the title *Waking from the Meme Dream*—had been well-received in the alternative health press. For Frank, the knowledge that he had been forced to develop about the relationship between reality and the imagination as divulged to him in the practice of meditation was worth the life-threatening attack of his disease.

Frank said: "Guided Imagery is really quite an art form. It comes from a lot of places, but the grand master was Milton Erikson." Frank shook his head in awe and feeling at the thought of the old, bald master. "Uncle Milty. Boy. That old guy was tough. You can tell it in his voice. He has this *ancient* voice going back to the patriarchs of the dawn of time. Slow and cracked and windblown. Mr. Erikson had to do about 6 HOURS of visualization work everyday! for pain, that was left over from polio.

"His poor wife. As she said, he wanted her to listen when he did his visualizations. It was something about the feedback. A kind of healing at a distance.

"The whole of NLP, Neuro Linguistic Programming, —do you remember that from the 70s? It was big in the 70s—grew out of people trying to understand the legacy of Milton Erikson.

"He had all these tricks and techniques. Like his guided imagery or hypnotic talk was always expansive. It was of the Receptive 'let it happen' type, rather than the Active "make it happen". He just presented the unconscious with alternatives and let IT choose. If you listen to his tapes you see how he was constantly reinforcing the patients' own ability to change, to feel, to heal. He actively played in the memory of his subjects, wove in compelling issues from their own lives for them. Like if they had children. And he was so very observant for signs of trance—fixed stare, eyelids fluttering in resistance and the more subtle body changes, blood pressure reducing—the Common Everyday Trance, he called it. He got the inductees in touch with their memory, with their feelings, their development patterns, evoking rather than programming."

"Like for example." Frank said, "there's one I do on the CD called just *Flight*. That one asks the listener to do a visualization of himself Flying. It uses Erikson's method of cleaving or separating the mind and the body. I start off with . . . '*I would like to remember what it felt like to be floating in water, maybe sitting on a floatation device, suspended, to be maybe straddling it so that you feel it in your center, actually like I was on a kind of recumbent bike, you know those kind with your feet out front of you, or some kind a thin saddle, and I could even lie back like I was the man in the moon, reclining with my feet up, just draped in the sickle arch of the cusp.*'"

"It goes back to a time when I was a kid. I remember as a young guy having dreams like that night after night for months. I couldn't wait to go to bed and dream. I would get a sense of being in a kind of motorcycle, but one that just floated, drifted, perhaps rose up and down on the waves, or that you could just straddle and float through the sky over things you wanted to see."

"One tries to adapt the visualization to your current position: '*standing in a crowded streetcar? Sitting? Lying down? It doesn't require that I get into any kind of position.*'"

"Anyhow do what you have to prepare to take flight. Get into the position. Most likely it has to do with an opening up of the support and an elongation. I get into this one, whenever I want to find my Fluid Body Self. We are something like 90% water. '*Could be just standing somewhere, I just need to move around a little in the waist and sink down a little to let my legs and gravity hold me up and just go into a kind of trust thing. Like I was some kind of being floating in gravity. I am.*'"

"Then after I have closed my eyes and imagined that I am flying, floating, hovering, over the world, I might try a test. It is a way to strengthen the experience. '*I find it helps to remind myself of the chains and anchors which are holding me back.*' That becomes a kind of tension test. And these tests don't have to be physical; *you can try to see, to notice all of the limiting beliefs and tired thoughts and old habits that you have woven together that you call yourself, that you think of as yourself. What is holding you back in life, or what do you think is holding you back. If you examine the metaphors and admonitions constantly running through our mind, and look at their textural and sensational meaning. Classify them. This is thinking mind. This is judging mind. Just follow. Fear for example. When we are afraid of something or always imagining it will happen we are linked to that fear, we are tied to that fear. For a moment try to really feel the weight of these attachment, these links which are preventing you from flying, from being free?'"*

"I take a moment and intellectually notice these impediments and try to give them both physical and mental texture. I try to see, are they Group Think, being so caught up in some group I identify with, I can't think outside of their reality. Are they Image Think (the image I hold up to myself of who I am or who I should be. The collection of behaviors and thoughts that grow out of these attachments, these intentions are the fruits, the allotypes of our memes. They are seed thoughts growing on the tree of our core belief system. They are the etiology of memes.

"And I wonder if these links holding you back could talk, what would they say? Perhaps they would say "you can't fly", and knowing that misery loves company, they might be saying "stay with us on the ground". But as you look closely at these binding links, you may be surprised to notice that however ferociously that these mental chains appear to be holding you down, you can know at least intellectually that these mental chains are memes. If you really look closely, you will notice that YOU are holding on to these interlocking links of the meme complex. Of course, here I give myself or the subject a chance to see, maybe just one of those memes. You are the one holding tightly onto these old habits, these disgusting limiting beliefs, you are holding yourself onto the ground. These chains, these interlocking concatenation of memes in a meme complex may be forged by the ideas and comments of others but you are the one holding onto them. And to whatever extent that you so strongly desire to live your life free and successful, you will let go of all chains and bad habits because you do owe it to yourself. You are your body's keeper, YOU are responsible for your own well being, your own happiness, your own success, your own freedom.

"There are some people who have actually done this. You can hear it in their writings. Often there is great simplicity. Some of the poets. Rumi. Neruda. They are flying up there in the sky. Winging their way to Parnassus. We can come into this world a crying child with nothing and go out a god. Hear it in their voices as they laugh way up in the sky, free from all chains. '*And to whatever extent that you so strongly desire to be free, you will begin to let go physically, let go of a chain. Simply make the commitment to let go of a limiting belief.*'"

Jack was kind of won over by this because he had read Rumi too. "*Yeah,*" he said with satisfaction.

Frank continued: "And you know, related to that, is—separating self—local self from higher self, which is non-local self. Erickson DID this cleaving, he had a whole bunch of techniques. He could really generate hope."

Frank looked around kind of furtive and wondered if Jack is the kind of guy who might be able to go into the more far out realms of the imagination. He said, "There are Hypnotic Realities, man. Everybody has the right to the Everyday Common Trance. It is perhaps related to concentration. Being absorbed by something. Some people think it is the action of the right brain. The intuition. The imagination. I think of it as entering the world of the imaginal.

Jack asked, "The Imaginal, what's that."

"I love that word the—imaginal—don't you? We slip in and out of these moments when we escape the conscious mind controlling us all the time and relax into the unconscious. These everyday common trances are like little mini-vacations to the imaginal, the place your mind goes when you send your thoughts on vacation.

"To me it is the WORLD of the," (and here Frank slipped into a reverent whisper) "*imaginal*, the place of possibilities, a superspace from which the imagined is a projection, a condensation. And reality is a further subspace, a further condensation of the imagined. I'm not saying it is some heavy duty thing, but we were raised on, we cut our teeth on, Carlos Casteneda. He talked about the Naugual and the Tonal. The task of the sorcerer is "seeing" into the Naugual. It is perhaps the perception of non-duality in Buddhism too.

"And Milton Erikson was the master of the Art of inducing hypnosis, and the indirect forms of hypnotic direction. He thought of therapeutic forms as extension of everyday processes of normal everyday living. He followed Jung's dictum: Seek to know the deity daily."

"You can go into the common everyday trance and come out of it with a fresh perspective. Solve problems. See the potential in an untoward situation. You should do this more often. Keep a diary."

Frank said: "This, combined with deep belly breathing . . . and relaxation are essential beginnings. It gets you into the imaginal, the multidimensional, the phenomenological."

Jack became a little peevish at this and said: "Yes. But is it the REAL."

Frank took this teasing in stride, he had heard this many times before. He said, "It is one of many *possible* realities. You've studied quantum mechanics. You know that the current moment of reality is a statistical average over a large ensemble of possible states."

Jack liked that. "Now you're talking my language. I get it. And one thing I have noticed in the little I have been able to see about visualization is that it is like a thing from engineering. Running the transducers backwards. Using what is normally something to sense signals, to actually generate them."

"Yeah!" Frank said. "Right! That's what I'm talking about! Reverse engineering! Metamemetics by guided imagery is reverse engineering!"

Jack said: "It's like turning a speaker into a microphone, funneling the sound down the cone to the vibrating membrane, and having that mechanical movement from the sound picked up through the transformer as electrical wave current. So instead of letting our senses drive the narration of our experience; we let the narration of experience drive our sensations."

"Right!" Frank's eyes got big, taking in the mutual sense of recognition and understanding. He smiled in agreement.

Jack said: "That's pretty cool stuff. Is it true?"

Frank answered: "Yes. I call it Being in the Flow of the Now. Being in the synchronicity. I'm just saying the world we live in is part of the universe and we are part of that universe and there is a lot more going on than just this little sample that our ego with its programmed senses lets us filter in. The ancient literature has names for the super-set of possible realities above those discernible by the senses and that is the space of the imaginal that we are trying to access. We in the west put it down by calling it psychic phenomena. But, FOR SURE, that points to what I'm talking about."

"What's that?"

"If we are unable to directly measure psychic phenomena with the normal set of senses it could only mean one thing."

"And what is that?"

"That psychic phenomena is *a priori* to the space of

phenomena. It is outside of the ordinary diachronic and synchronic of language-mediated reality."

Jack looked a little impatient. "What does THAT mean."

"It means you have nothing in the diachronic to hold on to. Look, we construct the world through language to be diachronic and synchronic. Diachronic—across time—is like the beginning, middle and end of things. The synchronic means with time, or outside of time. It is the data that can be put into the slots of the diachronic sentence. Subject / Verb / Object. Beginning, middle, end. But in meditation and trance, where you are constantly fending off the onslaught of chatter and received ideas, and trying to get back to a state before all the programming, you can slip out of time into the timeless. It is like that in a hypnosis. But the ego can be threatened. Listen and learn. After you have got yourself into the present, then you have got to get *induced*, introduced, to the juice of the imagination. Here let me take you under."

But Jack was too afraid to "go under". Yet still he could tell this was the path to the spontaneous self-healing he was on a quest for. This was further evidence that he needed Frank on his team.

Frank could see that Jack wasn't ready and he said, "Well . . .just listen and learn then. You'll catch on."

After that conversation, and feeling his own reticence to go into the psychic, Jack became certain he needed Frank on his team. Over the phone and by email, Jack started talking to Frank about him coming to San Francisco. Jack began telling Frank more about the opportunities at the UCSF Medical School. Jack could see that Frank wanted to access directly—through a higher language, the source of all healing from inside the individual, no matter what triggers it, and he put that out to Frank as a project they would work on together. Frank taught his subjects about what he called the Wonderful Modality; this included meditation, interactive guided imagery and visualization and internal prayer, even though he had a classical Russian science education which included lots of Math and Physics, lots of Quantum Mechanics. Frank had even spent a year exploring in the higher realms of analytical number theory—it was a course on the works of Riemann, especially the gamma function and his hypothesis about how prime numbers partition the energy of the physical world. This deeply penetrating understanding expressed by Riemann was for Frank a reflection of the Russian soul: that ability to stand in the light of an inexorable fate and be with that. Frank thought of his own practice as educating the Psychic Senses. For him it was clear that the unskilled imagination, manifesting as worry, had to have negative effects on your health by creating high levels of stress. He knew from his own experience that the key to *reversing this etiology* of stress, was to reclaim that pure innocent state of the child, whose imagination was unclouded by knowledge of how the world really worked.

In Frank Drown, Jack saw a prodigy who was exactly what he needed as his counterpart to bring about the PHASER. He could see that alternative healing was a matter of life and death for Frank. For Jack it was necessary to study these methods for the system he was trying to build to save his sister. Jack set about learning something of what Frank already knew very deeply. Basically it was to slip beneath the chatter of the thoughts, to be getting under verbal language consciousness to the world of imagery. This is listening to the wisdom of the body by speaking to it in its own language. Jack learned that though there were many styles and lengths for Guided Imagery, he could use a standard format. A guided imagery script had to have at least three main parts: the Induction or relaxation portion, the Imagery, and the Awakening (or, Return to Awareness). This way the imageries would be modular, or plug and play, increasing their versatility for different Reverse Etiology applications. That term Reverse Etiology was a term Frank had used to mean understanding the path down which a disease develops and takes hold in the body, as a sequence of steps, so you could make it—help it—go back UP that path to what it was before. Jack began to explore the reverse etiology as a kind of metamemetic programming. Neuro Linguistic Programming was a decent heuristic name for it. He thought of the structure of a guided imagery piece as a program. Set up the environment (environ-mental variables.) Making the statements (code) which had Function calls into the Unconscious.

The basic structure of the guided imagery had three parts: Induction, Imagery and Return. In the first part, the INDUCTION you get the subject to relax and close their eyes. This is in effect getting them to shut down some of their programming so you can run a reverse etiology program. It was necessary to ask the listeners to close their eyes. This is usually done with a big breath in and on the exhalation, the listeners should close their eyes and begin relaxation exercises. It was always a good idea to move the subject into abdominal breathing. Everyone required being reminded to breathe into a more expansive, relaxed state. He asked the listeners to give themselves the suggestion: "With each breath out you will become more and more relaxed."

Then came the IMAGERY. This is the main thrust of the piece, the actual image itself along with a period of silence so that the listeners can enjoy the experience and deepen it. The main image should guide the listeners into a beautiful, relaxing, playful, and positive scene. Your images should always be fun and positive. Don't forget to Pause for Silence. Always provide your listeners with a few minutes in which they can let their imaginations follow where you are leading them, or let them find their own source of imaginative wildness. This is often set up in an image with a statement along the lines of, "You will now have three minutes of clock time to explore, which is all the time you will need. You may begin now."

Then finally he brought them back with a RETURN or waking procedure This might be as simple as counting down from 5 to 1, telling the person "become fully alert, feeling totally refreshed."

With practice Jack got better at writing guided imagery scripts. The first one he did was for his sister. He read it into a tape and sent it to her. It was about trying to put her into that "I'm on vacation on a tropical isle" state of mind. It went like this with long pauses after each phrase: *Before imagining or listening to this scene, close your eyes and take three deep breaths. . . Breathe slowly and easily, in through your nose and out through your mouth....Now picture a happy, pleasant time, like those vacations you used to go on in Hawaii or the Caribbean . . . remember how you used to walk along the beach. . . and breath in the salt air . . . or maybe just sit in a chair on a verandah somewhere. . . or in a hammock even. . . this was a time when you have little or no problems or worries about your health. . .*

Fill in the details of that time. . . Look at the surroundings—is it indoors? . . . outdoors? . . . who is there? . . . what are you doing?. . . Listen to the noises. . . even those in the background. . . are there any pleasant smells?. . . feel the temperature. . . now, just enjoy your surroundings. . . you are happy. . . your body feels good. . . enjoy your surroundings. . . fix this feeling in your mind. . . you can return any time you wish by just picturing this happy time. . . .When you are ready, take three deep breaths. . . with each breath say the word "relax". . . imagine the word written in warm sand. . . now open your eyes—remain quiet for a few moments before slowly returning to your activities.

Of course Jack's analytical mind had to intercede and defend itself against what he saw as an onslaught of all this *imaginalia*. He found himself asking, Did these little guided visualizations, these hypnotic inductions follow the semiotics of a computer program?

He got more deeply into memes. Did Metamemetics deal with changing the percepts, concepts and the precepts. The three. Was this Peirce? The sign—induction, abduction, deduction. Except the meme is a lot more physical entrainment, has a programmatic action component whereas the sign is more mental. The seme and the meme. The seme was a higher level language, while the meme was a compiled language, driving the machine language of the body, whatever that was.

Frank and Jack started working together by email and plans were made for Jack to host a visit from Frank in San Francisco. Meanwhile, Jack continued his incremental development in both hardware and software. He created virtual spaces that you could walk around in. You could play in the spaces that others had created on the computer, like you might play a video. For example

Jack had always wanted to be able to go extra-vehicular from an airplane window and walk out onto the clouds. And VR he could sort of do that. Jack used 3D programs to create a beautiful space based on the paintings off David Hockney. It was a seamless suturing together of many of the artist's paintings in a virtual world. Using that style, expanding on that world. Hockneyspace, he called it. He could point the glove and fly away over a landscape of swimming pools through a beautiful space of the bright and diaphanous paintings of sunlight on swimming pool waters. Or you could just hover above it, floating high in the air, over eternal California summers. Or you could drop down and dip into the endless blue of cool aquamarine pools safely tucked away in everyone's private back yard. He made the figures too. He had gotten a lot better at creating beings.

He even started extending the experiments people were doing with using brain waves and eye movement to control interface interactions. Jack built a head-band and a skullcap of encephalopods. He called it his Thinking Cap. And working with some very creative people from the SRI, they got it to work together with his virtual reality data glove. He found himself feeling as giddy as Fred Astaire with the possibilities. He sang: "Yes, got my hat and my glove / I'll be as rich as Bill Gates / Just direct my love / through the virtual side of my fate." But really, Jack felt a kind of onerous sense of responsibility, too. First of all for his family. He had to somehow get this space he was creating over to the rich guys who could market it over to other people. The next step was an awesome responsibility.

Frank enjoyed the formalistic infusion of Jack's idea of writing visualization scripts as neuro-linguistic programming metamorphosized into metamemetic programming. Their activity of developing the guided imagery scripts took on a new rigor, for they were pleased to be working with imagery directly—because imagery is the major language of internal perception, memory, affect, and most importantly to their studies, physiologic response. The four functions of Jung. They were keen to explore how educating the patient to heal himself with meditation, visualization and interactive guided imagery allows the subject to use the powers of their own imagination to explore a particular area of concern, an illness, or just an area of interest. The process provides an opportunity for the subject to allow an image to form and to recognize some of these images are a direct communication from the unconscious, from the imaginal, from the superset of dimensions in which causality and experience were contained. Jung would say these communications were seen with experience to comprise the significance of one's life.

Frank called being able to vividly annex your imagination and have it effectively intercede with reality: Being in the Zone. He saw it as Jung's life-long Analytical Philosophy with its reward of being privy to and able to rely upon the processes of synchronicity. Frank developed this theory of how best to adapt the guided imagery to the learning style of the individual, based on Jung's Character Types, starting with how information gets into the being. He knew information gets into the being either from the outside as a sensory experience, or from the inside as a psychic experience. Sensory information derived from the recognized human senses of sight, smell, taste, touch and hearing as well as the secondary entangled perceptions such as temperature, pressure, balance, vibration, time, duration, body position muscle contraction and other known physiological responses. In meditation one could track these perceptions and think of them as communications from the beyond. Frank was a man of letters (he was aware that meant being possessed by one of the strongest memes which emerged with culture along with the alphabet). He was a man of words with metaphysical and mystical interests. He thought of the texts of visualization and guided imagery texts that they composed as prayers, incantations to bridge the gap between the local phenomena of the now across to the absolute, the agents of destiny, the non-local organizational principle.

They felt like they were developing a new mathematics, going back to the basic distinctions between what was sensible embedded in what was knowable. A sensory event is one that gives rise to the stimuli to which a known sense responds, and thus is measurable by instrumentation and the event's physical effects on the environment. Psychic information is data that does NOT derive from sensory experience. Psychic information derived from the recognized experience of intuition as well as the secondary perceptions such as clairvoyance, telepathy, synchronicities, ascension experiences. A *psychic event* gives rise to stimuli to which the psychic senses (intuition) respond. A psychic event is not a phenomenon measurable by today's equipment, though it can be experienced by *projection* on the senses. Psychic experience can involve a projection on the various sense mechanisms by running them backward. A hallucination for example. If several sense mechanisms are induced to be involved, the experience can be easily confused with the real. This involves "running the sense transducer backward". For example the same transducer, the eardrum that picks up sound waves in hearing can be vibrated from an internal projection and these vibrations are picked up as heard sound. Thus Jack and Frank were able to move from the engineering concept of reverse engineering a machine to the alternative healing concept of reversing the etiology of disease.

Jack continued with his VR studies. The design requirements and specifications for the project evolved. Frank began to take on the responsibility of developing the human software side, and Jack the machine side. One primary design requirement for the spec was that a patient would not only be able to truly interact with the game, but also able to write his or her own script, simply by making choices. Imagine playing an ultimate game in which *you* swing the sword and *you* made the decision about the scope and direction of the game. Left here or straight ahead? Fight or run away? VR would be the ultimate interactive roll-playing game.

Jack started getting more interested in playing with computer games because they were the most innovative interactive interface going. He got into the source code by using a decompiler and began modifying some of his favorite games, SimCity and Cyberpunk. He treated himself to the latest, screaming, state-of-the-art hardware; he purchased a ferocious rendering package called Vision, which puts users in the scene of the interactive 3-D modeling. It had 3D texture mapping which makes the objects photo-realistic. This was truly an advanced and literal interpretation of Object Oriented Knowledge Representation, a 3-D modeler that made it easy to create spaces and bring in characters to walk around in scenes. In addition to letting users create and render 3-D objects, Vision let you associate scripts with the objects, allowing them to function as front ends to background information. He used old school polygonal 3-D modeling and the new free-form NURBS and mesh subdivision techniques that had been rescued from academic mathematical oblivion. These algorithms made images look more realistic and render faster. You could create worlds that were totally photo-realistic or surrealistic, or any where on the spectrum between.

III

With his sister going in once again for a course of chemo therapy, Jack became very anxious to work towards the completion of Phaser. In their email correspondence, Frankand Jack began to lay out the plans for a company. They were surprised, shocked, but also inspired when they found that Siemans, one of the big players in MRI, had made good progress in the direction that they wanted to take their creative engineering. Frank and Jack got tickets and went to an exposition in Seattle hosted by the Certified Neurosurgeons' Society (CNS) in which they saw a presentation put on by Siemans of MR in the OR. Magnetic Resonance Imagining being used real-time in the Operating Room. It was a working presentation of what tomorrow's neurosurgical operating suite would look like. Siemens Medical Solutions, in collaboration with a company called BrainLAB, the leading innovator in the field of image-guided surgery, had built a model workflow-optimized neurosurgical OR. At the heart of this OR suite was a Siemens MAGNETOM, a 1.5 Tesla, high-field Magnetic Resonance (MR) scanner. The scanner would allow surgeons to verify whether a tumor has been completely removed while the patient is still on the operating table so that the patient doesn't have to undergo another follow-up surgery procedure. The imaging was done with powerful computer rendering of the MR data which was then moved over high-speed networking to get the pictures to the surgeon in real time. The Siemans marketing literature pointed out how MR in the OR meant surgeons can get instant feedback on taking the best possible path to a tumor, thus making operations safer and more precise. The suite was a state-of-the art integration of advanced technologies such as image-guided surgery, intra-operative MR, microscopy, visualization and data management. The workflow would be: Following an anesthetic induction and preparation, the patient is scanned in the MAGNETOM. The resulting images are transferred to a VectorVision, a ceiling-mounted image-guided surgery system where the MRI data is instantly downloaded and brought into registration with the patient's head position. Intra-operative navigation can be visualized on a VectorVision touch screen (image) connected to a network that accesses pre-designed exploratory and training visualizations to aid the surgeon in performing the operation.

Seeing this threw the partners into a panic that they would not be the first to market with their concept, and they moved into a frenzy of cooperation to best the competition. They realized their concept was the next step beyond what BrainSuite was working on with Siemans; they had MR in the OR, and it was for neurosurgeons. Jack and Frank wanted to take it to the next step: MR in the OR with VR. And to eliminate the surgeon, and have the MR images presented directly to the patient and have the patient do his *own* healing by using the real-time feedback of images of the area to be modified. What was intra-operative navigation visualized on a VectorVision touch screen image for the surgeon would be presented to the PATIENT as visualization overlays through head-mounted VR glasses connected to a network that accesses pre-designed exploratory and training visualizations to aid the patient in visualizations that make the changes in his own body.

Frank and Jack had realized this could be the basis of a feed back system that would invoke and enhance the body's own healing system. This would take place in an environment of visualization, guided imagery and meditation—what Frank called the general education of the imagination to develop the psychic senses. This environment required (in some cases severe) life style changes to include visualization meditation and dreams, art, movement, herbs, supplements, prayer, love—to stimulate one's own immune system. Frank and Jack realized what they had seen at the exposition was the basis for the technology they wanted to develop. So right away Jack called his broker and became an investor in the two companies, so that he could have access to their internal documents, and become a developer.

Frank began commuting to San Francisco, staying in a faculty housing sublease. Jack got him moved into a cubicle at the UCSF lab working with him and Paul. They hired a good grant writer and with the cachet of the medical school and a good sounding proposal, they got matching funds and ordered their own MRI system and BrainSuite. In their business plan, they said doing MRIs for hospitals and research institutes would become a source of making money for the school. They put in their order and waited. They got the University of California Medical School to give them more space in a basement of one of the buildings for the installation.

While they waited, Frank started what he called viral, self-organizing marketing by word of mouth. He got some cool, trustworthy friends at SRI (Stanford Research Institute), UC Berkeley, the Santa Fe Institute—Frank it turned out was an extrovert and very good at networking—who in turn fanned out and developed relationships with key individuals looking to do some supported research. Jack, at a distance over the internet, was able to speak to scientists in the language of science, talk molecular transport across cell membranes with biochemists, talk magnetics of encephalography with biomedical engineers. Frank and Jack put their money to work hiring the brightest and most capable minds they could find in the research hospitals, as components of their great plan. And this viral marketing spread. Soon they had a small team together: a molecular geneticist, a mechanical engineer (biomechanics), a computer programmer EE, and an MD. Also several capable graduate students. Being able to exchange science for science, or money for science or the opportunity to use equipment for grades, it wasn't long before they were able to start development on PHASER.

They took delivery of the giant 1.5 Tesla magnetom MR scanner and Brain Suite and began installation in the UCSF basement. Thus began on one of the greatest technical and philosophical hacks in modern times: PHASER Incorporated. That year one of the most creative collaborations in the history of technology took place, all instigated by Jack's money and Frank's connections. The mandate they gave themselves was to create a system powerful enough to enable a subject to examine the MRI images of his own internal structure through 3D glasses during a session. And to effect change in that structure, through a combined method of mental imagery overlaid and used in feedback with the real time imagery. To the user wearing the 3D glasses, the MRI images appear to be floating in the air in front of the subject. By reaching in and manipulating the image with the VR Data glove, the user would be able to rotate the image in space and look at it from any angle. What he sees can be augmented with "overlays" of computer-constructed images created either by CAD rendering of mesh, or by computational simulation methods. The user can also zoom down into domains: whole object- -> surface tissue- -> substructure underneath the surface- -> magnify individual cells- -> penetrate the surface membrane of cell to intracellular organizations- ->penetrate cellular entities to molecular models of cellular behaviors.

These real time data images are augmented by simulations. This simultaneous availability of richly detailed, high-resolution simulation, laid over the real-time MRI imagery with dynamic registration, required enormous computing power. To accomplish this, Frank Drown inspired his friends in New York, David and Gregory Chudnovsky, who were also Russian émigrés, to join the effort. The brothers were famous for building a parallel-processing supercomputer in their Manhattan apartment and programming the multiprocessing architecture to do numerical analysis—in particular, calculating π (pi) out to a couple billion decimal places. But it was because the MRI feedback healing project held out hope to Gregory, who suffered from debilitating myasthenia gravis, a muscular disorder that confines him to a wheelchair, that they came out to San Francisco, got into the program and put their shoulder to the wheel for the PHASER effort. Essentially, they built a supercomputer in the basement of a building at UCSF Med Center. They built it entirely out of off-the-shelf parts delivered by the big brown UPS vans, and the Airborne and Fed-Ex trucks constantly pulling up onto the curb at the medical school, their drivers pressing the intercom buzzer, being admitted for delivering new and picking up substandard parts. It was a parallel processing computer, with a back plane that ran for twenty feet down the middle of the room, and blades or cards stuck in the back plane bus. These cards were the fastest processors available being used for the real-time data processing and moving all the imaging work to and from the IO. The computer generated a lot of heat which rose up and was sucked out with fans. The computer was separated from the large magnet of the MRI installation—by a Faraday cage—to isolate it from the interference of RF and magnetic field noise.

The installation took up three rooms. The main room was the MRI installation. Before entering that you passed through a little anteroom where you could remove unnecessary ferromagnetic materials. There was a big sign that read: "Leave Your Credit Cards in Your Locker."

Adjacent to the main room, was the control room where the experimenters sat if they could not be in the main MRI room. Another adjacent room held the parallel computer which was running all the software and storage, and controlling the MRI apparatus. Here lots of custom software as well as terabytes of imported art, illustrations and animations and training digital video were instantly accessible in the way only truly parallel architecture can provide.

In the main room was the business end of the PHASER system: a Stand-up MRI. It was surrounded by its interface—a Brain Suite of sensors, data flow control routers, and monitors. These were networked through the heavy, under-floor cabling to the computer.

Several scientists from Stanford had been brought on board and one mathematician from the Santa Fe Institute. Among them they had cobbled together enough chutzpa to get a National Science Fund grant of 3 million dollars, which allowed them to afford all this high tech equipment. Soon they were logging time on the MRI system which they had affectionately begun to call, "Mr. I".

Mr. I. was a standard MRI system with serious modifications. The modifications included hardware to pipe the real time images to the user creating a feedback loop. Software algorithms used that feedback to control the magnetic and radio field strength at the point of interest. Other software presented an overlay of visualization and simulation imagery to the user, to enhance and enable his control.

They were embarked on a wonderfully heady time of engineering creativity and healing. And when they got their own MRI, people began lining up to do experiments and write papers. Fortunately, they brought grants with them, and they got their friends on board. This was the kind of viral marketing that Frank loved. They hired consultants and pressed graduate students (the second oldest profession) to instruct them in Cross Sectional Anatomy using their Magnetic Resonance Imaging device. Soon so many scientists and doctors were logging time on Mr. I, doing experiments and writing papers that they had to hire a full-time radiological technologist to insure that the facility was run smoothly and the many scientists coming through were not hampering each other's experiments—and were all up to speed on safety. Standard precautions of leaving magnetic strip cards (credit cards, bank cards, etc.) and watches in the console room were followed because the scanner wiped them clear. Rules were not as stringent as in other MRI installation however, because of the extreme fine-tuning and focused apertures of the Phaser magnetic field, and the radio beams of the Stand-up MRI.

Things really began coming together when they got some dons from Berkeley and Stanford interested and were paying them as part of the team. They began to have an illustrious crew of key scientists. One of them was Roddie MacDougall, an Associate Professor of Mechanical Engineering. He was Chair of the Biomechanical Engineering Division in the Mechanical Engineering Department and Co-director of the newly created Center for Biomedical Computation at Berkeley. Professor MacDougall's work draws on computational mechanics, medical imaging, and neuromuscular biology to improve treatments for neurologic and musculoskeletal diseases. He is best known for the development of highly realistic simulations of the musculoskeletal system. These simulations have been used to study neural control of movement, mechanisms of musculoskeletal diseases, and to design surgeries and medical devices. Another key scientist was Ahmed Korchemsky, a Professor of Computer Science at Cal Tech. Professor Korchemsky's research is in autonomous robots, human-centered robotics, human-friendly robot design, dynamic simulations, and haptic interactions. His exploration in this research ranges from the autonomous ability of a robot to cooperate with a human, to the haptic interaction of a user with an animated character, virtual prototype, or surgical instrument. There was Professor Omar Hourian who heads the Geometric Computation group in the Computer Science Department of Stanford University. He is a member of the Computer Graphics and Robotics Laboratories. Professor Hourian works on algorithms for sensing, modeling, reasoning, rendering, and acting on the physical world. His interests span computational geometry, geometric modeling, computer graphics, computer vision, robotics, and discrete algorithms. There was Dr. Wiley Lum-Wong, an Assistant Professor of Computer Science. Lum-Wong is interested in the applications of mathematics and computer science to genomic research. His current research focuses on alignment algorithms, comparative genomics, gene regulation, regulatory motif finding, and microarray analysis.

With all this talent and money starting to accrue, The Phaser Group opened their own clinic, and started small with a few clients—mainly as a research institute. They applied for grant money from the government. No one knew or needed to know about Jack's former life in crime. He revealed only parts of his plan to the others, for he felt that they would be overwhelmed and critical if they new the extent of his ambition. And he himself wasn't sure, that it might have a touch of hubris. The idea is to give the *patient* the power to see what the radiologist sees. Eventually to give the patient the power to control the fields of the MRI. And to present all this in an intuitive, easy-to-use interface. An interface that could be used in a very relaxed state of alpha waves that did not require a lot of cognitive work to accomplish, moreover one that helped precipitate and facilitate an altered state conducive to healing.

Thus what Frank and Jack started as a kind of hobby and experimental lab with some friends and associates from Stanford in a basement of the UC Med Center, eventually grew into a company which they called "Mind>Resource>Intervention." Jack and Frank became pretty good friends. They each benefited from what the other brought to further the effort. Frank brought great people skills for networking. And credentials. Jack brought can-do and longing. Jack appreciated being able to plug into this network that Frank created. Jack worked as interface designer, hardware engineer, simulations integrator, and trainer among many other titles on their PHASER system. Frank's input on guided imagery was very helpful, inspiring the user interface design. The method of healing: the reverse etiology, grew out of Frank's own routine for MS as a paradigm for the others.

Frank's self-healing paradigm involved creating tissue growth upon a scaffolding of hope. He was excited to take that paradigm and put it on firmer ground: hardware. First they collected a lot of good pictures and etiologies of the disease development. They got before and after pictures of the tissues of people who had reversed the process. They acquired microscopic and other imagery down to the cellular and even molecular level. They looked at tissue growth, in various substrates across a scaffold. He needed to create a mental scaffold in his mind but especially in the mind of the self-healer.

To stimulate development of the interface and the reverse etiology procedures, Frank began teaching a class in meditation and visualization across the street at UCSF Hospital. The participants were cancer patients and others who had been given a difficult diagnosis and were preparing to undergo surgery. Frank started them keeping dream diaries. His daily class became very popular. As he said, "For a developer of guided visualizations, he was in hypnagogic heaven." He taught the patients how to meditate, how to become sensitive to their own internal imagery and to develop their own visualization scripts. In the Dream / Imagery Group, Frank gave surveys and collected the imagery that people used to help them with their struggle recuperating from surgery or in their fight against cancer. He looked for correlation between spontaneously emerging dream imagery and guided imagery. He sought to have a cross fertilization from one domain to the other. This was crossing the conscious / unconscious / autonomic barrier.

Frank used a communications model to relate spontaneously generated imagery and visualization. For him imagery was an acknowledgment of a visualization signal. He explained the difference between visualization and imagery to the participants in his class this way: "Visualization is the consciously chosen, intentional instruction to the body. The relationship between visualization and imagery is like telemetry, the way a transmitter sends messages to a receiver, say an earth-base to a satellite. In telemetry an antenna is used both for broadcasting and receiving. The visualization acts as a message to the unconscious which is the receiver. This receiver includes the subcortical parts of the brain. The visualizations get translated into the body's own machine language, particularly the language of the limbic system, the hypothalamus, and the pituitary. These unconscious processes send images back to the consciousness, as acknowledgment in the communication loop. Imagery is the spontaneously occurring "answer," qualifier and modifier from the unconscious. Thus, a two-way communication is set up by the interplay of visualization and imagery."

"I usually give them some ideas for images. But first I try to help them find their own. I might say something like, "The idea for your image might come from almost anywhere. You might be inspired by one of the examples we do in the exercises, or by what we do in preparation for the treatment. Or you might just come in with some other image, something from art or TV."

Frank collected successful imagery visualization correlations and strategies and tried to put them in categories. He said: "Generally people regard their internal processes in one of five different types of imagery: (1) mechanical like a pulley; (2) religious like lights and haloes; (3) a feeling state, like white with fear or anger, or warm with love; (4) cellular or physiological, (I think you need to have been exposed to some biology for this); (5) psychological, these are the figures, or mental objects, or archetypes, where you might hold yourself like a soldier or a housewife, and maybe even shift among these organizations like in projections where, say you might relate to your boss at work like a father figure."

For particularly successful images, Frank sought to build a guided visualization around them. These he hoped to use later when he understood the personality of a user or subject and he could get the right match going. He surveyed the people in the Dream / Imagery Group about their dreams before, during, and after the diagnosis. And about the imagery they used to help them through chemo. Here are a few of the Dreams / Images that proved to be successful.

Dream: *I dreamed a crowd of people were trying to fix an old, railroad switch that was jammed into buried pipes. Sand and dust had gotten into these pipes and they was all rusty. I dreamed surgical images, such as cutting up a large piece of meat; repair of other broken objects, such as a stove and a car; and problems with the transport of fluids, such as a half-dried riverbed and a stopped-up septic tank.*

Imagery: *I imagined cleaning out lines, by sending pulses of air down them. Sometimes I actually used my breathing as the pulses of air.* *Allen S.*

Dreams: *I dreamed I was half way across a bridge when I turned and looked back and saw my family standing on the shore that I had left. I felt that they loved me, and I turned around to go back to them. As I approached my family I felt my heart filled with love and I realized how deeply I cared for them, and they cared for me. I realized that cultivating relationships with loved ones would facilitate my recovery and make "not crossing over to the other side" worthwhile.*

Images: *In my meditation and visualizations, I started building a bridge plank by plank. The planks were like affirmations, or like the "planks" in a politician's position. I realized I was bargaining with someone. So I would have to say the imagery I used was political. I visualize myself as queen and leader of my body, in charge and responsible for it, having to strategize, consider risks, take risks, and have some faith that in spite of unavoidable errors and weaknesses, I could lead my body through this crisis. I see myself healthy running in slow motion, muscular, strong.* *Maria R.*

Dream: *I am at the cooling pond in the plant where I work. I was watching someone in a lab coat on a ladder doing something with a queen bee. The bee flew over and landed on me, and then an entire swarm came and landed all over my body! I closed my eyes, tried to relax and breathe calmly, afraid of them going into my nose or mouth. I tried to walk to where my mother was, she was at the plant though she had never been there. But because my eyes were closed, I veered off course. And I ended up falling off the pump house into the lake. The lake was very dirty, but it kept the bees away.*

Imagery: *Though strikingly horrible, I used the bees. I let them come in through mouth and nose with breath; let them represent worry and annoyance; their urgent buzzing was like little electrical buzz saws stinging the cancer, and making it shrivel up.* *Robert W.*

Dream: *I am at the beach. There, oversized, shiny, bright orange, Alaska king crabs were ready to attack. They were as big as fork lifts, and had sharp steel blades sticking out of them. They chased me. They wanted to chop me with their scissors claws.*

Images: *When I breathed in very deeply I visualized breathing in healing colors of fuscia, teal and mauve; then exhaled orange. Watching this orange energy fight and devour the cancer cells* *Anne B.*

Dreams: *Dark figures/ shadow figures—representing my fear. Beautiful twins—representing my breasts (my beauties). Animals, especially cats—representing my instincts. I dreamed that my sister who died of breast cancer was with me and we were trying to stop a big tractor trailer truck from sliding down a grassy hill in the mud and the rain, and she was running around putting blocks under the wheels. She was going to get into it and drive.*

Images: *Salt water. Placing the breast lump and one affected node into the salt water and letting it be recycled. Army of immune soldiers protecting their Queen (me)—removing any troublemakers in the kingdom. Stream of gold moving through me, healing me (chemo drugs). Lisa P.*

Dreams: *The new house dream—used to make me feel grieving and lost for the old house. Now I like the new house and am glad to be there, looking around and seeing what is there that is interesting.*

Images: *I started to visualize myself exploring a beautiful new house, it was like something out of a Kincaid painting, with lots of lovely light and tapestry, and filled with lovely jewels and joyous objects. Jane L.*

Dreams: *When I was diagnosed with cancer my dreams turned dark as my thoughts. In them I was pursued by some psycho-killers. I dreamed I was being chased by scary violent animals. I had been given a death sentence. Then I dreamed of a pregnant woman. This was an image of potential new life. I began to see how precious life was, and that I had not time to waste on what little I had left. I began to see the existential challenge of taking responsibility for my life and I started doing more of the creative things I had always wanted to do, even in the face of death. Martin G.*

Frank taught the people in the Dream Imagery Group about the personae in dreams, "You might start to think of the personae in your dreams as Jungian entities. Anima, Animus, Shadow, Mythological symbols. Make friends with the Jungian entities in your dreams. Become a real oneironaut, a critical and intrepid dream voyager. Look for say the Animus. He appears when you are in touch with your male qualities and he lends strength, self-love and sometimes puts you in touch with your sexual creativity. He also might show up as angry with you when you ignore you gifts. It is very liberating to look at the dreams as a reflection of your life that way. Make friends with these powerful figures. They are representation of your instincts, and they will help you take care of yourself."

Frank taught the attendees of the Dream Imagery Group that it was very important to pay attention to the imagery of their dreams, because it would help them find a personal cancer fighting image that would really work for them. "It would come as a gift from the beyond," he said. "They are gifts that really enhance the meaning of your life. Perhaps the most useful place to look for imagery is the everyday commonplace tools and things that you are very familiar with in your lives. There is the Mechanical or Energetical image, where you might think of a body function in terms of anatomy. Or you might think of a stuck muscle in terms of a knot or pulley system that needs to be raised or lowered. I think that is a natural. People all through history have been drawn to the image of energy in the body. We just can't have too much energy. For some, the gift of energy is religious. Like the Chakras, a series of organizational centers that you can travel to and explore. There is a great deal of literature on the Chakras. This literature models the internal workings of the body as clusters or centers, each represented as a circular mandala. This subtle anatomy is related to the various glands of the body and is carried forward to give an understand of the insights and perceptions and organizations of reality that these glandular organizations give the body access to. Thus art becomes associated with an anatomical and physiological image. Also on the system of Acupuncture Channels. Also on Reflexology where every body part is mapped onto the foot. Or the Homunculus of the nervous system, where the body parts are arranged around the brain with the parts' size governed by the density of nerves running to it. It turns out the lips and the thumbs are big in that one. Or Iridology, where internal states of the body are mapped onto the eye.

"Most westerners who have not been brought up in a spiritual tradition find this very foreign. These 5 types of imagery are not the only kinds, nor are they clearly distinct types of imagery. In many systems of the world the spiritual imagery can be energetic. But usually the spiritual image is a great inspirational Person. Which can be both good and bad: we might be into hero worship here—the way control is maintained in a formal religion.

"Another important type of imagery is feeling state imagery, where you go to some relaxed warm beach or beautiful forest and have a pleasant fantasy or a day dream that you associate with how you are feeling and change how you are feeling.

"Another type of imagery is physiological or cellular imagery. This is where you get accurate, or it can by symbolic, physiological (or cellular) imagery: You might picture some part of the body that is troubled, uterus, ovaries, prostate, joint, lungs or the hormones functioning in an optimal, balanced fashion so you'll feel well. Imagine each cell in your body doing its task perfectly. People have had a lot of success imaging their T-cells as sharks devouring the cancer. We will be doing a lot of this kind of imaging around here at M>R>I.

"Another type of imagery is psychological. This is where you want to break the association between attitude and stimulus. Say if you have trouble with authority and bosses at work, you might think that goes back to your relationship with your father. Psychologists would say you are in this relating to the boss at work the way you relate to all authoritative objects, like the way you related to you father. Instead of associating your job with the pain of being subjugated by authority, concentrate on the job as an opportunity to study yourself in groups. Rehearse your response to authority or whatever the source of the pain is: Instead of becoming frustrated, allow yourself to relax."

To prepare the patients for sessions with Mr. I, Frank taught them meditation. He used his own practice of guided visualization for health, and an amalgam of many different kinds of meditation. He told his students: "There are many different kinds of meditation. In one sitting session a meditator might go through several inner landscapes to reach the desired destination. There may not even be a destination.

He would tell them, "In hypnosis we are trying to speak directly through indirect methods to the unconscious. In meditation we are trying to transcend thought and come to know Mind, the container of thought. The inner landscape. What is it like? What can you expect? Well, what have other travelers seen? Some see it as something going on in a space or a room, like in a dream. Others described it like a storm approaching. Others have even given a more scientific description, accessing various parts of the Brain." Frank liked the scientific approach to meditation.

His introduction started off with the traditional.

"Probably the simplest direction for meditation is 'Open your mind and relax.' Then we might get a little more detailed with 'Try to bring the mind back from its thoughts on the out breath. That is the place to look, for your relaxation.' You want to remain about 25% in this world. The idea is to appreciate the world around you in the moment and to be a part of that truth.

"Well this is good, but us westerners, we have got to have an itinerary, a roadmap, a guide book. We hate to just wander around. So you might ask, How do you KNOW you are present in the moment? How do you sense your own presence? Well you might look into the somatosensory cortex. This is a band of brain across the left and right hemispheres behind the frontal lobes. This is the proprioceptive band—that is, where the whole body can be thought of as represented by its sensations, spread across in a swath of left and right hemispheres. It is called the sensory/motor cortex, and it is just behind the frontal lobes where thinking occurs. It is the place in the brain where all the nerve endings from body parts come together. This is where the amazing 'homunculus' is—that is a map of the human body where the body part size is presented as proportional to the density of nerves running to that body part. Thus the size of the body part is seen as relatively large if it has more of nerve endings. The lips are large, as are the thumbs and the hands. Who knew how many nerves went to the hands? And of course they must, because the hands are capable of such fine motor activity, playing music, doing brain surgery, sewing, tying eyelashes into knots. The feeling and loving hands. You probably have seen drawings of this homunculus, or even a model. It has big fat rindy lips and a large face on a scrawny body with big feet. It is a striking image of an aspect of self. So to get under thinking, move your intention to feeling yourself present in the moment in your body by accessing the somatosensory cortex.

"But before we get there we might start by asking what is the object of meditation? When you meditate, there are Internal Lights. There is a huge amount of literature on this. But for now let us say you want to get in touch with this source of internal light, whatever it is. Say it is the light of dreams. Because it shines inside the dark. It is an ancient light, a mysterious light, that connects us to the universe, possibly a light of the future—an as yet unidentified light, one that may be a channel of communication in the future. One that psy-ops is already studying, one that telepathic tribesmen of the Amazon have known about for millennia, which may be the one that Tibetan Bardo travelers have explored for ages. Astrologers and astral travelers have tried to explain it as coming from the sun or the moon or the stars but their explanations, though they say a lot and it is an interesting essay on projecting the human personality onto the ecliptic, it is not a helpful content for our quest. We see dreams but not with our eyes. Our eyes are shut. What is going on here? Are we running the visual transducer system backwards, projecting the contents of the brain onto the visual perceptual system? Yes. How is this done? Well we might go back to our old physics book, inquire about the nature of the light. See mirrors bouncing laser beams around or waves coming through slits say in a sea wall or a particle beam being broken up into waves, coherent or going into a place of quiescence. What is the light itself? An ether? A wave? A particle? Or is it the internal light activity of the realm of being? I think it is the electrical activity in the human body of which there is so much, that sometimes there are coherences, when the waves just get together. The idea in meditation is to let the thoughts have the coherency of clouds, let the thoughts, going into complexes, behave the way clouds do. Why? Because these complexes are the structure of mind. Because we are pursuing the analogy: story is to image as thought is to mind. This we get from Rumi; he used metaphor and story and image as devices to help the meditator, the seeker, know the workings of the caring love-energy source in the world. Take his example—the story of the bath being heated up on the fire. He points out that the water is the fire's way of touching us. In meditation we will be using imagery and words to counteract the strong story you tell yourself about who you are, the story with the images that you have filed in memory, so that you can be touched by the fire, so that you can let it in, so that you may know the source that contains and cares for you.

"But our story is getting ahead of itself. Before we pursue the subtle anatomy of clouds of coherences, let us ask what distinguishes the mental occupation of meditation from ordinary thoughts as we are walking down the street. It is the difference between enveloping and being enveloped. Say the mind is like an intelligent entity, one of many in the body, and it works by a kind of enveloping, it envelops light waves, it envelopes sounds, and it uses these to construct a model of the world so that this embodied mind can push the body (that it develops by enveloping particles of matter) out into new territory. It is like a tree growing, pushing from the earth into the sky, the branching feelers of inference pushing from what is known to what is unknown, and as it absorbs more evidence it gets hotter and hotter on the trail of something; sometimes whole areas open up and we can get a ride on analogy. Logical deductions snap into place as we follow physical evidence, abductions, inductions, inferences. But these circulate around in a much bigger ocean—the ocean of being, the ocean of Mind. These are like clouds in an atmosphere of ocean. What would it be like to slip through the cracks and feel *that* ocean, that skin, that space working all around you like a kind of surface of a pond.

"The body drives the mind by creating anxiety scenarios, (pimples, burps, farts, poop, gas, dandruff, sweat, zits, ear wax, tumors, digestion, circulation and other yucky stuff) but also lures the mind by creating opportunities of pleasure. Imagine yourself drifting somewhere below and just looking at the thoughts going by like they were clouds. It might even be the case that if you have your eyes closed and you are looking up into the brain you see into the frontal lobes where the ideas occur, at least the planning and calculating. We want to put these thoughts at a distance from you, put them in containers and send them on their way. Give the thoughts names: That's worrying; that's planning; that's fantasizing—planning, worrying, fantasizing, being completely in another world, a world made of thoughts. You can take this further; might even have some fun with it. Personalize them. Like this. Treat them as aliens that have invaded the psyche There's Ambition shifting from one foot to another, impatient with you. Or the Stupid, a daring, rowdy young fellow with red cheeks who never thinks before he acts the—the class clown, he is sitting on a stool with a conical hat, the dunce. Or the Judge who watches us from afar in a mournful vigil, a little like your Mom. Who do they hang out with? Stupid hangs out with his old chum Denial, who covers for him. They are trying to avoid Regret, who is a sour young woman pretending to be a muse. Or there's Innocence. She's in a courtroom, on the stand; she is looking with her big brown eyes, like a puppy at the Judge and Prosecutor. The prosecutor Guilt is interrogating her. Oooohhhh, and there's Hate. It gets harder and harder to avoid him. He has spiky hair and always wears black, even in the heat of summer. He has forgotten what it was like to be happy. Many are attracted to Hate's dark spiteful eyes glowing with anger, but they soon tire at his loathing and complaints. He has a few friends. They are Pity, Anger and Depression. And there's Longing. She's got long dark hair and spends all her time in a dark room. She yearns for so much more than what she has but has no idea how to get anywhere else. She envies Contentment the way she walks so loose and free in the sun outside her window. There's Prudence and Gluttony eyeing a box of Valentine truffles. The old time Catholics were really big on personifying sins and virtues. So were the ancient Greeks, some way their gods were projections of a working psyche. Even Psyche herself, was a beautiful girl loved by Eros was a personification of the soul. Anyway this is a bit of a ridiculous exercise, but you get the idea. We are tracing thoughts back to their emotional clusters and putting them in a container created by this personification; once isolated and contained we can put them, like boxcars onto a train and move them out. Meditation is a mind storm we are calling down to derail the train of thought.

"How do you recognize and take part in a mind storm? You use the experience of putting the thoughts into containers and sending them on their way, to realized that the mind itself is in a container. One is asked to realize he is "thinking" when one finds himself in the world of thoughts. Mediation is like a quiet intentional mind storm to stir up movement of the thoughts by creating a vacuum into which the thoughts will rush to fill, like a tornado. Those thoughts are Reactors; they are around all the time. They are the story relating to the image the thinker has of himself, they are the content of sociology. If meditation is like a mind storm, the big thunder clouds that seem to suck up all the other clouds around them, that is the World View. The Reactors are swirled up into the World View. So to make a distinction between meditation and everyday walking around in the world consciousness: if you are walking down the street and observing the everyday contents of consciousness, most of that seems to be phatic, related to the pleasantries of social conversation, as stale as last nights TV. The phatic thoughts do not carry much of a charge, they are just what keeps the status quo. You've got cumulo status, alto status, these are the various kinds of inflated self-image you carry. The meditation storm is going, for a moment, to blow those out of the mental landscape, and you can just watch them coming through, maybe being swirled up into the World View with its rules of subjugation (are they the Memes?) The World View, where they just float away out of the top and then you are left with yourself, with the container of thoughts, the mind, and when the Mind comes through it sweeps down and settles for a moment, and the old timers feel this as a kind of hard, dull, shiver as the tyranny of how you are socially organized and held in your place is thrown off. I have noticed a couple of kinds of coherences going through: one sharp and almost hard. I often straighten my spine when it slices into me, like coming to attention. It's called the Shiver; some call it Kundalini. And then you might sigh right after that, and have a good relaxing Out-breath.

"The other kind of coherence is more of a warm flushing, a fluorescing in which you want to melt. You want to have it keep on coming—through you. The old yogis had names for these currents. They knew all kinds of subtle anatomy. We don't study that any more. The Shiver goes through you like an animal trying to shake off being held by its owner, as a pet. He is always in rebellion, this sub-personality. You get this sense of aloneness, like you are the only one here. Then there's the Fluorescence, she is what you are looking for, the warm, caring, sexy, intelligent one. This is the sub-personality you want to be with. And after you've been with her for a while, and it starts to feel so good, and you want to stay with her forever, there He is again, calling you back, as you must go back because it is necessary for the mind to create scenarios of anxiety to drive the body to support itself. You come back from having been with both these extremes and the world seems more and more permeable now, there is hope, for this is the Now, through which existence is strained and comes into your world and you can let more of it in.

"What if we did a sequence of meditation in which we visited the homunculus, because this is how we sense ourselves as present. This is a proprioceptive meditation; you are moving intention around through the homunculus, in which the meditator goes first to the part of the body with the highest density of nerves. We have spoken of the room, and the light that comes in the room, now we are talking about using the hand, going to the hand because the hand has the highest density of nerve endings, the biggest representation in the proprioceptive cortex and it is the first place to feel the intention moving—to feel chi, to feel energy. This happens when you curl up the forefinger and touch it on the thumb. Let that form a kind of "eye". Use this handy "hand eye" to "see" other parts of the body. Or at least to move your intention there, because this somatosensory proprioception is what lets you know you exist. You want to establish that, you want to get back to that base.

"You are moving around through the homunculus and the eye-ears—they are associated with sound. Sound is a wonderful thing to meditate upon because it comes and goes, and it is kind of related to fantasy because you have a lot of experience imaging what you hear, and localizing what you hear. So maybe just let the ears be like two butterflies that are outside the windows of the eyes. Let the ears hear the knocking at the door of your perception, and let the ears just let it go on through. The flitting butterfly ears. One hand can now see while the other one can hear. There is another knock at the door. A nose peers through and sniffs the air. Let this be about putting your attention on the breathing, the in and out of breathing. You can breathe in the colors of the world, mauve, teal, blue and green; and on the out-breath, imagine the air is orange, use your intention to shape this golden bright, healing orange air. This is like the light, the internal light that we are seeking. After a while you will be able to "movie" it around the body with your intention, to focus it on places where you are worried, or feel unwell. After the nose appears, start to feel the whole face that is attached to the nose. Let the hands like magic moving hands put the eyes into this head, and let the butterfly ears come over and go into the rightful place on this head, and let this head look up a bit to the light and let it balance on the neck and be a bit more intelligent. Feel. Because the face is the next most densely nerve-populated body part, you are moving around the homunculus. Two feet shoot in. We now have a head with the feet and hands joined on, creating a strange body-less homunculus. But it is present. And it is feeling, and you are probing the proprioceptive cortex with your intention.

"What is the next body part. You guessed it, after the feet the part with the most nerves is the genitals. So you want to place your attention down there. Suck it up. The whole lower part of the spine, slightly leaning over, you may get an intimation of the kundalini rising, the shiver may float through you.

"From there let the hands with their eyes, sculpt the rest of the body by gently feeling it with your attention, and saying this is my body, take this for this is my body, and it is what I use to feel what is real. As in seeing back into something very ancient, like a campfire in the mouth of a cave, casting shadows on the wall, shadows dancing, projected on the wall.

Frank wound up the talk with a little flippant humor. "There is probably a whole formal methodology of meditation that could take you deeper and deeper into more ancient areas of the brain. Although you probably can't access the thalamus with its flight / fright / freeze reaction, unless you meditate while bungie jumping or sky diving.

Frank developed exercises that trained people in the use of visual metaphor, in which they saw things they needed to see on monitors and TVs, or were something tangible they used like pulleys, ropes, dials and knobs. He told his subjects: "On the other hand, the imagery you use may have nothing at all to do with electronics or movies or tools or laboratories, but something else entirely. Your image could be suggested by an event in your childhood or from a scene in an old movie, a TV show or a book. What is important is that the image has meaning for you. It is the most wonderful thing in the world and the most natural thing in the world to be able to step in and out of the world of the real and the world of the imagination. One of the greatest travelers was Kandinsky. He had a great mental synesthesia. You too can learn to change the frequency and color of your mental world, but for our purposes we are focusing on healing.

"So, to sum up what we are doing with imagery here. You may find that it is easiest to first imagine how a system of your body would work if it were operating at optimal efficiency. This is a physiological or cellular type of imagery. Then you can imagine what the system would be like if it needed fixing. Once you know what needs to be fixed, you can create an image in which it is being fixed. The important thing is to be aware of the change. Finally, your imagery ends with the repair completed. This is the process type of imagery, it has a beginning state, middle and end-state imagery. When that is done, allow a feeling of healing and health to flow throughout the area that needs attention. Then expand that feeling so all of your body feels as well and whole as possible."

What Frank and Jack were about creating with Phaser was eliminating the radical intervention of elective surgery, and instead having the patient make his own changes—gradually, by applying what the patient has come to know as the Reverse Etiology. So Frank began to work on a kind of inverse dictionary of cures. Frank's typical day involved spending quite a bit of time reviewing patient developments, looking at test results, and consulting with the doctor. He also did follow-up with patients by phone. Frank conducted in-depth interviews and gave tests to find the patient's ways-of-knowing, that is their way of looking at the world, their character type, and their learning style. He developed imagery and language that was tailor-made to each individual.

Frank developed exercises to prepare the patients to become more active in their own healing, to change their life style, and to get them using imagery. He knew what they were up against: the use of imagery is surprisingly foreign to a lot of people in the west who tend to let experts and specialists, doctors and priests handle the body image for them. Or, they believed in the great meme-machine: television. The exercises that Frank developed matched the kind of imagery with the learning style of the patient. He gave tests to determine personality type to help the patients find the imagery that would be easiest and most effective for them. He told Jack: "I say something like this to every client. "You've got to create your own image, one that can help your body function as it should. You can use this image for a physical problem you are currently having or a problem you are concerned about. You can also create an image you plan to use on a regular basis to enhance your general health."

Frank talked to Jack about his posture once. It was at the point where Jack was doing a lot of computer work with interface design, and was looking overworked in hack mode and hunched over. Frank knew that mechanical imagery would appeal to Jack the engineer. That Jack would be more comfortable just using what he is familiar with, using screen monitor to display his own spine. Frank told him, "Here is one I use to get my shoulders to quit being hunched up and to keep one shoulder from being pulled up higher than the other. I seem to have this little toy soldier thing going on in my posture, where I stand erect holding myself up by my shoulders, rather than getting alignment from the base. To correct this, I use an image of two columns of liquid on each side of the spine. There is a red ball floating at the top of each tube. In order to bring the scapula down, the technicians in their control centers need to keep the fluid level even in both tubes so the red balls line up next to each other. And so, when I sense that I have one shoulder hunched up higher than the other, I imagine some liquid is poured into one of the columns until I can see the balls are once again floating side by side, quiet and still. Holding this image of the liquid body in my mind for just a few moments lets me get a better support for myself, and being better supported makes me more relaxed."

Frank liked to use one image in particular to help the subject think of themselves as big space. He called it Hotel <User name>. "I might start off with a place as space to hold the systems and functions of the body. *Maybe it is a big garage like you used to play with as a kid. One of those kinds with elevators and wide ramps out in front. You want something to house the structure, like a control room. The physical plant for a hotel maybe—or a big work of art. The emblematic country of the body. Welcome to the Hotel <User name>. There are many rooms in this hotel. You might see it as standing down town, or on a hill overlooking the city. Perhaps it has a round crown at the top of it or it is otherwise anthropomorphic, like yourself. We will want to visit a few rooms in this hotel, this infinite hotel. But first … of course you have to relax, and the fastest way I* *have found to do this is to get into belly breathing."*

After some deep relaxed breathing, he'd continue.

"The first room we might want to visit is the lobby, to kind of check in. Inside this building are many different rooms run by the various systems of your body. For example, there is one for your immune system, another for your hormone system, another for your circulatory system, and so on. The one for your... circulatory system might be the hallways connecting the rooms, or it might be the air-conditioning ducts, or just some kind of honeycombed system of tunnels going all over. The kitchen might be a place where food is prepared and used. The immune system, would that be something like a system of alarms, a kind of electronic security system invisibly permeating the Hotel <User name>.

"You might go down in the basement and investigate the furnace room. It heats water that goes up pipes to the radiators in all the rooms. It is controlled by thermostats and thermometers in these rooms. You might be able to zoom in on one of the thermostats / thermometers and adjust it up if you are too cool and this would cause workers down below to throw more coal on the fire, and you warm yourself in its heat. Or you might adjust it down and this would allow an air conditioner in the room to kick on.

"Or if you are... experiencing an upset stomach, in your imagination you might want to turn on the TV, select a channel or order a video on the pay per view. It's free. They have every video that you've ever seen, and every scene that you've ever seen and you can just ask some one at the front desk to put one on for you. Maybe a video of a beautiful lake with calm, smooth water on the TV monitor and you might imagine this is piped into the kitchen, where the flow of the beautiful

placid water image is connected to the flow of gastric juices in your stomach, and the stomach is calmed down by the video of the smooth calm cool lake.

"Or in this hotel there is a spa, a masseuse, or masseur that you can ask. He looks like Mr. Clean and he does wonderful work and doesn't say a word unless you ask him something. Perhaps Mr. Clean is high tech, and he can monitor your skeletal system. There is a work station on which a computer screen has an x-ray of your spine. The workers compare the x-ray with a picture of what your spine should look like. If the spine gets out of alignment, they push levers that move ropes and pulleys connected to the muscles in your back. This causes you to pay attention to the tension in your back and you feel the need to stretch or move around a bit. That helps your spine get back into a more healthy position."

Frank was very helpful in driving the development of both the kinds of visualizations that the patients needed to find within themselves and the computer imagery that the programmers made available to the user as part of the feedback overlay to enhance the healing authority. He told the development team: "You need to help them find ways to visualize their own body. It might be standard anatomy. We should teach anatomy here. It is wonderful the way the anatomists talk about the structure distributing force, the joints engaging freedom of dimension. But there are other systems—internal thermodynamic and endocrine systems, the sea of acids and digestive system etc." They realized that their ultimate goal was to use the feedback and control of visualization to drive the strengths and focus of the magnetic field and the frequency, as well as direction, of the radio beams that created the MRI image as well as the image in the patients visualization.

The called it Mr. I, though they thought of it as Mr. eye or Mr. Eeee as Wiley called it. Mystery indeed. And misery too. It was a long hard technical hack to get all the parts in place but now they were in place. Now Mr. I was in a place to send medicine on its way, into the future.

Frank frequently held meetings and talks with the core group. He was much more at home with public speaking than Jack and Jack was relieved when Frank naturally took on these inspirational CEO duties. In those talks he became excited and animated and had enough command of the technical issues to be able to talk the talk as he addressed the small group of co-workers at a round table meeting. It was at the meeting held about six months into their company that Frank first showed a video documentary walk-through of the current state of affairs. It was a particularly inspired meeting, the room was filled to capacity, with some team-members taking a second row against the back wall. As usual it was informal and Frank asked several times for commentary. It was a fairly typical weekly "what is to be done" meeting. In these meetings Frank often went to the white-board and sketched out ideas and architectures with multicolored marker pens. He had good readable printing which was a pleasure to see. Sometimes he used his laptop to project slides through an overhead projector. On this day he used his laptop to project their new DVD video walk-through on the overhead.

Frank introduced it with: "Well, we have finally finished our little documentary video." He looked with admiration at Jack. "Here is the long-awaited video that

Jack and I made. He paused for others to acknowledge their senior silent partner. "It is a simple walk-through of our procedures for perhaps investors, or the press. Let me know what you think of it. Lights, please."

As the lights of the conference room dimmed, Frank hit the space bar on his laptop to start playing the digital video clip projected on the big overhead screen in the front of the room. Amid some teasing oohs and aahs of the coworkers present, and fake gasps of amazement in the presence of a "media celebrity" it started.

Scene: Frank as a Tech in a white lab coat is leading a tour. He is entering through a door from the ante room into a larger room with the MRI installation. He is speaking into the camera. Over his shoulder, behind him inside the bright room—at a distance, we see a patient. She is a young woman. Frank crosses to the subject Claire who looks up at the camera. Claire is tall, athletic-looking with long blond hair and a good tan. She is a little shy of the camera, and does not look at it directly. She speaks only when spoken to, in a straight-forward unassuming way. Frank addresses her.

Frank: Hi Claire. It looks like today you will be looking at that sclerosis clean-up project on your knee. Have you been having any instability with standing?

Claire: Oh, no*oo*.

Frank: How's it going? Has the progressive repairing of the tissue damage along the nerve at your knee been preceding apace?

Claire: It's been going pretty good.

Scene: We see a metal band or collar around her knee. Frank points at the band around Claire's knee and camera zooms there.

Frank: We are in a typical BrainSuite, with a Stand-up MRI. The Stand-up MRI is a great improvement over the traditional claustrophobic tunnel MRI and even the only-supine "short bore" MRI.

Scene: He indicates the room with a sweep of his hand.

Frank: We call this set up MR in the OR . . . with VR. Let me point out the main components. *(He points to the various large modules of the system.)* We have the MRI, we have the computer imaging, and we have the control.

MRI in the operating room, (MR in the OR) has been used to verify the effects of surgery as it is performed, thus obviating the need for a second—invasive and costly—verification surgery.

But we have taken it to the next phase. In our system we present the MRI visual—formerly seen only by the surgeon—TO THE PATIENT, as a kind of feedback so the patient can effect his own healing. *Our* system uses the body's own healing power to effect changes in the tissue and at the chemical level. We teach the subject how to do visualization meditation, then to use a specially constructed program of guided visualization or imagery that is his own particular reverse etiology of his disease. These are step by step procedures of what needs to be undone and changed. They are presented through the conscious, to the unconscious, to the autonomic nervous system and thus across the brain / blood barrier. It is maintained by a regimen of meditation and visualization. Then gradually, by the power of the body's own healing mechanism—combined with judicious stimulation of the object of consideration with magnetic and radio energy—the unhealthy tissue is deconstructed (dissolved, absorbed) and new tissue is grown in its place. In effect we are performing surgery using the "knife" *(He makes "air quotes at the word "knife")* of magnetic field force and radio waves. This takes place in a much longer time frame than that of a traditional invasive surgery.

Scene: Medium view of Claire

Frank: Our subject, Claire here, has spent at least 6 weeks learning to do self-hypnosis, meditation and visualization. She has studied anatomy and biochemistry to educate herself in the etiology of what has happened and what needs to happen for healing to occur. We are building up to, and amplifying, the body's own healing ability.

Scene: Claire holds out a pair of computer goggles. They are like clunky rectangular wraparound sunglasses.

Frank: Claire is showing the 3D vision glasses. You can see the tiny LCD displays on the lenses of the glasses. These project a large 3D image onto the eye, in particular a real-time image of what the MRI scanner is looking at.

Scene: Frank touches the scanner collar around Claire's knee and indicates the heavy metal MRI transom behind her.

Frank *(continuing):* She sees what the scanner sees in real time. The PHASER system was the first to do that. Since the VR goggles are LCD screens and not monitors, they are not affected by the magnetic field. These VR glasses project a large space in front of the eye, so that the user can interact with the image using the suite of tools we have designed. We'll get to those tools in a moment. First we'll see what the subject sees.

Scene: Frank indicates Claire

Frank: The user is wearing VR glasses, and can visually look at the MRI image of the scar tissue from MS. We chose this situation for demonstration purposes because the healing process is quite dramatic. What the patient sees in her glasses is real-time MRI visualization. You see the same thing on your video screen at the bottom of your screen. We will, at times, see both our subject Claire in the room, AND we will see what Claire is seeing in the VR glasses at the bottom of your screen.

Scene: As Frank points to the bottom of the screen, a black and white MRI video image of a knee joint is seen to fill the screen.

Frank: Our problem of tissue removal and reconstruction of tissue involves procedures, called Reverse Etiologies, to remove the sclerotic tissue and grow repaired tissue in its place. This mixing of model and reality is accomplished by "Overlays" and "Cues" which stimulate the body's own ability to perform the desired actions on the tissues. The Phaser amplifies the body's own healing ability—the immune system—and other systems.

Scene: Medium view of Frank's talking head

Frank: The PHASER process, that's *(spells out)*, P-H-A-S-E-R for Phenomenal Healing by Amplification of Simulated Emission of Radiation. It is a long process that involves life change, diet change, learning to meditate. There is quite a lot of self-study that goes into preparation before the patient even comes into the MRI room. So the patient is quite well-prepared by the time we start to work in the MRI suite. We give the patient the correct procedures and the biofeedback of the real progress, the cells are grown where they need to be, on the substrate of the body part.

Scene: Screen inserts of progression of tissue growth. These are time-elapsed photographs of the same patch of tissue, with a wipe transition from one frame to the next frame in the sequence of growth. We see more and more skin cells populating the area. It looks like bubbles emerging from spaces in the grid.

Frank: This tissue regeneration was all done with visualization. During the long process, we have found that Virtual Reality amplifies the sense of immersion and hence the ability of the subject to visualize, to use guided imagery to ask the body to go about performing the needed healing alterations. How can we make such active yet somnambulistic (in the sense of being done while under an "induced" REM state) manipulation feasible? That's where the tools we have developed come in. We draw inspiration from Tangible User Interfaces (TUIs) which use physical objects to add *affordances* simultaneously to both the MRI data and the simulation overlay.

Scene: Frank smiles for the camera and gestures toward a couple of instruments on a little marble table beside the MRI station. He picks up what looks like a toy gun with wires coming out of the handle of the gun.

Frank: Here, for example, we have a TUI that acts as a Flashlight, or a Ray Gun, or a Light Saber.

Scene: He picks up the ray gun. We see a close of the toy gun in Frank's hand. The hand turns it so we can see the toy gun better. His other hands points to parts as he mentions them.

Frank: We built the RayGun tool by dismantling a toy gun, rewiring the trigger as the mouse button, inserting a motion tracker that senses movement of the gun, and modifying the hammer to display a pull down a menu when it is pulled back.

Scene: We see close up of his thumb pulling back the hammer. As his thumb moves the hammer up and down, a menu appears on the insert screen, and the highlight of choices moves up and down. CUT-TO Medium View of Frank's face. Frank smiles with satisfaction.

Frank (*continuing*): The physical shape and cultural connotation of this tool supports the metaphor of pointing at objects and blasting them with overwhelming futuristic power.

Scene: He sweeps the RayGun back and forth. A small inlaid image appears on the screen. Light is sweeping back and forth over it, in synch with his movements in the larger image.

Frank: If you look at the picture inlaid into your screen, you will see that I am using the RayGun as a flashlight to illuminate areas of the MRI data coming back in real time.

Scene: We see him moving the RayGun in space. The inlaid image is zoomed and we see the light beam sweeping over some surfaces of different densities. They are being illuminated by the light beam.

Frank: It has a light beam coming out of it, that moves over the surface of the visualization data—that is the real-time MRI imaging data. That took some real computing power, let me tell you!

Scene: A close up of his thumb pulling back the hammer of the ray gun. A menu appears on the insert screen with three choices.

Frank: I make a choice by touching the hammer menu and change it from a Flashlight into a Cutting Tool.

Scene: The insert scene of the ray turns into a blaster like blasting a wall clean.

Frank: The Cutting Tool is giving feedback to the user, as a virtual beam emanates from the gun's tip—adding precision to this choice.

Scene: A close up of his thumb pulling back the hammer of the ray gun. The menu item indicates another selection.

Frank: We can also use the RayGun as a flashlight, or a soldering iron, or a light saber. It is like the Phaser in Star Treck. 'Set your Phasers on stun.'

Scene: The inlaid image gets smaller and we are looking at Frank's smiling headshot. As he speaks, he gestures from the room, to the inlaid image of the data.

Frank: Our solution is a hybrid: we use the tangible affordances of TUIs to control a flexible virtual data representation to overlay on top of the real-time physical MRI observation data, all of which occurs in an integrated 3D space. AND, at the same time, the user is controlling the CAGE—the aperture, focus and strength of the magnetic field and the direction and frequency of the radio beams. That is how the imaging changes. We took some inspiration for our "RayGun" cutting tool from LASIK eye surgery which uses software to map the contours of the curvature of the eye and to find out the levels of tissues that need to be removed. Their software also controls the bursts of the laser cutting tool as it cuts away surfaces of the eye.

But our RayGun does not actually remove tissue with magnetics and radio.

Scene: Frank looks up from the Raygun and addresses the camera.

Frank: Not yet anyway, but we are working on it. Instead, our program projects an animation LIKE the lasik demo of tissue being removed; the actual removal is done by the patient's visualization, actualizing the body's own healing capacity. But like the way lasik controls the laser in surgery, our programs control the apertures of magnetic flux and radio beams from the MRI guns.

Scene: Frank poses like a gunslinger blowing smoke out of the pistol barrel.

Frank: This convolution of physical and virtual object breaks down the boundary between somatic space and digital space.

Scene: He sets down the toy gun and picks up a rigid net from the table near the MRI. He holds it in two hands.

Frank: This is what we call the Mesh, or sometimes the RiceField. I'll tell you why in a moment. The Mesh is a net or grid overlay that is placed over the real time MRI image of the sclerotic tissue to be removed, or other anatomical corrections to be made. This mesh becomes attached to the data, relaxes down around the image in a minimal surface mapping algorithm. It is used for DISCRETIZATION—for numerical methods.

Scene: Close up of hands, one holding the rigid net, the other turning a knurled knob at the right base of the net.

Frank: Turning this knob shrinks the net. It can be drawn tighter to squeeze the tissue. That is to say, we are manipulating the cage of the magnetic field and the radio beam of the MRI scanner with this interface. The basic functionality that the mesh supplies is to measure—in the imagery—the progress of scraping away and clearing of dead tissue that is to be done. And to provide a system of scaffolding for growing new tissue.

In our procedure of cutting away dead tissue, the net gives us the illusion of being close at hand, and allows us to pinpoint the bursts from the RayGun, which controls the changes in the magnetic field and radio frequency impinging on the tissue. It is analogous to the way a barber gauges the depth of hair to cut-off—by the thickness of his hand, or of a comb. So, using the Mesh helps the subject know what they should continue to focus—or focus more on.

Scene: Talking head of Frank.

Frank: Again, the main focus of this work is to enhance the body's own healing system with feedback, visualization and stimulus of tissues with magnetic and radio fields. We are not sure why it works but it does. In the PHASER, Autoimmune enhancement by stimulation of magnetic and radio energy of cells, through the mental pictures formed by simulation in your mind through visualization and listening to, or speaking, either vocally or sub-vocally, the incantations of neuro-linguistical programming, are used to control radio and magnetic field intensities at the cellular level.

Scene: In the room Frank nods and smiles to Claire.

Frank: OK. Claire is ready to begin. And I'll be walking her through the procedure.

Scene: Claire puts on the glasses.

Frank: Step One. You can see on the screen below the real time MRI imaging of the part of the body to undergo the healing.

Scene: Zooms in until the skeletal, black and white, MRI image of Claire's knee fills the screen.

Frank (*heard in Voice Over*): Step two. Claire will now overlay this with what we call the scaffold or the Rice Field. This is a TUI that the user controls by stretching a "net" device over the tissue of interest. Quick CAD mapping finds the contours and gets a good shape. Thus the volumetric mesh she will use, upon which to grow the replacement healthy tissue is a kind of scaffolding made out of magnetic field lines crossed with radio waves.

CUT TO:

Scene: Large, circular semiconductor wafer

Frank *(Voice over)*: Those of you familiar with crystal growth and wafer-fab techniques will see a lot of similarities to how we grow tissue. In tissue engineering, human cells are introduced into a scaffold or substrate matrix on which they grow and divide, producing replacement tissue.

Scene: Close up of what at first looks like the surface of a silicon wafer for chip making, then transitions into a similar image to what looks a fractal of a kind of soap film spreading out.

Frank: We adapted the work being done with tissue engineering on human cells to our system. Some of the basic approaches of tissue engineers also borrow from civil engineering: "scaffolds" are used for building tissues, providing biodegradable structures on which cells can grow. The key device we use is the concept of the "Rice Field," a vessel or container to shape the growth of living tissue. It is the "scaffold" on which cells grow and divide, producing replacement tissue.

Scene: We transition from a guy in a wafer fab facility, wearing a clean suit (a.k.a. bunny suit) in a clean room where they are hovering over electron microscopes to what looks like Paul's lab, with people working in the background at big slate lab tables, and various instruments and tubes.

Frank: In tissue sculpture we use some of the same techniques they have been using since the 60s in wafer fab for semiconductor etching.

At PHASER, our scaffold is a net of radio waves and magnetic fields which is the ultimate in biodegradability—it vanishes when turned off.

Tissue engineering is just now emerging from the laboratory into medical applications. Among the pioneers are engineers and scientists here at PHASER, Inc., in San Francisco. Our experiments have grown skin, cartilage, and liver tissue.

Scene: Before and after picture of dead cells tissue replace with fresh healthy new tissue.

Frank: This was all done with visualization! We just give the patient the correct procedures and the biofeedback of the real progress, the cells are grown where they need to be, on the substrate of that place of focus where they are needed.

Scene: View of an electron micrograph of the surface of cell.

Frank: The Phaser SYSTEM does not image at the individual cell level; what we see is tissue growing like grass on the surface of an organ. Or being cut away from the surface of an organ. You use the RayGun as a light saber, in conjunction with the grid, the RiceField mesh, to show progressively how much tissue has been cropped. In both cases, whether tissue removal or tissue growth, we use the net or scaffold as a kind of gauge of the progress the body is making on changing itself. Scaffolds are designed for specific tissues; this one is for skin. The sequence of cell seeding and growth can be seen in these photographs from the electron microscope and from the MRI images.

Scene: Three stills from electron microscope showing a surface growing.

Frank: Millions of living skin cells, called fibroblasts, have found their way into the area covered within the scaffold. The cells multiply on the scaffold, which is contained and nourished within our matrix device that we call the RiceField. In the Rice Field, the cells grow and multiply. As they organize themselves into three-dimensional layers of skin. The "scaffold" or net being made out of radio and magnetic fields changes with each session both to reflect the real progress being made and to enhance and encourage the body in carrying out that progress. Of course these fields go away when not in use.

CUT TO:

Scene: Back into the MRI room looking at the subject Claire who has her eyes closed in a trance.

Frank: How does this actually happen? For the purposes of this video, we will need to look at two screens: the subject and what the subject sees.

Scene: We see a split screen.

Frank *(Voice over)*: Screen 1 shows the subject in the MRI room and Screen 2 shows what the subject is seeing inside the virtual reality monitor glasses. And we will be showing you some screens that monitor the brain waves of the subject. In order to follow the events as they are triggered and occur.

Scene: Claire is putting on a tight fitting cap, with round white discs distributed on it. It is like a bathing cap with wires coming out of the little round disks. Franks explains.

Frank: These are encephalopods. They pick up brain waves.

Scene: A screen showing brain waves. We see the rectangular frame of an oscilloscope, it has a grid of horizontal and vertical lines. The background of the oscilloscope screen is green, and the trace of the wave is yellow. There are three wave shapes each with their own base line stacked vertically; each assigned to its own horizontal strip taking up one-third of the screen. The waves are on the same time frame, so that we are looking at simultaneous events in three different brain wave domains. The long slow alpha waves are pretty steady. The beta waves show clusters of spiking activity, corresponding with eye movement seen in the REM wave.

Frank *(Voice over)*: This screen shows the subject's brain waves. The main healing enhancement occurs in an alpha state. Here, as indicated on the brain wave monitor, the subject has slipped into a kind of dreamlike reverie, during which her mind is in a mild trance or hypnagogic state. At this point you may start to receive more directly the actual images generated from the body as it attempts to communicate through the unconscious to the conscious mind. We can't of course see these, but these communication images can be detected in increased internal vision—REM—(Rapid Eye Movement) activity. We know they are evidence of the eye scanning imagery. The unconscious communicates in a kind of Pictionary language.

At this point the stimulus to the glasses is dimmed to complete darkness. Or it may be that we superpose the real data with the simulation overlay, to get a suffusing of the two. This is light self-hypnosis that can be shaken off quite easily with any sudden movement of the body.

Scene: Medium view of subject Claire

Frank: In this state you are vaguely aware of things going

on around you, and at the same time you are aware of deep processes within your body. That is why it is called hypnagogic, it is a kind of waking sleep or dreaming reality. It is very pleasant and at the very least you will awaken from the experience quite relaxed.

Scene: Small window inset into the video of Claire—displays brain waves.

Frank: Here, through the evidence of brain waves, we can actually monitor the autonomic nervous system coming to the fore and performing the desired changes.

Scene: Bank of screens showing brain wave monitor

Frank: Here we see it is now, that the body has come to the fore and invoked the mind to enhance its own natural healing capacity. When this happens, the user implements a reverse etiology pre-program to facilitate the changes that need to be made at the cellular and molecular level. Using guided imagery—perhaps shrinking your internal observer down to a monad able to slip through the pores of your skin, or by making contact with the center for internal healing within yourself, however you do it—picture the slow changes you know need to occur. For example you might picture growing new tissue upon a scaffold you have carefully built.

CUT TO:

Scene: we see the subject with virtual reality gloves moving what looks like a mesh with knobs in each hand. She is turning the knobs.

Frank: In the future we hope to use the brain waves to control and trigger the amount of magnetic field strength and radio frequencies being focused on a very small high resolution. Surgeons are doing this now with ultrasonics.

CUT TO:

Scene: Electron microscope image of tissue close up. Caption in a corner of the image reads: PHASER, Inc.

Frank: This photograph shows skin cells that have multiplied. The cells have been tricked into thinking they are in their natural environment instead of an engineered structure, our scaffold. Several days after the fibroblasts have migrated to the area, they actually are in the natural environment. They completely fill in the space of the scaffold.

CUT TO:

Scene: Medium view of Frank talking into the camera

Frank: A few weeks of further growth will produce a piece of artificial skin large enough to replace what was damaged by MS. This method can be used for healing burns or replacing any diseased tissue.

What does tissue need to grow? We are working in situ, and we design the procedures to ensure the subject imagines the necessary ingredients. It is our belief that this liberates the body and encourages it to more easily and readily provide those necessary ingredients. Don't forget we have done a thorough analysis and have modified the life-style as well as the diet and the psychological profile (through meditation) of the participant.

When the user is away from the MRI, the magnetic and radio fields are turned off. Yet they still have nonphysical impact because these fields are in the memory of the body. The tissue of the body is changing and the image of this change is shown to the person. The person then asks for further change to conform with what is needed, what the process is designed to do. The next time the subject is hooked up to the MRI, they then get a new image of what the tissue looks like and can compare it with an image from the previous session.

Scene: We see a split screen, the left half shows the real-time MRI image and is labeled in small letters; the right side shows a slide of pink healthy tissue.

Frank: Then the mental image of what the tissue looks like is confronted with the real image shown from the real time MRI data, the person's immune system is enhanced—the person's own phenomenal to neumenal healing capability is enhanced—to relax the net down further, or to see cells and tissue growing in the rice field.

Scene: Frank smiles a smile of satisfaction into the camera.

He speaks directly to the audience.

Frank: With our Phaser system we are entering a new era of medicine—quantum healing. We are addressing the microcosm in its own language: the language of fields and forces.

FADE OUT:

Scene: Roll credits

IV

One year from the day they took delivery of the Brain Suite, at an Anniversary white board meeting, Frank was really awesome. He started this particular talk a little more formally than usual. He slipped into his "giving a paper" mode and started into what amounted to the Abstract of the paper: "This will be an informal discussion on current research here at Phaser in what we have come to call Teleomatics." He looked at the assemblage of scientists and coworkers around a large table and in chairs at the periphery along three walls. "We are at something of a cross roads now. We are in need of new models to carry our progress forward. The emphasis of my talk will be on computation methods applied to our clinical systems. I will begin by giving a brief overview of the current state of the work we are doing here, as I see it, of augmenting the body's own healing modalities with feedback. I will construct a model of how we induce the healing within the context of MRI data acquisition in simultaneous presentation with guided overlay visualization. I will then sketch out possible research paths where the framework we have developed here provides a perspective that would be useful in further developments.

"I'd like to start the talk by summing up what we have been doing in the year we have been here, what we are doing now. We are going through a paradigm shift. And I must tell you that I think we are ready to make an assault on curing cancer." Again he scanned those present as if looking for a fight. "And as we do, we are starting to have the AMA and the FDA cast even more scrutiny upon us. We are considering going public. So there is lots to talk about."

He paused for dramatic effect: "What is to be done. The actions that we will follow, will follow from our current model. SO I would like to describe the current standard model to see if we agree."

Frank then walked over to the board. He said, "We are seeking to approach the model of how healing works from two ways, the scientific understanding and the empirical approach." He wrote on the board:
scientific understanding -> ( ) <- empirical approach.

He looked at that for a moment, then continued. "And they meet each other at water."

Frank looked around the room at those present. "Today I come before you. . ." He paused, smiled, making brief eye contact with each of the major scientists who were contributing to the work at Phaser. "We will be looking at the work of three main groups here. They can be roughly grouped into the Empirical or clinical, the theoretical, and the computational." As he met each scientist with his gaze, Frank gave a brief, headline synopsis of their work: "Tony Mystelle and his group of engineers are building a network model of the immune system and the program language it uses. Gene Spector and his group are studying theoretical biology. Nicholas Bourbaki from the Santa Fe Institute and his group are studying theoretical and computational simulations. We are beginning to see the current model as an enlargement and expansion of the thinking process begun in the Nobel paper linking the immune system to generative grammar. This gets into evolution, thermodynamics and complexity.

Frank acknowledged with a nod some of the members of these groups. Roddie MacDougall Stanford Professor of Mechanical Engineering working on Teleomatics Fundamentals applied to concepts of Magnetic Body, developer of highly realistic simulations of the musculoskeletal system; Ahmed Korchemsky, a Berkeley Professor of Computer Science working on Transformation grammar model and engineering; Doctor / Professor Jacob Kornbluth, a department head at UCSF School of Medicine working on teleology of metastasis; Leonic Saladana electrical engineering of magnetic fields—loves computation with discrete algorithms. There is Omar Hourian and Wiley Lum-Wong computer scientists from industry working on alignment algorithms, comparative genomics, gene regulation, regulatory motif finding, and microarray analysis.

Frank said: "I am very proud of you all. In this talk today I would like to review the progress and discoveries we have made in Teleomatic Science in this our first year. And then to promote a discussion of what questions we should be solving on both the short term (say next 5 years) and the longer term (say the next 20 years) research horizon. I would be happy if at the end of this discussion we could write down something like a dozen questions in teleomatic healing dynamics for the next 20 years. This will not be a normal technical talk then, in fact I would be happy if it turned into more of a discussion."

Frank pressed the return key on his laptop; a PowerPoint slide was projected large on the screen in front of the group and behind Frank.

—[The slide had yellow letters on a blue background with standard Art Nouveau clip art framing. It had a list of three items]—

Frank said: "Where we are now is this. Given a certain kind of disease, I now have the analytic, numerical, and experimental tools to get a good local and global understanding of how the etiology of this disease influences, and is influenced by, the subject. I am genuinely impressed and delighted with this progress; it is a modest beginning, but it is also a solid one. We have learned,"—here he spoke about what he began reading from the slide—"1) We must understand and quantify (encode) the etiology of the problem under study. The specific guided imagery to help with visualization is crucial; from it comes the reverse etiology of the disease. 2) We are having great success adapting current mathematical machinery from Quantum Physics. 3) Generative grammar is leading us into the general concept of language and semiotics of the emergence of life in cells in a subsumption hierarchy."

"But first I want to say what we mean by paradigm shift. We are shifting our understanding of how we can aid in health from a mechanical local interventionist view, to a more unified mind_body connection with a non-local organization principle view. Our Phaser technology—by that I mean the whole feedback system we have developed here with the MRI instrument, the presentation of images to the client, and the prep work in subcortical linguistics—amounts to a new way that chemistry is being done or should I say, may be performed. With our visualizations and simulations we are specifying new designs for chemical systems. Because through the transmission of quantum signals by way of the magnetic and radio fields of our MRI machine, we are inducing changes in chemical potentials. This means the action is by action-at-a-distance, by field-effect rather than by proximate mechanical / thermodynamic chemical reactions.

"By paradigm shift I mean: In using our method of fields, images, and sub-cortical linguistics to communicate from the macrocosm to the microcosm and induce the human healing mechanism to perform its magic, we have learned to talk to," and here he paused for emphasis, "thc Microcosm! In its own language." He looked slightly taken aback, as though the import of that statement had suddenly shocked him.

"I am very impressed in that I can not see ANY other area of more fundamental interest than finding ways to communicate from the local world of phenomena to the non-local worlds of teleological purpose. With our simulations, we are stimulating cellular uptake of therapeutic macro-molecules such as antibodies and antigens, thus enhancing the delivery of drugs, and investigational molecules, as well as the ingredients of new tissue growth, to target cells in a biologically active form. We have an opportunity here I think to discover the quantum physics underlying the functioning of living systems. And that would be a huge, GIANT leap forward in mankind's understanding of nature. We would become part of History. We'd get the Nobel prize!

"Further, this discussion is important and appropriate for two reasons: first, we are at PHASER Incorporated, whose mission is basic research so it is appropriate that we think about "the BIG" questions here; second, this non-local, what we have come to call teleomatic healing, is being taken over by what I see as more traditional endeavors right here at Phaser. And this only reflects the fact that in general, a least in the United

States, this kind of healing is in a very precarious situation. The blunt fact is that both the AMA and FDA are looking into our technology and we have got to come up with some more satisfying explanations. We have had some clinical success, have experimented and tried a lot of things and some of them have worked—and worked well! The model we are constructing has empirical detail and theoretical underpinnings. It has data to explain, visual language, logical mathematical organization. But our own Tony Mystelle rightly criticizes us and compares it to a toolbox of techniques appropriate for a limited class of problems." He looked at Tony who smiled back.

"We are trying to understand the "complex" way of thinking from many standpoints. I see what we are doing as fundamental. And at the intersection of many fields. We have bootstrapped ourselves up on the science and physics of Magnetic Resonance Imaging to develop our PHASER system that combines: the physics of magnetism, and radio beam focusing, with the quantum mechanics of electrons, with the neuro-linguistics of the brain, and the psychology of healing. We are players in the fields of complexity.

"What I do hope to do is to begin to formulate a clearer VISION of what teleomatic science can and should be doing, and to articulate this vision to anyone interested in listening. I believe that by honestly appraising what PHASER has accomplished, and what we expect to learn in the near and longer term, we will be in a better position to develop our field both intellectually and in terms of resources. Not to mention getting grants and staying in business. So with charts and over head that we have prepared for clients and prospective investors I'm going to talk about getting, and continuing to get, MONEY.

"I would like to address a couple of, three, topics: Complexity, Evolution and Thermodynamics and Entropy / Information in the context of Generative grammar model of the immune system, and the Doctrine of Signatures. So to that end we'll continue our little slide presentation into some company history." Frank pressed the return key on his laptop; the next PowerPoint slide was projected large on the screen in front of the group.

—[The slide showed in bold yellow text against a blue background.]—

Frank stood aside and said, "The Title of my paper is," and he read off the material from the slide to the group in front of him: "Teleonomy and the Watercourse Way."

Several of the people present went "Ooh. Ahh." In a teasing but admiring way.

Frank smiled and waded into it. "Teleomatics. Yes. Teleomatics. Just to recap our sense of that term around here, it has to do with teleonomy, the biological mechanism that explains how the evolutionary goal provides a global informational constraint (teleonomy) to guide the efficacy of development. Teleology explains the evolution of biological Function. For example, predators developed binocular vision in order to chase down prey. Prey has a wide angle vision, in order to, escape predators. Teleology explains the phenomenon called crossover or homeomorphism across domains, which is where you have animals and plants using the same kind of mechanism to adapt to the same kind of media or niche even though these animals have no genetic material in common: like a beetle using the same kind of muscle to lift weight as a man does. We are looking into how this external guidance mechanism gets translated into internal structure, how it works on the molecular level, for example a genetic program's influence on its phenotypic expression. And, as we might have known, we have found the mechanism's substrate: water.

"The term Teleology found its way into modern physics through Prigogene in his work on statistical mechanics. Teleology was like the prime mover, the big battery of it all. For even time's arrow is an effect of the teleomatics of energy dissipation which causes expected and incessant change in open, self-organizing systems. The universe always seeks to maximize entropy creation, and does that by creating local pockets of anti-entropy where beings evolve with increasing complexity to become human beings, even greater wasters of energy in the long run. Our sense of this word teleomatics includes Telemetric, teleology, Mathematics. Telemetry is radio engineering and we do a lot of that with Magnetic Resonance Imaging, using electromagnetic means to transmit, and receive signals for recording and control of information to operate guidance apparatus. But not, as usual, between a ground station and a satellite or space probe but between our MRI cage and the subject. Telemetry has common root with telepathy, telescope, etc.

"Teleology is the study of the design and purpose of nature—that phenomena are guided not only by mechanical forces but that they also move toward certain goals of self-realization. Teleological and thus teleomatics is the study about how the non-local organization principle field impacts the local phenomenal field, and how to get control—or at least understanding—of that process."

He clicked the next arrow on his laptop. He said:

"We have discovered that the methodology of healing here at Phaser has three main components."

—[The next slide showed a wireframe surface with a grid structure embedded in it. Below this image was a list of three bulleted line items: • hierarchical model of turbulence, • dynamic finite volume decomposition of the space, • simplified linguistical model.]—

Frank said, "The current model of the methodology of healing here at Phaser is," and repeated the three items listed on the slide to the audience. He clicked the next button on his laptop.

—[The next slide showed cellular structure beneath the skin or grid of the a object of the previous slide. There were call-outs pointing to various structures. The title of the slide: FUZZY BLOBS was printed boldly across the top.]—

"We are using an advanced object-oriented architecture based on computer objects called Fuzzy Blobs in several of our simulations here. Fuzzy Blobs are like semi-autonomous computer agents with attributes, and hooks that take, as well as originate, Function calls. They have been developed in conjunction with the simulation model enables us to have a seamless feedback loop between the visualization part of our reverse etiology, and the animated presentation of real-time healing models overlaid on top of the changes that are occurring."

Frank clicked the next button on his laptop.

—[The next slide showed a binary tree with branches going up into the structure of the fuzzy blob of before.]—

"Essentially, the PHASER methodology of simulation stimulation by emission of radiation uses a hierarchical octree-like partitioning and quaternion representation of the space. The binary tree mimics the behavior of the tissue under study in the magnetic field crossed with radio beams. This cross convolution results in the increased possibility pathways and gets extended into the fourth dimension where it is accounted for in the quaternion formalism and the octree. We'll get into more detail on this later. Each grid level corresponds to a specific scale of the magnetic / radio / life field intersection, whose general behavior is obtained by applying a finite volume method of decomposition and recomposition of the structure corresponding to deconstruction and reconstruction of the cellular tissue."

—[The next slide showed the tree made more elaborate into a transformational grammar diagram.]—

"One area using fuzzy blobs is to model the immune system. We are doing a lot of work around here modeling the immune system in our efforts to understand metastasis. Basically the immune system is the system that recognizes self from other. That is the first distinction. Its program is to recognize what it not self, turn it into garbage and take out the garbage.

"Tony Mystelle and his group are studying the engineering network of the immune system to understand Teleomatic Healing dynamics. Viewed from the engineering standpoint, the immune system has various interesting features such as immunological memory, a level of tolerance, and pattern recognition. Tony's group used the basic ideas of Transformational Grammar, of how Deep structure communicates through Surface structure to interact with the outside world, as a model for the function of a robot they call the "Immunoid". Like the immune system, the continuity of the Immunoid actions can be seen as a judicious use of available energy. With this simplified immune / linguistic model they are studying how to stimulate the reverse etiology phenomena of healing. The immune system detects the non-self materials called antigen such as virus, cancer, and pollution and eliminates them by binding with them in an intricate pattern recognition and key-and-lock docking dance. This is the same kind of recognition that goes on in all protein synthesis activity of the cells. These are nano-machines at work.

"The Immunoid also supports itself, maintaining its own system against a dynamically changing environment through the interaction among lymphocytes / antibodies. These actually help dispose of the combined fuzzy blob pairs.

"From the linguistical standpoint the immune system is a decentralized consensus-concerting molecular communicating system, communicating in a kind of language or discourse with the outside world. In this model, staying alive is considered an act of linguistical competency on the part of the immune system in negotiating the many, MANY different invaders constantly threatening the entity. The Immunoid has to make choices about how much work it can do with the energy it has. It has to get its energy back up. At any moment the total energy of the system is dependent on the energy of the previous moment, minus the energy of walking around or being out of focus, minus the energy of creating and carrying the garbage to be disposed of, and minus the energy lost by running into obstructions. Surely this entity, conducting its actions by making distinctions, is the Embodied Mind.

"The immune system is an embodiment of mind just as the eyes are. But, on a much more basic scale, on the scale of enfolding and dealing with matter directly rather the eyes enfolding only the light in the reflection wavefront from matter. Even though both these processes involve enfoldment, the degree of entanglement for the Immunoid is much greater. The immune system is making us realize how our world is turned outside in; inside out across surfaces. Just as the Immunoid enfolds the outside world coming in to create antibodies ready to use against inflated attack, the brain creates memories to enfold the outside world and have this model of the world ready to use. Everything is computing, in a kind of organic computer, producing the right amount of ingredients and doing the chemistry on it, at the nano level. This embodiment of mind is like a kind of Artificial Intelligence—although compared to it, it may be that the intelligence in our brain is artificial. We are thinking of this Artificial Intelligence as a technique for reacting to a dynamically changing, material environment at the cellular to the macroscopic and neurological level.

Frank clicked the next arrow on his laptop.

—[The next slide showed the hierarchical tree transformed into the limbic system of the body.]—

"Tony Mystelle says that though important, using scientific visualization to stimulate the immune system is at this point just a bag of tricks, it is not a physical theory in the traditional sense. It is not like classical mechanics, quantum mechanics, or electrodynamics: it does not set out a grand framework for the definition and calculation of physical quantities.

"Tony compares it to a toolbox of techniques appropriate for a limited class of problems. According to this view, I think, teleomatics is most usefully viewed as an important and emerging branch of "non-local medicine", with close siblings in meditation and other cognitive disciplines—psychoneuroimmunology, psychosomatic illnesses. Allergies. Interesting and sometimes useful stuff, but not really all that fundamental. I agree with Prof. Mystelle that today Teleomatics is more like a tool box of techniques rather than a "real" discipline. Fun stuff. Nevertheless, something keeps pushing me to study teleomatics not just because it is fun, but also because it promises to be fundamental as well.

Frank looked at the group and smiled. "From clinical testing and anecdotal observations of patients who have successfully healed themselves giving, over and over, accounts of encounters with a "higher self", Gene Spector has articulated a much more visionary, but no less honest view, of the teleomatic dynamics of healing.

"We are starting to discover a lot of interesting parallels between the healing behavior our successful patients have undergone and the connection with higher selves. This Teleomatic Viewing, a sense of being watched over by a "higher self" starts occurring after one has gone through the autogenic training period and done some sessions on the Phaser. As the healing process begins with the visualization in conjunction with the Phaser machinery it then continues on its own without the use of the Phaser system. A process is set in motion, and the brain checks in to monitor what progress is being made every so often. And the process continues until the results of change are achieved. This is a direct viewing from a lower self to a higher self, a higher self of universals.

"Approaching from the non-local side, from the infusion of universals, Gene Spector has a much more visionary view of Teleomatics in his book *The Vector Space Theory of Biological Information Processing*. In that book Spector begins with a standard axiomatic refresher course on the useful parts of abstract algebraic structures: groups, rings, fields, vectors spaces and, algebras, matrices and operators and field extensions with liberal illustrations to biochemistry and molecular biology as well as traditional circuits, mechanics and linear optimization. He pursues analogies between the swirling information storm of chromatin in the cell nucleus condensing in and out of transcriptional phases, and uses the same mathematics on quarks condensing out of vacuum potentials in the quantum chromodynamics process of how they get their color. He uses the ideas derived from String Theory and Topological Gravitational Dynamics, of embedded subspaces and space-time sheets to study the effect of nested modulations on multiple frequencies to greatly enhance our present knowledge of the effects of electric, magnetic, and electromagnetic fields on biological systems. Gene Spector is attempting to derive *ex nihilo* and *ab initio* the basis of theoretical biology from the fundamentals of statistical mechanics. For him the language that teleonomy uses to write biology on the substrate of life is teleomatics and it is based on group theory. "

Frank said, "I must confess that the Pythagorean Romantic in me finds professor Spector's vision awfully alluring." Some of the scientists in the group shook their head in feigned disbelief; one rolled his eyes and looked heavenward and smiled as if to say 'Here we go.'

Frank continued. "Gene's view is shaped by his understanding of the child's development of universals as presented in the work of Jean Piaget, especially in his *Psychogenesis and the History of Science*. Piaget's vision of the mind is strongly shaped by his experience in studying children and the way that mathematical structures are unearthed in the developing mind. Piaget's account addresses the question: how do children acquire and develop a knowledge of universals? This search for universals has been the goal of physics—especially since Einstein's development of a frame of reference invariant to acceleration. The invariants are the result of group symmetries. When I was in school I wished I had been around to hang with Wigner and Weyl and von Neuman and the other *gruppenpests*, as they finally showed how the laws of physics are based on group symmetries of the universe. Piaget shows how, that at the end of infancy, young children already have access to a group structure as displayed in practical intelligence.

"I hope I am not inaccurately stating professor Spector's point of view when I say that when Gene speaks of studies in Teleomatics, he envisions a theory which is ultimately as rich as Morphogenesis theory, and which is the natural successor to Evolution theory. In his book *The Vector Space Theory of Biological Information Processing,* Gene expresses his vision of Teleomatics when he writes: 'Living tissue can be modeled as a polyphasic liquid crystal. Much of what happens can be understood as a consequence of life exploiting the many useful behaviors of water. Biology is the result of teleonomy programming the computer made out of these liquid crystals chips in the language of Teleomatics.' Water is ultimately a kind of Maxwell's Daemon. He calls it Solution Theory."

"Let me say that again. Water is a polyphasic liquid crystal substrate upon which biology runs its teleomatic programs, exploiting the many useful behaviors of water. The program Spector and his group have developed looks at the teleomatic coherency of water from the standpoint of its three main functions: it is the medium of suspension; it is the solvent; and it is the carrier of signals for our metabolic machinery. His group is studying how the qualitative nature of the solvent precipitates from the parameters suspended in the solution, a classical problem in fractal mathematics. In particular, they are focusing on the role of magnetism as a fractal field in the way DNA transcribes genetic code into biological structures. In short, Solution theory is the general study and classification of energy and information partitioning systems—at least according to Gene. Working backward, starting from studying the role of water in the differentiation between normal and diseased cells, its role in membrane function, in protein dynamics, in pharmaceuticals and even electrochemistry and corrosion, they began seeing a theory of health based upon the idea of "imprinting" on water.

"They have started to re-purpose the great work being done in Quantum Mechanics and Topological Dynamics. Basically what they did was re-purpose the multidimensional theories of wild and tame spaces—some barely differentiable spaces of nano-tesla and even femto-tesla fields needed to describe the much much smaller quantum domain—and aggrandize these models up to the nanoworld size. The differential topology of enzyme folding, and therefore combination, is an obvious area that benefited from this formalism. To find a metric for biological nano-space, they considered a space whose metric was not the Planck length but the Pressure Pixel length. The Pressure Pixel idea originated with J.G. Watterson as he puzzled about the number of collisions in a statistical ensemble of water molecules having way too much energy to be stable enough to stand as the fixed frame of reference from which to channel mechanical force. This seriously challenges the assumptions of molecular biologists modeling the machines of nanospace. Molecular biologists and biochemists have been modeling the denizens of nanospace as simple machines—cleaver, wedge, inclined plane, pulley, ratchet, gear, wheel—Newtonian machines writ small into the nanoworld. Watterson envisioned a (fuzzy) blob of water as being able to come into a much more coherent state and acting as a floor or fixed frame, the basis for the nano machines of biology to function from. This patch of coherent water he called the pressure pixel. It is the metric of the biological nanospace. Gene Spector and his group are getting lots of interesting direction from Topological Gravitational Dynamics. Basically, TGD considered all possible physics as a condensate of a higher space, embedding sub-spaces of a lower dimension in a higher dimension. String theory is one of its most famous incarnations. Classical physics is seen as a low-genus/low-energy special case of the more general quantum world. (Genus is the number of loops and perforations in a manifold. Normal flat space has a genus one. An ecology can have a very complicated space genus with all kinds of feedback loops. In an ecological system the different species 'support' each other in a way which cannot be understood by studying the competitive behavior of individuals in isolation.) This manifold and its non-local constraints and symmetries and how it stabilized itself from noise is what we are studying when we are study Teleology. Teleonomy is the organizing program working for the stability of the whole system. Indeed this spatial self-similarity at all dimensions is one of Teleonomy's great bag of tricks, as is the tickling of an ecological system with noise. Noise is teleonomy's potential.

"Topological physics on different space time surfaces embedded in higher dimension spaces extended information physics into a new domain, enabling an understanding of nano space interactions. Water and therefore living systems have macroscopic coherent properties that are quantum mechanical. Pressure-pixel scale interactions in a nanospace can be modeled on familiar magnetic flux-tube structures, whose mathematical structure is that of a differential fiber bundle. Similarly the cell boundary wall and the way they act as active filters, and the quasi-gel of coherent water that can have varying degrees of amorphousness, can be modeled on space-time sheets. Biologists have used genetic techniques, grafting a fluorescing gene from a jelly fish into an animal's DNA so that the endoplasmic reticulum of its cell glows. The result is that this organelle within the cell looks like the way we know that the lacy veil of constellation densities are draped over the bulges and currents and vortices of turbulence in spacetime. This is not just a similarity, it is an isomorphism. It is as though the external pattern that the living entity is trying to exactly replicate is a space time sheet that is always present as an idea, and which the phenomenal is always comparing itself against. It is as if this teleonomic pattern were a system's Soul, a subcognative but sometimes felt and known representation of the system. This space time sheet acts as a kind of sail, pulling the whole structure along on the polypeptide ocean. How the body loves to see—even if ever so briefly—the pattern toward which its vehicle is forever symmetry adapting. This certainly is a different perspective of the soul than that of the object of traditional religion, where one struggles, convinced that we are part of some moral experiment, conducted by a deity as far advanced from us as we are from the ants.

"In our picture, diachronic magnetic homeostasis with parallel synchronic teleonomic space-time patterns—the pattern that abides when we do not—is the mechanism that makes it possible for the system to entrain to the frequencies of various chemical transitions occurring in living matter. Our Phaser system which we affectionately call Mr. I, acts as an external Force which sets in motion a change. Once started, one doesn't need the outside force any more. This would make possible endogenous spectroscopies allowing the organism to consciously (not necessarily at the level of the entire organism) detect various chemical concentrations by magnetic quantum phase transitions induced at these frequencies.

"And why not. We evolved from the sea on a planet that is three-quarters water; our body is 90% water. Thus, water represents the interface between the 4th dimension in which we live, embedded in the 5th and higher dimensional sphere of the soul.

"I think that Gene would say—at least to a first approximation—is that Teleomatics is the general study and classification of non-equilibrium (either autonomous or forced) through information / energy sorting membrane systems. And that this classification, at the present time, strongly depends on dimension. Thus we study water and its mirror or dual, the space of logarithms and exponentionals, all in the context of group theory. Teleomatics is the next natural step after Evolutionary theory and the theory of groups should serve as a guide to show what this classification theory should look like. That is what, I think, professor Spector thinks.

Frank nodded at Gene Spector, and said, "Did I get that fairly right, Professor?"

Professor Spector smiled and said, "Well you are being very concise; and it works for us. I couldn't have done better myself."

Frank nodded and continued. "My own belief is that Teleomatics proper—as opposed to Evolution or Medicine, lies somewhere between Mystelle's toolbox definition," and here Frank indicated Tony with his right hand, "and Spector's program." Here Frank indicated Gene with his left hand, and stood there lifting his hands up and down like he was a balance, weighing each side. He said, "But it is not necessary or perhaps even desirable for us to provide a specific definition now."

Frank swung his open left hand indicating Tony. "Let us go back to the other opposing position of Professor Mystelle. His group took their inspiration from the Transformational Grammar of Chomsky. They programmed and designed a simulated immune system, the Immunoid. They are looking at the network programming language of the immune system and have developed the whole new field of Sub-cortical Linguistics.

"This is a wonderful new application of Chomsky. Papers mapping organizational systems onto Transformational Grammar are done for it's basic idea of deep structure communicating through surface structure to an outside world is a fecund one. These systems are as old as man's attempts to cross the barrier between the timeless (synchronic) world and the passing (diachronic) world in the forms of myths and spirit. In our time the functions of myth are taken up by science and models and mathematics; yet, since number is the archetype of order, this is still using an archetype to intercede between inner and outer to get our selves in touch with fundamental universal energies. The latest great incarnation of this debate about whether we are the angels gifted by the penetration of universals or the spontaneous patters of material hierarchy of organization network has been taken up by Piaget and Chomsky. Chomsky, then carried his method even further into political awareness.

"How does one harness and focus the energy of the immune system—the immune system that is the brain minding the body?" Frank paused for effect: "The body that we are, a swarm of evolved living organism, and get mind to do healing. The immune system is a decentralized consensus concerting molecular communicating system, communicating in a kind of language, or discourse with the outside world. Indeed there have been several papers relating the immune system to transformation grammar. I can see that I am repeating myself a little bit here.

"How is mind embodied in the immune system? The brain is there for 'minding' the body. The larger brain of the body is the immune system, that which distinguishes self from other and creates antibodies to enfold the intruder and dispose of them. The immune system, is a digital inverse fractal mesh that shapes itself in a way to attack antigens. There it is again—the basic teleonomy, as the immune system speaks a language of polypeptides flows. It is a language, a network protocol of the neurological and immunological pathways, and we can at least say, that it is a very competent discourse between what the world presents and how the body's immune system reacts to it. The preservation action of the immune system can invoke the neurological system by presenting the brain with scenarios that produce anxiety. And also joy. This is motivation. And this physical placing of the "net" around the object of interest, invokes myriad powerful sub-processes that speak directly to the brain in this language.

"The standard model of how psychoneuroimmunology works is that Anxiety is the driving field in the semiotic self, and this takes place in the organization of a subsumption hierarchy, with its origins starting down at lower levels at the interface of body and world. Especially the reptilian brain, the limbic emotional mind and the thinking cortex. This hierarchy is organized into a representation of self. We are a swarm of evolved living organisms, that harnesses and focuses the energy to do healing by making signs that communicate with various artificial and other intelligences, clusters, centers of attraction, in the dynamical sense."

"Anyway, I believe we now have several questions before us. First: Is this a reasonable vision for what teleomatics is about? That is, does past research give us any reason to hope that we can make some progress on this quest? Second, what specific research questions and programs should we follow for such a grand (hopefully not grandiose) vision? Third, can we begin to guess at what are the practical consequences that might result both in scientific and cultural understanding and specific (say medical applications) that would follow from theoretical results in line with this vision?" Frank smiled. "And forth, are the problems we hope to solve with break-throughs in Teleomatic Science better solved by other means? That is: what is our theoretical competition, and why do we think we can do things any better?

"We want to go into the next few generations of design for the PHASER system. I can see at least two directions we are going here at Phaser and they seem to be evolving into two cultures. Both involve obtaining strong radio and magnetic fields and we need to understand the dynamics of the interactions between molecular biology and the electromagnetic field inside our PHASER resonance cavity.

"One culture is using the cavity directly. We have developed techniques for destruction of malaria parasite by use of pulsed magnetic fields. It provides a novel method to kill malaria parasite without—or in combination with—malaria drugs. Magnetic field treatment of malaria is an alternative for drug resistant malaria which is spreading at an alarming rate in Asia and Africa.

"We are using our experience with this, now. And that leads to the most exciting of all, we are performing similar experiments on treatment of cancer with pulsed magnetic fields. Our work consists of development and design of exposure systems, computation of field exposure parameters, and taking part in clinical experiments. This work is being carried out jointly with our umbrella institution, the Medical School at UCSF."

"The other culture I have noticed, is using the field strength directly to do sorting of molecules. I notice that already some of you are taking on work here at Phaser experimenting with magnetic separation and transport mechanism to stimulate cellular uptake of therapeutic macro-molecules such as antibodies and antigens, thus enhancing the delivery of drugs and investigational molecules to target cells in a biologically active form. Though this on the surface looks like Phaser is taking in work and is being increasingly used in a more mechanical bioprocessing sense for experiments other than what we had originally intended, it may turn out to be good experience for the ultimate direction we want to go in. And that direction I think is to obtain stronger radio and magnetic fields and to be multiplexing and modulating these fields. And again, we need to understand the dynamics of the interactions between molecular biology and the electromagnetic field inside our PHASER cavity. This can lead to some big and useful products, we may even want to go into a direction where we use the Phaser to actually enhance transport across the cell membrane and deliver beneficial material, a sort of nano-teleport.

"So we see ourselves going in two directions, yet they both lead to a fundamental understanding of the physics of quantum healing. For myself, I am inclined toward pursuing the Magnetic Body model more—to actually analyze the vibrations and coherence of fields on the macroscopic, molecular, sub-molecular and even sub-nano level. What happens to the bundled field lines when they are pulsed and relaxed—modulated. Are we actually able to control these with our mind. We are finding these magnetic currents to be associated with internal speech. These currents of the brain are very faint indeed—nano-teslas and even femto-teslas—and we need to learn how to control the eddy currents of the MRI beam to be able to address and modulate these directly. Spector feels confident in the *Vector Space Theory of Biological Information Processing*, that we can. He calculates how to modulate these second-order currents as they are phase shifted, or frequency modulated or riding on a carrier joined in the focusing "cage" around the subject. He thinks we can know the required precise frequencies and mix of phase, frequency and amplitude modulations, as well as the correct intermodulation carrier necessary to obtain the desired effects.

"Thus we see that the strong magnetic field in the Phaser not only does standard MRI, that is: excites the hydrogen nucleus in the water of tissue after it has been orientated in the magnetic field, so that this hydrogen nucleus—proton—flips its spin, when the radio pulse is removed, causing the nucleus to return to its original orientation and in this action giving off measurable electromagnetic energy which is picked up and made into images of the density of the water at that point. But our big 1.5 Tesla Phaser also influences the fundamental quantum magnetic spin that is the basis (and the sub-space, the eigenspace basis) of all convolutions, both the coherent ones that stand and the incoherent ones that subside into noise. These are nested magnetic subtleties measured in nano-teslas and femto-teslas way down on the Plank scale, but they are the start of the layer upon layer of magnetic spin superheterodyning that creates the matter the way it is in the world, and creates (evolves) the mind that knows it.

"We see the nervous system as displaying a signature of at least six channels of brainwaves: alpha, beta, delta, gamma, theta, REM and spindles. These are like windows into the various waves of dendritic firings going on in the brain, and connecting to the body. These are not pure sinusoids, but superposition waves carrying information. These waves have complex nested modulations—carrier waves carrying signals superheterodyning on top of carrier waves. No one has ever decoded this information before. What these waves represent is the time averages of tuning going on by the nervous system, the Operators organizing and adapting in the life / consciousness loop. The Phaser is now intermodulating with the magnetic spins of the water of the tissues, and is thus contributing to these brain waves. We haven't, as yet, had the time to work out how this interacting is occurring and how to control it. We do know that we can have a lot of success in pain management by having patients assign colors to their pain, and changing say black and blue to orange and yellow. If I may make a joke, we are Hue-men after all. But really, what if in the next Phaser we can. Not only are we starting to have some success destroying cancer tissue but we could, for example using our tuning techniques, squelch or "jam" the process of the metastasis network.

"In *The Vector Space Theory of Biological Information Processing*, Spector uses the ideas derived from String Theory and Topological Gravitational Dynamics, of embedded subspaces and space-time sheets to study the effect of nested modulations on multiple frequencies to greatly enhance our present knowledge of the effects of electric, magnetic, and electromagnetic fields on biological systems.

—[The next slide showed two images side by side. On the left a complex diffuse cloud at the synapse between dendrites and on the right a superconducting Josephsen junction with base, emitter and collector called out.]—

"Gene Spector models the very metric of molecular biology—the pressure pixel—on the idea of the superconducting Josephsen junction which is a state of matter whose behavior changes at very low temperatures as it becomes a condensate so that it behaves as a kind of transistor. In our case the pressure pixel is being modulated with phase shifted radio and magnetic waves so that it acts as a transistor so that sub-cortical linguistic signals entering the base begin controlling the emitter-to-collector current across the dendritic gap. This is an explanation of how sub-cortical linguistics works. The visualizations are translated into the language of sub-cortical linguistics—a higher level compiled language that passes parameters and makes function calls into the physical machine language of the body's system of controlling and processing polypeptide flows."

—[The next slide shows side by side the levels of computer architecture, high level programming language, compiled language, machine language and the levels of language in the body.]—

"Thoughts and images are still (spoken) language. The whole theory of mimetics and perhaps memetics is based on this. As spoken language there are subtle mechanical and other frequencies, that can be entrained along with the magnetic field. To repeat: The modulated magnetic fields allow coding of these language frequency to magnetic transitions frequencies in the water molecule of the tissue. That is what sub-cortical linguistics is about. We used the term sub-cortical linguistics to differentiate it from Neuro Linguistic Programming. The modulated magnetic fields allow coding of these language frequencies to magnetic transitions frequencies—basically the frequencies of the water molecule in tissue. These fields are of a much subtler sort and of a much broader spectrum than microwaves. The operant word here is coding. The word made flesh. The Soluble Programmer. In *The Vector Space Theory of Biological Information Processing*, Spector assigned Operators to the various levels of organization in the hierarchical lattice—those constellations of perception and organization that he has called the Immunoid, or the Endochrinoid, or the Neuroid . . . He works with them as operators in a vector space. In general he thinks of each of these organizing entities as what he calls the Soluble Programmer, a kind of Maxwell's Daemon sorting and extracting information by operating on the infinite-dimensional statistical ensemble of thermodynamically available energy, organizing it into sub-spaces spanned by bases which represent how the operators have canonically adapted to group symmetries. Thus, evolution is placed on a firm theoretical footing.

"These operators are themselves organizations of different levels of sub-sumption hierarchy. In his expansion on the idea of surfaces and sub-spaces, we are given the whole sense of reality as an entanglement of clusters and quantum numbers. Quantum numbers, wave numbers, harmonics, that explain the bonds, the forces of attraction and construct the observables, in the sense that they are the measurable energy frequencies, constructing the wavefront of observable reality."

—[The next slide shows a picture of coherent water.]—

Frank looked wistful and said: "Allow me to wax poetic about water for a brief moment. Water. It is about the *water*. Water is composed on the most abundant element in the universe Hydrogen and the most life enhancing, Oxygen the building blocks of all animal life. These two form a stable tetrahedronal bond, but it has ambivalence in its orbitals as can be seen from the quantum mechanical picture of the probability wave bulging out of its orbitals and overlapping and being both bonding and lone-pair. Water. It has the macroscopic quality of pressure and the mesoscopic quality of surface tension and the microscopic quality of liquid and the nanoscopic quality of hydrogen bond. It is like the veil, the borderland, the boundary across which the Maxwell's Daemon, or one of these Soluable Programmers, sorts energies. Just as we posit for the sake of argument, these organizational entities, the Immunoid, the Endochrinoid, the Neuroid, there is a biological program helping them communicate. It is the teleomatics of teleology. And it operates on the substrate of water. (Don't we all?)

"It is the sorting demon between the macrocosmic variable of pressure and the microcosmic variable of intramolecular tension, the hydrogen bond. Water is the solvent in all the cells, it is the transport, the currency carrying necessary ingredients for all life to the just-in-time manufacturing systems of cells. Water is the "space" that carries signals propagating through its lattice for other parts of the body to perform functions. Blood is a solution.

"Water performs another great function, it is the veil between the macrocosm and the microcosm. The macrocosmic variable of pressure and the microcosmic variable of tension. It carries the world of forms, that is the group structure of universal into our world.

"It is the master of dimension, the fractal of fractals, the physical representation of the Tao, the water course way.

"And we are starting to develop great models, visualizations, theories backed up by large sets of Partial Differential Equations, Ordinary Differential Equations, Algebraic systems, and finite-element codes, which have a good chance of capturing and mimicking important dynamical features of these phenomenon."

Frank smiled at the math don, Nicholas Bourbaki that they had hired away from the Santa Fe institute. "Nick here is doing some great stuff with the Naiver-Stokes equations. He is making some great contributions to Solution Theory."

—[The next slide showed a long concatenation of mathematical symbols, the Navier-Stokes equation.]—

"Bourbaki's group is exploring the Navier-Stokes equation to accelerate the stimulation process and take into account the smaller scales of turbulence. They are using a so-called auto-similar form of the Navier-Stokes equations in wavelet space to model the inputs and outputs that a tumor experiences—the viscosity of the medium, the divergence of support, the pressure on the medium—instead of using the finite volume technique at the lower levels."

Frank smiled: "Thanks to our home-made parallel processing supercomputer build by the Chudnofsky brothers, we have the resources to do all this numerical simulation and model building, so that we can present the patient with a really precise, and individually-tailored reverse etiology program that is interactive and sensitive to real time developments."

Frank pointed at the equation in the slide. "This equation reduces to the Bernoulli situation that you have seen where the vacuum is blowing wind over a ball and holding up the ball with no visible means of support. This is how an aerofoil or a wing works in a substrate by creating turbulence which—through pressure differential—creates a lift under itself. A baseball does this; it curves by creating turbulence from the stitching so that there is a net pressure on the ball in one direction causing it to move in the away direction. Now by modeling the Navier Stokes equation in a wavelet space, a space whose dimensions are harmonics, we have in effect cast the model in a more natural setting, one that lets us speak easily from a general abstract thinking. Pressure becomes wave propagation through tuning at harmonics. Metastasis is this kind of propagation over the nodes of the body lattice. They are having great success by considering it as a quaternion equation in 4 dimensions."

Frank paused and looked at the group. "At this time

we need to present our efforts in what I call the "strong computational" school approach. That is, that we are going to be able to develop algorithms to run on our innovative parallel architecture hardware and these will provide effective, usable numerical simulation of the superheterodyning levels of existence. A level gives and gets by being a dual space for the next level. A dual space, superheterodyning—pulling signal out of carrier by entanglement with a dual inverse space (convolution)—IS the quintessential fractal exchange across dimensions.

"So we think that in the near and medium term horizon, that such simulations will provide "solutions" for most of the problems we are interested in. Because the strong computational view has a lot going for it, not the least of which, it is easy to explain to people and it is easy to point at the rapid progress in computers and algorithms in recent history. But we also want to have the theory to back it up."

—[The next slide showed a picture of the Phaser system.]—

"As a result, in PHASER, the depiction of healing is accomplished by using real time empirical MR data overlaid with simulations that mimic the visible geometry of the phenomenon. In our computations we used particle systems, stochastic model discretization meshes, noise based hypertextures and rule-based finite automata evolution (The Game of Life) that may or may not bare relationship to the real phenomenon.

"This real-time manipulation of stimulation simulation overlay are quite difficult to control, and because they are subject to the law of large times, i.e. the law of computational irreducability, they are taxing on computer resources, and require a lot of trial and error to reach a certain level of realness. But our system can handle it.

"And we expect to more and more relate these models to the physics of actual healing processes though they are extremely complex—involving conjugate heat transfer, radiation, chemical reactions and multi-phase flow not to mention the biochemical pathways of the immune system at work. Nevertheless, our simulation gives us a reasonable control over these processes." Frank smiled at David Chudnofsky.

The rest of the slides in Frank's presentation had to do with the importance of correct scientific visualization in conjunction with using it to stimulate the immune system. Frank also had a circle of little stick figure people illustrating the steps in the cycle of scientific revolution. He started the cycle from induction of the physical model, this leading to mathematical model, then this leading to programming, leading into a numerical model. This led to a simulation, and then this led to the visualization using images, which lead to understanding, which was back at the stick figure man, who took the understanding up the next level of the spiral to another intuition by induction. It was the growth paradigm of scientific revolution.

Frank had slides that listed their development efforts, the projects going on, the various hardware and other instruments in use. He had slides that showed how the analogy between words in language are reconstructed as images in the brain. Slides that showed how images for visualizations were the natural language that the immune system uses to speak with the brain. He got excited and admonished them that being scientists they were lucky to have the language of science that they needed to learn to speak to the immune system, for this was the language of nature which in the end did speak the language of engineers and scientists, in grid, in graphs of functions which convolve dimensions, in isoclines and surfaces, in vectors, waves, fields, tensors, numerical simulations.

Frank talked about this physical placing of the "net" around the object of interest, invoked a lot of powerful sub process that spoke directly to the brain in this language.

He ended up the talk simply with: "It is as if we are running Chomsky's Method backward: going from surface structure to deep structure. Where we find surface and beneath that new depth."

Phaser Inc. grew and grew and became quite a growing concern. There was tremendous successes with patients; the concentrated research effort ushered in a new era of non-invasive, adaptive, surgery and drug delivery; a whole generation of doctors published reams of technical and popular articles. But the increasing responsibility for the pace of innovation pushed Frank and Jack into roles they were not equipped to fill. The constant one-upmanship of the scientists jockeying and struggling for grants and achievements strained their relationship and eventually Frank and Jack had a parting of the ways. Frank walked away from tech altogether and retired in the mountains of New Mexico. But Jack couldn't keep his hands off technology, and he started a venture capital firm that did fairly well although it is the most terrifying thing in the world for an intuitive inventor to have management. The inventors and investors and the investigators of the inventors and investors gave him a lot of grief in life. He had to learn the hard way that sometimes when you put your money where your mouth is; it is only to kiss it good-bye.

The ending of Mr. I (Crossing the Brain / Blood Barrier), is kind of a 60s thing. That is, to not let the reader be lulled into some story. I wanted the reader to feel like he is a co-creator. One doesn't watch art, one constructs it. So that is why I tell you that it is a story, then take it down pretty fast at the end—sum up the rest of Frank's talk in a paragraph. It is like the monks dragging a hand through the intricate lacy trails of the sand mandala, then pushing all that order and organization into piles of inextricably merged colored sand. We see that the ending too as part of the mandala.

In Mr. I. (Crossing the Brain / Blood Barrier), I tried to narrate the coming into recognition of the microcosm manifested through the body. I thought to express the chutzpa of modern engineering by creating a character—Jack—based on engineering types I have grown up with, gone to school with, and known while working in Silicon Valley. This allowed me a place to express the technical creativity there. And to reflect on the basic precept of engineering, that our salvation lies in high-tech, that developing a machine will be our salvation.

Sensing the limitation of that perspective, I invented his other half—Frank—a humanist psychologist of the imagination. That allowed me to explore the education of the imagination, in visualization imagery, meditation and memes. As I went along, I felt like I was in the 60s aesthetic of a self-aware work and that at times it was mocking me. I felt that Jack and Frank were two representative icons of two worlds: the real and the imaginal, trying to drill across to each other through the microcosm. I had a scene in which we were watching a documentary film of the activities around Phaser Inc. that was about how they were creating informational object interfaces and they had developed tools for visualizing into their internal microcosm. This was later followed up by a scene of the CEO, Frank, an inspired leader and representative of the highly intelligent knowledge-workers of today performing his leadership duties and giving a slide lecture.

I felt like the character Frank emerged from the character Jack just as this modern aesthetic was emerging from me. For me Frank and Jack represent rapprochement in finding the common roots of psychic energy driving metaphor and its enactment in meme. I am trying to work out a better understanding between the religious and the scientific roots of creativity which in my time seem to be headed toward a great war, when really they are both different manifestations and engagements with the archetypes of order.

I do not expect the reader to get, Navier-Stokes or Riemann, or wavelet space, or Josephsen junction, but these are metaphors worth growing into. I do expect literature to ask the reader to take part in the (intellectual) action and passion of the times. Our world view is being very much influenced by exciting ideas. Some of them very old, seen by penetrating thinkers of generations past. Maxwell invented his sorting Deamon as a gedenkin experiment (a right brain conceptual heurism) back in the 1800s. It is a personification of how the statistical physics of large ensembles, which by sorting energy into potential through information, creates order. I think that concept ought not to be foreign for the modern educated person. Nor should the idea of the metric of a space—that there are spaces created by thinkers, which account for the behavior of phenomenon even though they are abstract spaces (this is well reflected in the modern aesthetic of abstract art.) And other ideas: the idea of fractal mathematics greatly expanding and radically changing our perception of the world; the idea of programming a chip as an analogy for life programming itself into the physical substrate of matter; the idea that the machines of nanospace are miniaturizations of the machines of the macro world and the very serious critique of that idea for its assumption that there is a fixed frame to support the reaction force. The idea of water having a behavior where it coheres to support that force is wonderful, and is the basis of imprinting, it treats water as an ASIC (Application Specific Integrated Circuit) that can be blown for the specific temporary use, then it can dissolve back into itself. Isn't it just thrilling to think of a deity, an intelligence creating life with these tools! Or maybe this is just me reflecting my current culture. (One cannot escape his own time.) How poignant. Don't you get a thrill just running with that? Even if you don't understand the specifics?

I understand now that my writing this story was an attempt to ameliorate my inadequacy around being the older brother unable to affect any slowdown in the impending demise of my sister. I felt so helpless. I tried to give myself something of an education. I tried to educate myself in a new psychoneuroimmunology paradigm of healing based on the mind working with the body, in hopes that I might be of some use. But perhaps I only held onto this story of a technical hack or the hope that a technical hack would save the day when really it was a distraction, an escape from my helplessness.

I suppose I spent a lot of time distracting myself in the possibilities of language, in all the many-faceted nuances that concept strikes, in particular the language of scientific visualization and the deep grammar of linguistical systems like the immune system, the DNA of our own make up, and memes. Memes as tapes and intentions that somehow go awry and cause the body to fixate on and to hold on to structures of its own death.

I wanted to write something that expressed the great intelligence of the young generation coming on now. In trying to understand the challenges they are taking on, my heart swells with great hope for them.

The Little Girl in the Corner

After my sister Anne called and told me the doctor thought this might be the end for Karen, I flew out of San Francisco the next day and visited our sister Karen in the hospital that night. Our brother Roux picked me up at the San Antonio airport. There was nothing in my background to prepare me for what I was to see that first night. They told me that they were holding off giving her her nightly major dose of morphine so that she might recognize me when I came in. Earlier in the day they had given her a spinal epidural, like what they give to women delivering babies. We got right over there so she could get her shot and ease the pain.

On the way from the airport Roux said, "Let me just kind of get you prepared, Walker. She's going in and out of being lucid. That doesn't bother me so much, I just try to go with her. But mom and dad don't know what to make of it. When you look at her, and see her eyes roll back up inside her head, you know, that's the morphine. And then when she appears to nod off she may start seeing things and talking to them and babbling to you. It's real crazy, man."

Looking straight ahead, moving, flowing, Roux (a consummate professional truck driver) was gracefully navigating the maze of San Antonio freeways. He was in emergency alert mode. "And there was some incident there today when the priest came to give her the last rite. It was this nervous little Irish priest, and when he reached up to anoint her forehead with the stuff, she reached up and grabbed his hand and said something like, 'Why weren't you there to protect me!' And Anne got down in her face—and I've never seen Anne so angry—she got right down in Karen's face saying: 'Please don't worry about that now. Don't bring that up now.' Anne got right down into her face, got all red in the face and shouted at her, 'Don't bring this up now.'"

Roux shook his head and looked spooked. "I don't know what it was about, man but I've never seen her react so strongly." We continued on in the fading light through a city panorama that had grown up so much I hardly recognized it any more. Roux continued, "They've got her on the good stuff, man. I've tried morphine. It's shadowy, and dark—frightening. That's some nasty shit."

I had to wonder a bit about my young brother's experience being in many ways more worldly than my own.

He continued, "And it never gives you any rest. You see shadows and dark things coming at you out of the corners of your eyes. She can't be getting any rest. That stuff makes you drowsy and you drop off and wake up in a startled fit and a cold sweat. You wake up in absolute terror. She can't be getting any rest, I'm telling you. And she's been like this for days."

We came into the hospital room, and there was our sister Anne and her husband Robert, standing by the bed. These two had started dating at sixteen, had grown up together and gotten married at twenty-one. Anne and Robert were a pair of eternal soul mates, the divine couple, now clutching each other and looking like frightened parents. The last time I was down to San Antonio we helped Karen move in with them. Anne had become the caretaker of her sister. Anne and Robert had built a separate little apartment for their house, out of the office downstairs, for Karen, with its own bathroom. Robert built a beautiful glass windowbox greenhouse attached to Karen's window so there were a lot of nice plants and little figurines to look at, and it gave more a sense of nature outside coming in. They had also done a nice job closing in the garage to make a room just for Karen's cats. Anne had had to take over all of Karen's dealings with the world, drugs, appointments, finances. She said, "It is a privilege and an honor to serve our sister." And so it was. This was the third bout with cancer. We had been through these struggles before, though never so extreme. Twice she had been cancer-free for over six months but apparently it had only gone into remission.

I went up to the bed and . . . and could see that Karen was all yellow from lack of liver function. She was not wearing her bandanna and she had very short hair, like a burr. She had usually tried to keep me from seeing her without her wig or kerchief.

Anne drew in close to Karen and asked, "Do you

recognize him? Do you know who this is?" Earlier that day, Karen had been talking to Roux and referring to him as John—Anne's oldest boy, Roux's nephew.

Karen said, "It is my brother, Walker," and burst into tears.

She kept looking at me and I held her hand and looked at her. I said something stupid like, "Everything is gonna be all right, I'm here." I don't know how to be around sickness. I'm a hypochondriac alarmist myself: fear the food, fear the air. I feel everything bad by an empathic contact low. They have long running jokes about me, for when I am in San Antonio I always go out to the health food store and buy tofu (because these Texans eat meat at every meal) and soy milk and granola. Mark, Anne and Robert's other son, age fourteen, talking like the redneck in Beavis and Butthead, will tease me in a good-natured way: "Dang long-haired hippie. You know where tofu comes from, don't ya? It's that guck you have between your toes, you have to leave it there for weeks until it becomes tofu." Though I had long ago run out of patience for the Texas Bubba style, yet could not avoid falling into it whenever I was back there and in my cups, it felt right and honorable to be there with my family. I would try to play-act. Put a more hopeful cast on things.

Beside Karen's hospital bed was a stand; it was a long pole, running straight up almost to the ceiling with short arms and curlicue hooks coming out of it. There were numerous bags of fluids—glucose and antibiotics and liquid morphine solution hanging on hooks. Thin plastic tubes snaked down from the bags around the stand into a pump about the size of a shoe box that was making an audible putt putt putt noise, and from the pump the tubes went into one entrance in her arm, and another beneath her clavicle. The room was a big gray hospital room, private, in a very good hospital. A little while later, I was shocked and taken aback when I noticed other bags of waste fluid hanging from the other side of the bed.

We made small talk. "How was your trip?"

Karen kept asking, "What's gonna happen now?"

I had helped her close down her apartment and move her stuff in to Anne and Robert's house the last time I was here. The sickness was taking all her money. She asked like a child, who had given up all rights of attorney and had put herself-had had to put herself-in the hands of her sister. "What's gonna happen now?"

She asked me about my son Bill.

And I said, "You should see my Bill these days. He's incredible!"

Without missing a beat she retorted, "You should see my bill for this hospital stay." I was shocked and delighted at the perspicacity of that. And she gave us a knowing wink, and we knew then that she was with us.

We hung out and tried not be in the way and tried to hang in and be there for her, all the while feeling bad for our sister and also honored that she would let us be with her in that. Sometime her eyes would roll back inside her head looking into what was going on inside her mind, and her conversation would just dribble on off.

And then she would awake with a fit and a start: "Red alert—red alert, red alert!"

She said, "Ohhhhhaaaaahhhhh." Her voice was like someone being stepped on, having all the wind squeezed out of it. Once we heard her murmur softly in a dry cracked voice, "Cancer. His face looked like cancer."

Karen was bearing the discomfort stoically, but occasionally she would go rigid and practically levitate off the bed in pain. She cried out: "OOO eeee !" And then said, "Oh, Oh, Oh, The devil is kicking me in the back!"

The nurse had seen this often before but it still stopped her in her tracks and left her aghast. The nurse would agree with her, "That devil must have big boots on."

And Karen said, "Oh yeah, he's got really big, steel-toed, cowboy boots."

Something had happened to her mouth too. And I soon saw what and I was deeply shocked to understand it. My poor sister: it was in the grimace she made when a stab of pain shot through her. She had been contorting her mouth going ooo ohhh, so much with the frequent savagery of the strikes of pain that the contorted configuration of her lips had engraved itself on her mouth. I shuddered and thought of the face on that dehumanized being in that horrendous picture, *The Scream*, of Edvard Munch, with its world set in a lava sunset of swirls of scrawled on slaps of spilled color.

She was moving her lips to form syllables of a statement, of a, of a question or sometimes—like a fish gasping for air. "What's gonna happen next?" she asked me, her big brother. "I don't know," I answered, trying to make sense of her words.

We all felt so afraid for her but wanted to present a brave confident face. I think we all believed that she was waiting to see each of us one more time before she gave up and let death take her. I really loved my sister. She was a wild one. She had been all over the world, many times. I tried to visualize her in better times. She had a kind of Texas women's liberation style, which is what they call a good-ole-girl, wearing blue jeans, talking soft and humorous, riding around on a the fender of a big Suburban, blasting snakes with a 20 gauge. Her car was a Wedgwood-blue colored Cadillac, with a gigantic set of Longhorns attached to the hood, centered over the grill like they had on *Dallas*—her favorite soap-opera. The longhorns almost spanned the width of the car and must have looked quite intimidating in a rear-view mirror. During Christmas season she always had a big flowery wreath hanging from the longhorns of her Cad.

She was in a really bad way, raving out of her head on morphine which had been given to her to manage the pain of bone cancer. She was getting 250 milligrams of morphine per hour. Her world was getting small and smaller. She was looking at it through the reverse side of binoculars, waiting for the next fix.

What horror must have been floating around her in that world, along with the love. What did she see. *The landscape of morphine was out there, reaching up its cloudy fingers and carrying her off, only to drop her more wretched than before. How . . . How was it that the floating world also suddenly turned to sharp edges and cliffs, to fall a long ways off.*

Even more than the pain she was going through, what shocked our parents was the fact that Karen was not lucid and was talking what appeared to be all kinds of non-sequiters and just crazy stuff. We thought that was all right. We knew what it was like to be around people who are vulnerable and on acid.

I even started trying to take her on some kind of guided meditation about going out on Lake Medina in a little boat. On a hot afternoon in the middle of the week when no one was out there. Take her floating along relaxed, lying down in an open boat. Floating out on the dark waters of the lake, looking up at the moon in the middle of the clear blue sky. I know she loved that lake. I started trying to talk to her about the sounds. "And that little putt putt putt sound that you hear, is a little outboard motor boat and we are just cruising out on the lake, and it is a warm day and you are all wrapped up tight in a boat blanket and you don't have to do anything, just let me drive and our boat is putt putt putting along through the calm waters of the lake. The moon is overhead. Karen. . . Karen."

Sometimes you could barely hear her, let alone understand what she was saying. While she was delirious that night, Anne kept trying to have her make peace with herself, Anne kept saying, "Be at peace, Karen."

And it frightened me.

Anne had said, "Put it to rest, Karen. Let it go." And I got afraid of what Anne meant, because I could not tell if she was just trying to quiet Karen down so she would get some sleep for the *night* or if she was admonishing our sister to just quietly, go gently into that good night and let it go. Finally, Karen dozed off.

Anne took me out into the hall and gave me a briefing on what has been happening. "The cancer has metastasized everywhere. It was popping up everywhere, her spine, her thigh, her liver, her pancreas. They did an MRI and found a lesion on her spine. That's what is so painful, it sends roots all through her movements. She can neither stand nor lie nor sit! They found another lesion on her thigh. It's bone cancer. And I don't know what is going on with her shoulder, even in spite of all this morphine they are giving her. She's been on a morphine drip of 250 milligrams an hour."

Anne looked tired and drawn out. Her face had that haggard look of consternation and resignation that made me think of the faces of those poor women in the Dust Bowl pictures who were still fighting but had really come to know despair at the hands of nature holding them in the grip of a long drought or blight. "It's been so hard, Walker," she said, "to keep this fight going. Her best friends have been really getting on my case: 'You mean she is still going to chemo?! You haven't got her into hospice yet?!'" Anne said this imitating the ridicule and incredulity in their voices. "And I answer them, 'It's up to Karen. As long as she wants to keep up the fight, we will be there for her.'"

Anne fell back, leaning against the wall as though she were about to collapse from the overload. "We are just trying to hang on for the occasional moments of peace."

I leaned against the wall too. I tried to remember seeing my sister in better times. I pictured us as kids meeting outside in the school yard leaning against a building. "Yeah, it was worrying me back there, you were talking about peace, I thought you meant the FINAL peace."

"Well in a way, I do! I want her to find some piece, WHATEVER it takes."

I, who had not been on the front line of this fight, was more hopeful. I tried to confront: "What did the *doctor* say?"

"The doctor said, 'It's not up to me. We'll keep fighting it as long as Karen wants to fight.'"

"And then the doctor told me it was the strangest thing she ever heard. When the doctor asked, 'Are you ready to die, Karen?' Karen said, 'I haven't had much experience doing this dying, but I don't think I am ready to go yet.' So by God, if she wants to keep up the fight, we'll do whatever we can."

I said, "Karen kept worrying about coming home. We got our hopes up and her hopes up about moving her home. There, she might be inspired to sit up, to go out into the garage to feed her kitties. Wow, just to be able to get outside and see the sunset would be so precious."

Anne said, "I just want to stop the pain."

Anne gave me a frightened, wide-eyed look. Shaking her head with dismay, she said, "Listen, something else has come up too. Did Roux mention to you about what happened with the priest today?"

"Yeah, he mentioned it briefly—she slapped away the priest's hand when he was giving her Extreme Unction!?"

"Yeah. Man, that was weird. Something awful was coming up, from her past and really bothered her." Anne, looking around, scared like some little child in a panic, said, "And we don't need that now, we need for her to be at peace. . . I think it is about some kind of molestation incident, Walker."

"What!? Wow. That's pretty shocking. Do you think so? That's terrible!"

"Yeah, I think some . . . I seem to have some kind of memory of it."

"What do you mean?"

Anne gave Walker a determined, not-to-be-inveighed-upon look. "Well, I don't want to get into it now. But it might be true."

With misgivings, but acquiescing to Ann's unspoken insistence, and figuring the sisters shared secrets that the brothers were not to be admitted to, Walker said, "Well, OK."

Anne continued, "She sure doesn't need this now."

Anne said, "She must have awakened from a sleep, drifting in and out on the morphine, and there was this . . . this little priest standing there in his black robe with the purple sash draped round his neck, and when he reached up to anoint her on the forehead she grabbed his hand and pulled him down to her, and lifted herself painfully up off the bed to get in his face and say, 'Why didn't you do something about what was going on.'"

"And the priest was really shaken. And he said, 'Well, now whatever is in your mind about what has happened in the past, let it go and be here now to participate in this sacrament now.'"

I tried to find some more positive thing to say, some other way of looking at it. I said, "Well maybe she just didn't *want* to get 'extree munch-on'." I said it like some kind of yokel redneck talking like it was some kind of extra rocket fuel food for a journey, partly to try and introject some kind of gallows humor into the sad situation and partly to express my waned belief. "Maybe it really scared her, getting the Sacrament of the Dead."

Anne gave me a pained look and said, "Wow. How long have you been away from the Church. They don't call it that now; they call it the Sacrament of the Sick."

"Yes," I retorted, "but what does it mean to Karen? You know we come from a generation in which we were taught by the Catholic Church that there is a Hell. We called Extreme Unction the Sacrament of the Dead back then. And that's probably what it means to her now!"

“Well now,” Anne insisted, “they call it the Sacrament of the Sick.”

“Maybe that frightened her.”

“No!” Anne was adamant, and got an argumentative look on her face. She was a realist and knew the pathways of the ego’s denial. “There was something coming up for her. I think there was some kind of molestation incident. . . She needs to have somebody like a priest come in and talk to her. Maybe apologize to her. I’m going to ask the priest who is a counselor over at St. Mary’s to maybe come over and apologize to her. We need to put this to rest. . . But she had recognized something, *something* from the dim past.”

The next day I was to do my first solo watch. We were going to be staying with Karen around the clock, Anne sleeping in the room with her at night, and my brother Roux and I splitting up the day. Because we wanted one of us to be there with her all the time. We did not want her to die alone. Anne briefed me on the kinds and types of drugs with names like Bastracin, Motrin, Lactalose. She reminded us, “If you go to radiation therapy tell them to be sure and use the gurney with the orange cushions.” I spent the morning with Roux, learning the ropes of how to care for Karen by watching him. She was in a really bad way, rambling out of her head on morphine for the bone pain.

My brother Roux is this big funny Texan, keeping a patter of wit and insight and good feeling going always, even though he is kept ground under the thumb of that paterfamilias state. You got to have a lot of soul to live in Texas and Roux has a lot of soul. He is a Virgo, a high speed workaholic always cleaning, tidying, ordering. When he comes over to my parents' house, he is busy pulling the weeds out of the cracks in the walks, fixing drainage pipes, taking care of stuff. I watched as he carefully spoon-fed Karen—ice chips out of a Dixie cup.

Watching my brother care for her, learning what to do from him, I was touched by the great love and high humor my brother and sister had with each other. He is one of those people with so much southern charm that he can say anything to her. They are always kidding. He told me about the day before when he was in the room with Karen and one of her best friends Cathy. Karen was raving out of her mind with some elaborate scheme of assigning numbers to each of her siblings. "Numbers: Walker is 15; Anne is 16; Roux is 17." He said, "Karen! While you're up there communicating with whoever you are communicating with, how about giving me 5 numbers between 1 and 50 so I can get a few million out of the lottery."

"Cathy laughed and said, 'Roux, you're going straight to hell.'"

Anne told me that Karen had been going on and on like that for days: "She was trying to get something out. 'Trip? Tap? Trip. Treck?' Karen was taking dictation from the life support machines around her!"

Anne explained Karen's erratic hand movement to me this way: "It was this whole elaborate thing, Walker. Patterns, patterns. It was all patterns that affected her memory. Like putting pictures and letters up on the wall. It was like Karen was back at her job, a teacher in the kindergarten room. She'd move her hands like she was putting pictures and letters up on the wall. She was just a little kindergarten teacher decorating her room.

"And she'll start talking about the little girl in the corner too, Walker. And this girl was perhaps one of her wards, her children. . . She'd say: *'You know. 3 years old. All the colors. She's messing with me. Here, there and everywhere.'*"

"'Who is it?' I'd say."

"'It's the little girl.'"

"What does she do?"

"'She holds my hand.'"

Anne told me, "When she was in the most intense pain, a little girl started to appear in the corner. 'Where is she?' 'She's over there,' Karen would say. *'She's moving about. . . She's wearing blue, red, white, yellow, green purple . . . she's very bright.'*

"It was a kind of Guide. She'd ask, 'Do you see her too?' I mean I have started calling myself the Cruise Director around here," Anne said. "Me and the nurses just kind of go along with her and I have kind of taken over and become a cruise director of the whole operation.

"She was taking dictation from the machines at the side of her bed in the hospital! She was doing it so much it would make her tired. It would make her so tired. She'd get exasperated with me and then go back into the dream. Look over at me and say something in this reality, and then go back into the dream. And she knew it too. And we just played along with it. Finally it came out that she wanted Roux here. Wanted to apologize to him for turning him on to dope. She really wanted Roux to come down and wanted to apologize to him for being the one to turn him on to drugs. That really seemed to bother her so much over all these years."

After a while Roux started letting me take over taking care of her. He let me do that. Karen was going in and out of morphine dreams, and even with the two of us we had to step pretty lively. Once she dozed off and he tried to read the newspaper. Later Roux and I went with Karen to radiation therapy. We were to do that because the boys driving the ambulatory had had to bump the fucked-up gurney they had—it was really hard to get its wheels to go down so they could slide her into the back of the van. They were nice young men though. One was a white kid with fine golden hair slicked back in ducks, looking strangely fifties in his blue cotton short sleeve uniform with the sleeves rolled up. I half expected to see a package of Lucky Strikes peeping over the rolled up shirt sleeve. Goes to show how looks can fool you—he was a pre-med student. His helper was a big Mexican. The big Mexican kept saying to Karen, "I'm sorry, I'm sorry." As she was screaming out in pain and them banging the gurney on the back of the van.

When I get around my brother I become loose and relaxed. He is really a comedian, and just a good-ole boy who acts right—straight from the heart. He is always so matter of fact and practical. He drives and loads trucks all day. He is tanned and built, with long sloping shoulders. He has the cynical smarts of a taxi-driver. Knows all about Houston and the Texas countryside, knows every honky-tonk and night spot from San Antonio to Houston covering a wide swath from Austin to the Gulf. Knows and loves little riverside dives in Seguin where the old women have let the gardens run as wild as Monet's gardens. He speaks fluent Tejano and Cajun and Ebonics, all with perfect accent. He heap big old

Houston swamp-rat bubba who keeps his humor going. When he was going to be leaving me in charge, he was to go out with our father later in the afternoon to buy a burial plot. Dad, from what I heard (I had not yet seen our parents yet on this trip), was being practical too. Taking care of seeing a lawyer and working out the financial details of a will. A while back he had taken Karen, when she was not so far gone, to pick out a coffin. Now he was writing her obituary for the newspapers. I imagined my father sitting at the big desk in his den, with pen in hand assiduously writing the obituary of his daughter on a yellow legal pad. Now that I knew what it was like to be a parent, I knew how my father must be suffering too. It must be so hard for a parent to lose a child.

Roux left and I was on my own. As soon as the initial fear of not knowing what to do wore off, I knew I was doing this on my own, and I could be nurturing.

In Karen's hospital room there was a TV mounted on a swivel arm from the ceiling. You could run through the channels from the bed. Karen had some favorite soap operas that she tried to get to religiously: *One Life to Live* and *All My Children.* We watched a little in the few lulls between the technical ministrations of the caretakers. I thought I would read a lot while she was sleeping, but she was in and out and being racked with pain, and I was trying to be there for her.

Karen kept worrying about Coming Home. I held out hope for it. Karen kept wondering what it meant *to be going home*. But I wondered, What was there left for her in life? Sitting and watching endless hours of daytime TV? But we were trying to encourage her. The psyche tries to protect itself. Tries to surround itself with a perimeter of hope in all situations.

Karen lay there in bed with all this technology and drugs around her listening to the putt putt putt of the pump. Somewhere outside, in the great hospital, we heard the screaming of some fretful baby, crying and being taken somewhere. Karen's eyes got really cloudy and her brow frightfully furrowed and out of the blue she asked: "*Does it have Dad's face. Whose face does it have?*"

Karen and I made small talk. She asked me about my son Bill. How was your trip. We talked about the plot of the movie *The Getaway.* At times her eyes would roll back inside her head looking into what was going on inside her mind, and her conversation would just dribble on off. Again she entered the Land of Morpheus conducting and being conducted by the machines. She indicated them with a wave off her hand. "I don't want this to take up all my money," she said. "I have left a little money, something like $20,000 for each of the nephews, for their education. Anne is going to administer it."

And then she would slip back into the dream, the movie. She asked a particularly attractive nurse, "Were you in that movie, *The Getaway*?"

"Do you think she looks like Kim Basinger?" I asked Karen.

The nurse said, "Oh thank you for getting me mixed up with Kim Basinger."

So the next time I saw that nurse I said, gasping with amazement, "It's. . . it's . . . it's Kim Basinger!"

The nurses in the oncology ward were perhaps the best in the hospital; they were great. In addition to Kim

Basinger there was Rachel. Rachel was very beautiful, had short red hair cut like a boy's and a lovely, lively female figure. But it was her snap and attention, and the brisk proficient way she moved and looked at everything and took care of everything that was so smart and caring it almost left you breathless to watch her work whenever she came into the room. You could tell her loving affection for Karen was real. She held my sister's hand and looked into her eyes and said, "How's my special patient doing down here, Karen."

Rachel noticed that Karen's left arm where the morphine and other drugs were being dripped in was starting to get swollen. "We better keep an eye on that, looks like the solution is not going in. I wonder if those veins have collapsed." A little while later she checked the blood return and it looked good. A little while later the swelling was continuing and it was decided to move the intravenous irrigation opening over to the right arm. They had to get permission from the doctor to use the right arm because when the breast had been taken, they had needed to damage the lymph nodes on that side as well.

That afternoon it took three nurses to find a vein. Rachel started trying to get the needle in a vein, and she looked up and down the arm, poked a needle into one spot. "It popped!" she said.

She tried again and the same thing happened. "I'll get Crystal to try."

The little one who looked like Kim Basinger came in, and she took Karen's arm in her hand and deftly ran her hand up and down Karen's arm. Up and down soothing and smoothing the arm, and said, "There are lots of good candidates here."

Crystal got here equipment ready, and put the needle in, and then she turned it around, and got ready to attach the opening to the lead needle and said, "OH oh. It popped. Sorry, Karen. Looks like you are going to be my pincushion today." Both nurse and patient laughed. Crystal preceded to try again. Meanwhile Rachel was bustling around behind and beneath Crystal, emptying out the bags of fluid into big plastic triangular graduated cylinders and I guess measuring it before she dumped it into the toilet in the little bathroom leading off from a door in Karen's room. "Oh oh it popped again. Damn," said Crystal. After the failure of the fourth attempt, she said, "I'll go get Adrienne."

When Adrienne entered the room a shock wave and an aura of competency and bracing focus of attention came with her. Adrienne was very petite and proper, a little wiry nurse, with a head of hair that was reddish brown and curly. Unlike Rachel, who wore almost stylish army fatigues with lots of pockets, and Crystal who was dressed kind of hip, Adrienne wore a starched blue nurse's uniform. It came out that Adrienne had lost all her hair due to cancer too, and it had grown back lush and marvelous and they all made comments about it. Adrienne had an almost fierce demeanor, yet she was a little nurse with the most delicate little hands I have ever seen. It came up that Adrienne had just returned from Goma where she had been volunteering her time to help work in orphanages for the little children who had been left alone in the world after all the carnage and blood bath of interracial genocide in Rawanda. The refugees had moved to Goma Zaire.

I was in awe of this almost preternaturally focused nurse with the alien look. It was as though her head was shaved back so that there was nothing but perfect attention to bring to bear on the situation. I have never seen such care happening. She got a hold of Karen's arm and started running her fingers around the veins, poked a needle into one, and said, "Bingo, we struck oil," when she got the blood back flow. And we all sighed a sigh of relief.

I had strict orders from Anne to keep the visitors away. But toward the end of the working day they started showing up. I could tell these people really wanted to be with Karen, and yet I felt so embarrassed at how awkward their humor was, and I felt so protective toward Karen. Robert had remarked about these people, "They don't come to visit you at home in life when you are well. They only come to visit you in the hospital when you are dying." He got all angry and protective too. "It's like a public place and they feel like they can just waltz in on you. And those nurses on the floor, they don't know who to keep out."

Finally Karen got quieted down and I could look at something else. Out of the window of her hospital room, you could see the straight needle of a radio tower. And you could see a huge water tower looking like a giant steel triple-decker hamburger or a flying saucer standing up on stilts like some strange virus of the macro-world. The sky was gray and tumultuous, filled with storms and shifting blustering clouds. You could also see some of the buildings of the medical campus, which went on for miles. The hospital complex was a modern city the size of a town. I got that famous picture in my mind, of a lion chasing down a monkey, and at the last moment the monkey had turned around to face the lion as it pounces. The hospital is the place you go to dance with the lion.

Because we have come to a point where we just have to give up and make our most fierce try and just give in and dance with the lion. Some of the buildings were so high they had lightning rods on them. Seeing the radio needle and the flying saucer side by side like that, two of my favorite symbols—radio, this wave voice penetrating space at the speed of light like the soul; the flying saucer, a mandala capable of travel from another dimension of the universe. I wondered about the beyond, and what universe my sister might be entering. The flying saucer and the radio, the great ways to escape from earth. Maybe one evolved from the other. Broadcast people? The Eschatology of All Beings (or just the higher ones.) Ah, but that is something we will never know.

We will never know death, because we will be gone. All we know is what we are conscious of now. It is all so psychedelic. We are like highly evolved snowflakes. We are in this big whirring buzzing clanking roaring sliding world with everything going on and all we know is that we are just an expression of it for a while. This is It. And we can know it for a little while. The End of knowing is so close, it is a parallel dimension running beside you all the time, and you do not know it, we cannot know it. Oh, we can get intimations of it from time to time. We are written in time hopefully to be read by those who know us. Born of a woman who fucked a man, we were loved at least by the big caregiver in the beyond. Karen was surrounded by a sea of love in the end. I wondered what my own end-time would be like. The first thing that comes to mind about my own death, is that there won't be any one there.

That evening, after a solemn dinner at Anne and Robert's place, we had a good sibling pow-wow with Anne on the back porch before she was to spend her night shift with Karen at the hospital. It was OK for Karen to be alone because it was visiting hour at the hospital and Karen had a lot of friends. Robert was kind enough to take the pre-teen to a pool hall, and leave us three surviving siblings to talk. Roux and I and Anne were crying and feeling so bad for Karen. Anne, as usual, had spent the previous night in Karen's hospital room. Anne was crying, and she said, "You take away everything and deep down inside she really is this loving person."

I said, "Karen kept worrying about Coming Home. I kept holding out hope for that with her."

Anne looked pained and doubtful and began to tell us about the incident with the priest the previous day. "She told me all about it last night. I asked, 'Do you want to tell me what happened, Karen?'"

"She said, 'I felt the cancer kicking and punching me, and I wanted to hit him back.'

"'Who?'

"'I saw Father O'Laughlin hit him.'

"'Who?!'

"'The man! The dirty, fat, little, Mexican man. He was so ugly, Anne. He looked like cancer and he made me do dirty things.'

"'Who?! What dirty things?! What are you talking about?!'

"'You know, that time when I was a little girl and the janitor used to make me meet him in the bathroom after baseball practice, and he did terrible things to me.'

"'Oh, my god. You mean he molested you?'

"'Yeah.'

"'When?'

"'When I was in the fourth grade. It started when I was in the fourth grade, and it went on for a couple of years.'

"'Who was it!? Who molested you?'

"'It was the janitor at St. Luke's. Pepito was his name, I think.'"

Anne looked at us brothers, and we were pale and shocked. She said, "I don't remember him. Do you?"

I said, "I remember Tony the janitor. He was a hip young guy. Married. He wouldn't have done anything like that."

"I don't remember him either," Roux said.

There was a huge rationalization starting to form itself in my mind as I guess I was trying to deny it. Because then I said, "Yeah, I kind of do remember seeing another big old janitor around there once or twice."

"Well I didn't remember him," Anne continued, "but Karen remembered him! 'Well it was!' Karen said. 'He did it with Abby Margolis, and with Lisa Doyle too.'"

Anne said, "I said to Karen, God! Lisa was one of my best friends! How come I don't remember any of this!"

"She answered, 'I don't know.'"

"I asked her, 'Did mom and dad know?'"

"'They asked me about it once and I said he touched me on the shoulder. I lied to them.'

"'Why did you lie to them?'

And then Anne hesitated for a long time. She looked at Roux and me. "She said, 'It was because he said he would hurt Roux if I told anyone.'"

Roux put his hand on his forehead and looked away.

Anne kept eyeing him.

"Oh, god damn," he said.

"It's not your fault that she was trying to protect you," Anne offered. "That's just the way she was."

I was really shocked. It threw me into despair. This was an assault on my family. I was the big brother, I should have been there to protect her. It was too horrible to contemplate. I went into denial, "Oh god damn. I don't remember any of this," I said. I tried to reason back and it seemed our younger brother was too young to even be in school. The ages seemed off.

Anne continued, "I was trying to make sense of this, but I was starting to remember it. I asked her, 'How did you know Father O'Laughlin hit him?'

"'I saw him! He hit that man hard and threw him out.'

"'You must have been at some meeting.'

"'Yeah, I guess so.'

"'Wasn't mom or dad there with you?'

"'No.'

"'Well, who found out about it!?'

"'It was Mrs. Tomain.'

"'Mrs. Tomain?!'" I asked. "'Our seventh grade English teacher!?'

"'Yeah.'

"Karen asked me: 'Why did the priest come here?'"

"'He came to give you the Sacrament of the Sick,' I told her."

I was pissed. I said, "Well, let's not have any more priests coming around here!"

Anne said, "I'm going to ask a priest friend of mine. She needs to hear an apology from a priest."

"Well, is it that important to her?" I wondered. "I mean, communion and all that? I know it's important for mom and dad. . ."

"Well, she seems to get some pleasure out of it; she had been enjoying it up to this instance."

Roux was fuming. He wanted to look up Mrs. Tomain and find out the truth. He wanted to go to the parish and get the employment records and find this monster, wanted to go get this "Pepito" if he was still here. He said, "If I ever get my hands on that guy, I'll tear off his head and shit down his neck hole."

That pretty much expressed how we all felt.

We all felt so afraid for her but wanted to present a brave, confident face. We ended up feeling pretty low, but galvanized together. Roux said, "You can't keep Death out. Death has lingered in this house way longer than most."

The next day, as I was with Karen, images of cruelty toward the child she was kept creeping into my mind. I couldn't keep them out. She was my sister; we had grown up together always. I could remember her, as a little child, when she and Anne got in trouble for getting hold of the scissors and cutting their own hair. And I feared this molestation incident was haunting her current suffering.

And yet my mind still would not let me believe the molestation story. Was it some kind of morphine fugue or was it real? Or was I denying it because of my guilt for not knowing, not having protected her? I tried to investigate it logically. How could that happen to her, what was the matter with them to think that they could just hit the janitor and fire him and that would be the end of it. Were the counseling skills of the Catholic school system that backward back then? Those nuns didn't know from nothing back then. And whatever happened to the other girls that were molested? How did their lives turn out? Well, Abby Margolis I heard did have a hard time. She was very overweight and had become a lesbian. And Lisa Doyle, she was fairly normal, wasn't she? When I asked Anne later she said, "Yeah, she got married and had a couple of kids as far as I know."

To go home. Karen kept asking, "What happens when I go home?" (She is ambivalent about this, somewhere in the back of her mind she knows this might be hospice). I tell her, "Our main hope is that you will be able to sit up and to stand up, we hope that you will be able to make it to a wheel chair and get around, and make it to the bathroom yourself."

During the day one of those quick summer storms you get in Texas blew in. It was so good to see a storm, to see a Norther come in, to see the wind blowing the branches and making the leaves dance and it kind of made you think that it was the hand of god coming down to clear the air. On the way over to chemo, I got Karen to look at a cloud formation: "It looks like a rabbit, yes a kind of big rabbit. See. . . its long ears there, and there are cherubs all around it, yes they are like little angel babies with wings and they are flying up to it, as if, as if they wanted to press noses with the big soft rabbit."

"Wow! Yeah, I see that."

"It's nice being out on a day like today with the rain washing everything off, and the clouds taking shapes and the sky is just beautiful. Isn't it?"

"Yeah."

"Wouldn't you just like to fly up into it though? Just get lifted off the earth, and flow up over the city and see the clouds on their own terms?"

She looked up at the wild blue yonder. "*Yeah*," she said wistfully.

And later back in Karen's room, the Little Girl in the Corner made an appearance, I think. But it was something about a baby, she kept on saying, "*Did you see the baby. Did you see its face. Who did it look like. I see the face. Does it look like dad?*"

"Where is the baby now?"

"They are taking it away. I didn't get to see who it looks like."

Later when I was relating this to Anne, we began to wonder if she hadn't had an abortion and if this was some memory of the child. I rather doubt it, we would have known.

I began to see the molestation incident as something that explains Karen's whole life. She never got married and always was associated with rich older guys who could really provide for her; they were father figures. The love that got twisted by a molester who could not contain his sexual urges made her look always for protection. There was always this need for protection, because no one had protected her when she needed it. And this marketing to older, more powerful men had made her such a "good ole girl," the kind of girl the older men liked: easy going, yet a challenge to their Republican, conservative ways, a flower child in their midst, whom they could protect and take all around the world, and who in some ways made them feel more a part of that world. It made me shudder to think of all that love she could have been capable of, for she really was a precious child when we were kids. All that love lost, down the drain with Karen's girl-soul after she had endured molestation. She should have gotten therapy. She should have taken on some young guy and brought some kids into the world. They would have been wonderful. She had really loved her nephews, they had been like her babies; she had always gone with Anne and Robert and idolized Robert so.

That evening Anne said, " It really shakes me up to think about how she felt dirty. How could such a good ole girl who everyone loved and who was so nice, feel so dirty? Dirty?! 'You don't think I am dirty!' she said with a kind of fear in her eye. . .

"She was so surprised that we loved her so much. For it seemed to her that she was dirty. And that cancer was a kind of punishment. 'It's been a 10 year sentence,' she said.

'"A sentence for what?"'

"'A sentence for being dirty.'"

God, this is awful I thought. To still be feeling guilty for being forced to have her tender young girlhood pressed against that fat, sweating, cancerous rot!

The next day it kept flashing across my mind all day. Our sister, as a child, a darling little Catholic girl in plaid, pleated-skirt uniform being pulled into the dark bathroom. What a moron that guy who would force himself on a child must be. And my sister having to spend ANY time with that creature. And he's supposed to be an older person, an adult, someone to trust. She had started remembering out loud, she couldn't help herself, deathbed confessions, floating out on the surface of morphine. "He told me I had to meet him. . . in the bathroom, OR he would hurt Roux. He would hurt my brother.

"I had to do what he wanted or he would hurt my little brother. He had a hold on my mind. He terrorized me. If I just let him do what he wanted he wouldn't hurt me or my brother. He told me not to tell anyone and I didn't."

A nurse came in to arrange things. As they rolled her over in bed, the cover was pulled away and part of her pajamas opened, showing a little bum, and the nurse teased her, "You're flashing, Karen!" And everybody laughed. Her personal space was slipping away. Everything was slipping out of her control.

And our mother, when she came to visit, was no help. Mom was suffering horribly too. Mom was so far gone now; there was no talking with her, no reasoning with her. Her own pain was so great, from tic doloroux (trigeminal neuralgia). She was completely addicted to prescription narcotics. She had become huge, pumped up on steroids, taking shoeboxes full of pills and making calls to her doctors, calls and trips to the doctor's office or the emergency room every day—hours every day in waiting rooms and emergency rooms—every single day. So that none of the doctors would talk to her any more or would call her back. Mother was their worst nightmare. She was even involved in a litigation for some botched operation in her past that left her irreversibly damaged. Nerve pain is a terrible pain. Long, chronic-term, protracted pain. She had been sentenced to live out her life in a pain-amplifying neurosis. They had even tried hypnosis and what she called mumbo jumbo visualization therapy, trying to get her to step outside herself and be another *observing* the pain—from the outside, not the one having it. Who was screaming in pain? It was like, supposed to be it wasn't even her.

Anne told us that Karen scowled when she saw their mother. She told Anne, "My mother, she has to be in here having her pain competing with my pain." And Karen actually did say to her, to our own mother, after mom had been going on and on in her litany of complaints, "Why don't you just go home and shoot yourself!?" We could commiserate with our sister.

Karen pulled us into the landscape of Morpheus again and again. It was a kind of theatre you had to enter because someone you loved was stuck in there. *It is a landscape that moved on its own and it moved through her, waking her up in fits and starts.* And it moved through you waking you up to what she was going through and causing you to go into all kinds of creepy justifications and sad heart rendering human saga.

She was moving her lips to form the syllables of a statement, of a . . . or . . . of a question? Or sometimes like a fish gasping for air. A kind of fish drowning in a polluted stream, sucking at the last bit of air.

What did she see around her in the half world. *The landscape of Morpheus. That was the mental landscape into which Karen had become rooted. She was captive, tied to a drip, a steady drip drip drip of morphine coming in a plastic tube that snaked down a chrome tree into a large pump mechanism about the size of a car battery going put put put with LEDs and buttons. On they went, tree branch and breeze with lights swaying on the tree branch, undulating on a river of breath, not moving in a moving landscape that flowed around the bed. And it breathed its own diastole and systole like some kind of inhuman thing looking through the round, lighted eyes of gauges and instruments with envy at people.*

The devil was able to bring up old feelings of physical revulsion and the horror of being trapped from those incidents of time and time again in the dark bathroom with that big ugly monster. And force Karen to relive them. And I was forced to imagine them, time and time again. *The ugly, dirty man's sweaty body pressing against her sweet school girl self, his face was all pocked marked and his nose was bulbous, he looked like cancer itself. Did she have to beg him not to hurt her? What did he make her do?*

She was fearfully trying to understand the devil's inner musings, conversations and calculations. She was haunted by some malevolent spectral entity, by energies buried in the grave of her unconscious.

I am taking this as a personal affront. What was wrong with our family, that she couldn't have told somebody? Where was I that she couldn't have told me?

The Land of Morpheus, it was shadowy like black trees moving against a black sky. We were drawn into these otherworldly visions that she was communicating to us. *Shadowy, drowsy, dropping off with fits of waking. The rack of cancer was the devil. The devil really had her, defiled her, making her body go rigid and toss to and fro, jerking and twitching, then Morpheus would get hold of her body and she would slip into a dream or a stream of consciousness.*

Karen wasn't getting any rest. When her eyes would roll back up inside her head and she would appear to nod off then would go to some place that was shadowy and dark. *Morphine dreams, the devil corrected.* Morphine dreams, I heard my ego explain. The visions of a brain, not getting enough oxygen. The effect of all the medication. Perhaps the last kindness of a beneficent god.

"What is going to happen to me now?" Karen asked abjectly, moving her lips silently, forming the syllables in the question. *"Why. . .," the devil answered, "you die!" And kicked her in the stomach so hard that she levitated off the bed, screaming "OH! oh, oh."*

Then her eyes would roll back inside her head again, looking into what was going on inside her mind, and her conversation would just dribble on off. *His debauched black eyes flashed; it was like it was projected into me, his face the horror floating around.*

I remember her in the Catholic girls high school playing the guitar and singing folk songs. She had a lot of friends then, as always. Yet none of *them* knew it either. How much ache she must have held inside.

How terrible that it would really feel or seem to her now that the molestation had festered into cancer.

What was I doing at this time? Fourth grade, she would have been nine. I would have been twelve. I was in the seventh grade when it started. I would have been there at the school. I used to take milk to the little kids' classrooms. I was running around wild with Mike Barnard and Bill Cox. We had to take ROTC all the time, marching around on the asphalt "playground" in the Texas heat and I just hated it. I was in a totally surly and rebellious mood. Wait now, little Roux would have been only three or four. He might have just started the first grade toward the end of it. Somehow things didn't add up. *Either she is having a false memory or perhaps he stalked her at church and knew our family!*

The devil really had her; he began to stretch Karen. The devil with the big steel-toed cowboy boots, was tuning Karen's body like it was some kind of an instrument, his plaything. Her body stretched out in bed was a long bass fiddle, that he could tune by turning these little white knurled knobs on the top of the neck, knobs made of shrunken human skulls, shrunken so small that their internal cavities had collapsed and they had become solid, and he could twist them between his thumb and forefinger making her body go rigid, stretching the chords and muscles tight as a string, to raise the pitch which was the voice of Karen screaming shrill in pain. He would twist them so tight it would make her head and face pull back, stretched over her neck.

She was only forty-three years old. A little kindergarten teacher; so sick in mind and body. It was like the stubborn gnarled roots of the sickness reached deep back into the depths of her mind as it was formed in childhood, and now, on her deathbed, with the help of Morpheus, the roots swelled up visible, cracking the ground of silence upon which our family had grown.

If I could have addressed her I would have said, I want to remember you riding on the outside of the truck, with a 30.06 in your lap when we drove down those dirt roads out at the deer-lease, hunting. I want to think of you sitting in the trunk of that giant redwood tree in Sausalito, the picture you had taken of you in your hippie days with your long hair, and then later when you came out to visit me as a young woman on your own. Or remember you as the world traveler, a temptress who delighted in tormenting Bobbies at their post in front of the Palace on her visits to London. She is only forty-three years old.

When I saw him, I asked my father, "What did you say in Karen's obituary?"

"I said she came from Canada, and that she was a kindergarten school teacher at Saint Rose's, and that she went to Ursline Academy. I said that she was survived by her brothers and sisters and gave your names and by her parents and gave our names. I said that she succumbed after a long fight with cancer."

I thought for a long moment about how writing an obituary was like being an accountant, trying to sum up a life, in a neat little blurb. It said nothing about her courage. It would have been nice to say something about her grace and courage and how she was so much loved by her friends and family and the health workers at the hospital.

Karen was freezing all the time as I took her back and forth to her chemo sessions at the hospital. Radiation treatment for cancer was attacking her immune system so bad that she was shaking and freezing even in the hottest Texas August summer. Inside it was severely air-conditioned. We were just trying to get her through her birthday, August 13. Her immune system was busy fighting a tumor elsewhere and consequently she was always shivering and cold and we had to pile the blankets up on top of her. At the hospital, her electrolytes and phosphates were falling and her bilirubin was up, and the life was slowly ebbing out of her and she worried about this a lot. The hospital could bring all these intense therapies and phosphates and electrolytes and other intense solutions with catalysts to bear and really work up her blood chemistry and keep the pain down, but her world had narrowed to just this hospital, just this room, just this bed.

I watched from the alcove as they wheeled her into radiation. The radiation machine looked like a star gate or a big astrolabe. The patient was laid out on a movable table that was threaded through the transom of the star-gate machine. The transom was so big and heavy it had to be supported on big steel I-beam girders. The business end was a big telescoping ceramic cannon pointing at the patient lying on the bed. These girders bracing the structure made it look like an altar upon which they were performing the sacred rites of life saving. The technicians of the sacred painted a target on her skin; it was a kind of sigil, an X within a square. That would guide them to the place they would expose for them to shoot the radiation into. I felt like I was looking at a gothic mystery play or something out of a Frankenstein movie, and I shrunk back out of that room and left her in the hands of the experts.

I stood around outside with the ambulance attendant Perry and his big Mexican helper. The two men began making eyes at the receptionist and some girl volunteers in crisp starched blouses at the nurse's aide station. The girls were all for it, teasing the strapping big Mexican boy in Spanish. I appreciated the give and take and tease, and then, thinking about the contrast between normal and predatory sexual attraction, became overwhelmed with sadness not only of Karen's situation but with the idea that she might have been sexually molested as a young girl. Thinking of this gentle dear innocent girl that I knew, reaching out her hand to things in life and getting burned by that.

I tried to have better memories of her. I think about her as a beautiful tall Texas hippie chick in the seventies and eighties. Bell bottom jeans. Vests, big blond hair with a ribbon in it. Tall well-built, curvaceous young woman. Ran with all these wild people. She was best friends with a skinny high-energy waitress whose brother was Big Bear, a biker and speed freak, and they had great parties on a farm out in the country. Then she settled into a job and a nice apartment. She became Gal Friday for a rich developer tycoon and ended up traveling all over the world with him, staying in the best of places. What a great life she lead. But how private too. Here I am her own brother and what do I know of her. Certainly not as much as her other siblings. Anne and Karen were really close, like two mothers raising sons and nephews. Then earlier when she and Roux were really close—Karen practically raised him. Then they turned into running buddies. What a pair.

Back in her room from radiation therapy, Karen slept, the sleep of the exhausted. And when she awoke, the little girl in the corner paid us a visit. Because Karen was in the most pain, a little girl, all done up in rainbow colors, appeared to her. The mind creates things like that, the psyche protects itself. A tiny—sometimes tiny and sometimes big—fairy-like person flits about the room. *(Tinkerbell, is that you.)* Impossible as it may seem, Karen blinked her eyes and stared at nothing. But to her she is not dreaming and there is, in fact, a little girl standing diminutively in front of her, in the corner of the room. Karen would wave her arm and beckon the little girl standing in the corner to come closer.

Now the little girl in the corner was flitting about the room here and there and everywhere. *She was all done up in these beautiful light and colors glinted and danced off her like her clothes were made of bits of mirror and glass, sequins, like snowflakes or phosphors, electric sparkles, pixie dust, or foam in the sea. And like the eyes of people who loved her looking down at her, the little girl in the corner seemed to be stretching out her hands to Karen, and Karen reached out her hand to take it at times.*

But as Karen is reacting to the unfolding strangeness, a black cloud of a devil under her back in the bed that she cannot see, pulls her shoulders back and sticks his boot into the base of her spine, wracking it, to send shivers of pain all through her body so that she almost levitates off the bed.

It must have been terrible for her and for everybody, the nurses around the clock. But in that hospital room sat the little girl in the corner, with a smile on her lips, laughing and teasing Karen, purring, propounding, and putting forth all kind of perplexing and preponderant pronunciations. A guide. To take her across. Trap. Trip? Treck? A spirit from another world, who does perhaps come to people who are in pain, because they need it. The mirror of torture got shattered into spangles of light, the shards of pain cutting into her got turned into flitting kaleidoscopic colors.

What would a psychologist tell us. That Morpheus is a two-faced god of death come here to release Karen from her pain? And take her soul, her life force, her essence, her self. In the land of Morpheus, Heaven goes round and round with Hell. Morpheus the Enatiomorph.

Both the devil / child-molester and the Angel / little-rainbow-girl-in-the-corner share the same body. When the devil wrings the most pain, that is when the Angel Girl in the corner comes to the fore. The body has the ability to generate a kind of neurologically induced halo that is a compensating mechanism for the pain and it released the body from the pain for a while.

A psychologist would tell us about the mechanism whereby a brutal child-molester devil wrings pain out of the female child that he molested over thirty years ago, and how it is still having a hold on her psyche. Still grabbing and holding onto her psyche as well as her body in his big meaty, pocky hands. Karen's pain summoned the little rainbow girl in the corner, as a kind of guide to lead her out of that dark place. The devil showed Karen these memories still potent from the past, locked in a frame that kept their energy radiating out and driving a great deal of her behavior. Is that what a psychologist might tell us?

Karen died Thursday, October 6, 1994 at 3:13 AM. Robert called us in San Francisco in the middle of the night: "Anne was holding her in her arms up until the last, Walker." He was really sad. I know he loved her very much. "She just let go. . . She spent the last day groaning."

I had been scheduled to fly out there that very morning at 11 in hopes of seeing her one more time, but it was too late.

Later that same night, after the call, I thought I heard someone ring the front door bell downstairs so I got up to have a look. I was fearful that some street person or worse, a reaper in a hooded shroud coming to collect my soul, would be standing there. But it was nothing, just the empty street in a tough neighborhood. I lay down on the couch downstairs and as soon as I closed my eyes had a lucid dream which started with Karen's face looking young and slender and tanned going by and smiling. I tried to hold her image around a little longer but it cut away too fast, shifting perspective, zooming up and down soaring out like I was being taken for a ride on the back of a spirit or a force that was looking for a way out, trying to find a path to get beyond the hills of San Francisco.

When I talked to Anne later in the day she said, "We were so relieved. She had been in and out of a coma the last couple of days."

She had gone down quickly since she came home from the hospital, and had gone into a hospice situation. She had become so childlike, appreciating everything, high on morphine pain patches.

It was about 7:30 that evening when I got to San Antonio. The hospice had taken her body to the funeral home, and my brother Roux took me straight there from the airport. We saw her in state that evening with Anne and Robert and their kids. It was very important to see her body, to have closure. They did the best they could. She had lost a lot of weight. We went home and continued working on a photo album of pictures of her throughout her life. It was a beautiful album. I never realized what a really gorgeous girl my sister was. According to Karen's wishes only the family saw her body. The casket was closed for the rosary attended by friends and parishioners the next day. People filed by and every one was in tears looking at her pictures in the album. Her obituary came out in the paper. Friends packed the chapel at the funeral hall. Teacher friends, nuns from St. Paul's and St. Luke's, parents of kindergarten students. She had so many friends.

That night a Norther blew in and we sat on the back porch watching it come in, drawing our chairs closer and closer as the rain drove in under the porch roof. Later we were almost knocked out of our beds by some earth-cracking thunderclaps following lightning strikes all around.

The next day, a cold clear clean Saturday, we had a big Catholic funeral at St. Luke's. The church was filled; everybody was crying at the beautiful eulogy given by Karen's friend, Father O'Gorman. There was a long funeral procession of many cars across San Antonio's expressways out to the graveside, where amid a wild cacophony of black grackles, she was lowered into the ground beneath a live oak tree. We had a wake for her after the funeral, people bringing tons of food and staying to share stories about her.

Afterwards, after the earth-shattering event that we felt that weekend, a lot of things got said. I will try to summarize here. Karen HAD been molested. By the Mexican janitor. She told us as much in the incident of the priest. She hinted at it later with me. She told Anne all about it that night, and Anne had corroborating memories of it that night. She did not go into any much more detail than that, and at first we tried to stop the impact of the revelation by denial and her just not being able to differentiate truth from the morphine ramblings.

She kept on telling us about the Little Girl in the Corner. Karen could perceive this sprightly entity, whose being shined with sparkling hair and rainbow auras, who flitted about and was sometimes in Anne's hair. I wish I could say that the little girl in the corner, the bright and shining personage with a kind of gossamer wings, like an angel, came along and Karen just said, Take me, take me with you, I'm ready to go. And it was easy. And she just breathed her last. And like a leaf floating back down to mother earth drifting calm and quiet and casual and comfortable, died. But it was not to be like that.

Anne said, "She spent the last hour trying to catch a breath, with her eyes open staring into the dark, never blinking. She finally let go. She caved down inside herself and her head and neck pitched forward and touched her chest and she just let go."

Her memories were not simply passing through her mind. They were activating muscular sensations in some cases, and we hoped that there would not be much longer to this torment. The horrible thought that the memories were somehow being associated in the dreams to physical sensations tormented us. That the visual image was linked to muscular sensations, thermal sensation, et cetera.

Anne said, "When we were going to have to work with her again, I asked for a female nurse. I told the coordinator that my sister had been abused. They understood and sent a female nurse."

We can of course never know what things she saw, some of the things she told us about. We have . . . pictures, some incredibly beautiful snapshots of her, just as she existed at that moment in time going through all the typical things a person goes through, in a high chair, walking in the park, standing by numerous cars, in a lacy first communion dress, high school graduation gown, throwing a party . . . The newspaper picked up on the obituary and did a story about the beloved kindergarten teacher who died young, and it appeared in the Sunday edition.

When I got back to San Francisco I was grateful to get back to my job, to be able to plunge my mind into a lot of detailed tech writing at Oracle. Of course one never has any friends at work. My manager actually said, "We step over the dead around here."

I am left desperately trying to recapture some threads of memory of her. It was making me crazy until I understood what I was doing: trying to reconstruct a past that we shared, and that I felt guilty about not sharing more of. I chose to live my life away from the family because you have to live your own life, and there's no sense in feeling bad about that, but I wish I had been able to spend more time with her, to have let her be a bigger part of my life. I'm still going over and over all this. My mouse arm is going numb from all the writing at Oracle. I'm almost on the verge of telling them to shove it, but that would be self-destructive behavior. It's hard to tell the difference between grief, depression, loss—and avoidance of these feelings. I'm just trying to get through these times.

Like anyone who experiences the death of a loved one, it has got me wondering what is the purpose of mortal life. Are we some kind of moral experiment? Invented, constructed by a higher being? For his amusement? I mean, he would be as far advanced above us as we are advanced above the ants. Who are we? Where do we come from and where is it all going. What is the meaning of the little girl in the corner. I hope that there is a Guide that leads us into the beyond. One of the Archetypes.

What is the meaning of it all? I am going with the Jung picture. I am hoping to learn what the body knows about its designer. Deep down inside us is the harmonious heterodyning of matter and form on an unprecedented scale, the gene intertwining and climbing up the wall of evolution to create us: probes—huge robotic space probes, to carry forth their assault on time. Is that the Self of Jung? The god at the center of each person?

In the body is the individuation process. As I get older, live longer, I hope to come to know my uniqueness, come to feel better about my life, come to know the truly profound gifts and the generosity behind them. I hope to have the time to mature in my personality, to feel the peeling away of the ego and the showing forth of the self who is the owner of the ego.

With aging I hope to get mellower, nicer. I for sure feel like I know more. I want to experience being nice, being of service, using myself for the good, just as she did. I used to be into banging heads and banging women, never seeing that in the center of each person is god. I am going to become a Jungian Buddhist.

The entity that bears your name (who else would it be?) is experienced only by use by us. Not by the other. YOU get it. (Who else?) You are the author of reality (who else). For in reality there is no other for whom reality is happening. (Who else could it be?) Your self is god. The knowing of that is a huge gift and responsibility. It is what the Buddha taught. And it takes time and it takes the disintegration of the body in old age to bring about the destruction of the ego so that you can come to know the self, the god for whom you are a probe. That is the meaning of the transubstantiation *take this body which is given to you* but I never could get it in Catholic school because they made the life around it so oppressive.

This soul, this self, levitates over the earth, the earth that lays itself out, filling every nook and cranny with life. There is no us, no me, no them. We are one of the many species pouring itself into the world each with eyes and a body to record and experience and remember and learn. And though we stand up on two feet and jet around in F-14s cruising the globe and dominating hot spots, the self is centered everywhere, each with eyes looking, and being looked at with other eyes, all looking over the rim of the world at what is coming around the bend.

Why are we here? And where are we going? I tried to put it in the larger perspective of Etiology and Eschatology. We are here to try to grasp the truth. This life, in this western hemisphere we are blessed to be born into, is based on the luck and rapacity of our forefathers' ability to conduct genocide and theft and survive in their ideals to develop democracy. We are here because our primogenitors were lucky enough to have developed immunities to the diseases that came from living together in large populations. They were living in cities because there were many grains and animals available for domestication in the wide Eurasian veldt. We are here because doctors developed defenses and inoculations, based upon petroleum compounds.

How can we continue to be here.

We have to survive the slaughter of nature's epidemics as well as our own narcissistic wars, famines and exploitations. We have to survive the ecological suicide of pesticide contamination creating an eternal silent spring, global warming and depletion of ozone, as well as the horrendous overcrowding in mega-cities and the relentless exploitation of the lower classes by the upper classes.

Okay. Then the next thing we have to survive is the nemesis collision with an asteroid like the last one which wiped out the dominant life forms on earth, the dinosaurs—indeed most of life on earth. But of course by then we will have good rockets and nuclear bombs that could knock such a doomsday planetoid off course or just destroy it.

Okay. Then the next great eschatological challenge would be the dying out of the sun in about four billion years. Our star will start to wink out, first becoming a red giant, expanding out to engulf all the inner planets including Earth in its fiery girth. Our blue-eyed baby jewel home and everything on it will be roasted into a burnt out charcoal cinder which will be spread into the consistency of dried chunky salsa before being ground into rings of fine dust before it disappears in vapor. But presumably by then the species will have moved off to other planets and taken some of your favorite books and CDs with them. Joyce and Shakespeare and Newton will go.

Okay. Then the final outcome of our eschatology is the end of the universe itself. Every star, every planet, every nebula, every galaxy, and every atom will run down, and become like every other atom and there will be no potential difference to do work. It's called the Big Freeze. The protons will cease to hold together. But not to worry, that won't happen for about 100 billion years.

That's 2500 times longer than humans have been on the earth. Essentially forever. And by then we should have the most advanced physics, to open a hole in space and travel between dimensions to go to a much younger, warming universe.

On a lighter note, my brother Roux, Anne, Robert and the boys and I went up to a country music festival in Greune, a little old Texas town beside New Braunfels. We enjoyed deep, soulful white-angst cowboy tunes with a side of zydeco and black blues, that you could hear very clearly word for word under tall oaks, down by the river. A very sweet area. Saw some old time gardens. Bought an antique Zuni button cover from Cactus Jack's antique store. It sure felt good being around the family, especially these nephews. I tell you what, those people in Texas know how to relax, know how to let if flow. That is quite an art, one I have long since lost living out here in the hustle. I might be looking for some greener pastures down there by and by.

How I Spent my Christmas Break

I was fifty-four and living with my semi-retired wife and our eleven year old kid. I was a dot. goner, the bubble had burst. I had not worked for two years, and had just brought out my fourth novel at the time. I was totally broke, run out of savings, run out of unemployment. (We were hoping Congress would give us the third extension but they had all taken off on vacation.) I was living off my wife and dreading Christmas. I was thinking man, I could use a break in life.

I don't know when I started not liking Christmas. I guess I was a bachelor too long; spent too many a Christmas on my own, far away from family. And being a writer, I was always so broke. I couldn't make any dollar votes in this great Christmas popularity election either.

My mood was swinging: at one moment I would be UP—just to hold this beautiful new book in my hands;

the next moment, I had stepped into one of the worst post-partum depressions that I have ever experienced, from having given birth through Art. The writing of that book had been an enormous effort that I should be taking a rest from. And yet, when I don't write I start to thrash about.

I hadn't fully realized it but I was coming to grieve over being dropped from even the *working* class. I'm in the Temp class, a slave of the information age. First to be let go, last to be hired back; no bennies, not perks, no options, no retirement. Being cannon fodder for the information age would just go on until I pitched forward at my workstation and my head crashes into the monitor.

I was looking forward to just hanging with my kid on Christmas break; that certainly takes your mind off your troubles. He has so much joyous energy in his basketball dance, his pirouetting around, his insanely genuine, free-style house-aping, hip-hop jive demeanor.

I had been to a job interview that morning, before I was to pick up the lad from school at noon to start his Christmas vacation. Me and the kid were going skateboarding. The job was for a network administrator at City College English Dept. I was sitting around the table with these swell-off department heads. They were like chameleons, turning their faces down to hurriedly read my CV for the first time, as I paced outside the glass cubicle, trying to figure out who I was. And it came out in the interview, (one of them had asked the usual question: What do you want to be doing in two years?) that I write novels and would like to keep on publishing them. We got tangential and one of them said, "Would you like to teach novel writing in college?" And I jumped at it, "Would I!"

We ended the interview with them saying, "Well, thank-you for your time," in that kind of patronizing, inconclusive, non-committal way people have when they hold all the power and you are expected to know it.

The skateboard bowl is out in Hill Top Park, part of the in Hunters Point area, up above the projects that you often see on TV at night. I was coursing around, riding the concrete wave with a grin on my face. We were a father and son teaching each other stuff. The skateboard flew out from under me and I tried to break my fall by getting my foot under me, and sat down on the ankle—breaking it in 3 places. My boy was brave going into a strange, all-black school that was not out for Christmas yet, calling his mom to pick us up. The foot was hanging, moving independently from the leg. *He* thought of going back into the strange school to get an Ace bandage to hold the foot in place while we waited.

Well, I did myself in good this time. Wow, what an unforgiving sport. I just got back from the hospital, where they kept me overnight after putting 9 screws in to hold the bones together. So now I'm hobbling around on crutches or doing the low scuttling crawl, while keeping the right foot elevated as much as possible. (The low scuttling crawl with one leg extended is more like a scorpion than a crab). I'm writing you sitting up in bed, on an ancient Powerbook 280c with a humble 28.8 internal modem. It's kind of nice, and old fashioned: 4 meg System, 2 meg MSWord, 1.5 meg Eudora. Got 16 megs to spare! I am bothering my mind trying to uncover the meaning of this set of affairs, as there are no accidents in the Freudian universe. I feel like such an old fool, trying to be a sidewalk surfer at fifty-four. Where was my mind!? Trying to have some of the joy of my eleven-year old I guess. What does THAT mean? Now I am even more of an unwelcome burden on my wife, who's got her hands full with her ailing mother. Oh, how I would like to be able to walk around again and carry stuff.

The operation was a success I think. Time will tell. I'll be setting off metal detectors for the rest of my life. My wife observed that my injury created a great deal of enthusiasm among the team of the famous osteopathic surgeon who was on duty when I arrived at emergency. They were excited to be going into surgery, to work on my foot with the master. I hadn't noticed until my wife pointed it out to me later - I thought it was just my own charm. I had a good intern, and he had a remarkably good assistant to do the initial bone-setting. When they were getting me ready for the operation they asked me how much I weighed. I thought for a while and said, "About 200 pounds." I told them about a calculation I had done recently comparing the weight of a ".1 ton man to the 6 million trillion ton earth." And how it is like a dust moat floating down on a city of skyscrapers—40 blocks by 40 blocks. The doctor twirled around and looked at me like he had been stung. He said, "Wow, that really makes you feel insignificant, doesn't it?" Something special happened between me and the doc at that moment, some kind of understanding passed between us. His assistant piped in: "And yet when we fall, look at how much damage it does."

He told me, "You have good bones." He said that the team he was on was headed by a great osteopathic surgeon, and I was lucky to have this team to work on my foot while on his shift. Somehow upper torso strength was mentioned, and one couldn't help but take notice of this young doctor's hugely-developed torso musculature with their long-sloping shoulders. Then later he set my bones in preparation for surgery. He got my foot into all kinds of ferocious wrestling holds and manipulated it into alignment. All the while, an orderly was pumping the morphine into my intravenous tap. I teased the doc: "You know, they say that long sloping shoulders are a sign of lack of responsibility, of one who sheds responsibility well, like water of a duck's back." That cracked everybody up. "Give him another shot," the doc said, as he twisted from the waist. And this cool orderly by my side squeezed some of this fast-acting morphine into my drip.

Then I said, trying to get an opinion from the medical establishment about certain alternative healers that heal by the laying on of hands, "What do you think of these osteopaths?

He snickered and replied, "You mean in general?"

I realized I had meant to say something else. I said, "OMYGOD I'm *surrounded* by a bunch of osteopaths." And trying to remember the name for those alternative healers I said, "What's the collective noun for a group of osteopaths, anyway?" Bone setters from ancient times. "Oh, I know! A *setting* of osteopaths." This had everybody snickering. They were telling me to relax. "I can't relax. I'm all tensed up!" Finally, they got the bones set and put on a temporary splint.

Fervor developed to work with the famous surgeon on the ankle of the disgraced, elderly skateboarder. They were definitely up late by the time they came to get me, After waiting hours in pre-op I got some experience with the bedpan before they finally wheeled me into the operating room. The ceiling of the OR room was almost entirely taken up by two, huge, flying-saucer disks. These were filled with smaller, high-intensity, variously-colored lights, to make the lighting on the situation perfect. The crack team transferred me to the operating table. The Anesthetician had me lean forward separating the backward gown and gave me a spinal injection. When I lay back down, I quickly started to go completely numb below the waist. One of the team raised and lowered his eyebrows like Groucho Marx: "Can you wiggle your toes?" Another intern starting lifting and pulling my mundged-up leg in all directions. I couldn't feel a thing. Groucho fluttered his eyebrows again and said, "Numb below the waist. It's kind of a (flutter, flutter) out-of-body experience."

I *did* feel cut off from my lower half. As the group of masked men congregated around my splayed leg I went into a panic. My mouth was dry and I was convulsed in a sweat. My eyes must have rolled back into my head because the Anesthetician thought I had gone into a faint and she slapped me and shook my face and she said loud, "Hey! Where did you go then?"

"Uh well, I think I'm having a panic attack. I've never had one before but I think this is it. Sweats, dry mouth unable to think."

I was hyperventilating and sweating. And the heart beat was racing on the monitor. I asked her, "Would you just hold my hand for a minute?" I had seen before that she had strong, capable hands, when she was explaining to me the choices among total sleep, spinal block and epidural drip.

And she said, "Yes."

And I took her strong hand in my hot hand—my hands were warmer than hers—and squeezed pretty tight but not too tight. After a minute, and remarking that my heart rate had stabilized, she produced a swab of water to wipe my lips. And in my panic it tasted like mango. "Wow, that tastes like mango!" I said.

I remembered: "It is one of my dreams to grow my own mangoes. Have you ever been to any islands where they grow mangoes?"

"You mean like Hawaii."

"Yea."

"They grow them in the Caribbean, too," she said.

"They do?"

"Yes, and Mexico. . . Have you ever heard of the Island of Bimini?" she asked.

"No, I haven't. Where is that?"

"It's about twenty-five minutes by seaplane off the coast of Florida, in the Atlantic. It's part of the Bahamas."

"Wow."

"My family has a place out there."

"Wow! . . . Ah the Bahamas I'd like that."

Trying to find some place else to put my mind, I wanted to go on some kind of an island fantasy. For the amber color of tropical island sun setting behind the palm trees is kind of mango. As is, perhaps, the color of spinal fluid. Certainly the dark iodine-tainted antibacterial swab they had liberally washed down my leg with was mango, as was the numb-butt feeling, imbuing my lower limbs. And from that sea plane ride, I was coming into her world, a little bay, a cove, an inlet. The two large flying-saucer shaped light containers in the operating room ceiling with their multicolored lights—some green, some red, others warm yellows, got into by reverie as we were lofting in for a landing. The water changed color from the darker emerald shade further out in the open deep sea into an aquamarine hue, a shade of light reflecting the life of multicolored corals underneath, shimmering up from the shallows. I am going under; I am undergoing.

The very loud whine of the high-speed meat-saw was like a jet turbine engine revving on a tarmac. With the help of this gifted Anesthetician, I was trying to escape into an island fantasy. I kept inveighing her with conversation leading to information about islands.

"What's the first thing you do when you get down there after you haven't been there for a while?"

"Go swimming in the ocean."

We had set down in a little island community with funky roads, kind of schematic at first—like a corny map from the drug store or the back of a comic book—but gradually becoming more real with volcanic cones, all covered over with fine green growth. There were highlands and lowlands and beaches . . .

To keep the fantasy going I asked her if she had ever seen the giant tree house on the Bahamas. And we got going on this tour of all the islands of the world; and it turned out that she actually had been to most of them.

The jet turbine of the high-speed bone-screw gun whined as the pilot throttled back and we took off to soar over islands on our way to another bright oceanic jewel. Bali, Isla de Mujeres, Tahiti.

Cloud forest in the highlands, that had little thatched huts overlooking vast primordial woodlands, on one side of a mountain. Then we talked about Salt Island of the coast of Vancouver.

"Oh, yeah. In the Juan De Fuca strait," she said. "There's some nice islands there."

I said, "I read about this one called Salt Island where they have these women who commune with the earth spirits, they have these pagan meetings in the woods. They claim to have been able to stop *developers*."

I could tell she liked the sound of that.

I told her about Deer Isle in the Bay of Fundy, how it was like going back in time, to be in the 1940s.

She took me on a lovely island fantasy, for most of the operation. Soon it was over.

They wheeled me into post-op recovery. Everyone was gone but me. So this cool old nurse was by my side attending to this, adjusting that, every 15 minutes it seemed. She had to use up her allotment of morphine and I was feeling no pain. When they were going to take me upstairs she asked me if there was anything I wanted. And I said, "I wonder if I can buy one of those bedpans at the pharmacy." She said, "Well here. Take one with you. Take two! Consider it a Christmas present."

Upstairs in my hospital room, I was pinching myself to make the numb-butt go away. The recovery nurse had said, "You won't be able to pee until you get the feeling back in your stomach. Don't worry about it. You'll feel a lot of pressure in your stomach, and if it gets too much, you'll feel the sheets getting wet. They'll just put a catheter in there." Man, I did not want the catheter. Anything but that! I kept praying for the control, and was thankful when it returned, and I did not have to have the catheter. I spent a sleepless night switching channels. Caught a little news about the impending invasion of Iraq and bombing in the no-fly zone. Next morning, I got some brief instruction in Crutch School from a physical therapist. Getting discharged took a long time. It was pouring rain when my wife picked me up. We had to wrap the cast in a plastic bag, and I sat on the back seat with my leg stretched out. On the way home, I saw the baseball diamond in the park resembled a large pond. At home, I slept as it rained.

I'm sad. Crazy old dad. Trying to be a skateboarder with my lad at fifty-four. Slowly it starts to . . . ever so slow it starts to rain. One day he'll say, My crazy father said to look for the rain drummer in the back yard.

He only comes out in the rain. The drummer in the rain is a child of the Rain God. Every yard has one. He only comes out when it rains. You've heard him. At first it's like the sound of a popping camp fire, little spitting, splitting explosions. Put-tak. There is an upturned pot out back getting attacked. It's not just the rain beating on the trash cans. The drummer in the rain is really fast, he's like Flash, jumping all around the yard. He makes it sound LIKE the rain beating on cans but if you close your eyes and listen, you can get a sense of him moving around the yard. It is a kind of call and response: one starts up close, then a whole chorus starts drumming and percussioning further away.

Bink: p-tock—burble, bubble. Is water boiling in the pot on the stove? No, it's the rain starting to strike the stove vent cover outside.

The beating of rain drums. It frightens me. I think the puddles and accumulations of rain around the house are going to start breeding West Nile Virus mosquitoes. Is there some way they can get through the windows? Through the foundation of the house?

It's hard to make an a-rhythmic drum beat like that -

so that it sounds like the rain beating on cans. It's the aleatory beat. It's a little like the krickety crack that the wind makes cackling and clattering those little bamboo stick hangings.

Dad got old all of a sudden. He'd open up the back door and, trying to keep his broken foot up, sit there and listen for the rain drummer to creep. Why? Because the rain makes him sad.

It rained and it rained and it rained. The storms that year were so severe. In some suburbs the middle class citizenry were hunkered down like refugees in bunkers. Storm water channels spilled over gutters and runnels of rainwater flooded streets and entered houses. Construction workers were idled, and some went Christmas shopping. The freeways that were not flooded with water were flooded with cars. Motorists drove through the downpour on flooded roads. The havoc wreaked by the heavy downpour in the night coupled with the weeks of relentless rain, saturated the hills and weakened the roots of trees which fell crashing into cars and across fences, or slid away on rivers of mud.

The Great Highway along the Pacific became like a river. While beyond, the ocean was crashing all the way up onto the sea wall, sending flotsam and debris way up onto the dunes. The Bay was another beneficiary of the rain gods. Rain swollen rivers flowing into it, discharged accumulated debris and garbage from the towns on its banks.

Time stops and gets all non-linear around Christmas. I started becoming a better Crutcher. The first time, standing at the top of the stairs on crutches, trying to remember how to do what they had taught me at Crutch

School about how to descend stairs, I could see myself tripping—mistaking and slipping—off the top one and sailing off the edge, falling to explode in a rage of bursting and *more* broken and expensive-to-repair body parts, gnarled bones: my misery ending in a compacting, lifeless mound of pulverized bone and bruised flesh at the bottom of the stairwell. I opted for ratcheting myself up and down stairs on my butt.

It is amazing how much trouble it is to be hopping around on one leg, reaching into the freezer for a piece of fish, and then carrying it in the bag—because you can't carry anything except that it's in a bag, hanging from one of your crutch hands. And I get so jammed up in my pectorals (is it?) Or under the arms. The underarms are just to steady the top of the crutch, one is really hoisting the body up on the forearms, and swinging the body as in a dip through the pulley of the hand holds. I get so tired. I start to scuttle. At least you can drag stuff along the floor; you can empty your own pee bottles for example.

Once while dragging my ass across the floor down below the book cases and the desk: I got this vision of being looked at by dust bunnies aligned along a downtown parade route. (I've gotten way behind on my vacuuming.) Looking up at the dresser, the desk, the filing cabinet from down below is like being down town looking up at tall buildings. And I'm a big gas-filled balloon bag floating down the avenue, tied to guide lines inexorably leading me. Dust bunnies are aligned / along the parade route, cheering.

One night, we watched the Nutcracker Suite on the Spanish Channel—Macauly Calkin in a little pink suit. I really appreciated the dancers. They spend so much time on one leg.

Christmas day my wife baked a delicious chicken with stuffing and trimmings. With her moma in her walker and I in my crutches, we were settled down in the parlor out of harm's clutches. The meal was fantastic. What an accomplished person my wife is. Later that night I found some Rave music on the radio, or Techno, or Trance—whatever the young people call it. I couldn't help but be doing a little one-legged jig held up in the sling of my crutches.

I have to try and understand what happened. Was it even an accident? At first I thought that it was my Shadow pushed me. That is disconcerting, (to say the least). To be inhabited by and entity who is trying to do you in. One who seems to have control over the CPU. Between the thought and the action falls the shadow. Maybe I can absolve myself from my own stupidity with that ploy. But what if there really is more going on in the unseen world than is imaginable, and that from the subtle action of a thought, gross results are produced in our physical world. There must be some better way to come into maturity than to be acting like a decrepit preteen.

What does the accident accomplish?

I don't have to do Christmas. I can stop the endless disappointing search for a job. But it is a huge burden on my wife, who is the sole support of her mother.

In an effort to slow the action down to its frames, I interrogate. What were you doing *immediately* before the accident?

I was with my kid. I was being a father to my kid.

What does it mean to be a father?

We were two beginners trying to teach ourselves something—skateboarding. I try, when I'm with him, to, I suppose, offer an image of masculinity, though mine is quite skewed, having never been interested in sports nor joining well the camaraderie of men. But when I slow it down and look at what was going on before the accident I see that I was angry from the job interview. I was with my kid and feeling like I was overcompensating because of feeling like an inadequate father.

Get to the Feelings! What was happening immediately after the accident.

Well, I remember about feeling so awful about having to be more dependent on my wife.

What was happening after the accident.

I put my arm around my wife and she acted as a crutch and helped me hobble across the park to the car.

What happened after that.

Well, when I had gotten myself folded up and crumpled up and dumped into the car seat, and my wife was across from me driving, and my kid in the back seat, and we were weaving in and out of the strange neighborhood trying to get to me hospital, I was feeling wretched about all this dependency I was going to have to be into with my wife. But now as I think about it, I was thinking how I can trust these two. And I am getting a feeling, it is something centered right in my heart, a kind of joy and gratitude that these two were with me.

HiT MoteL Press
www.hitmotel.com
These books can be ordered from any book seller or on-line, are deeply discounted on Amazon, and Barnes& Nobles. Check www.hitmotel.com for selections and recordings.

Boho Novels
The "Little House on the Prairie" Trilogy:
Cultivating the Texas Twister Hybrid, a portrait of the artist as a weed gardener (1998) ISBN 0-9655842-0-8 $20.00
The Secret of the Cicadas' Song, a peyote trip in poetry and prose (1998) ISBN 0-9655842-1-6 $20.00
Knight of a 1000 eyes, about Tai Chi, movement, Laban, and the I Ching (2002) ISBN 0-9655842-2-4 $25.00
others:
The Punctual Actual Weekly, about the life and times of a small mimeograph literary rag centered around artists living in a Berkeley warehouse and the Amphictionic Theatre ISBN 0-9655842-8-3
The Church of the Coincidental Metaphor, youthful adventures in Mexican radio

Novels: The "My Years of Apprenticeship at Love" Sextet:
Sex is the Anti-gravity of Metamorphosis, tales of romance and despair hitchhiking in North America. ISBN 0-9655842-9-1
The Indigenous Tribesmen of Neverland Bohemian life in Austin slacker enclaves. ISBN 0-9655842-7-5 $20.00
Dolores Park, Texan joins a California Tantric Buddhist commune (2001) ISBN 0-9655842-3-2 480 pages. $25.00
Seeing throught the Spell of Transference A cab driver's journal of psychotherapy. ISBN 0-9655842-4-0
A Blue Moon in August, about marriage and children late in life. (2005) ISBN 0-9655842-5-9
Thoughts on Vacation, a father is raised by his child and is enlightened by mortality. (2005) ISBN 0-9655842-6-7

Check into HiT MoteL @www.hitmotel.com for cover art, interactive Table of Contents, e-book sample chapters, recordings and other mindware.

Thoughts on Vacation

Thoughts on Vacation, pretty much sums up the subject matter and the style of this novel. It is a comedy of manners about raising children and how we are raised by them. It is away in the alternative frame of vacation, when thought is enriched by strangeness, that the modern family has meaningful experience with each other.

This is the 6th novel in the "My Years of Apprenticeship at Love" sextet. In it we watch the main character, Walker Underwood, as he matures into being a father.

The main theme of this book is the wounded artist struggling to capture, through his creative imagination a state of well being. This theme is reflected in the relationship between a father trying to maintain a creative spiritual environment and the son inviting the father to play. It is a novel in the form of Walker's emotional memories and creative experiences as he struggles to deal with the suffering and loss of a loved one. This compels him to query current thinking to understand our place in the world.

The story is told in third person narrative shifting into first person narrative through writing—intimate letters and moving stories. Within the stories we enter fantasy and dreams or exit outside the character through 'bookmovies'.

A long chapter—Mr. I (Crossing the Brain / Blood Barrier) presents the current zeitgeist in the hard-science style of sci-fi, a fiction that is a streamlined information space where the art is in the creative juxtapositioning of ideas. *Thoughts on Vacation*, gives a hopeful picture of this generation's thought and will raise your IQ if you let it.

$25.00 Sci-Fi / Philosophy / Psychology / Literature

www.ingramcontent.com/pod-product-compliance
Lightning Source LLC
LaVergne TN
LVHW091021080826
845145LV00002B/319

* 9 7 8 0 9 6 5 5 8 4 2 6 5 *